ALIEN ADBUCTION

Borgo Press Books by BRIAN STABLEFORD

ALIEN ABDUCTION

THE WILTSHIRE REVELATIONS

by

Brian Stableford

THE BORGO PRESS

An Imprint of Wildside Press LLC

MMIX

CONTENTS

ALIEN ADBUCTION

CHAPTER ONE

LEARNING TO RELAX

Steve had never thought that the time would come when he would be glad to see Rhodri Jenkins, but the deputy head still seemed to be the only member of staff who was talking to him—or, at least, the only one who was actually prepared to sit down opposite him in the school canteen—which seemed like a very large and lonely place without any pupils in it. Although there was still an entire fortnight to go before the new school year started, the staff had been summoned to pay homage to the latest idol adopted by the local authority: Continuing Professional Development. The "refresher" course had sucked them all in, from the Newly Qualified—a category from which Steve had only just escaped—to those with thirty years service, like Jenkins.

Steve had hoped that the new year might be a chance to start again with a clean slate, but four weeks of absence had not been sufficient to make the hearts of the female staff grow fonder, or the inclination of the male staff—who were in a conspicuous minority—to withdraw their manifest support for the outrage felt by the female staff. The Tracy/Jill affair obviously would not be forgotten for some little time to come. The school's deputy head, however, could not sensibly refuse to talk to any of those to whom he had occasionally to assign additional duties, so Jenkins actually made a point of filling one of the empty chairs on the table where Steve would otherwise have been condemned to eat alone.

"Don't look so depressed, boyo," Jenkins instructed him. "If you're in that sort of a mood now, imagine what you'll be like after thirteen weeks of teaching. Can't let it happen. Give in to the pressure and you'll go under."

"CPD is enough to make anyone suicidal," Steve told him. "It's ten times worse than teaching. I thought I'd put that sort of bullshit behind me when I got through my probation, but now it looks as if I'll have to put up with it for the rest of my career."

"The secret," Jenkins assured him, "is to let it wash over you. You have to learn to relax. Mind you, a young fellow like you ought to be perfectly relaxed after four weeks' holiday. You're still young enough to go on those Club 18-30 jaunts, aren't you? Unlimited sun, sangria and sex, so they say. Or did you run out of prophylactics and catch some horrible venereal disease?"

Jenkins pronounced the first syllable of "prophylactics" to rhyme with "toe" and the second to rhyme with "pie". Steve had never figured out whether it was a purely personal idiosyncrasy or whether everyone west of Cardiff pronounced it that way.

"I didn't manage to get away," Steve admitted. "Never got out of Salisbury, in fact—and now I'm back on site, everyone's picked up exactly where they left off in July. You're the only one who's addressed more than a monosyllable to me all day."

"Ach, it won't last. Once the kids are back and life reverts to normal, they'll relax the freeze and issue your return ticket from Coventry. They have to go through the motions first, to teach you a lesson. This is a special kind of community, not like uni, where you can play Don Juan to your heart's content. Here, the rule is *don't shit in your own backyard*...or if you do, keep it quiet...and if you can't keep it quiet, ration yourself to breaking one heart per term."

Steve looked glumly down at his corned-beef-and-salad sandwich, which he'd painstakingly assembled and wrapped in clingfilm all by himself that morning, because the canteen staff wouldn't be returning to duty until the pupils were back. He couldn't meet Jenkins' eye for the moment, because he knew that the old man was right. If he'd just been able to keep a lid on his affair with Tracy, everything would have been fine, but a messy break-up in mid-term would have been bad enough even if the cause hadn't been his taking up with Jill—and to break up with Jill with two weeks still to go until the end of term had been fatal. Even Steve thought that he fully deserved the universal cold shoulder, and wasn't yet fully qualified for remission and rehabilitation.

"Still playing cricket to keep fit, are you?" Jenkins asked.

"Yes," Steve replied. "Saturday league games for the seconds and Sunday friendlies. Took three wickets yesterday, and a good catch down at long leg."

"Don't confuse me with technical terminology, Boyo—I'm a rugby man, as you know, and was only asking to be polite. I'm sorry the school doesn't have a cricket pitch, but you could always volunteer to help us out with the rugby. Mrs. Jones would be glad to have you aboard. No chance of an injury that would spoil your looks while playing with kids, is there?"

"You're joking," Steve said. "I'm only five-nine—half the boys in the second year sixth are taller than I am, and the ones who play rugby are mostly two stone heavier. I manage to stay fit in the winter without risking a broken neck. I get plenty of exercise." That wasn't strictly true; his sporting interests over the winter consisted entirely of watching horse-racing on Saturdays, while betting on the internet exchanges, and playing internet poker—neither of which activities did much for his muscle-development.

Jenkins sighed. "*That* sort of exercise won't do you much good in the long run," he said, obviously thinking that Steve meant sex. What you ought to try, by way of learning the art of healthy relaxation, is hypnotherapy."

"No way," Steve said, immediately. "I'm not letting anyone put me in a trance—and no matter what you and everyone else might think, I *don't* need treatment for sex addiction."

"For once, boyo, I'm not only thinking about sex," the deputy head informed him. "I'm thinking about getting through the working day, week after week and term after term. Hypnotherapy's not about trances, if there's any such thing, and it's certainly not about planting posthypnotic suggestions that make you think you're a chicken and act accordingly. A proper therapist would no more dream of playing that sort of silly game than your GP would dream of using leeches. If there's one thing people in this job need more than anything else, it's the ability to relax when the stress mounts up. If you can't get through a two-week refresher course in Best Practice without tensing up, that GCSE group of yours will drive you to an early grave. Since we aren't allowed to switch *them* off, it's a great advantage to be able to switch off ourselves, whenever we need to. It's pricey, mind, but worth every penny."

"I don't think so," Steve said, dubiously. "It's not my sort of thing."

"Don't knock it till you've tried it, boyo," Rhodri told him, in the kind of authoritatively patronizing voice that schoolteachers of thirty years' experience invariably cultivated, whether they were Welsh or not. "I only wish I'd known about Sylvia—or someone like her—when I was your age."

"Sylvia?" Steve repeated, questioningly.

"Sylvia Joyce—my hypnotherapist. You can take that lustful gleam out of your eye, mind. She's a handsome woman, but she's old enough to be your mother. If she were of an age to have her heart broken, you can be certain that I wouldn't let you anywhere near her, the way you carry on."

Steve honestly didn't think that having slept with four of his female colleagues in two years made him into a Casanova, even if two of them had been in the same term. After all, none of them had been married—which was probably more than Rhodri Jenkins could claim about all the female teachers he'd slept with in the course of his long career. Even so, Steve had sworn an oath never to get involved with a colleague again after the Tracy/Jill fiasco.

"I'm going out with someone else now," he said, defensively. "Not a teacher. From now on, my sex-life is strictly out of school hours and off school premises."

"Glad to hear it," Jenkins said. "Not an ex-pupil, I hope?"

"No," Steve said, patiently. "She went to the other one." Although Salisbury qualified as a city, by virtue of possessing a cathedral, it wasn't even as big as Swindon, so the staff and pupils at its two large comprehensives were always able to refer to "the other one" with perfect clarity.

"Better and better," the deputy head said. "You're a local boy, aren't you—is that where you went to school?"

"No," Steve said, "I went to the boys' grammar."

"Perhaps as well," Jenkins observed. "A young Adonis like you would have got into all kinds of trouble in a sink of iniquity like this—probably have been paying three lots of child support all the way through uni. What does your new girl-friend do?"

"She works for Thomas Cook, in the pedestrian precinct."

"A travel agent! No wonder there's a *verboten* sign on Club 18-30. Still, you should have been able to get away easily enough, to somewhere nice. Travel agents always bag the best deals for themselves and their nearest and dearest, I dare say."

"Well, we didn't," Steve said.

"Plenty to keep you at home in the first flush of enthusiasm, I dare say. You're of an age to start thinking in the longer term, now—settling down and getting married. Keep you out of trouble, at least for a while. Think on. You'll want to get way at half-term, I suppose—or a Christmas break in the sun. Can't tell whether there's a future in a relationship until you've gone away together. A travel agent's ideal for fixing that sort of do—she's probably thinking along the same lines."

Steve didn't say anything in response to this network of suggestions, because there was nothing he could say. The truth was that he had only been on a foreign holiday once, when his parents had dragged him to the Canaries at the age of thirteen, in spite of his loud protests. He and they had both sworn never to repeat the experiment. Since then, he hadn't even been as far afield as Wales. He wasn't only phobic about flying, but also of driving over large bridges. He had never been over the Severn Bridge, even as a passenger, but he had once been taken over the Clifton Suspension Bridge by his parents, while they were still optimistic enough to think that he might get over his phobia if he were forced to confront it. That was another experience they had never attempted to repeat. There had been one more occasion when they had tried to cajole and shame him into boarding a plane to Malaga, but they had failed miserably; then, like sensible folk, they'd given up and reverted to taking their last few family holidays in Bournemouth, Poole or Weymouth—all of which could reached by car, provided that the route was properly planned, without crossing any rivers wider than thirty yards.

Unperturbed by Steve's silence, Rhodri Jenkins rambled on "I don't go abroad, myself. Why would I, when I can go home to the lovely mountains and Cardigan Bay? I never dated a travel agent, mind. I'm not much of a boozer, mind—these days, binge drinking is all the rage, so I hear, and Spain is very cheap for that."

"Just because Janine works for Cook's," Steve told him, wearily "it doesn't mean that she's addicted to foreign holidays. She doesn't go binge-drinking either." He wasn't entirely sure about the final item, because Janine still went on occasional "girls' nights out" with her old school friends Milly and Alison, from which boy-friends were banned—so strictly that he hadn't yet met Milly or Alison. When she was with him, though, Janine was a very moderate drinker, and had not yet shown any conspicuous interest in dragging him off to foreign climes. If she were to start measuring him up for a permanent relationship, though, it would only be a matter of time....

"Better get back to the classroom, boyo," the deputy head said, cutting off Steve's train of thought. "It's doing us good, I don't doubt, to be put in the kids' shoes for once. Just let it wash over you."

"On second thoughts," Steve said. "It can't actually hurt to explore new possibilities, can it? What was the name of your hypnotherapist again?"

Jenkins beamed, like a man who had just made an unexpected breakthrough in pastoral care. "Sylvia Joyce." he said, as he stood up and lobbed his sandwich-wrapper into the nearest bin, while pocketing his half-full bottle of Evian. "I'll pop a card in your pigeon-hole, but she's in the yellow pages, if I forget. She'll do you the world of good—teach you to cope with any amount of stress."

Steve didn't hurry to keep up with the Welshman, but lingered a few moments more over his can of diet coke before tidying up in a slightly more decorous fashion and making his way back through the corridor at his own pace.

The exchange had given him food for thought. It was just possible, he thought, that a hypnotherapist might be able to help him with his phobias—which had become a considerable nuisance even before he'd started going out with Janine, if only because of the absolute necessity of concealing them from his colleagues and pupils. If ever it got around the school that he was incapable of getting on a plane or driving over the Severn Bridge, he'd be a laughing-stock till the day he retired. Maybe, if Sylvia Joyce were such a hot shot at teaching people to relax, she could also train him not to have panic attacks whenever he so much as thought about the Avon Gorge. At least he'd be safe confiding in her, if she were as scrupulous a practitioner as Rhodri Jenkins claimed.

"After all," Steve said to himself, as he paused in the doorway of the classroom and stiffened his back in order to face up to the mute hostility of his colleagues and the patronizing smile of the instructor, "it can't do any harm, can it?"

* * * * * * *

Steve was able to book a two-hour appointment with Sylvia Joyce for the following Tuesday evening. She talked him through a relaxation procedure by way of demonstration, and suggested that he ought to make a personalized relaxation CD on his PC, which he could play to himself whenever he went to bed alone, in order to practice the technique. "Can you do that?" she asked. "It works best if you lay down a backing-track of soothing music, then put on a voice-track taking you through the various stages I've mapped out for you."

"Sure," Steve said. "I've got mixing software, and a huge collection of MP3s. Ambient chill-out isn't really my thing, but I can find enough to make a long lullaby, and I think I can do the sonorous voice."

"Eventually," she said, "you'll internalize the CD, so that you can play it to yourself in your imagination, as it were—you can summon it up in the classroom, or if you're in a queue, or any other time you feel tension building up."

"Would that help to combat a panic attack, if I happened to be having one? Steve asked.

"It might," the therapist told him. "Why—do you often have panic attacks?"

"Not often," Steve said—and then shut up.

"We're supposed to be compiling an issue-profile here, Steve," Sylvia said, maternally. "I can't help you with your problems unless you tell me what they are. When do you have panic attacks?"

"Mostly when I go over bridges," Steve admitted. "But that's only because I never travel by air or look over the edges of cliffs and tall buildings."

"You mean that you suffer from acrophobia."

"Yes. I get panicky about heights, especially if they involve air-planes and rivers. Viaducts aren't so bad. I'm not helpless, mind—I can do short spans with little more than a slight shiver. If I can learn your relaxation techniques well enough to reduce the shiver, and maybe let me get on a plane once in a while without tranquilizing myself into oblivion, that would be useful."

"Well, you'll certainly find that the relaxation techniques will help. If you really want to get to grips with the phobias, though, I can do much more than that. If we could search out the cause, by investigating your childhood...."

"Regression, you mean?" Steve said. Psychology wasn't one of the sciences Steve taught—he'd done chemistry and physics along with biology at A level before going to university to train as a teach-er—but he wasn't entirely a stranger to psychological theory. He'd read a fair amount in his time, although he didn't read nearly as much now that he'd got so heavily into the internet. He was vaguely familiar with the notion of hypnotic regression, and with the Freu-dian notion of abreaction, whereby repressed memories had to be dredged up and confronted in order to obtain release from the irra-tional anxieties they transmitted from the unconscious to afflict eve-ryday behavior.

"Regression's one term we use," Sylvia confirmed. "It's not so different from what any psychotherapist would do, though. It's all a matter of getting you into a state of mind to skip back in time, to re-cover the full sensation of your early memories. Think of it as a fur-ther stage of relaxation—that's all it is, really, although some people call it a trance."

"I don't know about that," Steve said. "It might be opening a can of worms."

"That's the whole point of it," Sylvia told him. "Better a can of worms than a can't of worms, I always say. Sometimes, you have to regress before you can progress. The recovered memories can be painful—they probably wouldn't have been repressed in the first place, and wouldn't be causing you difficulties now, if they weren't—but it's not a good idea to let them fester indefinitely. This is as safe an environment as you're likely to find to reach out and touch them, I can do a swift demonstration now, if you like. Nothing heavy—I'll just send you back five or ten years, if you like, so we won't risk touching on anything too stressful, and you can see how it works. Then, if you're agreeable, we can try to go deeper next time I see you."

Steve hesitated. "I'm not sure I believe in that whole thing," he said. "It would be convenient, I suppose, if all our problems could be traced back to childhood traumas, and then surgically excised by confronting the relevant horrors, but I really don't think my phobias have that sort of cause. I think they're jut some sort of random neurophysiological accident—so I'm more interested in treating the manifest symptoms than going in search of potentially illusory causes. People start coming out with all sorts of rubbish when they're regressed, don't they? Past lives and false memories of being abused as children, and all that sort of crap. There's a risk of increasing the problems instead of solving them, I think."

"Memories of child abuse aren't necessarily false," the hypnotherapist told him, "even if the people cast as abusers deny it. I don't agree that there's any risk of increasing your problems, although it's true that people who do begin to remember traumatic things sometimes find recovered memories hard to deal with. Can of worms or not, I believe it's best to get such things out in the open."

"I'm not sure that I can agree," Steve said. "You might be right about memories of child abuse—but memories of past lives are certainly false. If delusions as blatantly ridiculous as once having served in Nelson's fleet at Waterloo or as one of Cleopatra's handmaidens can carry as much conviction as they're said to do, how can anyone trust recovered memories of any sort? Regression can't help me if it turns out to be nothing but an invitation to fantasize, and I sucker myself into believing my own fantasies."

"You don't have to believe anything you might recover, Steve," Sylvia assured him, "and the recovered imagery might be revealing and helpful, even if it's a blatant fabrication. The unconscious mind doesn't send us these messages unless it's trying to help. What do you have to lose?"

Steve didn't know what he had to lose, and that was what worried him. He didn't like taking leaps in the dark.

"Maybe it's time to bite the bullet, Steve." Sylvia Joyce said, gently. "Maybe the time has come to stop procrastinating. You're here, aren't you? Why not make the most of it? You can stop at any time."

"Okay," Steve said, eventually. "It can't hurt to give it a go, I suppose, Give me a gentle introduction, mind. Just a brief trip into a safe and familiar yesteryear. *That* can't do any harm."

Ten minutes later, those had come to seem like famous last words. As promised, once he had begun to drift away with the fairies, Sylvia had asked him, in her most soothing and reassuring tone, to go back to the age of twenty-one, when he'd been in his third year at university, and as happy and carefree as in any period of his life before or since. The last thing he'd expected was to go into a full-blown panic attack—but that was what happened.

He felt the physical symptoms first—the cold sweat, the nausea, the dizziness. If he'd been able to faint, he probably wouldn't have obtained any conscious sensations at all—but he was lying down on Sylvia Joyce's couch, and the blood couldn't drain away from his head under the pull of gravity. After the horrid physical sensations came the horrid psychological ones: a fully-fledged hallucination; a waking nightmare such as he'd never experienced before...or never, at any rate, allowed himself to remember after he awoke.

"Wow," said Sylvia, after sitting him up giving him a glass of water from which to sip. "You really do suffer from phobias, don't you? I've seen reactions like that before, but never in a first session and never in response to such a minimal regression.

"It was just a dream," Steve said. "A nightmare. I don't remember having suffered from nightmares like that at uni, but I suppose I must have. It was crazy."

"Can you remember any of the images?" the therapist asked.

"I can *now*," Steve told her, accusingly. "I was aboard some sort of spaceship, looking down at the Earth from a great height—from orbit, I suppose. The Earth was dark, devastated. I think the sun was about to explode. I was up so high...higher than I could ever go in real life. I felt such an awful vertigo...." He handed the glass of water back, and lay down again, to armor himself against the possibility of fainting.

"That's okay," Sylvia said. "It's enough, for now. You're going to have to deal with it, though, if we're to get on the root of your phobias—not just *this* nightmare, but others, maybe even worse."

"A can of worms," Steve murmured. "Just like I said."

"And we *can* work on it," the therapist insisted. "It's not insuperable. It just needs time."

"It was only a dream," Steve said, sharply. "It wasn't *real*. It can't have anything to do with the cause of my phobias. It's just one more stupid symptom."

"It would be a mistake to back away from it," Sylvia advised him. "Even if it was only a dream, it might well have significant meanings wrapped up in it. You really need to recover more of it, and get a better grip on it—and you probably will recover more, now, even if you try to put it back in its mental box and throw away the key. In my experience, once these things begin to resurface, they usually continue to bubble up. It's far better to control that process, to the extent that we can, so that we can try to make some sense of it. If you resist, you'll just make it more difficult for you to deal with it."

"No way," Steve said, remembering the flight to the Canaries and the crossing of the Clifton Suspension Bridge. "No more regression. Not now, not ever."

"I don't want to abandon you, Steve," the hypnotherapist told him, presumably meaning that she didn't want him to abandon her. "You need to deal with this. I won't regress you again, if you don't want me to, but you may be in greater need now of learning to relax properly than you were before."

"Is this how you drum up business?" Steve asked, angrily. "Is this why Rhodri Jenkins has been coming to you for donkey's years—because he's getting further and further away from a cure for whatever ails him with every visit?"

"I can't discuss another client, Steve," the therapist said, soothingly. "And I don't *drum up business*. I don't have to. The world does that for me. You're *not* further away from finding an answer to your problems than you were before—you're closer. You just need a little more help in completing the journey."

"No more regression," Steve repeated. "I won't bin the relaxation treatment, but that's all I need from you, okay? I don't need to be *cured*, in the way you think I can be—I just need to get my head into a state where I can step on a plane, if need be, or cross the Severn Bridge, without being reduced to a gibbering idiot. That's all. We need to focus on that. Management, not cure. Forget about hypothetical causes, let's just treat the symptoms."

"If that's what you want," she told him, "We can do that. You're the client."

As long as you get your money, he thought, *it doesn't really matter which particular brand of old rope I buy, does it?* Aloud, though, he only said: "Just a couple of sessions more, mind. No point in throwing money away if it isn't working." The reason he said that was because he thought there was just a possibility that she might be right, if only about more bits of the "recovered memory" resurfacing. If that proved to be the case, he might need someone to talk to about them—and who else could he possibly tell, apart from his therapist?

"If it's the money that bothers you, Steve, there's something you might try for free," Sylvia said, still full of apparent concern. "There's a local support group for people who've had...experiences like yours. It's called AlAbAn. That's short for Alien Abductees Anonymous. They couldn't call themselves Triple-A because that was already taken. They meet in East Grimstead every second Thursday."

Steve was flabbergasted by the suggestion that he could be put in the same bag as lunatics who thought they'd been abducted by aliens, but the reflexive denial died on his lips. "East Grimstead?" he said, weakly, when he had recovered himself. "Isn't that where the Scientologists' headquarters are?"

"No, that's East Grinstead with an en, in Sussex. This is East Grimstead with an em. Unsurprisingly, it's a couple of miles the other side of West Grimstead, after you've taken a left turn off the A36 in Alderbury. You don't have to worry about any big bridges, once you're over the Bourne. Here's the address—they meet later this week." She handed him a piece of paper, on which she'd been scribbling while she spoke.

"I don't need a support group," Steve said. "I haven't been abducted by aliens—I've just been suckered into having a bad dream in a hypnotherapist's comfy chair."

"It doesn't matter whether you were abducted by aliens or not," Sylvia assured him. "What matters is whether or not you can get to the bottom of whatever it was that produced those images in your mind. AlAbAn can help, believe me. I've referred people there before, and they've always got something out of it, if only a nice cup of tea and a few biscuits. It's free, as I said, and they won't pressure you into telling your story if you don't want to. Just go along and listen for a week or two. It can't do any harm, and you might be surprised by how helpful it is."

"That's what you said about the regression," Steve reminded her.

"And I was right about that, too," Sylvia told him. "We just have to work through it, to see what your unconscious is trying to tell your conscious mind. If your conscious mind were in a more receptive frame, maybe communication with your unconscious wouldn't be so difficult, and you wouldn't have cultivated your phobias in the first place."

"I knew it would wind up being my fault," Steve said. "It always does with you people, doesn't it?"

"Absolutely not," Sylvia told him. "There's no fault involved. That's one of the things of which you have to convince yourself. We can get there, if you'll give it a chance. You really should go to AlAbAn—it might be interesting, even if it isn't helpful, and it can't hurt."

Steve finally consented to take the proffered piece of paper, but he had no intention of going to the meeting. He didn't think he was *that* crazy—not yet, at any rate. He didn't want to reopen the can of worms into which he'd accidentally peered, so he didn't want to do anything that might jiggle its lid, let alone anything that might help him get to its slimy bottom.

* * * * * * *

Steve hadn't yet told Janine that he was seeing a hypnotherapist, because he didn't want to let on about his phobias yet, and it would be direly difficult to do one without the other. He wasn't yet sure that their two-month-old relationship had the sort of future that entitled her to know such things about him, and wasn't even sure whether he ought to hope that it might.

In the past, he'd always told himself that he wouldn't be ready to settle down for a long time yet, and that he had many more notches to put on the bedpost before he began to contemplate trading in the bachelor life, but he knew that Rhodri Jenkins might have a point. While he remained conscientiously young, free and single, conspicuously regarding every young woman he met as a potential conquest, it wasn't going to be easy for him to settle into the kind of community that the school's staff-members were trying to be: one that could set a good example to the students as well as preserving its own harmony.

There was no doubt in his mind that Janine was one of the finest conquests he had ever made, not just because she was so good-looking but because she was bright and witty. She hadn't been to university, but he gathered that it was because she'd been too desperate to win her independence in order that she could leave home and set herself up with an entire new life. He'd met her parents once, and couldn't see that they were particularly terrible, but there was obviously more there than met the eye. He could imagine himself living happily ever after with Janine—or as close to happily ever after as any real people could ever get. He'd have to get to know her more thoroughly first, of course—meet her friends, for sure, and maybe go away on holiday with her, if only as far as Weymouth—but he couldn't see any reason, at present, why he shouldn't try to prolong the present relationship indefinitely.

It seemed to Steve, moreover, that Janine was thinking along much the same lines. They'd already reached the stage in the relationship in which she felt entitled to be curious about how he spent the time he wasn't spending with her, and what sort of things he considered adequate excuses for delaying their meetings. She'd accepted that cricket matches sometimes dragged on, so that he couldn't always be on time for Saturday night dates, and understood that he sometimes felt the need to spend whole evenings alone with his PC, checking the videos on YouTube, playing poker, listening to his music or just surfing. She showed every sign of being adaptable to his habit and hobbies, and no sign of turning into a nag—although he knew that early appearances could sometimes be deceptive in the latter respect.

When he turned up half an hour late to meet her at the wine bar, after the appointment with Sylvia at which he'd come up with the "abduction experience", Janine had the ideal excuse for demanding an adequate explanation and not being put off by any casual evasion, but she didn't press as hard as a committed nag would have done.

"So you've been seeing another woman, "she said, lightly, when he returned from the bar with two large glasses of house red and explained that Rhodri Jenkins had sent him to a hypnotherapist, in order that he might learn to relax, and thus be better able to cope with the stresses and strains of classroom life.

"She's older than my mother," Steve told her, "and not so good-looking." Janine had met Steve's mother, and had complimented her by saying that it was obvious where Steve got his looks from. Steve's mother, in consequence, thought that Janine was a "very nice girl—better than you deserve".

"Did she hypnotize you, then?" Janine asked.

"Of course—that's what I went for. It's not like stage hypnotism, though, or old movies with swinging watches and rotating spirals. You don't really go into a trance. She'd told me that I ought to make a CD in my computer that will take me through the stages of relaxation in the comfort of my own home. Do you want eat here, or shall we go on somewhere else?"

"Might as well stay here," she said. "I know it's only Tuesday, but I'm already feeling a touch of end-of-the week apathy. Can I get a copy—of your CD, I mean? Then we could both learn to relax."

"I think it needs to be personalized. Besides which, you're relaxed enough already. I don't know how you do it, since you're dealing with members of the public all day, but you seem perfectly able to shrug it off even when someone does have a go at you."

Janine shrugged, as if to demonstrate how it was done. "Shit happens," she said, in an insouciant one. "You have to take things in your stride. You get upset for a moment, then you wind down."

"I find it much more difficult than that," Steve admitted. "Things get to me, I guess, and gnaw away at me. I worry.

"I've noticed—but I didn't think it was so bad that you'd have to seek professional help. Is there anything more I should know? If you've got dark secrets, I'd rather know about them sooner than later."

Steve contemplated brushing the question off with a flippant remark, but he found himself in the unaccustomed position of not wanting to tell his girl-friend an outright lie—not, at any rate, an unnecessary outright lie.

"Stress can really take its toll on teachers," he said, earnestly. "It's not a trivial matter. You're fortunate to have a natural resistance to that sort of thing."

"Oh, it's not natural," she said. "I got a lot of practice at home. My mother got upset over the slightest thing—so much so that she was almost impossible to live with. She loved me, I suppose, but I was such a worry to her that the love never got a look in—and Dad just armored himself by withdrawing into his obsessions. I'd never have believed that a man could treat a pub quiz like an Olympic final if I hadn't seen him in obsessive action. I just went the opposite way. Shit happens—that's my motto. Accept it and move on. That's easy to say, mind, while I'm not put under too much pressure. I suspect that I've got my breaking point. Is it really so difficult to deal with stroppy children?"

"The A level groups aren't so bad," Steve said, "but the year elevens are awful. Most of them will reach the age of consent during the year. Combined with the fact that they'll be sitting their GCSEs next May, that turns the classroom into a witches' cauldron of seething hormones, fear of being left out, terror of not being in with the crowd, anxiety about not being able to cut it...you must remember the recipe from your own schooldays."

"Sure," Janine said. "Alison, Milly and I were witches all right, cackling away like the best of them. Gave our teachers hell, I suppose, although we didn't think of their poor nerves at the time—or, if we did, only about how better to get on them in the hope of inducing a comprehensive breakdown. Okay, I take it back—stroppy adolescents probably are far worse than people complaining about their holidays from hell and whining about the inadequacy of the travel insurance they never wanted to buy. Can your hypnotherapist and your do-it-yourself relaxation CD take care of that, do you think?"

"Maybe," Steve said. "Can't hurt, at any rate. Shall I place our orders at the bar? What do you want?"

There must have been something in Steve's tone that he hadn't intentionally incorporated into it, because Janine picked up on the fact that there was something he wasn't telling her.

"Something else happened, didn't it?" she said, after she'd made her selection from the menu. "Either that, or there's some other reason you went to the therapist. You don't have to tell me, of course—but I really would prefer it if I didn't discover some dark secret six months into our relationship that you could have come clean about much sooner. That wouldn't be nice."

Steve could have fenced that off by saying that six months was a long time, relationship-wise, and that maybe she was being over-optimistic, but he knew that wasn't the right thing to do, in the circumstances. "I have a phobia," he said, reluctantly, when he returned from the bar clutching a numbered ticket "I don't think Sylvia will be able to do much about that, though, except maybe ameliorate the symptoms. Then, in the faint hope of deflecting the obvious question, he added: "She wanted to try regression, and persuaded me to agree, but it turned into a farce. I didn't even get back to my childhood. I only remembered some stupid sci-fi nightmare. Sylvia took it seriously, though—she tried to persuade me to go to some support group for nutcases. Would you believe that there's actually a group called Alien Abductees Anonymous, and that they have a branch in Wiltshire?"

Janine astonished him by saying: "Oh, I know all about that. My friend Milly goes regularly—she's been trying to persuade Alison and me to go with her for ages. They meet over in East Grimstead—she must be serious about it, because she takes the bus."

Steve seized upon the unexpected opportunity to draw the conversation into what seemed to be safer waters. "Your friend Milly thinks she's been abducted by aliens?" he queried. "When? What happened to her?"

"Oh, she's never confided in me or Alison," Janine said, with a slight hint of bitterness. "I don't even know whether she's ever told her story to the group. She says there's no pressure on people to talk about their experiences if they don't want to, but that it helps just to listen. If you ask me, she just got addicted to support groups after the other one. That one cured her, after a fashion, so she's being more careful this time—eking it out, so to speak."

"What other one?" Steve asked, glad for he opportunity to take control of the conversational tempo. Even though he didn't know Milly, he was fully entitled to ask about her, because Janine had brought the subject up and left the information she'd supplied tantalizingly incomplete.

"It was a group for people with Eating Disorders."

"You mean she's fat—or was."

"No, the opposite. When we were at school she got very thin after GCSEs. She used to make herself sick after eating—even after school lunches. Mind you, that wasn't so very unusual once we got to year eleven. Alison and I were never in the sick club, but there was quite a clique. The pressure of the A levels that we never got around to taking, I suppose. We could have—we were all clever enough, Ali especially, but none of us wanted to. Milly's bulimia just gave us one more reason for resolving to get out. She never committed herself fully to the clique, mercifully; Ali and I remained her crucial connection to normality. As I said, she's cured now, and had to move on from the Eating Disorders group. She eats normally, and works out a quite a bit at the police gym. Did you know that traffic wardens are allowed to use the police gym? She gets preferential treatment housing-wise as well—a special flat for key workers, Ali's got one too, but travel agents don't qualify."

"Teachers do," Steve said, "but I prefer my own place—I like older houses. So, is Milly contentedly plump now?"

"No. She's bigger than me—nearly as tall as you, I suppose—so she can carry more weight that I can without looking fleshy. Actually, she looks very good—the broad shoulders and big bones give her an athletic look. Beside her, I look like a fragile doll. She needs that sort of appearance, mind—being a traffic warden's definitely a high stress job. Victims of road rage are even worse than rebellious pheromone-crazed adolescents. Should I recommend your hypnotherapist to her, do you think?"

"Maybe," Steve said. "Sylvia's a fan of AlAbAn, at any rate. She'd approve of Milly going, even if you don't."

"I don't disapprove," Janine said. "I just prefer conventional girls' nights out to support groups."

"You get free tea and biscuits, so I'm told," Steve rambled on, "although I don't suppose that's much of an attraction, if she's paranoid about what she eats."

"She's not, any more," Janine reminded him. "She'd really appreciate it if we gave her a lift, mind. The bus service is terrible. She doesn't drive herself, you see—doesn't think it's becoming for a traffic warden to fraternize with the enemy."

"I wasn't actually thinking of going," Steve said. "I know perfectly well that I haven't really been abducted by aliens. The ones who think they have wouldn't want someone like me there, sticking my skeptical oar in. Your Milly probably wouldn't like it either. Hang on—that's our number. Back in a sec."

When he came back with the two plates and the cutlery, Janine was quick to take up the thread of the conversation. "They don't mind skeptics, apparently," she said. "According to Milly, they're very tolerant—she says it's a very *supportive* support group—much more so than the Eating Disorder group, which tended to be much stricter and more censorious. There are rules, though, that everyone has to follow. I don't think you're allowed to accuse the other members of the group of being deluded or telling lies. I think we should go, though; it might be fun."

Steve gathered that Janine was at least slightly curious about her friend's involvement with AlAbAn, and was not ungrateful for an excuse to relent in her refusal to attend the meetings. Steve wasn't so sure that Milly would be pleased about it, but when Janine insisted on ringing Milly's mobile there and then, without even finishing her food, she carried through her mission with irresistible aplomb.

"That's settled, then" Janine said, as she put her phone back in her bag. "You'd better pick me up first, between six-thirty and six forty-five. I said we'd get to her before seven. The meeting starts at seven-thirty, but they like people to be prompt."

"Right," said Steve, uncertain whether to be mildly annoyed because the decision had been take out of his hands or mildly pleased because Janine seemed to have forgotten all about his reasons for seeking hypnotherapeutic assistance. "I guess that's a date, then."

* * * * * * *

The very concept of a "support group" had always sent a vague shiver through Steve's body, and the notion that someone like him might be in need of an institution like AlAbAn was slightly horrifying. Under the circumstances, though, he was able to justify his impending attendance at the AlAbAn meeting as a means by which Janine could introduce him to one of her closest friends, and thus move their relationship forward by one more small but vital step.

As Janine had mentioned. Milly lived in one of the brand new flats that had been built near the city centre, in one of the smaller ones reserved for occupancy by "key workers". It was a nice flat, with central heating—which Steve's flat didn't have, being reliant on an old-fashioned gas fire for winter heat—but it was rather tiny. Milly was, indeed, built on a more generous scale than Janine, but she was wearing flat heels, so she was still a comfortable inch short-er than Steve. She wasn't as exquisitely beautiful as Janine, but the relative boldness of her features was matched by a boldness of atti-tude and manner that chimed in perfectly with the style of her looks. Steve wouldn't have cast her as Helen of Troy—although he could see Janine in that role—but he reckoned that she would have made a strikingly imperious and satisfyingly voluptuous Cleopatra. She greeted Steve warmly, telling him that she'd heard a lot about him.

"All good, I hope," Steve said, lazily falling back on the con-ventional cliché rather than trying to improvise something wittier.

"Oh yes," Milly said. "Quite an ad, really—but Jan's always po-lite about her boy-friends. Ali's the one who always runs them down. Jan always thinks she might have got hold of a good one at last—but in your case, she's certainly not mistaken about your boy-band looks. You'd make a very handsome couple if you weren't so much taller than she is."

"Don't mind Milly," Janine put in. "She's a past master of the back-handed compliment. It's me she's insulting, in what she thinks is a subtle fashion, not you."

"I like to think of myself as a connoisseur of delicacy as well as beauty," Steve said, ostensibly to Milly. "I like Janine's perfect economy of form as much as I like her perfect facial symmetry. She's practically my ideal."

"Oh dear," Milly said. "*Practically* your ideal. And Jan thinks I'm one for back-handed compliments. You'll have to watch out for that margin, Jan—the next thing you know, he'll be referring to your *almost* perfect economy of form and your *almost* perfect facial symmetry, and it'll all be downhill from then on. I'm all ready—we can go."

Fortunately, Milly didn't have time to quiz Steve about why he was going to the AlAbAn meeting during the journey to East Grim-stead, because she was too eager to instruct both her companions in the nature and etiquette of the group. "They're not at all doctri-naire," she told them, wriggling slightly to settle her backside more comfortably into the rear seat of Steve's Citroen. "It's not in the least unusual for the stories they tell to be wildly different, even mu-tually contradictory, but everyone's supposed to be supportive, no matter what improbabilities they're faced with, and everyone is. You mustn't challenge anything anyone says, even if you think you've found some crucial logical flaw or elementary violation of the laws of physics. It's taken for granted that everyone's experience is valid, no matter how peculiar it might be, and that everyone's equally deserving of trust and moral support. If you listen quietly for two or three meetings, you'll find yourselves slipping into it very easily.

"Amelia, the hostess, is one of those incredibly polite and pleasant old dears that everyone wishes they had for a granny, and Walter, the chairman, has a remarkable way with people. If anyone steps out of line, he just eases them back into it with the utmost gentleness. I never knew anyone so good at compelling politeness. He'd probably have been the greatest traffic warden the world has ever seen, instantly quelling the worst road rage with a slight frown and a few soothing words, but I'm not absolutely certain what he actually did before he retired—something to do with insurance, I think. You'll find that a lot of the crowd are pretty old, although all age-groups are fairly represented.

"Walter and Amelia have been running the group for more than forty years, since the 1960s—although it wasn't always called AlAbAn. Walter reckons that everyone in the world has been abducted at least once, but that the aliens have some kind of device for blanking out the memories. He thinks that the people who remember what happened are a tiny minority, who often need help to bring the buried memories back to the surface as well as help in coming to terms with them, but he also thinks they're enormously privileged, because they obtain glimpses of possibilities far beyond those available to our narrow lives. He considers AlAbAn members the most privileged of all, because they have the chance to see how their glimpses fit in with others. Not that there's any overall pattern that I can see, although you often catch echoes of one person's story in another."

This last item of news didn't surprise Steve in the least. He figured that the real purpose of the group, for most of its members, must be to assist in the elaboration of individual confabulations. People went there, he assumed, in order to plagiarize bits of other people's delusions to make their own more detailed, and perhaps more satisfactory. He hoped that by forewarning himself of this fact he might forearm himself against any similar effect, although he didn't think that it would do him any great harm to start dreaming about other people's supposed alien abductions, or even projecting himself into such dreams, provided that he remained fully conscious of the fact that dreams were what they were. He was confident, as a man of science—even the second-rate kind who taught science to school kids rather than actually doing it—that he could resist the temptation to start believing in nonsense simply because it was sometimes spouted by people who had the gift of the gab, capable of sweetening the tempers of road hogs and selling ice to Eskimos.

Before picking Milly up, Steve had vaguely assumed that the AlAbAn group would meet in East Grimstead's village hall, but by the time they had passed through West Grimstead Milly had disabused him of that notion and had given him fair warning that the front room of Amelia Rockham's so-called cottage could get a little crowded.

Steve was surprised to find, when he, Janine and Milly arrived, that there were already twenty-five people gathered, most of them perched on folding chairs with no space to stretch their legs. There were more than enough tea-cups to go round, though; Mrs. Rockham was obviously used to catering for such numbers. She greeted the newcomers warmly, and told them not to be shy about grabbing their fair share of the biscuits, because no one else would be.

When Milly introduced Janine and Steve to the chairperson, Walter Wainwright—who was even older than Mrs. Rockham— Steve felt vindicated in his anticipations, because the old man seemed every inch a slick salesman, of the type who could easily transfer skills learned flogging second-hand cars or dodgy stocks and shares to the context of a church, a cult or a support group. Walter hardly glanced at him, though, before greeting Janine much more warmly, claiming to know her parents quite well. Steve immediately added "old lech" to the list of pre-prepared insults he had organized, but the conversation was brief because the old man had other people clamoring for his attention and there were other newcomers to be introduced to him.

Milly obviously had a seat reserved for her by the other regulars—an old armchair that had seen better days, and she only paused briefly before taking it, making an apologetic gesture to Janine because the folding seats to either side of it were already occupied. Janine nodded to indicate her appreciation of the situation, and drew Steve across the room so that they could sit together, almost directly opposite Milly's position, on a settee that was even older than the armchair. It was upholstered in a synthetic fabric whose brief fashionability had evaporated before Steve was out of short pants. "It's called Naugahyde," he whispered to Janine. "My parents had one once. So sad."

He looked around then, and tried to gauge the composition of the audience. He, Janine and Milly were probably the youngest people in the room, although there was one other man and one other woman who were probably under thirty, There were half a dozen people apparently in their thirties and half a dozen apparently in their forties, but the remainder were over fifty, and at least ten must have been senior citizens. There were more men than women, although not so many more as to form an overpowering majority. Steve noted, though, that apart from himself and Janine there were only two obvious couples in the assembly; he suspected that the proportion of widows, widowers and divorced people in the group might be substantially higher than was manifest in the population of Wiltshire as a whole.

There was no round of general introductions when the meeting got under way, and no minutes to be read. Walter Wainwright's welcome seemed to Steve to be more like a warm-up man's patter than a preamble to the kind of meeting that he had to attend at school once a week or thereabouts, but he wasn't displeased by that. The chairman ran briskly through the rules that Milly had already summarized, but didn't labor the key points; when he asked whether anyone wanted to speak, Steve dutifully stared at his shoes, but the precaution was unnecessary. One of the non-debutant members seemed only too eager to introduce himself—as "Jim"—and to volunteer to tell his tale.

Jim, it seemed, had come all the way from Ringwood to attend the last few meetings, because Dorset apparently didn't yet have its own branch of AlAbAn. He gave the impression that he wouldn't be back once he'd got his story off his chest, although that obviously wasn't typical, given the size of his audience and the attentiveness of its members.

Steve tensed himself for a painful experience. Within a very few minutes, though, he had to admit to himself that Jim's story wasn't at all what he'd expected or feared. It wasn't an account of alien abduction at all, although Steve could see why the guy had brought the story to AlAbAn in search of a sympathetic hearing rather than broadcasting it to the regulars in his local.

CHAPTER TWO

CREATIONISM

I work in Southampton so my normal way home is the motor-way and then the A31, but I'd had to visit a client that day whose offices were on the north side of Romsey. I'm in corporate insur-ance. We finished late—after seven—and instead of driving back to the motorway junction I let the SatNav guide me home by a more direct route. It took me through Awbridge, Sherfield English, and Plaitford, and then to a place that's actually called Nomansland. It was south of there, aimed vaguely in the direction of Fritham, that it happened.

This was late November, so it was pretty dark and the road was empty. Because it was a B-road, I wasn't doing much more than thirty—fifty at the most—and I was keeping my eyes peeled for headlights coming in the opposite direction. I didn't see the deer un-til I was almost on top of it. It wasn't a big deer—a roe deer, I guess, and not fully grown at that—but it was plenty big enough to put some hefty dents in the radiator and the bonnet if I hit it head on. I braked hard, but I didn't think it would be hard enough, because the damn thing stood stock still until the last possible moment, when it suddenly leapt sideways.

I will gladly swear on every Holy Book there is that there was nothing else on the road before that moment—but when the deer bounded from my side of the road to the other, it was suddenly in front of another vehicle, which appeared out of nowhere, coming in the opposite direction without its headlights on. Even if he'd braked, the other guy would have been certain to hit the stupid creature, but it didn't seem to me that he braked at all. Instead, he swerved—which, as you know, is entirely the wrong thing to do. If he'd swerved my way, he'd only have clipped my back end, because I was still moving forward even though I'd slammed the brakes on. In fact, he went the other way, straight into a tree.

I didn't actually see him hit the tree, because he didn't have his headlights on and mine were pointed in the wrong direction, but there was an almighty bang. I came to a halt shortly afterwards, and jumped out immediately—well, almost immediately—to see if there was anything I could do. I left the door open in the hope that the car's internal lights would give me enough light to see what was what.

I took my mobile with me, and began thumbing 999 before I noticed that there was no signal—which was peculiar in itself, given that I wasn't exactly a million miles from civilization, even if they have just made half of Dorset into a National Park.

I'd only got the vaguest impression of the other vehicle as it went past. It had seemed bulky, so I'd assumed it was some kind of four-by-four, but as I first set off towards the wreck it seemed even bigger than that—minibus-sized at least. The thought crossed my mind that it might have been carrying a whole bunch of kids—but as I ran towards it, it vanished as suddenly as it had appeared. One moment it was there, a mass of shadow suggestive of the kind of mangled metal mess you'd expect to find, given that it had just run into a tree doing fifty-five or sixty; the next, it was gone. The vehicle, that is; it had left its driver, or one of its passengers, behind.

The guy was lying on the roadside, apparently having been thrown clear on impact—or maybe having jumped just before the impact. For a moment, I thought he was dressed in something like a big plastic bag, but that must have been a trick of the poor light. When I knelt down and put out a hand I found that he was wearing a dark suit just like mine—made of identical cloth, it seemed. He started when I touched him, and tried to sit up.

"Don't do that, mate," I said. "You're supposed to stay still until the ambulance gets here, so they can put one of those collars on your neck."

He didn't take any notice. First he tried to look at his wristwatch, and then he started fiddling with his belt.

"Honest, mate," I said, "You really need to take it easy." I was so caught up in the moment that I'd mentally shunted aside the fact that no ambulance was coming, because I hadn't been able to call one, and the fact that the guy had jumped or been thrown out of a disappearing car.

There was a noise behind me then. I turned around, expecting to see some farmer or householder who'd heard the bang and come running. It was the deer. It had taken a few steps forward, as if to see what havoc it had wrought. Its eyes caught what little light there was, glowing in the eeriest way. I had the impression that it was staring at the chap on the ground, in fascination or in terror. Then it turned aside and bounded off the road, disappearing into a thicket.

The accident victim managed to sit up. His face was badly scratched, presumably where he'd hit the road. He wasn't bleeding much, though. He was still trying to squint at his wristwatch, while his other hand was groping at his waist. He was staring at me in the much the same way the deer had stared at him, in what seemed to be fascination and terror.

"Well, okay," I said. "If you can move you can move. I can't get a signal on my mobile anyway—we must be in a freak blank spot. You'd better get into my car, so I can drive you to A-and-E in Ringwood. You're going to need X-rays, probably some stitches."

I put out a hand to help him up, but he wouldn't take it. He got to his feet by himself and looked as if he was about to bolt, following the deer into the bushes. Then he changed his mind. He looked at me, and at the car behind me, and then he turned around to look at the place where his own car should have been but wasn't. He cursed. I didn't recognize the language, but it was definitely a curse.

"Odd, that," I said, trying to inject a note of humor into the situation. "I didn't know they'd started making four-by-fours that vanish into thin air when they hit trees."

He cursed again, in that unknown language, and fiddled some more with his wristwatch and his belt. Now that he was standing up I could see that his suit really was identical to mine—not to mention his shirt and tie. I'd just begun to wonder exactly what his face had looked like before the road bashed it up so badly when he suddenly said: "What year is this?"

"2006, mate," I said. "You got amnesia? Do you remember your name?"

If he did remember his name, he didn't tell me what it was. His face was in no condition to go white, but I never saw a man look so scared. He looked at me in sheer panic, and then he looked at my car again. I never saw anyone look at a Volkswagen Polo like that.

"Okay," I said, "it's a couple of years old, and it doesn't vanish on impact—but it goes, and the brakes still work. I'm not the one who came off worst in this little business. Get in, and I'll take you to A-and-E."

He started fiddling with his belt again. It looked like an ordinary belt, just like mine, but I'd begun to cotton on to the fact that appearances were deceptive, and that it might be something more like Batman's utility belt. It didn't have a holster attached to it, but all of a sudden there was something in his hand that looked uncomfortably like a gun, and he pointed it at me.

"Come on!" I said. "I could have just driven off. I stayed to help you. I'm trying to get you to hospital. Believe me, you're not fit to drive. You don't even know what year it is."

He seemed to have second thoughts, and lowered the gun, which now looked like something you might see in a cowboy film. Then he brought it up again, and said: "You drive."

It was my turn to curse, but I got back into the car, and didn't even try to drive off while he was going round to the passenger side. He couldn't get the door open. I had to do it for him. I got my first clear sight of him as he got in. He was my height and build, and his shoes were brown suede, just like mine. If his face hadn't been so badly cut and bruised, he might well have looked exactly like me. The gun was, indeed, an antique Colt revolver.

"Well," I said, all the more desperate to make light of things, "either you're some alternative version of me displaced from a parallel world, or you're some kind of alien chameleon who's automatically taken on my appearance and is plundering my fondness for old movies in deciding what a gun ought to look like."

He still looked terrified, but now he looked amazed too. "You know that?" he said. "You understand?"

"Sure," I said, although I felt anything but sure. "I even know how to put a seat belt on—which apparently you don't."

If he really had been me he wouldn't have been able to look any more frightened than he already did, but alien chameleons obviously have an advantage in that regard. He did put his seat-belt on, though.

"Drive," he said.

"Where to?" I wanted to know.

"Turn around," he said. "Go back the other way."

I made a three-point turn, and headed back towards Nomansland.

"You really do need X-rays," I told him. "It's a miracle that you survived, and I'm really grateful that the cuts on your head aren't bleeding nearly as much as I'd have expected, but you could have broken something. You really should have had your headlights on, you know, even if that thing you were driving was only pretending to be a car. It's way too late for making crop circles, you know—the harvest came in three months ago."

He didn't say anything, but the hand that was pointing the gun at me was trembling. I should have been terrified myself, but I wasn't. However absurd it might be, I thought that I was in control of the situation.

We should have reached Nomansland—the village called No-mansland, that is—within three minutes, or five at the most. We didn't. The road just kept on, silent, dark and deserted. It didn't take a genius to work out that we weren't in Wiltshire or Dorset any more—and I don't mean that we'd somehow skipped into Hampshire.

I was shaken up, I guess. At any rate, I wasn't myself. In any normal frame of mind I'd never have done what I did, which was to slam on the brakes without warning and grab the gun out of his shaking hand when he lurched forward. I turned it on him. It felt strangely comfortable in my hand.

"Ordinarily," I said, "I'd just tell you to get the hell out, and then drive off. Unfortunately, I realize that it might just be a bit too late for that, and that I might not be able to find my way back to any place my SatNav can recognize. So tell me—where are we?"

He cursed softly in his alien language. "Not 2006," he said, eventually. "Too dangerous."

"2006 is too dangerous for you?" I said. "What year do you come from, then?"

"Too dangerous for everyone," the alien chameleon said, resent-fully. "We no longer keep count with clocks and calendars. We know when it is, internally." He was watching me very carefully as he said it. I'd already managed to give him the impression that I knew and understood far more than I did, and I wanted to hold on to the intellectual high ground

"Do time travelers often crash into trees while avoiding stray twenty-first-century deer," I asked him, "or are you feeling like a bit of a chump just now?"

He muttered something that might have included the words "your fault" and "stupid asshole", but he'd obviously inherited my habit of strangling undiplomatic remarks as well as my physical appearance. He pulled himself together and said: "What now? Do you want me to drive?"

I looked out at the bare patch of road illuminated by the head-lights. It didn't seem unreal, but I knew that it was only pretending to be a bit of English B-road. It was actually a very different high-way.

"Where or when were we driving to?" I asked him. "Surely not all the way home? Converting second-hand Volkswagen Polos into time machines can't be that easy."

"A...lay-by," he said.

"Right," I said. "Presumably, you could get a signal on your unwristwatch, even though I couldn't get one on my mobile, so you were able to call the temporal AA. One up to future technology. Are you thirty-first century or forty-first? If you were still counting by means of calendars, that is."

His eyes were fixed on the barrel of the gun, and he was literally quaking with fear, but he forced himself to reply, seemingly trying to humor me and make sure that I didn't do anything violent. "It's not a matter of centuries," he said. "My cra is a billion years from yours."

"A billion years," I repeated. "You just crashed a time machine from a billion years in the future into a twenty-first-century oak tree?"

"It wasn't an oak," the time-traveler said. "It was an ash."

"You picked up the language very cleverly," I observed. "Almost as cleverly as you picked up my appearance. What do you really look like, inside your plastic bag?"

"Would you like me to drive?" he asked, again—in a manner suggestive of some urgency.

"All you had to do was say," I told him. "All you had to do was say: *Please don't take me to A-and-E in Ringwood, because I need medical help from my own kind.* All you had to do was say: *There's this little interdimensional lay-by not a million miles from Nomansland, and if you could drop me there I'd be ever so grateful.* And I'd have said: *Sure—always assuming that I can get back again.* Can I get back again? I mean, you wouldn't want to rip me out of the time-stream permanently, would you? That would be tantamount to changing history, and I know how sensitive you time-travelers are about that sort of thing. Even if we humans are no more to you than a Mesozoic butterfly might be to us, you never know what changes might unfold over a billion years if you were to take me out...not to mention my poor little Volkswagen."

"There were no butterflies in the Mesozoic era," the pedant couldn't help saying—but he knew what I meant. "Yes, you can get back. I'm sorry I didn't ask politely. It just seemed...such a very dangerous time."

"Is it really that bad?" I asked, curiously. "So the ecocatastrophe's scheduled to unfold quickly enough to cause a major economic collapse before the century's end?"

"Worse," the time-traveler replied tersely.

"How much worse? Extinction of the species?"

"Yes."

"Before the end of the century?"

"Yes."

"So, when I say *Can I get back?* I really ought to be asking *Do I have to go back?*"

"Yes."

"Well," I said, after a few moments thought. "Do I?"

"Yes. I'm sorry about that—but you wouldn't like my world."

"Why? It must be a lot better than 2006 if the thought of being stranded there is so utterly terrifying. I wouldn't be that bothered about being the only human being alive, you know, even if I were in a zoo. I'm not long divorced, you see—I've no ties and I'm suffering a certain amount of endemic disenchantment with the world of corporate insurance. Anyway, it would beat imminent extinction."

"You still wouldn't like it," the time-traveler insisted.

"I might," I insisted, in my turn. "What exactly were you doing in the twenty-first century, anyhow, if it's such a frightening time?"

"Passing through. Is there any way that we can settle this quickly and be on our way? If I don't get to where I'm going soon enough, I won't be anywhere—and neither will you."

That raised all sorts of questions. How could time be a problem to a time-traveler—even one who'd crashed his machine? What would happen to us if we didn't get to the lay-by? How come we were stuck at all, given that the chameleon had such awesome powers that he was able to conjure up guns out of nowhere? It was obvious, though, that he really was in a hurry. He was obviously up against some kind of deadline.

I wound down my window and threw the revolver out into limbo. Then I put the car into gear again, and moved off. "I figure you owe me one for that," I said. "I know you didn't really understand what you were doing, but some people might get upset at being treated the way you've treated me. Personally, I'm still happy to get you to wherever you need to be, even if I do have to take a detour outside the universe, but I want to know where you come from, and why I wouldn't like it, and what you were doing in these parts. I don't want any more terse bullshit, like just saying *yes* and *passing through*. You owe me as much of an explanation as you can give me, okay?"

He thought about it for a few seconds, and then he said "Okay"—exactly as I would have done if I'd have been in his shoes, instead of him being in mine.

* * * * * *

I can't put what he told me in his words, because most of his words weren't in English, although I seemed to understand them well enough at the time. He obviously still had tricks up his sleeve, even if they hadn't done him any good when I took him by surprise and turned the tables on him.

What he told me, in a nutshell, is that life on Earth a billion years hence is very different from life now. Evolution has moved on, as you might expect, although you'd still be able to identify most of the animal species that exist as analogues of the ones that have existed for the last few hundred million years. Some are adapted for life as herbivores and some for life as carnivores; some fly, some swim and some crawl. The most important difference is that all the animal species that exist then, and most of the plants too, are conscious and intelligent.

That might seem surprising to you, given that you're probably used to thinking of humans as the top of the evolutionary tree, but human intelligence will come to seem like an evolutionary disaster in the not-too-distant future, when the species becomes extinct. The intelligence that's widespread a billion years hence is the result of an adaptive radiation a long way in the future, by which time the whole apparatus of complex animal species will have rediversified from worms a dozen times over. There'll be a lot of interesting times between now and then, so I'm told, although he couldn't give me details. The inhabitants of the future a billion years from now don't call the Earth's ecosphere by a name equivalent to our Gaia; they call it after a mythical creature whose nearest contemporary equivalent is the phoenix.

There are creatures that look not unlike humans in that future world. At any rate, they're as similar to humans as humans are to baboons. They don't live much like humans, though. The human monopoly on contemporary intelligence makes animal husbandry uncomplicated, but in a world where all animals are intelligent the politics of meat-eating are much more complicated. Even the politics of herbivore lifestyles can be awkward, in an era when so many plant species are as smart and knowledgeable as animals—smarter and more knowledgeable, he said, if the claims made by some of the million-year-old trees and fungi can be believed. He didn't seem to believe it himself.

You might think that the situation would be a recipe for all-out warfare, with herbivores forming alliances to wipe out carnivorous species and carnivores trying to enslave or lobotomize whole populations of herbivores, but it doesn't work that way. Smart predators are very well aware that what's good for their prey species is good for them—and that what's good for the plants that feed their prey species is also good for them. Similarly, the prey species recognize that it wouldn't actually be a good idea to exterminate their predators, because the consequent explosion of their own populations would only lead to famine and warfare—though not to disease, since the larger creatures in this future have long since come to a proper understanding with their indwelling bacteria and viruses. The top predators are, of course, vulnerable to exactly such population explosions, and have to be smart enough to find their own ways to avoid them, partly by birth-control and partly by regulating inter- and intraspecific competition.

To cut to the bottom line, prey species a billion years hence—and the smarter plants that feed herbivorous prey species—accept that a certain proportion of their population will go to feed other species. Just as the predators take measures to regulate their own numbers, the prey and smart plant species do their utmost to take control of the process, and manipulate it to their advantage. A billion years hence, evolutionary selection is a wholly conscious process, with every intelligent species devoting itself to eugenic planning—and because every species is doing it, they all compete to do it as artfully and as productively as possible.

Some species are content to be as they are, and merely seek to refine their own imagined perfection, but the great majority are intent on further change, on metamorphosis into something finer. There are, inevitably, disagreements, both within and between species, as to the directions that the evolution of individual species and the collective ensemble ought to take. Politics a billion years hence is an extremely complicated business, although there's only one fundamental political philosophy, whose name can best be translated as "creationism". A billion years hence, evolution isn't something that intelligent beings merely believe in, or don't, but something that every intelligent species is actually *doing*—a cause to which everyone is committed, and work that everyone takes seriously.

No matter how much they may disagree about details, everyone who lives a billion years hence is interested in intelligent design. Everyone, the traveler assured me, is trying with all his might to make the design of life and the design of destiny better than any kind of nature could ever contrive unaided. No one then seriously expects that the Phoenix will never die again, but everyone is determined to make sure that it becomes as glorious as possible before some cosmic accident puts an end to their particular adventure. It certainly sounded like a world that was—will be—very different from this one. I think he was trying to be kind when he said I wouldn't like it, trying to soften the blow of his not being able to take me with him.

Obviously, I couldn't get my head around all of this immediately, and I knew that we were running out of time. Rather than simply let him ramble on—as he surely would have done—I started asking questions again, in the hope of focusing his account on matters of more immediate interest.

"And the time travel is part of that project, is it?" I asked him. "You're trying to apply intelligent design to the past as well as the future—laying the foundations for your wonderful world by inventing things like the bacterial flagellum and dumping them in the pre-Cambrian. Why doesn't it lead to paradoxes? Or are you just hiving off new alternative prehistories into an infinite manifold of possible worlds?"

"Time travel is part of the project," he agreed, "but not in the way you mean. There's only one Earth, only one history of life. We need to understand it, but we can't change it. We can sample it, in certain relatively unobtrusive ways, but it's mostly a matter of copying information for future use."

"Only one Earth and only one history of life?" I said. "What about all the other worlds in the universe—all the other Phoenixes? Surely ours will develop space travel eventually, even if humans die out before we can master the trick—and even if our world doesn't, some of the others surely will."

"Maybe," he said. "We don't know. Our view is that space travel simply isn't practical."

"Unlike time travel?"

"Time travel is definitely practical, provided that you're very careful. The lay-by's just up ahead."

If the road was really a road, then the lay-by was probably really a lay-by—but I didn't believe it. I pulled off just the same, and parked the car. There was nothing outside but the shadows of trees; I couldn't tell whether they were oaks or ashes.

"Where were you going, in your very careful fashion, when that deer got in your way?" I wanted to know.

"Home," he said. He was being annoying again, probably to pay me back for the ironic remark about his very careful fashion.

"Where had you been, then?" I asked. "Collecting dinosaurs?"

"Much further back than that," he told me. "Collecting alternatives to DNA, from the era when there was a chemical contest to determine the fundamentals of Earthly life. You can imagine how many individual moments I had to pass through in a five-billion-year journey. They were all supposed to be vacant of solid material—until you changed history."

"Me!" At first I was outraged, but then I caught on to what he meant. I'd been supposed to hit the deer. The deer shouldn't have jumped sideways. But he was still wrong. It hadn't been me who's changed history—*his* history—but the deer. I remembered the way it had looked at me before it left the scene of the accident...if it really had been an accident.

The time traveler had implied that history couldn't be changed, but what he'd actually said was that he and his kind couldn't change it, and it seemed to me that his remarks about the practicality of time travel might imply that he actually meant "wouldn't" rather than "couldn't". For them, perhaps, there really might be only one time-track, one history of Earthly life...but they weren't arrogant enough to think that they would be the end of the Phoenix's story, or the very last word in intelligent design, and they weren't stupid enough to think that everything they couldn't do was necessarily impossible or impractical.

"Your friends might not be able to come and pick you up," I said. "If that bloody animal wiped out the history of the next billion years, your entire world might have been blanked out of existence."

"They're already here," he countered, smugly, pointing to the driving mirror.

When I'd pulled into the lay-by it had only been big enough to accommodate one car, but now there was an empty space behind us, in which another vehicle was forming. It didn't have its headlights on, but its shadowy form was uncannily similar to a Volkswagen Polo.

The thing that got out of the driving seat, however, didn't look anything like me. It was wearing a plastic bag, but it looked vaguely reminiscent of a shaggy crocodile walking on its hind legs, although it bore about as much resemblance to a twenty-first-century croc as a twenty-first-century croc does to a lichen-encrusted warthog.

The time-traveler turned towards me, and stuck out his hand. "I'm truly sorry about the gun," he said. "I didn't know you as well then as I do now. You've been you for an entire lifetime, so you're probably used to that awful chaos and confusion of motive and desire, fantasy and perception, but it was all extremely strange and disturbing to me."

He opened the door as he was speaking. The car's internal light came on. I saw that the cuts and bruises had almost healed, and that his features were almost exactly like those I see in a mirror when I shave—except, of course, that they were the wrong way round. I'm not the most symmetrical person in the world, alas.

Automatically, I took the hand in my own and shook it.

"You couldn't give me a few tips, I suppose," I said. "Tactics for avoiding the worst effects of the world's impending end—that sort of thing."

"Study Stone Age survival techniques and move to Antarctica," he said. "That's if you want to drag it out. Otherwise, don't wait too long before buying that antique revolver and blowing your brains out."

"I really would like to come with you," I said. "I might not like your world, but...."

"No can do, Jim," he said. "Very sorry. Thanks for the lift. Just turn around and go back the way we came. You'll be home in no time at all." Then he shut the door, and walked back to the other car with the shaggy crocodile in the plastic bag. They seemed to be arguing about something as they went, but they certainly weren't doing it in English.

The time-traveler got into the other Volkswagen's passenger seat. The vehicle moved off a minute or so later, swerving past me and continuing along the road in the direction of the unknown.

For a couple of minutes I thought about following it, but I knew that time travel couldn't possibly be as simple as that, and that I'd probably get lost in limbo. Doomed or not, the familiar world seemed the more attractive option. I put the car into gear, did another three-point turn, and headed back the way I'd come.

I had a lot to think about, and whatever the time traveler had said about "no time at all" I'd had a very long day. I was so used to the fake road being empty that I wasn't really paying attention. I didn't notice the road become real again, and I didn't see the deer until it was far too late.

It wasn't a big deer—a roe deer, I think, and not fully grown at that. I braked hard, but I knew it wouldn't be hard enough, because the damn thing just stood stock still until I hit it. In the last split second before the impact, I stopped wondering whether it might be the same deer as before, realizing that it had to be *exactly* the same deer. This time, though, it wasn't going to leap aside. This time, the time traveler's history would be conserved.

The luckless deer slammed into the windscreen, and the windscreen broke. A deer—even one that's hardly more than a fawn—can really make a mess of your face when it's traveling along with the shards of a windscreen at God-only-knows-how-many miles per hour, but it didn't knock me unconscious. To tell the truth, I think most of the blood must have been the deer's, not mine. I was able to bring the car to a halt, unbuckle my seat belt and step out on to the road.

"The bastard," I said. "I wonder whether he and his mate fixed things so that it never bloody happened, or whether the dent in history was just snapping back into shape." I was glad, though, that I still remembered every moment of what had happened, even if it hadn't happened any longer. Neither he nor history had been able to take that away from me.

I couldn't be absolutely sure, of course. How could I begin to guess what the temporal AA, or the natural resilience of the time-stream, might be able to achieve?

I stuck the deer in the boot, although rumor has it that collecting road kill still counts as poaching in the eyes of the law. I got a friend in the business to butcher it for me, and split the legs and rump with him. Unfortunately, every time I eat a bit I remember the way the damn thing looked at me that first time, immediately after it had caused the time machine to crash. I don't know for sure, but it still seems to me that the deer had known what it was doing. Perhaps, in some parallel universe, it still does—but in ours, it seems, intelligent designers seem to be content to work in less ambitious and more mysterious ways.

CHAPTER THREE

TAKING THINGS SERIOUSLY

In most of the places that Steve had hung out in the course of his life, a story like Jim's would have got a round of deeply ironic but sincerely admiring applause, assuming that the audience could have tolerated its enormous length—which was unlikely, given the shortage of modern attention spans. Even respectful applause, however, was evidently not *de rigueur* at AlAbAn meetings. When Jim finished he was greeted with a polite murmur of approval and an assortment of sage nods.

Steve hadn't been planning to tell his story anyway, even if there had been time left for a second one, but he realized immediately that he was going to have to remember a great deal more, and organize it far more comprehensively, before he could even begin to think about taking the floor in Amelia Rockham's front room. Even if Jim's performance wasn't typical, it had certainly set a standard. Steve wasn't the kind of person to obsess about the possibility of falling below an established standard, but he felt obliged to make some effort to uphold the honor of the teaching profession, science, and youth.

The group was not only scrupulously polite, Steve observed, but exceedingly stubborn in maintaining its supportive appearances. When Walter Wainwright invited questions and comments, the gist of the opening remarks was that Jim's experience must have been unusually disturbing, and that he was obviously coping with it extremely well, not only emotionally but intellectually and imaginatively.

Jim, who had obviously been slightly worried about the kind of reception he might get, even though he had scouted out the group before diving in head-first, blossomed in the warmth of the praise.

He admitted that he was, indeed, coping very well, not only emotionally but intellectually and imaginatively, and that he was a fortunate man to be able to pass on the legacy of his experience to such understanding people.

Steve was mildly surprised that nobody even ventured to hint, let alone to suggest forthrightly, that Jim might have fallen asleep at the wheel and hallucinated the whole experience—or the ideative seed that he had since nurtured and brought to maturity by careful confabulation—in the split second before or after he hit the deer. Nor did anyone imply, by the merest word or gesture, that he might simply be telling a tall tale. Indeed, it seemed to Steve that some of the private glances exchanged between the group members were signaling that Jim's story had made even more sense to them than it had to its teller, not just because it dovetailed with their own experiences but because their own experiences cast some light on its murkier elements. Steve was tempted, just for a moment, to throw a spanner into the works by making some slyly snide remark, but he didn't have to make an effort to suppress the temptation; it withered and died of its own accord.

"That wasn't quite what I expected," he whispered in Janine's ear.

"Nor me," she replied. She was looking across the room at Milly, who was nodding sagely and making murmurous approving noises along with everyone else, and who seemed to have identified as forcefully with the narrator as anyone else had. Neither of the women who sat to either side of Milly, one of whom looked to be in her thirties and the other in her forties, could match her robust figure, but they didn't seem at all frail: there was color in their cheeks and a marked liveliness in their manner a they fed on one another's fascination and good will.

None of which signifies, Steve thought, *that they're anything but completely crazy, intoxicated by the chance to pool their craziness*. Such was the atmosphere of the meeting, however, that Steve felt ashamed of the judgment as soon as he'd formulated it. He decided, on due reflection, that it didn't matter whether he believed Jim's story or not, or whether anyone else really believed it, or even whether Jim believed it himself. It was the kind of story that had to be treated earnestly and represented as actual experience in order to take full effect. If it were only to be reckoned a traveler's tale, like a mariner's account of singing mermaids, a salesman's account of some farmer's daughter or a scaremonger's account of a brief encounter with a maniac serial killer, it had to be treated exactly as the members of AlAbAn were treating it in order to generate its particular *frisson*—and that *frisson* was something to be valued in itself, as a kind of intoxication far more delicate than alcohol or ecstasy could produce. As someone who prided himself on being a connoisseur of delicacy, Steve thought, he ought to be wholeheartedly in favor of that kind of thrill.

Amelia Rockham made a second huge pot of tea, although many of her guests politely refused, and began to drift away in ones and twos. Steve and Janine waited politely until Milly signaled that she was ready to depart, and then they bid farewell to their hostess and Walter Wainwright before making their way back to the Citroen.

"Is it always like that?" Janine asked Milly, as they got into the car.

"The group, yes," Milly said. "The story wasn't typical, by any means. Most are closer to the stereotype: little aliens in saucer-shaped spaceships, with operating tables and bright lights, with or without lengthy dialogues in which one of the aliens explains the reason for the whole enterprise, usually involving the imminent extinction of the human race by virtue of nuclear war or ecocatastrophe, or both."

"Is that the sort of thing that happened to you?" Steve asked, tilting his head so that he could see Milly's face in the mirror.

"Yes and no," she replied, shortly, blushing.

"Have you told your story to the group yet?" Janine asked, as Steve switched the engine on.

"No," Milly said. "Nobody hassles you to tell, if you're not ready, I think Walter might worry about me, a little—he makes paternal comments occasionally—but the others have the patience of saints."

"I've seen that kind of paternal interest before," Steve said. "Some teachers are the same way—the kind who used to be always patting the kids on the head or the knee, before all physical contact was outlawed. It's usually harmless, of course—the ones who fantasize about taking it further don't last long in the profession—but it's still slightly suspect."

"Walter's not like that," Milly replied, with conviction. "He's absolutely sincere."

"That's the salesman's motto, isn't it?" Steve said, as he headed off towards Alderbury. "Sincerity is the key—once you can fake that, you're made. Did you say that he was an insurance salesman, in his working days?"

"I don't know," Milly said. "I think someone mentioned once that he used to work for the Prudential, but I've no idea what his job was."

Steve couldn't suppress a brief smirk. *Walter Wainwright, the man from the Pru*, he thought. *Back in the days when the outfit prided itself on the individual attention it gave its customers, always sending its agents round to collect premiums, long before England became the Empire of the Financial Advisers.* Aloud, he said "Is there something going on between him and Amelia Rockham?"

"I doubt it, at their age" Milly said, dryly. "They've known one another for years—since they were our age, at least, and probably since their schooldays. Amelia told me once that they knew one another before they married their respective spouses, and there might have been a wistful note in her voice, but I'd hesitate to drawn any conclusions from that. They're both widowed now, though, and they seem to be close—they certainly see one another outside the meetings, although I doubt that it involves any hot sex. I'd like to think our friendship would last as long as that, wouldn't you, Jan?"

"Yes, I would," Janine replied, "Although it's bound to be difficult once people start pairing off and getting married."

"I've got no plans," Milly said, "and Alison seems to specialize in dating men who are already married nowadays. How about you?"

Steve glanced sideways, knowing that it would be Janine's turn to blush. She didn't reply to Milly's provocative question.

"It needn't matter, anyway," Milly said, as soon as it became clear that Janine had no comment to make. "None of us would marry the kind of husband who'd monopolize us, would we? We'd carry on being friends no matter what."

"We ought to get together with Ali next week," Janine said. "It's been too long."

"Absolutely," Milly said. "She's bound to have some tales to tell. She's well on her way to becoming the Town Hall tart. Have you met Alison, Steve?"

"No," Janine answered for him. "I've explained that boy-friends aren't allowed on our girls' nights out."

"We could arrange something more decorous that he wouldn't find quite as shocking," Milly suggested. "A weekend excursion to the coast, maybe."

"Steve plays cricket," Janine said. "Saturdays *and* Sundays, most weeks."

"Well, no one's perfect," Milly said. "At least he's remembered his abduction experience, even if it did need hypnotherapy to help him remember it. You should try that, Jan—dredge up your own experience. Everybody's had at least one, you know."

"I'll leave mine safely buried for the time being," Janine replied. "I'm sure it won't be as lurid as yours."

"We really must try to get Ali along to the next meeting," Milly countered. "Hers is *bound* to involve alien sex. I'd love to see the expression on Walter's face while he listened to one of Ali's adventures. Amelia would just nod her head maternally, though, and sympathize. She's imperturbable."

While this exchange continued between the two girls, Steve kept his eyes on the road, looking out for stray deer and wishing that the unlit stretch connecting West Grimstead to Alderbury didn't look quite so much like a road that wasn't really a road at all, mysteriously heading directly to nowhere. On the other hand, he thought, how wonderful would it be to belong to a world in which intelligence was everywhere, and in which the only fundamental political philosophy was creationism?

Janine and Milly's private discussion petered out as they reached Alderbury. "Shall we stop off for something to eat?" Steve asked, as he turned on to the A36. "I didn't get away from school until half past five, so I haven't had a chance."

"I'm okay," Milly said. "I had a snack before I came out."

"We can stop off at the Chinese takeaway on the corner of my street after we drop Milly off, if you like," Janine said. "We can eat at my place."

"Good idea." Steve said.

"You will be going to go to the next meeting, won't you?" Milly put in, quickly.

Janine tried to save Steve from the necessity of answering by saying "I don't know," and would probably have gone on to say that she could let Milly know when they got together the following week, but Steve had already decided that he didn't need saving.

"We can pick you up at the same time, if you like," he said. "I'll give it one more go, at least. It's free, after all—and anything's better than watching TV."

"Thanks," Milly said. "I appreciate it. The bus is awful, and I don't like begging lifts from the others, even though a couple of them drive through Salisbury on their way further west."

"Warminster used to get a lot of UFO activity, didn't it?" Steve said. "Cley Hill was quite famous back in the fifties and sixties, so I hear."

"Some of the long-term members remember it fondly," Milly said. "The whole of Salisbury Plain was said to be a hot spot. That's probably why Wiltshire has its own branch of AlAbAn—most of the others are in big cities, although I think there's one in Devon."

"They used to get a lot of crop circles in the Pewsey area," Janine said, "but I think the fashion's passed. Maybe the aliens are attracted to Stonehenge—they probably built it, along with the pyramids."

"The armed services have a long tradition of using the plain for military exercises," Steve pointed out. "Lots of helicopters ferrying men back and forth—and all that empty airspace higher up for testing new aircraft."

Milly didn't object to the injection of skepticism. When they dropped her off at her flat, she seemed to be in a very good mood. She thanked Steve profusely for the lift, and told Janine that she would call her to firm up arrangements for the following week.

"Milly doesn't seem the AlAbAn type, somehow," Steve said, as he drove away in the direction of Old Sarum, where Janine had a bedsit in a triply divided terraced house. "How did she get involved in it?"

"I'm not sure," Janine replied. "I think it was someone she knew from her old support group who got her involved."

"But she really does believe that she was abducted by aliens?"

"To tell you the truth, I don't know. It's the only thing I've ever known her to be reluctant to talk about. She's always urging Ali and me to go with her to meetings, but she won't tell us what supposedly happened to her. Now I've seen the group, though, I can see why she likes the atmosphere, and the etiquette. You don't get a lot of feedback when you spend all day handing out parking tickets. She's been threatened with violence on many an occasion—one white van man told her in great detail exactly what he was going to do when he raped her. She took a bit of the color out of his cheeks by telling him exactly what she was going to do by way of reprisal, but it shook her up just the same. She can strike an intimidating attitude, but she's not as strong as she looks. She can be very moody—but you saw how tonight cheered her up. I know it seems a bit silly, but I think the group does her good, and probably does its other members good too. It's harmless, at least. I was surprised that you were so quick to offer her another lift, though. Fancy her, do you?"

"I thought it would be interesting to take another look," Steve said. "At the meeting, not Milly. I'd like to see if the other stories they tell are as enterprising as that one. If they are...well, it'll be *much* better than television, and it's only once a fortnight."

He found a parking-spot not far from the house where Janine had a top floor flat. The house wasn't dissimilar to the one in which his own flat was located, but he had a ground floor apartment which, though slightly smaller than its own upper-level companion, was considerably more spacious than Janine's garret. It was only a short walk to the Chinese restaurant. While they waited for their order to be cooked and boxed, Janine said: "Do you think going to the meetings might help you remember more of your own nightmare?"

"Maybe," Steve said.

"And that's what you want to do?"

"Maybe," Steve repeated. "I honestly don't know. Part of me thinks that getting deeper into this will only make me crazier than I already am, part of me thinks that Sylvia might actually be right, and that I might learn something useful—from the group as well as from the nightmare. It's the uncertainty as much as anything else that makes me think I ought to go back at least once. I can stop at any time, can't I?"

"So you're taking it seriously—the alien abduction thing?"

"It depends what you mean by *seriously*," he parried.

"What do *you* mean by *seriously*?" Janine pressed on.

Steve shrugged his shoulders. "What Sylvia Joyce would mean, I guess. Even if the stories can't be taken literally, they might still be revealing in psychological terms—generally as well as personally. In a sense, the stories might be more interesting as dreams to be interpreted than mere accidents of happenstance."

"You never did tell me exactly why you went to see the hypnotherapist in the first place," Janine reminded him. "What is this phobia you have?"

Steve looked away, as if to study the menu posted on the restaurant wall. "Like your friend Milly," he said, although he knew full well that he was merely procrastinating, "I'm not quite ready to tell you everything yet. A mystery or two helps keep a relationship interesting, don't you think?"

"Perhaps it does," she countered, "but only in the sense that it provides a target to aim at. Am I supposed to winkle it out of you by guesswork and experiment?"

"No," Steve said. "Just let me work up to it for a while. To change to subject, the advice Jim's time-traveler gave him was pretty sound. If the ecocatastrophe does accelerate, survival skills might be a good thing to have. There's a course starting at the old technical college next week, still open for enrolments. It's ten weeks in the classroom—Wednesday evenings, so it won't clash with AlAbAn—then a field trip in December, with two nights sleeping rough on the plain. We could do it, if you like."

"Why not?" Janine replied. "It's always good to know how to catch, skin and cook a rabbit—and as you say, anything's better than having to watch television. I'm not moving to Antarctica, though, no matter how hot the weather gets."

* * * * * * *

When Steve saw Sylvia Joyce for a second time on the following Tuesday, the therapist was almost as glad to hear that Steve had gone to AlAbAn as Rhodri Jenkins had been to hear that Steve had gone to Sylvia Joyce. When Steve added Milly's gratitude for the forging of an extra link between herself and Janine and the convenience of regular lifts of East Grimstead into the equation, he seemed to be delighting a great many people—which made a pleasant change from all the alienating he'd done as a result of the Tracy/Jill fiasco.

"How's the relaxation going?" Sylvia asked.

"Too soon to tell," Steve reported. "I made the CD, as you suggested, last Friday night, and I've been playing it to myself regularly. I've only spent two days in the classroom since, so I can't tell yet whether it'll have a lasting effect on my stress level at work. We were playing away on Sunday and I had to cross the Test, so I tried to go through the process while I was on the bridge. Maybe I felt slightly less queasy than usual—I'll need a lot more experiments before I can be sure."

"That's all good," the therapist assured him. "I'm sure you'll see the effects soon. Have you had any further thoughts about attempting another regression?"

"I'm not sure there'll be any need," he said. "I think I might be able to make more progress consciously. The AlAbAn members may be a little bit crazy, but it might turn out to be a constructive kind of craziness. I've only heard one report so far, and that one didn't even get as far as outer space, but it's already triggered some ideas."

"Have you recovered any more of your own experience?"

"Not really," Steve admitted. "I haven't had any recurrence of the nightmare itself—so far as I can remember—but the imagery does keep on niggling at my mind. I think I prefer trying to deal with it while I'm fully conscious, with the aid of a scientific outlook, rather than having it seize me by the throat while I'm off guard."

"Isn't that just beating around the bush?" Sylvia asked him. "You can think of any number of excuses for not trying to get to grips with it, but there's no substitute for head-on confrontation."

"I don't think head-on confrontation is the best way to go," Steve said. "Some things are best approached by stealth, and a scientific attitude is never a bad thing. I need time to practice the relaxation techniques, and to bring them to bear on all the different aspects of my life in which they might be useful. This might be one race that slow and steady really can win.

"If that's the way you want to do it, Steve," Sylvia said, blandly, "that's fine. I can't talk about my other clients, as you know, but you wouldn't be the first who wanted to talk all around his problem as a way of not facing up to it. You know, don't you, how many psychotherapists it takes to change a light-bulb."

"Yes I do," Steve said. "Only one—and pretty much any one will do—but the light-bulb has to want to be changed."

"Do *you* want to be changed, Steve?" the therapist followed up, relentlessly.

"My filament hasn't gone yet," Steve told her. "I know you're used to working with the traditional brand of light-bulb they still sell in Sainsbury's, but I'm the new sort—the low-energy, long-life, curled-up-radiant-tube sort. I'm not the reckless type, in spite of what Rhodri Jenkins may have told you about my love life."

"I don't talk to other clients about you, either," Sylvia told him.

"Of course not," Steve said, "but that doesn't prevent your clients from talking about each other, does it? I bet he's mentioned me to you, since he found out I took his advice—just by way of being helpful, of course. You might not be an orthodox Freudian, but he is, at least in the sense that he thinks that sex is the root of all psychological problems. He thinks I'm a Don Juan because I've had four of my female colleagues in the last two years, while he's only had half a dozen of them in twenty, despite being made deputy head—and most of them were probably married ones bored enough to bonk anyone who could make them feel more attractive than a soggy chip. Actually, my attitude to sex couldn't be healthier, and I'm perfectly happy with my current girl-friend. That has nothing at all to do with my phobias, or my classroom-induced stress."

"Are you familiar with the quotation, '*The lady doth protest too much, methinks*'?" Sylvia asked him.

"It's from *Hamlet*," Steve said, relieved to be able to retain the intellectual high ground. "Shakespeare's hymn of praise to methodical madness. I was just trying to make the point that my phobias aren't symptomatic of some sexual hang-up, in spite of what you might suspect or Rhodri might have hinted to you."

"Thanks for sharing that with me," Sylvia said. "You'll forgive me, I suppose, if I reserve my judgment until we can resume our attempts to get to the bottom of the problem."

"It's possible, isn't it," Steve said, "that some problems don't actually have bottoms—that they're just what they seem to be, and nothing more? And it's possible, too, that some problems are better solved by whittling away patiently, rather than attempting to blast them open with dynamite?"

"Quite possible," Sylvia conceded. "But I wouldn't be doing my job, would I, if I didn't explore all the possibilities available to us?"

* * * * * * *

Steve and Janine went to the first meeting of the survival course on the day after Steve's second session with Sylvia Joyce, but it turned out to be a formularistic introduction session, with the standard icebreakers that now seemed to be universally accepted as "best practice" by teachers of every sort, although Steve loathed them. The icebreakers were followed by a long pep talk on the necessity of self-sufficiency in a fast-changing world.

On the Thursday night Janine went out with Milly and Alison, but Steve didn't mind being deserted, because it gave him a chance to play poker on-line. He played for four hours, ending up thirty pounds down—an unusually bad result. He always played in low-stakes games that were too trivial to attract predatory sharks, and was usually able to come out ahead, but the competition had been atypically disciplined and the cards he'd been dealt had been profoundly unexciting.

On Friday he and Janine met up at the wine bar again to celebrate the beginning of the weekend.

"Did you have a good time last night?" he asked.

"Great," she said. "And before you ask, we hardly talked about you at all. Milly told Alison how extremely good-looking you were, and that you were one more reason why she ought to start coming to AlAbAn meetings with us, but Ali didn't seem impressed."

"Her description obviously didn't do me justice," Steve observed. "I can't imagine why Alison wouldn't be prepared to go to the ends of the earth just to get a glimpse of me, if my magnificence had been properly explained. You must have run me down, so as to keep the opposition to a minimum."

"It was me who suggested that we give Milly a lift to AlAbAn, remember?" Janine said. "I'd hardly have done that if I were afraid of opposition. Don't worry—I'm sure you'll meet all my friends eventually. You haven't introduced me to any of yours yet."

"They're all cricketers and schoolteachers," Steve said. "You'd find them incredibly boring. Besides which, I'm not as brave as you—I wouldn't take the risk of introducing a girl as stunningly beautiful as you to any of my male friends. I may be a young Adonis—I'm quoting my deputy head there, so it must be true—but I'm too good a poker player to take that sort of reckless risk."

"They'd probably find me boring," Janine said. "I'm just a travel agent. I'm getting to the age now when I wish I'd tried a bit harder at school—sad, isn't it? Milly was saying the same thing last night—she's beginning to get a sense of unfulfilled potential. She never used to crack a book when we were at school, but she reads a lot nowadays. I told her that she ought to go to the tech and do A levels in the evenings. She might, if Ali or I would go with her—but Ali's got a career path of sorts already mapped out for her in local government, and I'd be better off doing an in-house management training course. I've been thinking of putting in for one."

"Why not?" Steve said. "Go for it. Might as well take advantage of any opportunities that are going."

"Milly and Alison said the same. None of us is likely to get on to the property ladder any time soon unless we can bump our salaries up, even if we find a suitable partner."

Steve was well aware of the problems of getting on to the property ladder, even if one could find a suitable partner with whom to bear the burden of a mortgage , but he didn't want to start discussing his relationship with Janine in terms like that just yet. "Milly gave me the impression that your girls' nights out were far too lewd for tender ears like mine," he said. "It's a bit disappointing to discover that you spend your time comparing salaries and promotion prospects."

"Oh, we did the X-rated stuff too—not me, I hasten to add. They wanted all the lurid details, of course, but I maintained a diplomatic silence. Ali's the one who usually provides that sort of entertainment, although Milly's had her moments. Don't let your imagination run riot, though...on second thoughts, maybe I should have let you carry on thinking that it was all shop talk. What do you talk about when you go out boozing after your cricket matches?"

"We talk about all the reasons why the umpire's decision to give us out LBW was an absolute atrocity, how many times we nearly found the edge while bowling but didn't quite, how many times we thought about hooking their fast bowler for six while batting, but decided to duck instead, and whether the Pakistanis really were guilty of ball-tampering in the final test. It's riveting stuff, at least as interesting as the average teachers' drinking session, when everyone complains at great length about the iniquities of CPD and how much we all hate the beginning of term—that's why I always sneak off early to get together with you, if I can."

"Well, I'm glad I can attract you away from such strong competition," she said. "That makes me feel really good."

Unfortunately, that Saturday's game was an away fixture, and by the time Steve got back to Salisbury Janine was beginning to wonder, audibly, whether she really wanted to spend as much time hanging around waiting for him to favor her with his belated presence. He assured her that winter was not far off now that Autumn had begun, and that the season would be over soon enough. They patched things up on the Sunday, but they didn't meet up again until Wednesday, when the survival course made little progress, being mostly concerned with nutrition—highlighting the deficiency diseases that might result from inadequate vitamin provision—and the elements of paramedical improvisation, which Steve had previously thought of as "first aid".

On Thursday, Steve picked Janine and Milly up in quick succession on the way to the AlAbAn meeting. Milly seemed to be in a much more buoyant and frivolous mood than she had been on the previous occasion, presumably because Steve was no longer an unknown quantity and she no longer felt the need to be wary of him. She asked how their survival course was going in a flirtatious manner, and Janine countered by asking Milly, in a much more earnest tone, whether she'd thought any more about going to A level evening classes.

"I don't know," Milly said, dubiously. "I don't really rate the tech, you know. I did a martial arts course last year, remember, and I was a bit disappointed. I wanted to learn to hurt people, but it was more about learning how *not* to hurt people."

"A levels aren't quite the same thing, are they?" Janine said. "You get a much better class of homework."

"You're only saying that because you were too scared to let me practice on you." Milly retorted. "Ali let me throw her—mind you, she's not much bigger than you are, so it wasn't hard. If you'd been going out with Steve then I could have borrowed him, and found out whether big people really do fall harder."

"I'm not exactly a rugby player," Steve pointed out. "You'd be taller than me if you wore high heels."

"I think the answer I was looking for," Milly said, "was: *You're welcome to throw me any time, darling.*" She giggled as she said it, revealing that she had a rather infectious laugh

"That might have been the answer you were looking for, *darling*," Janine said, stifling the infection that made her want to giggle in her turn, "but if you'd got it, you'd both have been in trouble. You'd do better to set your eyes on Walter Wainwright, Milly—an affair with an older man would do you good, or at least calm you down."

"I wouldn't dare," Milly said, breezily. "Amelia looks innocent and harmless, but so did Lucrezia Borgia."

"According to the head of history at school, Lucrezia Borgia was much maligned," Steve put in. "She really was sweet and innocent, but horribly exploited by her relatives and direly besmirched by historians."

"Is the head of history one of the ones you seduced?" Milly asked, clinging insistently to her flirtatious vein. "Jan told me all about your checkered past."

"Good god, no," Steve said. "And it's really not that checkered."

"Are you going to tell, your story tonight, Mil?" Janine asked—a question that immediately dampened the mood. Milly took some time before muttering a denial. Steve glanced sideways, attempting to judge whether the move had been deliberate, but Janine wouldn't meet his eye.

They got to the meeting a little earlier than they had the previous week, although Steve wasn't consciously aware of having pressed the accelerator any more firmly, and had time to watch the greater number of the faithful arrive. Janine drew Milly aside when they'd collected their cups of tea, so Steve slipped into scientific observer mode and studied the AlAbAn regulars—especially Walter Wainwright, who was busy greeting people as they came in. After watching him for a few minutes Steve decided that his initial judgment had been a little hard on Walter Wainwright, even if he did turn out to be an ex-Man from the Pru. On observing him more intently, Steve decided that Walter was neither as much of a lech nor as much of a con man as he'd first elected to believe. Beyond the insistent amiability and quasi-paternal attitude there was an aura of authority and competence, and there was a genuine warmth in the way he addressed people.

Walter Wainwright must have observed Steve observing him, because he came over just as Janine returned from her intimate chat with Milly. "It's good to see you again, Steve," he said. "I'm glad you decided to return—I'm always disappointed when people don't give us a second chance. It's good to see you too, Janine. I saw your parents on Saturday, and mentioned that I'd seen you. I hope I didn't put my foot in it—they seemed rather surprised that you'd been to an AlAbAn meeting."

"I hadn't had a chance to mention it to them myself," Janine said, vaguely. "I really must give them a ring some time soon—thanks for reminding me."

Steve knew that Janine was rather dilatory in the matter of keeping in touch with her parents, although he wasn't sure exactly why. On the one occasion when she'd taken him to meet them, on a Sunday when he didn't have a game, they'd all gone to the local pub for lunch. It had seemed to him to be a fairly comfortable experience, as such experiences went, but Janine had been very glad when it was over. Steve had remarked that Janine and her parents didn't see eye-to-eye on a good may issues, especially the propriety of working as an "office skivvy" for Thomas Cook's, but they hadn't seemed to be any harder on her than the average concerned parent Obviously, they'd expected better of her, and would presumably have been more content if she'd had a job more akin to Steve's, but he'd seen far worse performances at every parents' evening he'd ever been forced to attend.

"Is there anything you'd like me to say to them if I see them this weekend, my dear?" Walter said, radiating concern, "or anything you'd particularly like me *not* to say."

"Nothing at all," Janine said, with a furtive smile. Steve took this to mean that she was perfectly prepared to let her parents suspect that she might think she'd been abducted by aliens. From her point of view, he supposed, that was probably an alternative preferable to letting them believe that she was in a steady relationship with a man who thought that *he*'d been abducted by aliens

Steve couldn't resist saying: "Do Janine's parents know that you believe that *everyone* in the world has been abducted at least once, Mr. Wainwright?"

"Call me Walter, Steve," the old man replied. "And yes, of course they do. I don't hide my opinions. It wouldn't do me any good if I tried—it would only lead to people in the pub pointing at me slyly and whispering: *That's nutty old Walter Wainwright—he thinks that everybody in the world's been abducted by aliens.* It's better to be open about such things, don't you think?"

"I guess so," Steve agreed, wondering whether the old man was hinting that *he* ought to be a bit more open about things, even though he couldn't possibly know how open Steve was or wasn't.

"Friends of Milly's are particularly welcome here," Walter added. "We're all very fond of Milly."

"She's been my best friend for years," Janine said. "This is the one thing we haven't shared, until now. She's never told me what happened to her, though."

"It often takes time," Walter said. "We all had to wait until we were ready, and we understand perfectly why it takes some people longer to reach that point than others. You must both take all the time you need. Excuse me, please." Walter allowed himself to be drawn away by Amelia Rockham.

Janine was still smiling, and Steve could see that she had no intention of explaining to Walter that she was only here to keep Steve company.

"You want your parents to worry about you, don't you?" he said.

"You're the one who thinks that a little mystery spices up a relationship," she retorted. "Let's sit down—we're about to start."

They took their places on the Naugahyde settee, which was already beginning to feel like "their" seat. When the preliminaries were over and newcomers had been duly advised of the rules, Walter invited "Mary"—a middle-aged and very well-furnished woman, who gave the impression that she had certainly never suffered from an eating disorder of the sort that had once afflicted poor Milly—to tell the story of an encounter she had had some twenty-five years before, in 1981. The prospect did not seem overly exciting, at first—but Steve found out soon enough that appearances could be quite deceptive.

CHAPTER FOUR

THE CATALYST AND THE CHRYSALIS

This is something I've always remembered but always kept quiet about. I didn't need psychoanalysis or hypnotherapy to dredge the memory up, but it wasn't something I wanted to tell anyone at the time, or at any time since. It wasn't that I was afraid of being laughed at, or being called a liar or a fantasist. It was just something I needed to keep to myself for a while. Now, though, it seems that the time is right. I've been coming here for a couple of years now, listening to everyone else's stories, and I feel that I'm ready to let it go.

Some of the younger members won't have any memory of 1981, and it's not a year that has gone down in history for any particular reason. It's probably enough to say that it was two years into Mrs. Thatcher's reign of terror, with the economic recession getting ever deeper and unemployment rising fast. I was married then, and my husband, Mike, was one of the people who lost his job.

We had been doing reasonably well until then, and weren't exactly plunged into instant destitution. I was working at the local hospital as a nurse, but my pay wasn't enough to pay the mortgage and sustain any kind of decent standard of living. Unfortunately, Mike didn't react well to unemployment, or to my becoming the breadwinner. The vague plans we'd made to start a family went right out of the window, and although the prospect of having children had never seemed a particularly big deal before, the fact that we were no longer able to consider the possibility suddenly seemed to become one. At any rate, it became another thing for Mike to get bitter about—another thing to fuel his disappointment and his drinking.

We were soon struggling, getting gradually deeper in misery and debt. Being in debt doesn't seem to mean much nowadays, when everybody under thirty seems to live on credit, but in those days we didn't think about owing money as something normal and natural. It was bad, and it preyed on our minds—which only served to increase Mike's disappointment, and drinking, even further. You can imagine how the spiral worked.

I did my best to increase our income, working extra shifts and studying hard for the exams I needed to pass in order to get promotion, but that only made the fact that I was supporting him increasingly conspicuous, burdensome and annoying. The state of the marriage went downhill rapidly once the slide began, and I think we both knew that it was only a matter of time before something broke under the strain.

The abduction itself was like a dozen others I've heard described here. I'd worked sixteen hours on the trot, from six o'clock in the morning to ten at night, and I came home exhausted. Mike was already asleep when I came into the bedroom, so dead drunk that an earthquake wouldn't have woken him up. I should have been equally oblivious once I'd dropped off, but I woke up suddenly in the early hours of the morning. I glanced at the clock on the bedside table, which said that it was twenty past three. I got out of bed and went to the bedroom window.

The window was open—it was August, and we were three days into what passed for a heat wave in those days. There was a huge disk floating over the house, silent and unilluminated. I was paralyzed, and then grabbed by some kind of tractor beam. Its manipulators maneuvered me out of the window easily enough. I was a lot thinner in those days. I lost consciousness when the thing swallowed me up.

When I woke up, I was in the kind of laboratory space that we've heard described so often. I was lying on my back on an operating table, with a white sheet draped over me. My limbs were immobilized, although I couldn't see any solid restraints.

There was a bright light directly above me, bright enough to hurt my eyes. There were various items of equipment massed on the left-hand side of the bed, all seemingly idle. I had lines in each arm, and one in each leg. The one in my left arm seemed to be an intravenous drip, and the one in my left leg also seemed to be carrying a clear fluid—probably bodily wastes. The ones that caught my attention, though, were those in my right arm and leg, which were full of colored fluid. The tube connected to the leg appeared to be carrying red fluid out, while the tube connected to the arm seemed to be carrying a blue fluid back again.

It didn't take a genius to guess that the leg-tube was carrying oxygenated arterial blood while the arm-tube was returning deoxygenated venous blood. The flow was slow but steady. I didn't appear to be breathing any more deeply or rapidly than usual, but the air I was sucking in had a slightly strange taste, which suggested that it was richer in oxygen than Earthly air.

It wasn't easy to see where the blood was going, because it was below the level of the operating table, but I could crane my neck just far enough to see that there was something in a kind of cradle resting on the floor. The cradle must have been about four feet long and two wide, and the thing fitted into it fairly snugly. It was dark brown in color, with a shiny surface. It put me in mind of a big balloon, or a giant rugby ball, or some sort of monstrous egg. My blood was being slowly pumped into the ovoid at one end, and pumped out again at the other, then returned to the vein in my arm.

My first thought was that I had fallen victim to alien vampires, but that didn't make sense, because the blood—or something very like it—was being returned. Then I wondered whether the ovoid might be some kind of dialysis machine, but that didn't seem very plausible either.

I must have been lying there for an hour or so before anyone—or anything—came in. I felt quite calm, perhaps because I was being fed tranquilizers through the incoming drip as well as nutrients. I didn't scream when the door finally opened, or experience any dreadful sensation of shock. I'd already prepared myself mentally to see something that wasn't human, and was, in the event, slightly relieved to see something that wasn't quite as horrid as it might have been.

It was a bug of sorts—a six-limbed thing that used its four hind feet for walking while its two front feet were modified into something more like arms. Its wing-cases curved around its upper body like some sort of fancy jacket, colored dark red with black spots like a ladybird. The body would have suited a head like a praying mantis, but that's not the sort of head it had. Its skull was big and rounded, and its face was like some kind of Halloween mask, with big round eyes positioned in front and a big smiling mouth with nice white teeth. It didn't have a nose or ears, but the eyes and the mouth were just enough to provide a hint of apparent humanity even before it spoke.

"Hello Mary," it said, in a strange fluty accent. "I'm Imhotep. I'll be looking after you while you're here. I hope you're quite comfortable."

"Wasn't Imhotep the guy who built the Great Pyramid?" I said. "You're not going to tell me, I hope, that the pyramids really were constructed as landing-pads for alien spaceships?"

"The legend connecting Imhotep to the Great Pyramid was something of an afterthought," the bug informed me. "You're absolutely right to identify it as a pseudonym—you wouldn't be able to pronounce my real name—but it was selected because of a different legend, which makes Imhotep the father of medicine."

"You mean you're a doctor?"

"Absolutely."

"And what, exactly, are you treating me for?"

"You're not the patient, I'm afraid," it said, in what might have been a crude attempt to fake an apologetic tone. "You're the treatment."

I looked at the thing in the cradle. "That's your patient?" I said.

"Yes it is. Perhaps I should have said that your blood is the treatment—but I assure you that our using it won't do you any harm at all. Blood is essentially a carrier, you see. At the risk of stretching the metaphor, you might say that we're using your hemoglobin and its associated cofactors as a kind of catalyst, which facilitates certain chemical reactions but is then regenerated, so that it can be used over and over again in an endless cycle."

The bug said all this rather blandly, as if it didn't expect me to understand, and didn't really care whether I did or not, but wanted for some reason to put on a show of honesty. It obviously didn't know that I was a nurse, or that I'd been desperately revising my anatomy and physiology of late.

"Isn't there an easier way to pump oxygen into the damn thing?" I asked it. "Taking an interstellar trip, then using a tractor beam to kidnap human beings from their bedrooms, merely in order to use the hemoglobin in their blood as a means of infusing an egg with oxygen, strikes me as the most ludicrously uneconomic project imaginable."

"It probably would be," the pseudonymous Imhotep agreed. "As it happens, though, we've disguised our apparatus as a spaceship for reasons of convenience. We haven't had to take an interstellar trip, or even an interplanetary one. And yes, if it were only a matter of oxygenation, we could find simpler ways to do the job. Unfortunately, it isn't. It's a much subtler process of catalysis—which, I have to admit, we don't fully understand ourselves. Also, it's not an egg; it's a chrysalis."

It took me a minute or two to work my way through the complexities of the triple denial, but I got there in the end. I figured that I ought to take things a little more slowly.

"You're not from another planet, then?" I said.

"No," it said. "The little silver-skinned guys with the big eyes apparently claim to be extraterrestrial, and they're probably not alone, but we don't socialize with them any more than we socialize with others of our own kind. We often disguise our vessels as theirs, though, in order not to attract overmuch attention from other travelers. Everyone's used to seeing the little guys hanging around this era."

"So where do you come from?" I wanted to know.

"Earth, about three hundred million years downstream."

"Downstream?"

"Down the time-stream—about three hundred million years in the future. The Third Arthropod Era. The insects of your world are our remote ancestors. Some of our scientists think that might have something to do with the fact that we still have a vestigial dependence on—or, at least, a vestigial affinity with—human blood. Personally, I don't believe it. The hypothesis that we're descended from human parasitic lice is at best unproven and at worst silly. The chain of evidence is broken in half a dozen places—global catastrophes and their consequential extinction events tend to mess up the fossil record somewhat. On the other hand, our adults do seem to need the catalytic infusion of mammalian blood if they're to pupate successfully, and human blood does seem to work far better than any other kind. Whatever the explanation is for that, it's bound to be at least a little crazy."

By the time Imhotep had finished that speech I had several things on my mind, and it wasn't easy to figure out which to tackle first. "So you got to be the way you are by having human blood pumped into you when you were a chrysalis?" I said, figuring that I really ought to demonstrate that I was capable of keeping up with his arguments.

"That's a neat inference," the bug conceded, "but I'm afraid it's mistaken. I know that I look something like an adult, with the wing-cases and the legs and all, but actually I'm the result of what we call pedogenetic pseudometamorphosis. I never pupated—which might be regarded as a blessing, or as a lost opportunity, according to your point of view."

I was now way out of my depth. Rather than ask it what the hell *pedogenetic* meant, though, I thought it might be more productive to change tack.

"You don't have any humans in your world," I inferred, "so you have to travel back in time to acquire human blood."

"That's right," it said. "I'm sorry to be the bearer of bad news, but your species becomes extinct in the not-too-distant future, when global warming causes a catastrophic release of methane from sea-bed clathrates. Most vertebrate species go with you, although a handful of rodents get through. The insects do better—though not as well as the worms, of course. The worms always pull through. Ar-thropodan Eras are relatively rare events, although they might be more common downstream of our time. As I said, we don't socialize with time-travelers from our past or our future. It's too dangerous. Nobody wants to create an unhealable rift in the fabric of history."

"But snatching twentieth-century humans from their beds doesn't count as changing history?"

"No. It happens all the time, thanks to the little silver-grey guys, and it never changes anything, even though their memory-wipes are always liable to go awry. Not that ours are perfect, mind—but our timing's much better. The silvers are always returning people hours, or even months, later. With us, you can be sure that you won't lose a single minute. You'll be back in your bed within a few seconds of getting out of it, no matter how long you're here. You won't have aged measurably either—that cocktail we're pumping into you to keep you healthy and happy is good stuff."

"That's good to know," I told it. "Even so, you're not exactly observing the principle of informed consent, are you? I know you're calling yourself Imhotep rather than Hippocrates, but that doesn't free you from the demands of medical ethics. Or do you think that just because you're a giant bug, who isn't even a true adult, while I'm only a long-extinct mammal, you don't owe me any ethical con-sideration at all?"

"That's fair comment," the bug conceded. "To tell you the truth, we have occasionally tried to observe the principle of informed con-sent, but we've found that it leads to a drastic shortage of volunteers. Time travel isn't as impractical as space travel, by any means, but it's not so convenient as to allow us to waste a great deal of energy and effort. It's an ethical compromise, I know, but we tend to skip the consent part—and I have to confess that even the information component is a bit of a swizz, considering that the memory-wipe will surgically remove all the information I'm currently giving you. The odds are a thousand to one against your actually remembering any of this when we put you back—and even if you do, the fact that you'll only have been gone for five or six seconds will make it very difficult for you to believe that it was anything but a wacky dream. In that event, your brain will probably do its own memory-wipe, just as it does when you wake up every morning, to protect you from the possibility of mistaking your dreams for real experiences."

"Actually," I told it, "I'm quite good at remembering my dreams—and my nightmares too—although I rarely mistake them for real experiences."

"That's unfortunate," Imhotep said, with all apparent sincerity. "I'd offer to treat you for it if I could, but it's not my specialty. I'm a metamorphologist."

"Right," I said. "The overgrown football is your patient. I'm just the unconsenting blood donor. So what's the problem you guys have with pupation? Why does your average chrysalis need a three hundred million year time trip if it's to produce a healthy adult?"

I got the impression that it had been asked the question a dozen times before. Its answer was as casual and as practiced as the rest of his spiel. "It's a question of pedogenesis," it said. "There are a few pedogenetic insects around in your era, but they don't get the same kind of publicity that ants and bees get, so the idea isn't exactly common knowledge. You might be familiar with the general notion, though, in an amphibian context. Do you know what an axolotl is?"

"No," I said.

"Pity. Well, briefly, an axolotl is a kind of tadpole, which has the genetic apparatus to metamorphose into a kind of salamander—but if there's plenty of water around, it doesn't bother. It grows sexual organs while remaining a tadpole, and breeds without ever producing a true adult. We think it's a fairly common reproductive pattern in certain evolutionary phases—lots of new species seem to emerge during phases of rapid adaptive radiation by taking neotenic short cuts, so that larval forms begin reproducing themselves rather than completing their supposedly-full life-cycles.

"In your world, some insect larvae that feed on material that's rare in general terms but tends to crop up in massive quantities when it does occur—the rotting wood from falling trees, say—have the option of developing sex organs as larvae and breeding as juveniles, often going through twenty or thirty generations like that before finally running short of food, pupating, and producing flies that hurtle off in every direction looking for another juicy fallen tree. Do you see the logic of the situation?"

"Yes," I claimed, bravely.

"Well then," Imhotep said, settling down on his oddly-jointed legs as if for a long lecture, "imagine what might happen to an insect species that developed intelligence in its larval form—and developed agriculture along with it. Agriculture provides the means to secure a permanent food supply, while the prospect of a reversion to idiocy provides a strong motive for trying very hard to avoid metamorphosis. My ancestors—like the ancestors of most of the species that developed self-conscious intelligence in our era—had the pedogenetic option, and they took it. Adults became very rare, and then almost mythical. Pupation came to be regarded as a fate worse than death, and for centuries those individuals unlucky enough to pupate were ritually destroyed. After a long period of time, though—during which our fledgling civilization flourished, and eventually gave rise to science—attitudes began to change. Pupation became a mystery to be solved, and an opportunity to be explored. We began to produce adults again—but the adults our nearer ancestors produced seemed to be defective, even by comparison with our modest expectations.

"We had to go back to our myths and legends to figure out exactly what we ought to expect of our adults, and why we didn't seem to be getting it. We gradually began to realize that we'd lost something vital. Like most intelligent species, our early emergence from animal stupidity had corresponded with a massive extinction event, during which we'd wiped out a great many potential competitors. Our larval form was vegetarian, but our adults had been blood-drinkers, and the species we'd killed off included almost all of those from which blood could be drawn in any quantity on a regular basis.

"We realized, too, that blood-drinking hadn't just been a matter of adult nutrition. Long before our larvae developed self-conscious intelligence our adults had developed a number of parental care strategies, which not only involved the protection of eggs and larvae but also the boosting of pupal metamorphosis by injections of blood. Over the course of time, our pupal form had got so much benefit from those injections that it became heavily dependent on them—a process whose interruption might well have been another key factor encouraging the development of pedogenesis.

"Now, of course—our now, that is, not yours—we don't actually need to produce adults at all, and some of our people think that we shouldn't even try. If we don't, though, that leaves us with an awkward ethical problem in disposing of the chrysalides that occasional result when individuals spontaneously pupate. Another school of thought holds that if we are, in fact, morally or practically compelled to produce adults, then we ought to do everything possible to produce the best adults we can. Some of those individuals hold to a quasi-religious faith that if only we can find the right sanguinary catalyst, we might produce adults far better than those that nature used to produce in the remoter eras of our evolution. The ultimate goal, I suppose, would be an adult that retains, or even improves on, larval self-consciousness and intelligence.

"In the meantime, of course, a combination of natural mutations, selective breeding and—more recently—genetic engineering has allowed us to reproduce various aspects of adult form within essentially larval bodies. That's what I meant by pedogenetic pseudo-metamorphosis. Some of us, inevitably, think that's the way to go to produce something resembling an intelligent adult. Others, especially those inclined to various versions of evolutionary mysticism, disagree. Our explorations in time revealed soon enough that antique blood is better for our pupae than contemporary blood, and that blood from the mammals of much earlier eras than ours seems to be better still.

"The present experimental run—that's your present, of course, although it's ours too, in a peculiar sense—is only part-way through, but the results so far have proved astonishingly variable. There's something in human blood, especially late twentieth-century human blood, which encourages mutational metamorphoses. Some of us entertain high hopes as to what the run might ultimately produce. Others, admittedly, see the project as a matter of mad scientists running amok and producing monsters—but you ought to understand that little disagreement well enough, if what I've seen in your movies is anything to go by.

"That's the whole story in a nutshell. That's why I'm here, and why you're here, and why you're hooked up in this admittedly undignified fashion. I'd say I'm sorry if I thought you'd believe me, but the fact is that I'm doing what I'm doing because I think it needs to be done, and you're just one of the means that I believe the end justifies. Such is life—and now I have to go."

The bug doctor didn't wait for any further questions, but turned and made its exit. I got the impression that it was embarrassed by what it had told me, and that it really was a little bit sorry for the way I was being treated—but it didn't come back again before I went to sleep. I have no idea how long that was, or how long I slept, but I didn't get bored and I woke up feeling better than I had for some considerable time. It was a holiday of sorts, and—to tell the truth—it was a relief simply to be free of Mike's increasingly resentful and accusatory presence.

* * * * * * *

Imhotep came in again on the second "day" of my confinement, and we talked again for what seemed like an hour or more. It filled in a bit more detail about the nature of the Third Arthropodan Era and the politics of time travel, but didn't add much to the basics of his explanation. I got the impression that it was distracted, and that its heart was no longer in our conversation now that it had done what it considered to be its explanatory duty.

On that second day I put Imhotep's distraction down to concern for the progress of his experiment. It certainly spent a lot of time hovering over the bloated football and making unobtrusive measurements of its progress. On the third "day", however, Imhotep wasn't alone when it came in. The newcomer didn't introduce itself, and ignored me completely while it inspected the chrysalis with the utmost care, but it was easy enough to see that it and Imhotep were at odds. They clicked and whistled at one another incessantly, in what was obviously their native tongue, but Imhotep didn't translate any of what was said for my benefit. Indeed, it seemed to be ignoring me, just as its adversary was—but it came back later to explain and apologize.

"As you probably noticed," it said, "you've become the object of a minor controversy. Well, not you exactly, but the effect that your blood is having on the chrysalis."

"Why?" I asked. "Am I turning it into something horrible? Something from the *Outer Limits* of the Third Arthropodan Era?"

"In your situation," Imhotep observed, "I'm not sure I'd be able to see the funny side of that particular joke. But yes, something like that—something, at least, that we haven't seen before."

"But you don't think it's horrible," I guessed. "You're the crazy optimist who thinks it might just be the messiah you've all been waiting for: the superadult with brains as well as legs and a fancy carapace."

"Let's just say that I'm hopeful," the bug said. "Hopeful, at least, that the thing won't rip me to pieces and gobble me up when it hatches. I'm the one who'll have to be here, you see, when it does emerge. I'm the metamorphologist. On the other hand, if it does rip me to pieces and devour me, I won't have to listen to anyone saying *I told you so*."

"That's monster movies for you," I said. "Don't expect any sympathy from me—I'm just the nubile underdressed starlet supinely helpless on the mad scientist's operating table. According to the script, all I have to do is scream. Given what you've been feeding that thing these last three days, isn't it more likely to devour me than you."

"You blood isn't feeding it," Imhotep reminded me. "It's just a catalyst. It provides oxygen, and that mysterious something extra—something, I presume, that the immunoglobulins do, or maybe the clotting factors...."

"You need to find out, then pop back in time to tell yourself how to do the job properly," I said. "What's the point of time travel is you can't tip yourself off when you need a helping hand?"

"It doesn't work like that," it said. "You can't socialize with other time-travelers, and that goes double for yourself. This is the finding out part of the story all right—but once we have the information, we'll only be able to carry it forward. Trying to tie time in knots is worse than making material changes in history. It's the sort of thing that's likely to lead to elimination."

It sounded genuinely anxious—almost as if it were worried about the possibility that it had already shot some kind of hole in the continuity of history—not, of course, by removing me from the cold marital bed to which it would ultimately return me, but by using my blood as a transtemporal catalyst to produce a kind of adult that its species had never known before, and might not like very much.

Personally, of course, I didn't need to care—except, maybe, about the slim possibility that the damn thing would turn on me and do horrible things to me. Whether Imhotep and its snooty buddy regarded the product of my catalysis as a monster or messiah was all the same to me. To me, it would just be another bug, a louse writ large.

I couldn't help being interested, though. Even if I wasn't really the damn thing's mother, or even its midwife, I was doing my bit. It would owe its form—and perhaps even its thoughts, if it were capable of having any—to me.

* * * * * * *

Imhotep's adversary came back repeatedly on the fourth day and the fifth, sometimes on its own—but even when it didn't have Imhotep around it pointedly refused to look at me or talk to me. It obviously had a very different view of medical ethics, or the degree of ethical consideration owed to a mere extinct mammal. Imhotep apologized for its colleague's behavior, but I could tell that its heart wasn't in the apology.

On the sixth day, the chrysalis began to crack. As soon as that happened, Imhotep came in with no less than three others of its own kind, two of them far more obviously larval in aspect than it or its familiar adversary was. The three others soon cleared out, though, leaving Imhotep to supervise the emergence solo. I soon developed a nagging pain in my neck straining for a better view, but I never gave up no matter how irksome it became. This was a once-in-a-lifetime opportunity, and I didn't want to miss a thing. Nor did I.

Bit by bit, the thing emerged, and I watched every moment of the process. I had been harboring the vague hope that my catalytic blood might produce something more human than bug, but that hope was dashed as soon as the thing began to ease itself out, wing-cases first. The ground color of the wing-cases was yellow rather than red, and its ladybird spots were very faint, but there was nothing particularly unusual about them. The wings themselves, when it had stretched them to their full extremity and dried them, were beautifully diaphanous, but very obviously insectile. The legs, which it poked out one at a time, were darker in hue and somewhat sturdier than Imhotep's, but they too were exactly the sort of thing one might expect to see on a giant grasshopper, save for the forefeet ingeniously modified as manipulative hands, which looked exactly like Imhotep's.

"This thing's related to you, isn't it?" I guessed, as I watched Imhotep busy itself obsessively with its machines and various items of movable apparatus. "Not just in a species sense, but in a kin sense. Is it a sibling?"

For a moment, it seemed that Imhotep would refuse to answer the question, but then it thought better of it. "My offspring," it said, shortly.

It was the first time I had cause to wonder whether I was really correct to think of it as "it". "Are you its mother or its father?" I asked.

"Neither," it said. "Sex is the prerogative of adults. Pedogenetic reproduction is a short cut in more ways than one. It's my clone—or was. It still would be, if it weren't for its capacity for mutation. Thus far, though, it doesn't seem...."

The reason Imhotep stopped was that the head of the adult had finally appeared. Imhotep's own head, I remembered, was the result of pedogenetic pseudometamorphosis. There was no reason to expect the head of its clone-sibling's adult incarnation to resemble it closely. It did resemble it very closely, though; it had similar big dark eyes, and a similar mouth with similar teeth and a tongue, shaped for pronouncing the syllables of human languages as well as well as those of its own species.

Except, of course, that it didn't know any human languages. Imhotep's clone-sibling had not had the same opportunity, or the same motive, to learn any language that Imhotep had learned while it was a larva. Imhotep's larval clone-sibling had only known its own language—a language it ought to have forgotten, if the normal course of specific development had been followed.

Once the monster's head was free, it was able to stand up slowly on its four hind legs, and to use its hand-like forefeet to free itself of the debris of its cocoon. While it did so, it looked down. Not until it had finished did it look up—not at Imhotep, but at me.

It looked at me with intelligence in its eyes, and with compassion. It looked at me with love. It didn't say a word, because it couldn't, but I understood. Imhotep understood too. Imhotep understood that I had worked the miracle, that I had catalyzed the production of the first self-consciously intelligent adult that its species had ever produced.

Imhotep spoke to its recently-metamorphosed clone-sibling, but the clone-sibling made no reply. It continued looking at me, and its silent gaze told me everything I needed to know.

I'm not claiming that we exchanged ideas telepathically, or even that there was any kind of quasi-magical empathy between us, but there was a bond, and there was understanding. I knew it, and so did Imhotep.

The monster took a single step towards me, which brought it close enough to be able to reach out with one of its vast and clumsy hands to caress my throat. All the while it was looking directly into my eyes—and now it came close enough to be able to do so without my having to strain my neck.

I was able to lie back, and make myself more comfortable, while the creature from the chrysalis moved its head to a position directly above mine, so that it could look down at me gratefully, fondly and admiringly. It didn't matter, just then, that I was a long-extinct mammal, while it was a God-knows-what from the Third Arthropod Era. There was a bond between us more intimate than that between any Earthly mother and child, or between any Earthly pedogenetic clone-parent and clone-sibling.

I felt perfectly happy, for the first time in my adult life.

Then the others burst in, all armed with ugly ray guns, and shot the thing to pieces.

Imhotep tried to stop them, and was gunned down too.

That was when I started screaming.

I must have blacked out soon afterwards, presumably because whatever was in charge of my drip feed doctored the input with a powerful narcotic. When I woke up, I was back in my own bed.

The clock on my bedside table said that it was twenty past three, but it wasn't—not so far as I was concerned.

It wasn't the end of the world, either, but it certainly wasn't twenty past three—not for me.

I remembered everything, probably because the confusion aboard the alien timeship had been too great to allow them to do the memory-wipe properly. My brain might have attempted its own kind of memory-wipe, but there was never any possibility of it taking effect. Nor was there any possibility of my confusing the experience with a dream or a nightmare. It was real. It took no time, according to the clock, but it was real. It was more real than Mike, more real than the divorce, more real than the ovarian cysts, more real than the hysterectomy, more real than any of the thousand diseases and hundred deaths I witnessed week by week and year by year at the hospital. It was the realest thing I ever experienced, or ever will.

It's possible, I suppose, that the time-travelers got the wrong idea. It's possible that they thought that the adult was attacking me, and that the hand it put to my throat was about to strangle me. It's just about conceivable that they thought they were doing the right thing, the ethical thing. They were, after all, afraid of what Imhotep and I might have wrought...and, for that matter, of anything and everything else that their project might yet produce.

They didn't understand. They couldn't understand.

They were not, after all, adults themselves.

I *am* an adult. I do understand. I understand better than they did, and better than Imhotep did. Nothing can ever take that away from me, even though it's no longer my secret, my private torment, my heaven and hell on Earth. Whatever anyone says, *it wasn't twenty past three to me*.

CHAPTER FIVE

REVEALING THE TRUTH

Steve thought that Mary's story was even more interesting than Jim's, in terms of potential psychological insights. He couldn't be certain whether the elements of coincidence between the stories were just that, or aspects of a pattern, but he was enthusiastic to find out. He was tempted to ask Walter Wainwright whether the coincidental aspects had cropped up before—and how frequently they recurred, if so—but he knew that the chairman wouldn't appreciate a question like that being raised in a meeting, even in the casual chat phase that preceded the general retreat.

In any case, Steve thought, even if it were to be confirmed that the coincidental resemblances were more than merely coincidental, that would only open up a new set of questions. The overwhelming likelihood was that AlAbAn members borrowed from one another in reconstructing their own stories, perhaps unconsciously—a turn of phrase here, an interpretative guess there. It was entirely natural, he supposed, that some such process should occur; every AlAbAn group, and perhaps every other group remotely like it, must develop its own idiosyncratic culture as its particular membership formed a social microcosm, which newcomers learned and then passed on. The mild sensation of intoxication that the group was able to conjure up in its meetings probably had more to do with that petty kind of creationism than with the exotic content of the stories that were told, although the particular stories told by Jim and Mary certainly lent a distinctive flavor to the experience.

Janine had wept a few discreet tears at the spectacle of Mary's distress, although she'd tried to wipe them away discreetly with her sleeve, but Milly hadn't. Steve wasn't surprised by that—not because he had assumed that Milly's relative physical fortitude was reflected emotionally, but simply because Milly was an old AlAbAn hand. From her viewpoint, Mary's story must the thirtieth or fortieth in line rather than the second, and must have contained enough familiar details—even if they were purely coincidental ones—to make parts of it seem stale.

Amelia Rockham was the real heroine of the evening, though, in Steve's view. She had been able to comfort Mary, and had even persuaded her to listen to a few spoken responses. Needless to say, no one asked any questions. The only people who spoke offered warmly sympathetic comments, as they were supposed to do. Neither Janine nor Milly was among them, but Steve saw Milly nodding and murmuring in the general chorus, as was apparently her wont. When they left the cottage, though, Milly seemed more subdued than she had been on the outward journey, and she made no further attempts to flirt with Steve.

"I suspect that AlAbAn meetings must proceed rather differently in the branches based in London, Birmingham and Manchester," Steve said, pensively, as he waited for two other cars to pass before easing himself out into the unexpectedly busy traffic. "Urban stroppiness must surely override the genteel etiquette of the shires, and turn the meetings into slanging matches. Wiltshire isn't even your common-or-garden shire, like Hampshire or Hertfordshire, or all the other places where hurricanes hardly ever happen and everybody knows the price of elderberry wine. It's a shire squared, like dear old Dorset: quaintness run riot. It would be the perfect home for an organization like AlAbAn, even if it weren't such an intense focal point of UFO activity."

"That must help, though," said Janine. "If Walter's right, and everyone in the world *has* been abducted by aliens at least once, so that the victims in need of support are merely the unlucky few whose memory-wipes have failed, it's hardly surprising that Wiltshire had more than its fair share of rememberers. There's so much *talk* of UFOs hereabouts, even nowadays—so many props and prompts to struggling and faltering memories."

"And it's hardly surprising, either, that the Wiltshire rememberers should include veterans like Amelia Rockham and Walter Wainwright," Steve added. "They must have been way ahead of the wave of fashionability if they remembered their own abductions way back in the fifties. That was long before everybody else began to get in on the act and forging crop-circles became a popular summer pastime. They're entitled to get a little merry on the success of their enterprise."

Milly listened to this exchange from the back seat, but didn't join in. It wasn't until Janine turned round and began chatting about the possibility of another night out with Alison that Milly broke her silence, and not until Janine asked her what kind of week she'd had that she found an occasion to deploy her infectious laugh, in an anecdote about road rage on the school run.

"You can come with us to the Chinese if you like, Mil," Janine said, as they came back into the city. "I'm sure Steve wouldn't mind driving you home, later."

"No, that's all right," Milly said. "Drop me off first and have yourselves a ball."

Steve stopped the car to let Milly out, and turned his head to let her kiss him on the cheek before she got out. She kissed Janine, too, saying: "Same time on the twenty-eighth?"

"Absolutely," Steve said.

When Milly was safely inside, Steve turned to Janine and said: "You actually warned her off, didn't you? Just because she made that remark about throwing her any time?"

"You think a lot of yourself, don't you?" Janine retorted. "Do you really think that I'm so desperate to hang on to you that I'd read the riot act to anyone who invited you to call her darling?"

"I'd like to think so," Steve said, as he steered the car in the direction of Janine's flat and the nearby Chinese take-away.

"Well, I didn't. I think it was Mary's story that cooled her down. She's always been that way—up one minute, down the next. It gave me a shiver or two, although it certainly made me grateful for modern hygiene. Thank God there's no possibility of my entertaining the ancestors of countless potential sentient races in the Second and Third Arthropodan Eras. Imagine if you caught head-lice from one of your filthy kids, and had to use that disgusting medicated shampoo, wondering whether every vigorous scrub might be exterminating potential ancestors of sentient species to come. Every swipe of the nit-comb might be changing future history."

"My kids aren't any dirtier, on average, than your customers," Steve said, although he wasn't usually in the habit of defending his charges. "Schools only suffer from epidemic outbreaks because there are so many people gathered together in one place. Anyway, we needn't think of it in terms of exterminating potential ancestors. We could take pride in being the instigators of such a rigorous selective regime, hastening the evolution of insect-kind. We might be making a small but crucial contribution to their eventual rise to sentient intelligence. One of those stinky scrubs or deft flicks of the nit-comb might be selecting out the Mitochondrial Eve of future Arthropodan culture and civilization."

"And that would be something to take pride in?" she said.

"Why not?"

"As opposed, say, to scrubbing just a little bit harder, wiping out the ultimate ancestor of arthropodan civilization, and paving the way for a new evolution of something much more like us instead?"

"Or something even less like us, which not even a maternal Mary could learn to love?" Steve countered. "Changing history is a tricky business, especial when we can't tell one louse from another, so we've no way of identifying the ones with potential. You have to remember, too, that head-lice aren't the only kind we have. If I had to bet which kind would be most likely to give rise to intelligent offspring a couple of hundred million years in the future, I'd go for the crotch-crabs every time."

"Now you're being deliberately disgusting," Janine said. "Unless, of course, you're trying to be superior, because you know something I don't. Will there be pubic lice in the story that you're working your way up to telling?"

"If there are," Steve assured her, "that's a part of the dream I haven't remembered yet. In the meantime, if ever I get an itch down there, I won't hesitate for an instant before taking the cure, even if I might be exterminating the ancestors of a thousand potential sentient species. In matters of that sort, the principle of informed consent simply isn't relevant." He pulled on the handbrake by way of punctuation, and switched off the engine.

"What a busy life we're beginning to lead," Janine said, with a contrived sigh, once they had reached the Chinese and placed their order. "Survival studies on Wednesdays, victim support every second Thursday. When you throw in your Tuesday sessions with your psychotherapist, and all your staff meetings at school, you must be exhausted by Friday—and yet you still manage to lead me up the garden path every now and again."

"Cricket keeps me fit," Steve told her. "It's a pity, in a way, that the school doesn't have a team. If I could do a bit of coaching, Rhodri mightn't be on at me so often to supervise computer club or run plagiarism checks on his wretched assessment projects. That's the trouble with being young and computer literate—the old hands get you to do all their dirty work for them. Mercifully, it's only the second week of term—that particular deluge doesn't usually start until the end of October. On the other hand, it's better than helping out with coaching rugby. Rhodri and Mrs. Jones the PE are welcome to that one."

"She's Welsh too, is she?"

"Her husband is. He *was* a rugby player in his time—built like an ox, although he's running to fat now. She can hold her own in a scrum, mind. Do you know the old joke about nothing good ever coming out of Wales but rugby players and loose women?"

"My wife's Welsh—what position does she play? Yes, heard it a million times. Is that still going the grounds in the playground?"

"I doubt it. I try not to listen to playground talk—way too filthy for my tender ears."

"Especially the bits about you, no doubt. It's really quite decorous in Tom Cook's, considering the reputation reps have. I thought of becoming a rep, you know, if only to give Mum and Dad heart attacks, but I'm too good on the computer. I'm going to put in for management training, though, given that you think it's a good idea. It involves the occasional weekend course, but they'll be child's play compared with the survival course we're planning to do in December. Nice seaside hotels or jaunts to London—you know the sort of thing."

"Not really," Steve admitted. "It's been a while since I went as far as Bournemouth, and I don't go to London at all if I can possibly help it."

"Is it crowds you're phobic about, then?" Janine said, striking so unexpectedly that she caught Steve completely off-guard.

"No," he said, shortly.

"You'll have to tell me eventually," she said. "You do realize that—unless you're planning to dump me if I get too close."

"No," Steve said, again, then had to add: "That's no to the second part. I don't plan to dump you. I know I'm going to have to let you in on it eventually—but give me time, okay? If I can just make a start on breaking the phobias down, it'll be so much easier to confess to having them. Bear with me, will you?"

"Sure," she said. "As Walter Wainwright says, it sometimes takes a while. I'll be here when you get around to it, just as I'll be here in a fortnight's time, when you need your next dose of victim support. In fact, I'm quite looking forward to it. I'm beginning to understand how Milly got hooked—but I hope the next story has a little more zip in it."

"So do I," Steve said.

* * * * * *

The weekend went well—especially the Sunday, when Steve was able to enjoy a long and uncommonly productive bowling stint in the friendly, finishing up with four wickets, and then won forty-three pounds in a long poker session. He turned up at school the next morning in a state of absolute exhaustion, but the kids didn't care and most of the staff still weren't talking to him. Rhodri Jenkins made a muttered remark *en passant* about travel agents and marathons, but he was far too busy to stop and chat.

On the Wednesday, Steve and Janine went to the third seminar of the survival course, which mostly had to do with the necessities involved in procuring and using a supply of fresh water in the absence of any kind of tap-supply. Thirst, the course-leader alleged, might be the most urgent problem, but it wasn't the only killer to be feared. His account of the possible and probable consequences of bad hygiene was suitably blood-curdling, although substantial compensation was offered in the practical part of the demonstration, which explained how to improvise a still.

Steve met Janine again on the Friday; they went to a comedy club in Swindon, where there was an open mike night. Steve preferred open mike nights to gigs featuring big names, partly because he was naturally antipathetic to TV-brokered celebrity and partly because it seemed so much more exciting when some youngster who was still only practicing turned out to be funny against all the odds.

There was no one particularly promising in the first batch of three, but Steve was still hopeful that the next batch might throw up a surprise or two. In fact, though, the surprise came earlier than that, during the break, while he was doing his best to enjoy a Red Bull because Janine didn't approve of his having even one alcoholic drink when he was driving.

"I won't be able to come out next Friday," she said, "and I'll have to miss Thursday's meeting too. I booked on to a management training course yesterday, and the induction session's next week. It's a bit short notice, I know, but that's the way we like to do things in the travel business—the last-minute deals are always the juiciest. I'll be away from Thursday afternoon to Sunday morning."

"Okay," Steve said, heroically. "You have my full support in your bid for promotion, obviously. Does this mean that you're now firmly committed to a career in travel and tourism?"

"I suppose it does," she replied. "I only took the job as a fill-in, to begin with. I was desperate to leave home, and I needed an income to pay the rent on my flat while I looked around for something more suitable—but nothing more suitable ever landed in my lap, and I never really went out searching. Everybody my age seems to be permanently *looking around for something more suitable*—jobs, flats, partners, whatever—but we rarely do much about it, except for scanning the job ads in the local freesheet, pausing to look in the occasional estate agent's windows, or, in your case, staring at some other girl's tits while you're supposed to be listening to me."

Steve immediately locked gazes with her again, although he'd actually been staring into empty space while he wondered exactly what significance he ought to attach to the fact that Janine had really decided to go for promotion, rather than just chatting about it. Did it mean, for instance, that she was thinking of moving her entire life forward a stage, making vague but highly symbolic preparations for saving up for a deposit on a house, with a view to eventually having a family?

"The travel business is as good as any other, I guess," he said.

"Thomas Cook is a huge company," she told him. "It offers a lot of scope to interested and willing employees."

"Is that what it said in the ad for the course?"

"It's in all the staff literature. Anyway, if I do eventually want to look around for something more suitable in time to come, it'll be far easier to do that from half way up the ladder than the bottom rung. Any potential employer will want to know how I used the time spent in my previous post, and it's no bad thing to have hard evidence of enterprise and ambition."

"None at all," Steve agreed. "Whether you stay with Cook's or not, the course will do you good. You're wasted on the front line. You've got the brains and the personality to do much better."

"If not the tits," she said, sarcastically, to register the fact that she could recognize idle flattery when it was presented to her on a plate.

"Management trainees in travel and tourism don't need the same qualifications as models in lad's mags," he said, "but as it happens, there's nothing wrong with your qualifications in any regard. Trust me, I'm...."

"A connoisseur of delicacy," she finished for him. "Sometimes, I'm not so sure that's as complimentary as you try to make it sound. I can be indelicate when I need to be, and I'm certainly not made of porcelain. Anyhow, I'm sorry that I'll have to miss AlAbAn and Friday night. It can't be helped."

"I'll probably give AlAbAn a miss too," Steve said. "A couple of quiet nights in will give me a chance to catch up with the kids' course-work. I certainly won't be shedding any tears when GCSEs and A levels go back to all-exam assessment. In the meantime, I'd be happier if my lot plagiarized far more off their work off the Internet—that way I wouldn't have to wrestle with their tortured spelling and grammar."

"You don't need me to hold your hand at the AlAbAn meeting," Janine told him. "You're going on doctor's orders, remember—and we promised Milly a lift after the last one."

"Sylvia's not a doctor," Steve said, unable to resist correcting the error. "She doesn't have an M.D.—although she does like to decorate her wall with certificates, and has a string of letters after her name much longer than my meager B.Ed."

"I wasn't speaking pedantically," Janine assured him. "Therapist's orders, therapist's recommendations, whatever...the point is that you're supposed to be going for the benefit of your health."

"I suppose I am," Steve admitted. "But *supposed*'s the operative word, isn't it? I suspect that what it's really *supposed* to do, from Sylvia's point of view, is to make me more receptive to the idea of being regressed again. The idea is to help me remember-in-inverted-commas more of my abduction-experience-in-inverted-commas, so that it will be fit for exposure at AlAbAn. In Sylvia's mind, that will help me move on to the next step in delving down to the actual source of my anxieties."

"Which is wrong because...?" Janine left the sentence dangling, inviting him to complete it

"Because that's not the direction in which I want to go. I think the whole regression plan's a red herring, and that I'll be much better off sticking to the relaxation techniques. They seem to be working well enough, thus far, even though progress is a bit slow."

"You've been working on your phobias, then? Confronting your demons every night you're not with me?"

Steve blushed. He *had* been taking the occasional drive along the Bourne, crossing and recrossing it as the bridges came along, quieting his racing heart as best he could. "It's most obvious at school," he said. "I'm coping better with the everyday stresses, just as Rhodri Jenkins said I would. I reckon that if I can just keep chipping away at the other things, I can gradually wear them away. If that's the case, AlAbAn's just a pleasant distraction. I don't need to go to every meeting."

"But you enjoy it. The performances we've seen in East Grimstead are better than the ones we just saw on stage—and future ones are just as likely to be better still as the ones that we'll be seeing after the break. Mind you, it might be a lot simpler if you just told me what you're phobic about, so that we can stop beating around the bush."

Steve could see the sense in that, and his inhibitions seemed to have taken a short break, even though he hadn't touched a drop of anything more powerful than caffeine. "Flying," he said, contriving to throw caution to the wind just long enough to expel the two syllables.

"Is *that* all?" Janine said, in frank amazement.

"No," Steve said, only able to contrive one syllable this time.

Janine was flustered by the brutal simplicity of the reply, momentarily unable to connect it up with her own remark. Eventually, though, she worked it out. "Heights?" she guessed.

"That too," Steve admitted. He was breathing more easily now; the barrier was down and he knew that he could continue if he wanted to. After a moment's pause, he decided that he might as well seize the opportunity. "Especially as seen from bridges," he added.

Janine took another pause in order to be appropriately startled. "*All* bridges?" she queried. "Or just very high ones?"

"The extent of the panic is proportional to both the height and width of the bridge," he said, scrupulously. "The equation might need a couple of specific constants to being it to perfection, but the basic relationship is obvious enough. More width, more panic; more height, more panic." He paused, but then carried on. "Short road bridges over the Wylye and the Bourne only give me a nasty *frisson*. I've never dared attempt the Severn Bridge, but the Clifton Suspension Bridge was my idea of hell on Earth until I read about the opening of that new bridge connecting Sweden to Denmark. I can't watch *Charmed* on TV because of those scenes set on top of the Golden Gate Bridge, and every time there's a movie on with a literal cliffhanger I turn into a quivering wreck. I went to an i-max cinema once, just to see a wildlife documentary, and nearly had a heart attack. So now you know."

"I can see why you keep saying that anything's better than watching TV," Janine murmured. "Look—I'm sorry. I can see now why you found it so difficult—why your pride seemed to be on the line, and why you wouldn't want your pupils finding out. I'm glad you told me, though. I'm glad it's not a secret between *us* any more."

"It stays between us, right?" Steve said. "You won't tell Milly?"

"No, I won't. Jesus—you went to Sylvia Joyce because you started going out with me, didn't you? You wanted to be better able to travel, because I'm a travel agent?"

"Partly," Steve said. "You're not the only one thinking about taking steps forward in life, though. I'm just as close to the dreaded thirty as you are. I can't avoid flying, tall buildings and long bridges forever, can I? Well, actually, I suppose I could—but, as you say, my pride is on the line. I'd rather not be that kind of coward if I can avoid it."

"Phobias aren't cowardice," Janine told him, as she was honorbound to do. "What happened when your hypnotherapist regressed you, then? Did you have a panic attack?"

"And how. Usually, it's just the queasy feeling, maybe with a little nausea thrown in. Sometimes there's cold sweat, and breathing difficulties. In extreme cases, though, your arteries constrict. I've never seen it, of course, but when the blood-flow to your brain cuts off you go a remarkable shade of grey. Usually, you come back after you've blacked out—but not necessarily. People really can die of fright, even in nightmares of their own manufacture. Best not to take the chance."

"And that's why your therapist suggested that you go to AlAbAn? She thought that if you could relive the experience, in safe and supportive surroundings, you might defuse it? And that might be a crucial first step in defusing the whole complex?"

"I told you that you had the brains and personality to be management material," Steve said—but the discussion was cut abruptly short then, because the next hopeful amateur had come to the mike. The local protocol demanded that people in the audience shouldn't talk over the opening of an act, although judicious heckling was allowed after the first couple of minutes or so.

Steve didn't sigh, but he did feel relieved. It was all over, at least for a while—except, of course, that it had only just begun, Janine would start thinking about it now. In fact, she probably already had, in spite of the fact that the act had started. The first amateur up was an obese bloke in his twenties who obviously thought that his falsetto Liverpudlian accent was funny enough to get laughs even though his material was a great deal thinner than he was—thus leaving plenty of vacant mindspace for the various members of his audience to go exploring.

Janine's curiosity, Steve knew, would have been whetted rather than soothed by the revelations with which he'd just parted. She would be keen to know exactly what experience he'd had when Sylvia Joyce had regressed him, and exactly why it had generated such a powerful panic attack. She would not be put off for long by the excuse that he couldn't remember much of it himself, and wasn't at all sure that he wanted to try, even with the aid of a very supportive support group. How long, in fact, could he be content with that excuse himself? For all his expressed doubts about Sylvia's tactics, he had to admit that she probably had a point. If he *could* bring the nightmarish fantasy into some sort of completion, especially if he could add the kind of narrative trajectory to it that the AlAbAn story-tellers achieved, then it might indeed reveal something about the ultimate source of his phobias, and might indeed assist the hypnotherapist in reaching further back into his psyche in search of answers, if not possible solutions. The only thing stopping him from taking that route was fear itself—a phobic response to his own awareness of his phobias.

Steve also knew that Janine would not simply have become hungry for more information. She would also start to process the information she had. She was probably sitting beside him right now, ignoring the weak-kneed scouser while she wondered what the symbolism of his fear of bridges might be. All women, it seemed, thought of men as inherently commitment-phobic, and she would probably wonder whether his bridge-anxiety might somehow be reducible to a fear of crossing existential or experiential rubicons. She had already guessed that he had been inspired to take up arms against his sea of troubles by the fact that he had started going out with her, and was bound to wonder whether it might be the character of the relationship rather than the nature of her employment that had turned the screw and moved him to act. Among the other things she'd be hungry to know, she'd be bound to ask whether he'd revealed his awful secret to any of his previous girlfriends—and if she believed him when he said no, she'd be bound to read something into that regarding the potential future development of their couple-dom.

In fact, though, when the Liverpudlian went off and there was a half-minute respite before the next act was introduced, the question that Janine asked was: "Are you going to go, then?"

"Where?" Steve asked, thinking about bridges.

"To AlAbAn. Next Thursday. Will you give Milly a lift, or shall I ring her and tell her that she'll have to take the bus?"

"Oh," Steve said. "Yes, sure, if you don't mind. I'll go—why not?"

The next act—a bottle-blonde whose repertoire mostly consisted of jokes about tampons and the many inadequacies of the phallus as an instrument of female pleasure-seeking—gave him plenty of mindspace to wonder whether that had been the right answer, and to think of possible reasons *why not*. He was suddenly unsure exactly what he ought to read into Janine's apparent insistence that he should go to the AlAbAn meeting with Milly. Did Janine mean that, in her opinion, he needed the support group's support so desperately that he couldn't afford to miss a meeting? Did it mean that she suspected that he and Milly were both hooked on the members' confessions, and was merely giving her permission for them to get their fix? Might she be making the point that she trusted him to spend an evening alone—except for the twenty or so other people who would be at the meeting—with Milly, because she trusted him implicitly? Might it, on the other hand, mean that she didn't trust him as far as she could throw him, and wanted Milly to keep an eye on him for her, to make sure that he didn't get into mischief while she was away? Presumably, Janine trusted Milly implicitly, whether she trusted him or not, given that they'd been friends since the year dot—except that he still wasn't convinced that Janine hadn't ordered Milly to keep her hands off at the commencement of the last AlAbAn meeting.

Steve wished, briefly, that his experience of relationships had had more depth than variety in it, so that the practice they'd provided would have improved his understanding of womankind rather than further confusing it. The comedienne wasn't helping, either.

"I wonder whether she'd dare to do that set in a working men's club?" Janine said, when the turn ended.

"Sure," Steve said, "Even horny-handed sons of toil are new men these days, and it wouldn't be macho to let on that it might be getting to them. What would take real courage would be doing it at the mother's union."

"Is there still such a thing as the mothers' union?" Janine asked.

"How should I know?" Steve replied. "Probably. It's a hell of a lot more likely than AlAbAn—although having a baby must be very similar to being abducted by aliens. Less than half the population has to go through it, of course, but they're more likely to remember it."

"My mother certainly remembered it," Janine said, hurrying to get the last word in before the next act reached the mike, "and never forgave me for it. That's why I'm an only child."

Steve was an only child too, but his mother had never given him an explanation for that—even an explanation as fatuous as remembering what it had been like giving birth the first time. On the other hand, he thought, as an unsteady flow of attempted political satire began to build up pace on stage, perhaps it wasn't as fatuous as it sounded. Maybe women did have to forget the pain of their previous childbirths in order to be ale to contemplate going through it again. Maybe they had built-in memory-censors to ensure that they did exactly that—except that the censors occasionally failed in their duty, permitting the horror of the event to remain *in situ*, blighting everyday intercourse as well as instilling a deep-seated phobia regarding the possibility of future conception.

That reminded him of Mary, and her fantasy of nurturing a chrysalis with her blood, exactly as every mother nurtured an embryo inside herself whenever she brought another human being into the world—occasionally accompanied, so it was rumored, by hemorrhoids and varicose veins, not to mention episiotomies and umbilical cords.

Steve quickly shut such thoughts away, although the queasiness they made him feel was quite different from the queasiness he felt whenever someone was hanging off the edge of a high-rise in some TV melodrama, and concentrated on the political satire. There was something ineffably cozy and relaxing about mocking politicians, relentlessly making fun of their vanity, their ambition, their incompetence and their incessant peccadilloes.

One thing Steve *had* contrived to learn from his previous bouts of relationship fever was not to ask Janine any of the questions that had occurred to him regarding her possible motives for urging him to go to the following Thursday's AlAbAn meeting with Milly even though she would not be with them. He didn't raise the issue again that evening. Nor did Janine, who was apparently quite satisfied that his earlier reply had settled the question. As Steve drove back to Salisbury, feeling conspicuously sober, Janine told him a little more about the management training course, but the only hard fact that Steve was able to ascertain was that it would be in Brighton—a place to which he had never been, even though it was by no means notorious for the size or multiplicity of its bridges.

* * * * * * *

When the following Thursday rolled around, Steve went to pick Milly up at her flat.

"It's just me, I'm afraid," Steve explained, although he knew that Milly must have been thoroughly briefed. "Janine's away in Brighton doing extreme geography."

"I know," Milly said. "She asked me to keep an eye on you."

Steve had no idea whether that was true, or what it might imply if it was, or what it might imply if it wasn't. "Bang go my chances of chatting up Amelia Rockham, then," he said, figuring that there was always safety in absurdist humor.

Milly was still in her uniform, having only just finished her shift, and Steve had to wait for her to change. Unlike Janine's bedsit, Milly's flat had a separate bedroom, so there was no possibility of any undue embarrassment. Steve was able to sit on a sofa studying the sparse furnishings while the operation was completed. He had glanced around on past visits, but had never taken the time to consider the implications of the various visible objects. He observed that Milly had a CD collection, which fitted into a pair of forty-slot towers, but he didn't know whether that signified that she wasn't particular fond of music or whether she had moved on to MP3s as soon as the opportunity presented itself. The pictures on her walls were mostly prints of flowers, ranging from Monet-esque studies of water lilies to intimate Georgia O'Keefe-style close-ups. She had a rowing-machine propped up beside the window that overlooked the street, and a flatpack set of bookshelves crammed with paperbacks.

Figuring that the books were more likely to offer an insight into Milly's personality than anything else, he squinted in an effort to make out the titles. They all seemed to be fiction, but there was no evident genre specialization and many of them were far from contemporary. She did seem to like thick books whose page-count offered value for money, though: *Gone with the Wind* sat beside *Doctor Zhivago*, *Star Maker*, *Atlas Shrugged*, and *Lady of Hay*.

Milly came out of the bedroom dressed in a pink T-shirt, blue jeans, and trainers while Steve was still leaning forward and squinting. "The non-fiction section's in the bedroom," she said. "Self-help books are my preferred material for reading myself to sleep, but if I get really desperate I've got an old copy of the *Highway Code*." She laughed before adding: "I always buy second-hand—it's much cheaper."

"I used to," Steve said, smiling in response to the laugh, "but I spend so much more time on-line these days that I don't have time for reading, except for the occasional text-book. Even that's rarely necessary, given the amount of stuff there is on-line."

They left the flat and went downstairs. "Good day?" Steve asked, once they were in the car and on the move.

"Fair to middling," she replied.

"Made your ticket-quota without any difficulty, then?"

"No problem. The world's full of people who can't see a double yellow without wanting to park on it—especially mums on the school run. They seem to think that motherhood sets them above the law—not that they behave like madonnas if they catch me in the act. They go off like cluster-bombs, spraying expletives about like the Israeli air force."

"They probably think you're failing in our duty as a member of the great sisterhood, rather than doing your duty as a police auxiliary," Steve said. "It's a question of priorities."

"No they don't," Milly told him. "They hate me more for *not* being part of their sisterhood of breeders than for being a traffic warden. They think I should be pumping out kids, taking my share of the misery. They're not as likely to accuse me of being a lesbian as male drivers are, but that's only because they think that would somehow be letting me off the hook. On the other hand, they never threaten to rape me—just to gouge my eyes out with carefully-painted fingernails."

"Must be a fun job," Steve observed. "Any prospect of moving up to management, like Janine, and getting out of the firing-line?"

"Not really," Milly admitted. "Janine's lucky in that respect, at Tom Cook's. There are far more career-paths mapped out there than in my line. On the other hand, I am a civil servant of sorts, like Ali, so there'd be a possibility of transferring to some other line of work within the sector, if I wanted to."

"But you don't?"

"Maybe, in time. For the moment, I'm still in the frame of mind where I'll be damned if I'll let the bastards grind me down. At the end of the day, I'm the one who hands out the fines, so I always get the last laugh—at least until someone really does gouge my eyes out with fake fingernails or bend me over a bonnet and fuck me up the back passage. Has any of your pupils pulled a knife on you yet?"

"Not yet," Steve admitted. "I've never even been punched, even though they know I'm not allowed to hit them back. A year eleven girl kicked me in the shin last year, but she was wearing trainers, so it wasn't a crippling wound. She's in the sixth form now, but she isn't doing Biology A level, so I'm no longer at risk from that direction. The present year elevens are mouthy, but so far it's all obscenities and bad breath—no one's tried to bite."

"It's the same with my lot, really," Milly admitted. "All talk and no action. They know as well as I do that it's not me they're really angry at. I just give them an opportunity to let it out."

"I don't have that consolation," Steve said. "It really is teachers that make the kids angry and frustrated, because we're the ones who have to try to discipline their behavior from nine to four—or, increasingly, to half-past five or six, because we have to hold on to them till their parents get home from work. Somebody has to do it, I guess. Janine mostly deals with people in search of leisure pursuits, so she gets a much more hopeful and even-tempered class of client, on the whole."

When they went into Amelia Rockham's front room, Milly immediately went to her usual armchair rather than moving towards the settee with Steve. Steve took one to the folding chairs, figuring that he ought to leave the Naugahyde nook to a couple, but he took one opposite Milly rather than in parallel with her.

As things turned out, there were no newcomers at the group that night, and it was one of those occasions when nobody wanted to relate any new experience. A few of the regulars looked at Milly in a speculative fashion, but no one looked at Steve. Steve didn't know whether or not to feel insulted by that, but decided to believe that it was just a matter of seniority. Milly was evidently not yet ready to step in and plug the gap, and Steve was certainly in no rush to fill the breach, so there was a full minute's awkward silence before Walter Wainwright began talking again.

Walter explained that when occasions such as these presented themselves, the normal practice was to ask whether one of the long-standing members might care to retell a story that the younger members of the group hadn't yet had the opportunity to hear. After all, he went on to say, because the group was very scrupulous about not keeping minutes, stories sometimes needed to be retold, so that recent abductees could discover what their forebears had gone through in the difficult days when abductees hadn't had the same opportunities for obtaining a sympathetic hearing.

Steve hoped, briefly, that Walter might be about to retell the story of his own abduction, or at least ask Amelia to oblige by retelling hers, but in the event the chairman followed his preamble by asking a man named Arthur if he would mind repeating his story, for the benefit of all the people who'd joined since the last time it had been told. Arthur, it seemed, was only too happy to oblige.

CHAPTER SIX

THE FERTILE IMAGINATION

I haven't been in the group quite as long as Amelia and Walter and I thought at first that I didn't really belong here. If I've ever been properly abducted, before or after the events I'm about to describe—which happened way back in the seventies—I don't remember it at all. Walter very kindly told me, though, that AlAbAn meetings are open to anyone, and more than willing to offer support to people who've had any kind of alien encounter whatsoever. The members have always been good to me, and I hope that's not just because of the boxes of organic vegetables I bring along in the season and the jars of chutney I give out as Christmas presents.

As those of you who haven't heard my story before will have guessed from what I just said, I'm a keen gardener. Now that I'm retired, of course, it's my sole occupation, but for twenty years before I turned sixty-five it was a convenient way of not getting under Mildred's feet too much. Mildred is my late wife. She liked to keep the house nice, and didn't approve of clutter in her territory, so it suited us both for me to spend Sundays and summer evenings in the garden. She used to joke that if we ever got divorced she'd get custody of the house and I'd get custody of the garden shed, but of course we never did. Forty years without a single argument, and then the silly old girl goes and gets cancer. What can you do?

Anyway, I found the tuber—the tuber that the story's about, that is—in a bag of tulip bulbs I bought at the local Garden Centre. I could see immediately that it didn't belong, and my first thought was simply to throw it away, but I didn't like to do that without knowing what it was. I tried to look it up, obviously, but it's actually very difficult to identify the species of a tuber unless you've got a dissecting kit, a set of stains and a high-powered microscope. If, on the other hand, you plant it and let it grow, you can usually tell what it is as soon as it begins to produce leaves—or, at the very latest, once it produces a flower.

Flowers are, of course, the structures that provide the fundamental plan of the Linnaean classification system. The move was very controversial at the time, I understand, because flowers are a plant's sex organs and most amateur botanists back in those days were clergymen, some of whom thought that Erasmus Darwin's poetic account of *The Loves of the Plants* was an exceedingly racy text.

Anyhow, I decided that the simplest thing would be to plant the anomalous tuber and see if it would grow. I had no idea what kind of soil would suit it, or how much water it might need, or how much shade it could tolerate, but I wasn't that worried. I just bedded it down it in a five-pint pot in early March and shoved the pot into a quiet corner that I wasn't using for anything else, in a little covert between the edge of the patio and the back wall of the garage. I left it to its own devices, fully prepared not to give it another thought if nothing actually materialized.

I suppose I must have glanced at the pot occasionally during the next three weeks, but it wasn't until a shoot began to appear that I actually took any notice of what was happening. The shoot was mostly white at first, as shoots often are, but the first time I saw it I noticed that its sprouting tip was tinted purple rather than green.

That's not entirely unknown, of course; these days, you see that crunchy purple rubbish in all the bags of mixed salad the supermarket sells. Not that I'd ever buy such a thing, mind. You don't grow fancy lettuce from tubers, but I already had the suspicion that the thing might be an exotic kind of potato, and I had the vague idea that some potatoes with purple skins also had purple tints in their foliage.

In South America, where potatoes come from, there are thousands of different kinds, although Europeans only imported the ones that were best to eat. Globalization hadn't really got off the ground in the seventies, but there was a certain amount of new interest in exotic vegetables even so, and it seemed perfectly plausible to me that the Garden Center's suppliers might have been investigating neglected potato species, and that one such sample might have gone astray and accidentally fallen in with the tulip bulbs.

There's nothing very exciting about potatoes—even exotic ones—so I didn't pay any special attention to the purple plant during April, even though I was mildly surprised by just how purple it was. It wasn't until May Day—I always spend the whole of Bank Holiday Mondays in the garden—that it became obvious that the thing had become far too bulky for the five-pint pot and that I'd have to plant it out. When I did that, I took the opportunity to take a good look at the root system, to see how the new potatoes were getting on.

That was when I realized that I'd made a mistake. There weren't any new potatoes forming amid the roots. The original tuber was still in one piece at the centre of the tangle, and it had grown considerably. The roots themselves looked like any other roots—white, thin, expanding in every direction—but the thing that now sat at the bottom of the stem was like nothing I'd ever seen before: round, plump and very solid. It was a lighter shade of purple than the stem and leaves—Mildred would probably have called it mauve—but that still seemed odd. It brought it home to me for the first time how strange it was that all of the plant's upper body was colored deep imperial purple. Obviously, it wasn't using chlorophyll for the purpose of photosynthesis but had substituted some other compound of similar efficiency.

When I planted it out, its growth rate accelerated. On May Day the stem had attained a height of about two-and-a-half feet, and the leaves had expanded in a spray that was maybe two feet wide. Three weeks later, the thing was nearly as tall as I am, and it was pushing out branches that were four and five feet long—not woody branches, mind, but branches whose texture was more like plastic. In fact, the whole thing looked suspiciously artificial. If it hadn't been growing so enthusiastically, it could easily have been mistaken for a giant version one of those plastic plants they put on restaurant tables, which had been mistakenly cast in the wrong color of polystyrene.

It was late flowering, but that didn't surprise me, and the buds it eventually produced grew to be as big as my head before they began to open, but that didn't surprise me either. By then, I thought nothing would surprise me. If the thing had unfolded flowers like a Venus fly-trap's, with a gape like a crocodile, and started catching cats and urban foxes while building up to a career as a man-eater, I'd have been alarmed but not surprised. I knew, you see, that I had to be dealing with something alien—the product of some Arrhenius spore carried across the interstellar void by the wind of some ancient supernoval explosion, which had fallen to Earth in a meteor shower.

I thought I was ready for anything. I even bought a new camera so that I could record its further progress—we were still in the predigital era, alas, so I suppose I paid over the odds for something that would soon be obsolete. However, as even those of you who haven't heard the story before will probably have anticipated, I wasn't ready for anything at all. When the buds opened, they weren't like hungry mouths ready to devour anything they could get their teeth into, although they did eventually develop mouths of a sort.

At first, when the flowers opened, they looked like huge carnations, with multitudinous petals. There was no scent at first. By most surprising thing about them by far was their color. The sepals folded around the buds had been purple, of course, and the tips of the corolla protruding from the bundle had seemed to be grey, but when the flowers expanded, it turned out that they were more silver than grey, if they were any color at all. I say *if they were any color at all*, although it doesn't quite make sense, because the whole ensemble was strangely reminiscent of a mirror. I say *strangely* reminiscent because the petals didn't form a smooth and shiny surface at all; they bore no more resemblance to a bathroom mirror than they did to a dandelion-clock. There was still a sense, though, in which the flower was *reflective*: capable of capturing and reproducing an image.

The images took time to form, but it was only a matter of days. They weren't consistent or stable—if you looked at the plant from a distance they looked like little cumulus clouds or bundles of cotton wool—but when they had some nearby presence to reflect they became much more clearly-defined. When I was there, they immediately began to look like me. The only other Earthly face I ever saw in them was next door's cat. I never asked Mildred to come out of the house and take a look, because it wasn't her sort of thing. I did take a lot of pictures with my new camera, though, so I do have proof, of a sort.

I've got pictures of flowers reflecting the cat as well as pictures of flowers reflecting my own face. Pictures don't lie. Unfortunately, they don't always tell the whole truth either, and they came out rather fuzzy. I did my best, but I never could get the images in the flowers properly in focus. When I showed them around here, the first time I told this story, most of the members could see what I meant, but when I showed them to Mildred, she couldn't see anything at all.

Cameras don't record sound, either. You couldn't get camcorders back in the seventies—not at the sort of price I could afford, anyway—and I didn't have a Dictaphone, so the second aspect of the flowers' marvelous properties went unrecorded. The reflections weren't just surface appearances, you see. The flowers had depth, and those plastic stems obviously had versatile xylem at the core. As to what was going on underground, where the central tuber must have been much bigger than a football by then, I could only speculate. At any rate, the flowers soon began to reflect more than the appearance of my face. By the second week of July, the plant was able to talk.

I've always talked to my plants. That's not the sort of thing I confess readily, even in a safe environment like this, because I remember the reception poor Prince Charles got when he said that it was a good thing to do—but it *is* a good thing to do, even if you never expect them to reply. It helps them to flourish, to make the most of themselves. I talk to my tulips and my geraniums, my rosemary and my fennel, my rose-bushes and my pear tree. I always have and I always will. So I'd been talking to the purple plant ever since I first transplanted it from its pot and started taking a greater interest in it.

I suppose I talked to the purple plant—which I had begun to call "my purple emperor", although a purple emperor is really a kind of butterfly—more than any of the other plants in the garden, especially when it got to be about my height. I had no idea that it was actually listening, but it must have been. It must have been smart, too, to learn English simply by listening. It didn't say a word until it had mastered the language; it wasn't the sort of creature to go in for baby talk.

I don't know how many times I'd put questions to it before I finally got a reply, but it must have been far more than a dozen. They were all intended rhetorically, of course. The answer, when it eventually came, had obviously been carefully considered. It was right at the end of July, on the thirty-first, when I asked it for the umpteenth time what the hell it was, and it told me.

* * * * * * *

"Essentially," it said, "I'm a dreamer. Unfortunately, the soil in which you've planted me isn't doing a great deal to fertilize my imagination. It needs assistance."

As you can imagine, I was somewhat taken aback by this revelation, but I won't embarrass myself by trying to repeat exactly what I said during the next half hour, while I belatedly convinced myself of the obvious. Eventually, we got back to the nub of the matter.

"What kind of assistance?" I said. "There's a young man at work who's always bragging about tripping on LSD. I expect he'll know where I can buy some."

"I'm not talking about human-active psychotropics," the plant said. "Do I look as if I have the kind of brain chemistry that could be stimulated or inhibited by the same things that play havoc with *your* neurotransmitters?"

"You do when I'm staring one of your flowers in its temporary face," I said. "But that's not the point, I suppose. You don't even look as if you have the same kind of carbon-fixing chemistry as your neighbors, so I'll presume that we're in a whole different ball-park, if you'll forgive the Americanism. So what *do* you need?"

"I'm not exactly sure," the plant confessed. "This isn't a milieu I know anything about, and I haven't a clue how I wound up here. I've sent out roots as far as I presently can, in order to sample the local resources, and the most promising location seems to be roughly north by northwest, on or above the surface."

It took me a few seconds to work out which way that was, but I eventually figured out that I needed to look towards the far corner of the garden, at the shady covert sandwiched between the back end of the shed and the fence, diplomatically shielded by the bole of the pear tree.

"Oh," I said. "The compost heap. You want composting."

"There appears to be something in the soil in that region that has a stimulating effect," the plant informed me. "I can access it by means of my exploratory roots, but it would be more convenient if you could transport the active compound to the immediate vicinity—and more convenient by far if you could identify it and procure more."

"That might not be easy," I said. "I compost all sorts of things—not just cuttings from the lawn and the usual sorts of garden waste but potato-peelings and apple cores, and leftover food when Mildred gets a rush of blood to the head and makes a bit too much for our feeble appetites to cope with. She means well, bless her, but I wish she wouldn't try to *feed me up*. I'm a solicitor's clerk, not a Sumo wrestler. I also buy fertilizer at the Garden Centre and mix it in with the stuff in the heap—not that vile chemical fertilizer, of course, but *natural* fertilizer: horse manure and the like." In those days, of course, green politics was just getting off the ground, and there were only a few prophets of doom anticipating ecocatastrophe, but as a keen amateur gardener I already had many habits that would nowadays be thought progressive.

"That's good," the plant said. "It will make it easier to experiment. Just pack a few forkfuls of compost around the base of my stem, for now. Starting tomorrow, though, we'll test out the elements of the mixture one at a time. We'll do the household leftovers first, and then we'll move on to the things you can buy at the Garden Centre."

"I don't have a lot of control over the kind of leftovers we generate from day to day," I said. "Menu-planning is Mildred's department, and she's very keen on my respecting her boundaries. That's only fair, mind, because she's just as keen on respecting mine—

which is why you haven't met her, and probably won't. She's not a garden person. She hates bugs and gets allergies."

"We'll take things as they come," my purple emperor assured me.

And that's what we did. I forked some general compost into the soil around the plant's roots, and then I started adding more specific things day by day: potato peelings, cold spaghetti Bolognese, eggshells, used lard from the chip pan...you know the sort of thing.

The general composting perked the plant up a bit. The purple in its leaves became a little more luxuriant, although it didn't grow any taller and didn't extend its branches any further. The flowers also acquired a scent for the first time—pleasant enough, I suppose, but certainly nothing that could compete with my roses. The real difference, however, was in the way it talked.

"That's better," it told me, in a much plummier accent and a much more satisfied tone. "I'm beginning to dream a little more effectively now."

"What do you mean by that, exactly?" I asked.

The plant explained to me, little by little, that there are significant differences between plant consciousness and animal consciousness, and hence in the kinds of intelligence associated with them.

Animal consciousness, it said, is the evolutionary product of relentless movement, and of the continual need to evaluate new situations by comparing them to others, in order to figure out how they might develop and thus make rational choices. To some extent, that's a matter of locating food and avoiding dangers, but, according to the purple emperor, the primary evolutionary motive of all consciousness is sexual. In that respect, animal consciousness is very much orientated to the matter of finding and pursuing mates. Animal consciousness is busy and alert, always *wakeful* even when an animal goes to sleep. Animal dreams are busy too, always manufacturing bizarre situations for comparison with experienced ones, further exploring the potential and testing the limits of choice.

Because plants are mostly rooted, and very limited in their capacity for movement, the consciousness they develop—in evolutionary circumstances where they do develop it—is much less concerned with the needs of meeting new situations and making choices. It's far more meditative. The sensoria of plants—even plants like the alien in my garden, which could develop organs of sight and hearing by reflection—are markedly different from those of animals, far more sensitive to the interplay of chemical substances and fundamental physical forces. The same applies to the sexual aspects of plant consciousness, which are closely akin—if only in a symbolic sense—to those of flowers. There's no discovery and pursuit involved; it's all a matter of reception and sensation. Plant consciousness is very luxurious and very voluptuous; plants, my purple emperor assured me, are the true connoisseurs of sensuality.

The plants with which we're familiar are extremely primitive by comparison with the intelligent plants that are the dominant species in whatever world my purple emperor had strayed from, but they possess the rudiments on which true plant intelligence is based. That's why it helps if you talk to them—not because they can experience sound as animal ears experience it, let alone decode human speech, but because thy can experience it as a form of nuanced physical vibration, a subtle component of the great universal symphony of matter in motion, and something essentially erotic. There's not a lot that humans can do for plants in terms of erotic enhancement, but a soft tone of voice is apparently quite nice.

It would give the wrong impression to say that intelligent plants are telepathic, or even intuitive, but when they dream—which they do while fully conscious, because they never sleep, even while their photosynthetic activity ceases at night—they possess a particular kind of perception, of which humans can only obtain the merest glimpses at the extremes of psychotropic experience. The younger members of the group have probably sampled magic mushrooms and ecstasy as well as LSD, and maybe more exotic things too, but, if what my purple emperor told me can be trusted, the best trip ever experienced by any animal in the history of the universe can offer no more than a thousandth of the enlightenment that's routine in the course of a sophisticated plant's dreaming.

"With the right chemical stimulus," my purple emperor assured me, in a voice that was getting more rhapsodically elevated by the day, "a plant like me really can tap into the cosmic consciousness of the universe entire, sensing its spatial breadth and its temporal depth, from the moment of the Big Bang to the Omega Point. It can tap into the essential sexuality of the universe—the perpetual echo of the infinite orgasm. If I guess rightly, that's probably what my people were doing when I got lost: searching the great erotic symphony for new nuances, experimenting with the long-lost organic produce of the Dark Eras. Do you happen to know, by the way, exactly how old the Earth is just now?"

"No," I said. "I think current estimates vary from six thousand years to four billion."

"That young?" it said—although I don't think it was talking about the six thousand years. "Well, no matter, I won't need to find anything particularly exotic to dream what I need to dream, in order to figure out exactly when I am, to restore empathy with my species and obtain a measure of relief from dreadful frustration. I'll die here, obviously—almost certainly unpollinated, in a crudely literal sense—but I needn't die alone, if only I can find a moderately powerful stimulant. We just have to keep trying."

So that's what we did. In the latter part of August we moved on from leftovers to the opportunities offered by the Garden Centre—and that's how we discovered the miraculous efficacy of horse-manure.

* * * * * * *

The moment I started spreading the manure, the plant got very excited. "That's *good*," it said. "That's very, very good. Do you know how it feels when you've been looking for something your entire life, without even knowing what it is, and then you find it?"

"Actually, no," I said.

"Well," my purple emperor assured me, "it's good. In fact, it's wonderful. Yours is a direly ineffectual language, you know—it can't even begin to express the merest fundamentals of vegetal dreaming, let alone the greater rewards."

"That's not something that English has a lot of call for," I admitted. I hoped that the plant might go on talking anyway, in spite of the inadequacies of the language, in order that I could get a slightly better grasp of what it was talking about, but it didn't. I did, however, manage to catch a glimpse—a literal glimpse—of the substance of its dream. Mostly, its fancy flowers only reflected entities outside of itself, but they were also capable of other modes of reflection. They could change their apparent color and apparent shape in all sorts of ways, as if they were little three-dimensional windows into other worlds. They could change their scent, too, and when I breathed in their finest perfumes I became better able to make out the images within the flowers

I didn't recognize any of the shapes, of course; if any of them were faces I couldn't tell. To me, they were all just different kinds of flowers—but I've grown a lot of flowers in my time, and I can assure you that these were flowers like none on Earth. I took a lot of pictures, but they didn't come out any better than the pictures of my face and the cat's; there was some kind of light-trickery involved that was too subtle for the camera. I was able to stand in front of my lovely bush, breathing in its exhalations and watching its flowers change, though—and sometimes, while watching them change, I managed to fall into a kind of trance, to experience what modern jargon calls an "altered state of consciousness".

I'm not going to tell you that I actually gained a full appreciation of the great universal symphony of matter in motion, or that I made any kind of empathetic compact with the infinite orgasm extending from the Big Bang to the Omega Point. I didn't feel infinity in the palm of my hand and eternity in an hour, let alone get a grip on the essential secret of existence—but I did sense the incredible multiplicity of possibility, the vastness of space, the sheer stubbornness of Earthly life in the face of perennial adversity, and the essential voluptuousness of vegetal identity. Even in my poor suburban human brain, there was some slight potential—which I'd never learned to tap before—to think somewhat after the fashion that a superintelligent, supersensitive, and supersensual plant might think, and to dream in a strange way distantly akin to the way that such an organism might dream. I must have nodded off the first time, because I woke up with quite a start.

"More," was all that my purple emperor said, like a drunken Old Etonian. "Much, much more."

* * * * * * *

I shoveled on all the muck I'd bought, and then went to wash my hands before dinner, but when I went out into the garden the following evening, the plant demanded more. It also demanded to know everything I knew about the fabulous substance that had given it the ability to dream with such awesome and unexpected power.

When I'd explained, my purple emperor immediately decided to investigate the properties of every other kind of manure I could lay my hands on—which seemed to me to pose all kinds of practical difficulties, as well as being a trifle unsavory. I won't go into the details; suffice it to say that I did my best.

The summer was drawing to a close, and there was already a hint of Autumn in the air. By the end of September, the plant had experimented with forty different kinds of animal manure, if you count the various kinds of bird and bat guano. I'd had a horrible suspicion, at first, that it might turn out to like human waste best, but it didn't. In fact, it reckoned human manure to be distinctly inferior as dream-nourishment, even by comparison with horses.

What my purple emperor like best of all, it turned out, was elephant-dung—which was rather inconvenient, given that the nearest zoo was in Bristol. I made what heroic efforts I could—which didn't do the boot of the Escort any good at all—but I was desperately anxious that I wouldn't be able to meet the plant's increasingly desperate demands. Not that it was exercising any terrible power of command over me—mine was just a gardener's passion for the products of his art.

As it was, things came to a head more rapidly than I'd ever imagined. Almost as soon as I began to transfer my precious final cargo of elephant-dung from the boot of the car to the place where the bulbous structure at the foot of the purple emperor's stem now protruded a couple of feet above the surface of the soil, I could tell that the plant was in dire distress. It wasn't a matter of withdrawal symptoms—quite the reverse. The poor thing was overdosing on the stuff of vegetal dreams.

I wanted to stop, but it wouldn't hear of it. It insisted that I keep shoveling, until the boot and the wheelbarrow were both empty. Perhaps I should have insisted, but I didn't have the heart—and I couldn't imagine, at that point, that the poor thing was actually going to die.

Its purple leaves turned black, and then began to get brittle. Its roots began to emerge from the ground, not just in the vicinity of the overgrown tuber but all over the lawn, writhing like tormented snakes. As for the flowers...well, as soon as I stopped shoveling I was entranced, just as I had been entranced before. I experienced the merest, slightest hint of that final vegetal dream, and it overwhelmed me. It was a dream of sex and death—of individual sex and individual death as well as cosmic sex and cosmic death—and it was magnificent.

Human consciousness, the existentialists tell us, is blighted and crippled by an awareness of the inevitability of its own extinction; the fundamental mood of human existence is *angst*. You might think all consciousness would be similar, and I suspect that all animal consciousness is. Animal consciousness, you see, is fundamentally a matter of action and exploration, of being busy and making rational choices, of pursuing and finding potential mates—or trying to. Plant consciousness isn't like that. It's fundamentally quiet, sedentary, meditative, sensual and self-indulgent. That's not to say that it welcomes eventual death, or even that it's fatalistic about the necessity, but the fundamental mood of plant existence is neither blighted nor crippled by angst. Even humans, so it's said, can sometimes find compensation for the awareness of death in erotic experience; flowering plants have no difficulty at all.

In human beings and most other animals, sex and death are only loosely connected, both existentially and symbolically, but flowers retain a far more intimate connection in the process and ideology of seed-production. My purple emperor never got to make any literal seeds, because whatever pollination mechanism it had in its own world was lacking in ours. That might qualify, from our point of view, as a lucky escape, because I'm not sure that the human race is quite ready to share its world with a race of superintelligent plants, but from the purple emperor's point of view it was a tragedy of sorts. It was, however, a tragedy considerably ameliorated by dreaming—and my purple emperor was a dreamer before it was anything else. Its manure-nourished dreams reflected the great ballet of gametes in motion, the purpose and existence of every flower that had ever lived and ever would: the great and mighty thrust of an orgasmic evolution that will lead, inevitably and inexorably, to the floral Omega Point that will become the glorious seed of a whole new universe.

That, at least, is what it dreamed, and what it believed; it probably had no special insight into the actual fate of the universe.

The plant didn't have to die so soon. It didn't have to overdose on ecstasy—but I think it chose to go that way. It chose to go out on a high. There's a sense in which it was poisoned, but there's also a sense in which it found its own destiny, and met it gladly.

Somehow, I don't think there are any elephants in the world from which it came, and probably no horses or humans either. It never said so, because it didn't know—how could it, growing up, as it did, as an orphan, probably countless light-years away from its point of origin. That, if you think about it, must be the fate of almost all the infinitesimally tiny minority of Arrhenius spores that ever make planetfall; the vast majority must, of course, drift eternally and dreamlessly through the interstellar void, without any such hope.

In the end, the massive globe at the foot of the stem collapsed like a punctured football and shriveled up, exhaling the most appalling stench. I had to throw my clothes away. Luckily, they were old ones reserved for gardening, and my current set of work shirts were already reaching the end of their allotted span, so Mildred didn't get upset.

I put my purple emperor's remains on the compost heap. I think that's what it would have wanted.

CHAPTER SEVEN

TAKING THE WRONG DIRECTION

When the meeting was over, Steve expected to drop Milly off at her flat and then make his way straight home. He was mildly surprised when Milly raised the possibility of getting something to eat, although he remembered that she'd said on prior occasions that she'd had time to eat before the meeting, which she obviously hadn't been able to do on this occasion.

"Sure," he said. "Janine and I usually get a takeaway from the Chinese at the end of her street, but that's a bit out of our way. We can get a burger, if you like, or we could stop off at the Pizza Hut in the town centre—it won't be crowded on a Thursday—if you'd prefer that."

"I don't eat burgers," Milly said, flatly, hastening to add: "They may not actually be made of elephant-dung, but they always look a bit iffy to me."

Steve suspected that Milly was worried about what Janine might have told him about her past problems with food, so he was quick to say: "I'd prefer a pizza myself. We can split a large one, if you like—your choice of toppings."

"That's fine," she said.

When they got to the centre of Salisbury, Steve had to double-check with Milly that it was okay for him to park in the side-street near the restaurant, despite the single yellow line, given that it was after six o'clock and that he was on the right-hand side of the thoroughfare.

"You're a driver," she told him, after consulting the relevant notice and confirming that it would be okay. "You really need to be able to understand restriction notices, even when they're a little complicated and badly-expressed. Look at it as a matter of simple economics, if not moral duty."

"I do," Steve assured her, as he opened the restaurant door and ushered her through. "Luckily, I'm still a parking-ticket virgin, although I once got caught by a speed camera."

"It's only a matter of time," Milly said, ominously. "Everybody gets a ticket eventually—everyone who drives, that is."

"Have you ever been tempted to learn to drive?" Steve asked, while they waited for the food to arrive. Milly had ordered a strong cider, but Steve thought it best to stick to diet Pepsi, given that he was dining with an officer of the law.

"Not since I became a traffic warden," Milly told him. "I'm not that much of a movement-freak, to be honest. I'm more the sedentary type—although I'm very grateful to you for driving me to East Grimstead once a fortnight. Catching the bus is a pain, especially if it's raining.

"You've never been tempted to leave the old home town, then?" Steve said. "You don't dream of the gold-paved streets of London, where they have red routes and a congestion charge as well as double yellows?"

"If I were to be tempted," Milly assured him, "that wouldn't be the kind of bait I'd go for. What about you? Do you dream of getting a plum job in some public school? Winchester, if not Eton or Harrow?"

"Not really," Steve said, honestly enough. "I wasn't comprehensive-educated myself, so it seems like a strange new world to me, but *real*. I was only at the grammar, though, so my image of public schools is mainly based on cinematic depictions of Hogwarts Academy. I don't think I could make it as an instructor in Defense Against the Dark Arts, alas." It was supposed to be light banter, but Steve couldn't help shuddering as he remembered the flying car from the second movie in the series. He had probably been the only person in the cinema who'd wanted poor Harry to remain at the mercy of the giant spiders. If Milly noticed the shiver she must have put it down to a slight chill in the autumnal air, although September had been unusually warm ever since day one.

Milly didn't show any conspicuous symptoms of an eating disorder when the pizza arrived, although Steve ended up eating five slices to her three, which he tried to do unobtrusively, without any apology or comment on his own greediness. Steve's mobile didn't vibrate once during the meal, even though it was ten o'clock by the time they left the restaurant. He didn't know what to read into that absence. Did it mean that Janine was so busy on her management-trainee course that she hadn't had time to ring him, or that she'd tried the landline at his flat first and had then opted to leave a message on the answerphone rather than ring his mobile number?

"I can walk home from here," Milly told him. "You'll be heading in the other direction."

"Nonsense," Steve said. "I know it's not Friday, but you can't walk through the pedestrian precinct at this time of night—too many binge-drinkers who haven't quite reached the point of falling over in the gutter. Suppose you get spotted by someone you've given a ticket to? I'll drive you back—it's no trouble at all."

"Well, if you're sure," she said.

"Janine would never forgive me if I didn't," he told her. "She may not have commissioned me to keep an eye on you, but she'd expect me to do it."

"Well, we wouldn't want you to disappoint Janine, would we?" Milly said, so lightly that Steve thought nothing of it, even when she invited him to come in for a quick coffee before he went home.

He really did intend, when he crossed the threshold, to drink the coffee and go. He wasn't quite sure, afterwards, exactly when or how the quick coffee had turned into a long slow screw up against the wall—and not in the harmless cocktail sense.

* * * * * * *

By the time Steve actually got home it was after midnight, and the red light on his answerphone was blinking in a fiercely accusatory manner, of which he had not hitherto thought any mere machine capable. He only had to hear Janine's voice apologizing for having missed him and wishing him a good night's sleep, in a warm and affectionate tone, to feel that the world was dissolving beneath his feet and that he was about to fall into a very deep abyss.

He didn't ask himself what he had done, because he knew perfectly well what he had done, but he did ask himself, over and over again, why on earth he had done it, without being able to find any answer beyond the observation that it had somehow seemed like a good idea at the time. The reason he asked himself so repeatedly was not that he expected to find some further and more satisfactory answer if he only cudgeled his brain sufficiently, but because the repetition helped him to avoid moving on to the next question. That next question was, of course, what would happen now—"now" being, in this particular instance, the moment of Janine's return to Salisbury. Steve had no alternative, however, but to move on to that uniquely awkward question eventually, and it preoccupied him for the whole of the following day.

His Friday morning timetable was full up, so he had to mingle his tentative planning process with instructing year eleven in the heady delights of elementary optics—always a trial by fire, given that the only uses any of the pupils could think of for a convex lens involved magnifying one another's less attractive features and focusing the sun's rays on pieces of combustible paper—and teaching the sixth-formers about the arcane mysteries of the digestive system, all the way from the mouth to the colon. In the circumstances, it wasn't surprising that his thought-processes became somewhat constipated.

Steve wasn't on duty during the lunch-hour, but his one chance to grab a solitary cup of coffee and make a little mental progress came to nothing when he was buttonholed by Rhodri Jenkins. "You look terrible, boyo," he said. "Sylvia's relaxation techniques letting you down, are they?"

"Actually," Steve said, "I'm getting some real benefit out of them. It's just that today is a particular taxing one."

"End-of-the-week syndrome, eh? Never mind—got a date tonight, no doubt? A chance to get legless—or your leg over."

Steve made a face. "My girl-friend's away on a course," he said, without thinking. "Management training."

"Moving up in the world, eh? Good for her. Too many people your age are slackers. I know you all think the ecocatastrophe's going to hit before you grow old but that's no excuse for not trying to better yourselves in the meantime."

"Of course not," Steve said. "I'm thinking of going for a public school position myself. Winchester, maybe. They have their own nuclear bunker, I understand."

"You'd stand as much chance of becoming Professor of Potions at Hogwarts," Rhodri retorted, cruelly following a train of thought similar to the one that Steve had boarded the previous evening, before he'd somehow gone off the rails. "Sylvia may be a miracle-worker, but Jesus himself couldn't turn you into public school material. It's an ill wind, though—I need someone to supervise computer club tonight."

Steve realized, too late, that he'd made a ludicrously elementary error and violated the first rule of talking to the deputy head—which was *never*, under any circumstances whatsoever, to let fall the slightest hint that one might be available for extracurricular duties. "I can't," he said, reflexively.

"Why not?" the Welshman countered, with deadly skill and entirely accidental accuracy. "Not two-timing the poor girl, I hope? Thought you'd had enough of that lark after Tracy and Jill."

"It's Friday night, Rhodri," Steve complained, "and I've got a bugger of a day. I'm back to the digestive system in five minutes, and then I have to explain the principle of the telescope to the terrible elevens."

"A nice quiet session in the computer-room is exactly what you'll need to wind down, then. They're no trouble, so long as none of them manages to get around the blocks and start using the head's credit card number to download porn. Mostly, they don't even try—too busy playing Grand Theft Auto. You can try to nudge them in the direction of something more wholesome if you want to, but it's not compulsory. And you do get extra pay—help you save up for your first mortgage. You'll need that if your girl-friend's stepping up in the world. It won't be just her office she'll be managing, will it? You'll be hooked, cooked and hung out to dry in no time."

Steve just managed to get "Can't you ask...?" out of his mouth before the deputy head vanished, as expertly as any ghost in an academy of wizardry, leaving him well and truly stuck with the computer club once he'd finished failing to explain why telescopes allowed people to see further while microscopes only made things close at hand look bigger—a distinction he didn't feel that he'd entirely mastered himself.

Rhodri Jenkins was, however, right about the relative lack of mayhem kicked up by the computer users, who were indeed perfectly content to play violent games to while way the time. Steve tried to console himself with the thought that Milly was pounding the beat until six o'clock again, and that he couldn't possibly make ay meaningful plans until he'd talked to her about the situation, and that he too, therefore, had nothing to do with the hours between four and six but while them away. Had he been able to absorb himself in the fiendishly difficult task of getting through to Level Two of Apocalypse Now or Slayride he'd probably have done it, but his position as a teacher-in-charge forced him to play the much less exciting game of Keep a Watchful Eye on the Little Bleeders instead, quietly envious of the twelve-year-olds who were probably through to Level Four of Faculty Massacre already.

In the meantime, Steve had a certain amount of spare mindspace in which to consider his situation and get his calculative juices flowing. If Janine found out that he'd screwed Milly, she would almost certainly dump him. She had, therefore, to be prevented from finding out, if that were possible. Could Milly be persuaded to keep quiet? Quite possibly, if she didn't want to let on to her best friend that she'd shagged said best friend's boy-friend as soon as said best friend' back was turned. Perhaps, in fact, Milly would be so eaten up by guilt at what she'd done that she would want to repress the memory and never speak of it again. On the other hand, perhaps she wouldn't. Perhaps, in stark contrast, Milly now expected *him* to dump Janine, and form a couple with her. That wouldn't necessarily be a worst-case scenario but it couldn't qualify as a preferred outcome either. In any case, he wasn't prepared to take on the burden of dumping Janine, not only because he didn't want to do it but because it would make him out to be the bad guy—the vile seducer of his innocent girl-friend's innocent best friend—and he was pretty sure that he wasn't. Even if Milly couldn't be condemned out of hand as a heartless scheming bitch, he was pretty sure that what had happened had been six of one and half a dozen of the other, with a helping hand from the inexorable logic of the unfortunately-stereotyped situation.

No, Steve eventually decided, if Milly wanted or expected him to dump Janine, he'd have to refuse—which meant that he had to hope that she could be persuaded, if she hadn't already made up her mind, to keep quiet. Perhaps, if she wasn't consumed by guilt already, he could magnify whatever inclinations in that direction she might have. Would that be fair? Fair enough, he supposed, given that she really *ought* to be eaten up by guilt. After all, *he* was.

At five-thirty Steve made his way home, which was a more-than-usually frustrating process because of the rush hour traffic, although he contrived to resist the emotional depredations of road rage. At half past six he called Milly's mobile and asked if it might be possible to get together for a drink and a chat.

"I'm just on my way home," she said. "I've got to pop into Sainsbury's, then I'll need time to change out of my uniform. You can pick me up at seven, if you like." She didn't sound like a person eaten up by guilt; her tone was light and cheerful.

Knowing that the occasion might call for a strong dose of alcohol, Steve left his car parked and walked to Milly's flat. It was more than a mile away, but he had time in hand. The weather was clear and balmy, so it would have been quite a pleasant walk had the circumstances been different.

He was five minutes late knocking on Milly's door, but she still hadn't changed out of her uniform. She smiled at him, but it was a friendly smile rather than a possessive or conspiratorial one.

"Sorry," she said. "Frightful queue at the check-out. It's Friday night, so everyone's stocking up on food and booze for the weekend—including me, I suppose, so I've no right to complain. Did you bring the car?"

"No," Steve said. "I figured that we could go somewhere local, if that's okay."

"Fine by me," Milly said, still giving not the slightest evidence that overpowering guilt might be corroding her inner being. "The Pheasant's my local—it's relentlessly old-fashioned, but very cozy. I bought some cans of cider at Sainsbury's if you'd like to have one while I make myself decent."

Anxious to fortify himself for the coming ordeal, Steve agreed. Milly went into the kitchenette and came back with two cans, seemingly intent on keeping him company while she swapped her uniform for civilian dress and put some make-up on.

Steve prowled around the room rather than sitting down, inspecting the items that he hadn't inspected the night before. It only took him two or three minutes to check out the CDs in the racks and pass on to Milly's computer, which was a five-year-old Compaq sitting on a wheeled desk neatly stowed away in the corner opposite the one in which the rowing-machine stood. After that he went to the window and stood looking down into the street, watching the pedestrians go by. Milly's flat was on the first floor, so the elevation only gave him the slightest of *frissons*.

He turned round when Milly's bedroom door opened, and experienced a *frisson* of a different sort as she emerged wearing nothing but a towel. She waved negligently in the direction of the bathroom door, saying: "I think I'll take a quick shower, if it's okay with you. It's been a long day, and the weather's been unusually warm and sultry for September."

Steve contrived a nod. When he heard the hiss of the shower he decided that it might be better, after all, to sit down. By the time Milly emerged from the shower, he had finished his can of cider. After that, events moved on with a seemingly-relentless pressure of their own, one thing leading to another and all roads to the bedroom.

Steve didn't have much opportunity to study the books Milly employed in reading herself to sleep, although he did take note of the capaciousness of the bookshelf beside the bed. By the time he finally got around to beginning the chat he'd planned to have, they were back in the front room cracking open two new cans, and Steve was trying to figure out whether any of his prepared script was still viable.

"That wasn't supposed to happen," he said, finally. "I only wanted to talk about last night."

"Actions speak louder than words," Milly pointed out.

"Yes," Steve admitted, "but sometimes, they don't make as much sense. Janine...."

"Mustn't find out," Milly was quick to put in. "I only borrowed you. She doesn't need to know. Not that I haven't borrowed her things before, you understand—we've been friends for ever so long—but I've never actually borrowed a boy-friend, and she might consider that to be overstepping the line, especially after she ordered me to stop flirting with you last week. That was a bit unnecessary, I thought. Anyway, I'd certainly mind, if I were in her situation—and I speak from experience. Not that Jan's ever borrowed any of my boy-friends, so far as I know, but Ali did, once. I forgave her, of course—Ali's a slut, and can't help it. Jan would probably forgive me—after all, she's very fond of shrugging her shoulders and saying *shit happens*—but she might not. I'm not a slut, by the way. I'm very keen on people only parking where they're allowed to park—but as I said, it's always just a matter of time, once you've learned to drive. Anyhow, best keep it to ourselves. There's no need for Jan to be upset unnecessarily. We're friends, after all. Not that we've actually broken any rules, mind. It was after six o'clock, and Janine was in Brighton." She giggled, but the laugh wasn't as quite infectious as it usually was, in the circumstances.

Steve clutched at the one straw that seemed capable of saving him from drowning. "She mustn't ever find out," he said. "As long as we're agreed on that, we should be okay. You won't lose a friend, I won't lose a girl-friend."

"You shouldn't look on the dark side, Steve," Milly told him. "Think of in terms of gaining friends, not losing them. This time yesterday, you and I were just nodding acquaintances with one secret apiece. Now we're the best of friends, with one apiece and one shared. Twice as rich—unless, of course, you've got some other secret I don't know about, and some other girl-friend that Janine doesn't know about."

"We shouldn't have done it," Steve said, dolefully. "You're supposed to be Janine's best friend, and I'm supposed to be her steady boy-friend. Can you imagine how she'd feel if she knew?"

"Far better than you can, I suspect," Milly retorted. "You could always confess everything, if you'd prefer that option. You could say that I seduced you, like some irresistibly wicked *femme fatale*. I'll back you up if you want to do that. I've always wanted to be an irresistibly wicked *femme fatale*. I'll tell her it was all my fault, if you like, and beg her forgiveness. She's more likely to forgive me, if I confess that it was all my fault, than she would be to forgive you, if she thought it was all your fault, so we might just get away with it.

We can play it that way if you want to—but there's probably less risk in simply keeping quiet."

"It wasn't all your fault," Steve said, glumly.

"That's a shame," Milly said, not at all glumly. "As I said, I always wanted to be irresistible, wicked and deadly. I think it's a bit unkind of you to puncture the illusion. You weren't thinking of trying to take all the blame yourself, were you? That would make me seem rather pathetic, don't you think? I can't let you do that. I'm a traffic warden, and I have the honor of the uniform to protect."

"So it's all just a joke, is it?" Steve said.

"No, it's not," Milly retorted, her face suddenly becoming very serious. "That's almost as insulting as your trying to take all the blame. At least you didn't say *just a bit of fun*. It was more than that, Steve, and you know it."

Steve took another gulp of cider, as he tried to focus on what seemed to be the one remaining issue to be settled. "Yes," he agreed, for tactical reasons, "it was. But it has to stop there. We have to put a lid on it."

"And pretend it never happened?" she countered, arching an eyebrow. "Well, if that's what you want. It takes two, after all, and either one of us has the power of veto. If you've decided that it'll never happen again, then it'll never happen again, because you have the power to make that decision. You don't have to consult me about it. I'll go along with whatever you decide. If you want to pretend that it never happened, I'll pretend too. I'll never breathe a word to anyone. I can keep a secret."

Steve felt that he was being mocked. Everything Milly said was true. He did have the power to make the decision. He'd had it the previous evening, and he'd had it tonight. Somehow, though, he'd failed to exercise it on both occasions. Milly was obviously unconvinced that he'd be able to do better in future—and if he were honest with himself, he had to admit that he was a trifle doubtful himself. He remembered, uncomfortably, that Rhodri Jenkins had adopted a similarly mocking tone at lunch-time, when he'd hazarded a wild and entirely unserious guess about Steve's two-timing proclivities.

"What would you rather do?" he asked, defensively.

"I'd rather not make any promises I couldn't keep," Milly told him. "I'd rather not maintain any pretences, between the two of us, whatever pretences we maintain with Janine."

Steve took that to mean that Milly didn't want to rule out the possibility of their doing it again—and again—if ever they found themselves in the mood."

"I'm an idiot," Steve said. "I'm the pathetic one, not you. I'm the one who's out of his depth. How on earth do I get myself into these situations?"

"It's not the first time, then," Milly said, perceptively.

"No—but I swore that the last time would be the last."

"There you go," Milly pointed out. "Why make promises you can't keep, even to yourself? You have to learn to read the signs, Steve. Why are you seeing a hypnotherapist?"

The abrupt change of direction took Steve by surprise. "What's that got to do with it?" he asked.

"You asked me a question. *How on earth do I get myself into these situations*? I can't tell you the answer unless I know all the facts. I asked Janine, but she was very cagey about it, so I'm asking you. If you can tell me why you're seeing a hypnotherapist, I might be able to tell you how you keep getting into situations you don't want to be in."

"Maybe I'd be better off telling my hypnotherapist about you," Steve opined.

"Maybe," Milly agreed, "but I don't charge, so I've no interest in spinning out the process. You don't have to tell me if you don't want to. Have you even told Janine?"

"Yes I have," Steve retorted—but then realized that if he now refused to tell Milly, it would look like another insult, another implication that what he'd done with her was *just a bit of fun*, of no real consequence. "Phobias," he said, shortly. "I'm trying to use the relaxation techniques she's taught me to conquer some irrational fears I happen to have."

"That's what I thought," Milly said.

Steve felt mildly insulted himself. "What do you mean, *that's what I thought*?" he demanded. "Why would you have thought anything?"

"Because I've experienced the other symptoms first hand. Phobias fit—they're exactly the sort of thing you'd expect to find in the same package. Don't tell me your hypnotherapist hasn't pointed that out?"

"I've no idea what you're talking about," Steve confessed, helplessly.

"Emotional incontinence," Milly told him. "You get carried away—by lust, by fear. They're the same thing, really, in purely physiological terms—you're a biologist, so you ought to know that. At the level of true causation, they're essentially similar petty excitations of the nervous system and bursts of hormonal activity, which the conscious mind interprets in different ways. Given that you have trouble containing and constraining your particular lusts, it's entirely expectable that you'd have trouble containing and constraining your particular fears. In a sense, fucking me when you really want to be faithful to Janine is exactly the same as throwing a panic attack whenever you see a spider—or whatever it is that you're phobic about. Remembering an alien abduction is just another way of representing the problem to yourself."

It occurred to Steve then that perhaps he ought to have paid more attention to the bookshelves in Milly's bedroom, instead of allowing himself to be so totally distracted by her anatomy. She obviously wasn't the kind of girl who lulled herself to sleep with Mills and Boon or the latest issue of *Heat*. He'd read Carl Jung's book on *Flying Saucers*, by way of attempting to understand his own predicament, but she'd had a lot longer to extend her research, and had evidently not been wasting her time. He remembered that she had mentioned self-help books. She was obviously not taking the same approach to the solution of her problems as he was, but she was obviously working just as hard.

"Emotional incontinence," he repeated, dazedly. "That's what I've got, you reckon?"

"It's very common nowadays," she told him. "You probably see as much of it in your line of work as I do in mine, although you probably write it off as adolescent behavior. We're all adolescents now, apparently—long into our forties, at any rate. I'll make an exception for Walter and Amelia, although some of their friends are a bit suspect."

"You too?" Steve queried.

"Certainly. I used to suffer from eating disorders, as Janine presumably told you. I was shaping up to be a real wreck, before I went to the support group, started work as a traffic warden and began figuring out how to pull myself back from the edge. I'm much more disciplined now. I think I've nearly got it beaten, but I'm well aware of the possibility of self-delusion."

"So last night and this evening were some sort of relapse?" Steve said.

"Oh no. *You* were overcome by emotional incontinence. *I* knew exactly what I was doing—borrowing Janine's luscious boy-friend. That's why I can be so reasonable about it all, while you're shitting yourself at the thought that she might find out. Don't worry: it's our secret. I think I'm almost ready to let go of the other one—the abduction experience, that is—but I'm perfectly happy to keep this one for as long as necessary."

"And how long will that be?" Steve wanted to know.

"Who can tell? We'll just have to see how things go. Maybe your hypnotherapist will cure you, and you'll find the means to control your phobias and your lusts. Maybe she won't. I saw a therapist when I had my problems—not the same one you're seeing—but her contribution to my cure was minimal. The support group was more help, but at the end of the day, therapy and support can only help you to help yourself. You can take pills, though. Have you tried Prozac?"

"I'm not depressed," Steve said.

"It's not just an antidepressant," Milly told him. "It gees up your brain in all sorts of ways. I don't take it any more, though. You can get dependent, and that's bad—especially for people like us."

"People like us?" Steve queried.

"Teachers and traffic wardens," she explained. "High-stress jobs that involve us in continual confrontation with hostile adversaries. Did you think I meant alien abductees? When you've been coming to meetings a little bit longer, you'll see that they come in all shades and sizes—as Walter Wainwright says, *everybody*'s been abducted by aliens. You and I have much more in common than that."

"You want me to dump Janine, don't you?" Steve divined. "You want me to say that I've seen the light, and that I want to be your boy-friend, not hers?"

"That would be a nice compliment," Milly admitted, "but I'd only want you to say that if it were true, and I'd only want you to do that if it were what you really wanted. At present, all that's happened is that you've given way to your emotion incontinence, and now you're feeling guilty, confused and scared half to death—which is entirely understandable, given your emotional incontinence. You really ought to work on that. If you don't, you'll never be able to make a reasoned decision as to what you want out of life, or carry any decision you do make through to a successful conclusion."

Steve had to remind himself that he wasn't listening to some irresistibly wicked *femme fatale*, but merely to someone who had read a lot of self-help books, because she had thought she needed them in the days before she became a traffic warden and made contact with her inner control-freak. He still felt that he had as much freedom of action as the average glove-puppet, but he had to admire the brilliance of Milly's passive-aggressive technique. Here, he thought, was a woman who might actually be able to reform him, given a chance—but she wasn't as good-looking as Janine, and she certainly didn't seem to be as nice as Janine, and she might well prove to be far too robust for his delicate sensibilities.

Milly appeared to be dead right, though, about his so-called emotional incontinence. He really did need to work on that, and quickly—although he had a strong suspicion that he wasn't going to be able to do it quickly enough to save his relationship with Janine, whether Milly stuck fast to her promises or not. It occurred to Steve, very belatedly, that Janine's casual insistence that he go to the AlAbAn meeting without her might have been a kind of fidelity test—in which case, he'd failed spectacularly. Animal intelligence, he decided, had some pretty obvious defects. Given that he was trapped within it, though, he figured that he needed to put it to good use if he could. The first thing to do was to make sure that things didn't get any worse.

"We just got carried away," he said to Milly. "It happens. As you say, adolescence lasts well into our forties nowadays. It's only natural, given the kind of creatures we are. We just have to keep our heads in future."

"Absolutely," she said. "Shall we go back to bed, now?"

* * * * * * *

Steve was worried that the evening of the next AlAbAn meeting might precipitate the disaster that he and Milly had been scrupulously keeping at bay for the previous fortnight, but they all fell into their normal behavior-pattern without any difficulty. As he drove to East Grimstead the conversation between Janine and Milly was as light and inconsequential as usual. Janine gave no hint that she suspected that Steve was two-timing her with Milly, and Milly gave no indication that she might let the cat out of the bag, accidentally or intentionally. Fortunately, it wasn't totally out of character for Steve to be quiet on the journey, except for the occasional terse response to a direct question.

Steve felt a good deal better than he'd expected to feel, partly because the situation had proved more easily manageable than he'd dared to hope during the previous fortnight, and partly because there was a certain undeniable sense of satisfaction in having a mini-harem at his disposal.

He and Janine had never got to the stage of seeing one another every night, and now that Janine had started management training she felt that there was a certain pressure on her to do more in the shop, to play a larger part in team meetings, and to do extra tasks at home. They had regular dates every Wednesday at the technical college and every second Thursday at AlAbAn, and Friday night was also sacred, but on every other evening of the week—including Saturdays, if the second eleven was playing away—it was permissible for one or other of them to offer working late or having to take work home as an excuse. That left plenty of space for Steve and Milly to get together twice a week without either one of them having to put a strain on their authentic extracurricular commitments.

Steve was no longer under any delusion, however, that his liaison with Milly could be excused as merc emotional incontinence. It had started that way, but it was definitely a full-blooded affair by now, consciously maintained and managed. He was no longer a hapless idiot but a thoroughgoing rat. He didn't like to think of himself that way, but there was no way around it.

Unfortunately, there didn't seem to be any way back. Whenever he broached the possibility of giving up seeing Milly and putting the affair behind them, she blithely agreed that it was entirely up to him, and assured him that he could trust her implicitly never to let on to Janine that anything had ever happened. It wasn't that he didn't believe her, although he was pretty sure that she was using reverse psychology—a topic that he knew to be well-covered in her bedtime reading, now that he had had abundant leisure to examine her bookshelves—but he couldn't believe that the thing could simply be closed down and buried, especially while he, Janine and Milly had a standing arrangement to attend AlAbAn meetings every second Thursday. Even if it had been feasible for him to cut Milly out of his own life, it would not have been feasible to cut her out of Janine's, and while she was still in Janine's life, she was still implicitly in his; merely cutting out the AlAbAn meetings couldn't and wouldn't solve the problem.

Steve hadn't told Sylvia Joyce about this aspect of his predicament, nor had he suggested to the hypnotherapist that his phobias might be aspects of a more general phenomenon and problem. He was still working hard at relaxation, still hoping to chip away his difficulties bit by bit, in spite of the fact that they seemed to be increasing and multiplying while he worked.

Because Milly knew about Janine, while Janine didn't know about Milly, Steve now found being with Milly intrinsically more relaxing than being with Janine, even though he preferred being with Janine because he liked her even more now than he had before, in spite of the fact that he also liked Milly, quite sincerely and quite a lot. They were quite different in bed, partly for purely dimensional reasons and partly by virtue of their contrasting techniques, and he found the variety exhilarating, like the spice of life it was rumored to be. All in all, though, the complexity of the situation was getting to be a bit much. He felt that he was being slowly but inexorably overwhelmed, crushed by the weight of so many expectations. He could not, in his heart of hearts, believe that he was making progress in any respect whatsoever.

In the meantime, however, Janine continued chatting to Milly as they drove to the AlAbAn meeting with all the cheerfulness that might be expected of the blissfully ignorant, while Milly chatted to Janine with all the blitheness that could possibly be manufactured by a successful deceiver. Every time Milly's infectious laugh bubbled up, Janice's echo followed close behind. Neither of them seemed to notice that Steve never laughed once during the entire journey

Once they had arrived at Amelia Rockham's cottage and were safely ensconced in the front room drinking cups of tea, Steve eased himself away from both his lovers. Instead of sitting down on the settee when Janine took her usual place he buttonholed Walter Wainwright and offered an unnecessarily profuse apology for the fact that he hadn't so far got himself into a frame of mind in which he felt that he could tell his story. He was able to spin the conversation out further with similarly profuse enthusiasm regarding the group's utility.

"I think you've done a wonderful job with it," Steve said. "It works very smoothly, and I'm sure it does a great deal of good. It's certainly doing me good, even though all I've done so far is listen. It's been a real eye-opener."

"I'm delighted that you're finding it helpful," Walter said. "Don't worry about taking all the time you need before telling us your story. Newcomers rarely arrive in the group with their recovered memories complete and coherent; we old hands all know what it feels like to have to piece things together, like a jigsaw puzzle, and we all understand why listening to other people's stories helps the process along. Members often feel the need to feel perfectly at home before they can reveal themselves, and that can take a long time, as it has with your friend Milly."

"I don't know anything at all about Milly's abduction experience," Steve was quick to say, "but I know that she really appreciates the group. She says that it's the most supportive support group she's ever attended. She has experience in that respect, because she used to suffer from eating disorders. As a traffic warden, of course, she doesn't get much moral support in the everyday context."

"She's very lucky to have friends like you and Janine," the old man said, with such sincerity that Steve felt an unusually sharp pang of guilt about the quality of the friendship he'd recently been supplying to Janine. He was mildly relieved when Mrs. Rockham started clearing the tea-cups away and he had to take his seat. He hoped that the confession would be interesting enough to distract him from his problems.

The woman invited to tell her story gave her name as "Zoe". Although she was some fifteen or twenty years older than Janine and Milly, she was still moderately attractive, having obviously had some cosmetic surgery. She was conspicuously well-dressed, and Steve concluded that she was probably an executive wife from one of the Winterbournes or the Winterslows. She had been to at least as many meetings as Steve, but this was apparently the first time she'd plucked up the courage to tell her tale.

CHAPTER EIGHT

THE FORCE OF DARKNESS

I've listened to enough of your stories by now to know that the earlier part of my experience is tediously commonplace. It happened in the early hours of the morning, in December last year, a few days before Christmas. I'd been feeling a little lower than usual, because I suffer from Seasonal Affective Disorder. My husband Josh thinks that's an imaginary disease, like restless leg syndrome and CFIDS—that's chronic fatigue and immune dysfunction syndrome—from which I also suffer, but it isn't. Josh and I sleep in separate rooms, and I'm certain that he slept through the whole thing. The window in his room faces east, while mine faces west, so he wouldn't have seen the bright light that woke me up and drew me to the window like a magnet.

The light was moving in such a strange swirling fashion that I couldn't make out the shape of the vessel on which it was mounted. The window wasn't open, but when the whirlpool of light emitted a single ray that fixed itself on me and paralyzed me I was conscious of being moved. I lost track of time completely. When I returned to my senses I wasn't in my bedroom any more, and my night-dress had vanished.

Most people the aliens take seem to find themselves on operating tables, usually restrained in some way, and I'm sure I wouldn't have liked that either, especially if I'd had a fit of restless legs, but the situation I found myself in seemed at first to be much worse. Perhaps it makes me seem like an awful prude, but for the first couple of minutes after I woke up I couldn't think about anything but being stark naked, and having nothing to cover myself up with.

I wasn't even lying down, let alone tied down, but I was in a kind of glass case, like one of those round display cases people sometimes keep stuffed birds in. There was nothing else in there—not a stick of furniture, not a scrap of cloth. There was a kind of box built into the glass wall just below shoulder height, and the inward face was grooved in a way that suggested that there might be little doors in it that could be opened, but I couldn't get any of them to budge at first, even though I broke a nail trying.

The other side of the box, outside the glass cage, was joined to an opaque wall. I thought of that as the back of the cage, because there was a bigger open space on the other side, which had some weird equipment in it. The wall beyond the open space had a big window in it, through which I could look into another room—although the view was doubly distorted, because the window of the room seemed to be curved, like the wall of my glass prison. It was difficult to figure out what the real shapes might be of the objects I could see between the two glass walls and beyond the more distant one. The other room put me in mind of a control room, though, because there seemed to be some kind of console underneath the window on the inside, and there seemed to be chairs lined up so that people—or aliens—could sit at the console.

Only one of the chairs was occupied, and I wasn't at all sure whether the thing sitting in it might qualify as a person, or how much of its strange appearance was due to visual distortion. I was aware of its existence for some time, while I grappled with the unyielding box, before I could bear to turn around and face it. I was terrified, of course, and horribly embarrassed. I admire the way that some other members of the group seem to have sailed through their experiences without undue alarm, but I felt simply awful. I think that was due to not having been desensitized to weirdness by watching a lot of TV. Josh won't have a TV in our house, although I keep telling him that we ought to get one now that the kids have left home and we don't have to worry any more about the possibility that it might rot their brains.

I couldn't actually meet the alien's eyes, because it had three of them. I thought at first that might be an optical illusion, but I soon became convinced that it wasn't. The extra eye was mounted in the middle of what I had to think of as the creature's forehead. Its mouth was pretty much where you might expect a mouth to be, given the position of the two eyes set below the single one, but if it had a nose and ears I couldn't identify them, and I couldn't begin to make a guess as to what the various smeary protrusions and excrescences distributed about the rest of its face might be. If I'd been able to look at it directly, without the distorting glass, it would probably have looked something like a slug with virulent acne. What I could discern clearly, though, was the color of its moist and rubbery skin, which was a vivid scarlet.

I screamed for a while, and writhed a bit—because I was trying to cover my breasts with one hand and my nether regions with the other, not because of my restless legs—and when it first spoke to me I screamed some more. Eventually, though, I calmed down when the familiar CFIDS numbness began to take hold. At least the lights were bright, and they never went out, so the one good thing about the early part of the experience was that it kept the SAD at bay. Eventually, I was able to listen. Josh says that I've never been a good listener, and I suppose he's right, but I did my best.

The monster wasn't really *speaking* to me. The voice was synthesized; it was as if the words materialized in the air close to my ear. "Please don't be alarmed, human lady," it said. "We are neither cataloguers or analysts, and we mean you no harm. If all goes well, we shall return you to your home within a matter of days. We shall do our utmost to minimize the apparent lapse of time between your departure and return, and we shall do our best to obliterate your memories of this disturbing experience. In the meantime, we shall keep you informed of everything we are doing and the reasons for our actions, in order to reduce your temporary distress and perhaps obtain your cooperation. You may address me as Kitten."

"Kitten?" I echoed, incredulously.

"There is no actual resemblance, I know," the alien admitted. "The name is meant to be suggestive of something humans find familiar and non-menacing."

"Arrows by any other name would wound as deep," I said, feeling quite proud of myself for being able to be witty, even though I'd stolen the quip from Josh's standard repertoire. He always attributed it to Saint Sebastian, but that was just part of the joke.

"You may call me Rose if you would prefer to do so," the monster said. It could recognize an English play on words when it heard one.

"No thank you," I said, politely refraining from making any remark about the impossibility of believing that the foul thing could possibly smell sweet. "Kitten it is. I'm Zoe."

"Thank you, Zoe," it said. "I apologize for frightening you. It would have been feasible for me to replace the glass panel in front of me with a TV screen, on which I could project the false image of a human being, but that would be a lie. We do not approve of the manner in which the cataloguers and the analysts lie so frequently in order to confuse the increasingly-large number of humans who prove resistant to their primitive memory-obliteration techniques."

"Can I get some clothes in here?" I asked. "A dressing gown, maybe?"

"I'm afraid not," the alien replied. "You are being held in a maximum security biocontainment facility. We need to be extremely careful about any kind of matter-transfer between your environment and ours."

"Well," I said, "I'm sure it's very kind of you to go to such lengths to make sure that I don't catch any of your diseases, but I really would be willing to take a small risk in the interests of having something to wear. A hospital gown would do, or the kind of paper suit the police give you to wear in a rape suite, when your own clothes are taken away for forensic examination."

"We are a gnotobiotic species," the monster said, "but even if we were not, you could not possibly be infected by micro-organisms from our ecosphere, which is very different from yours. The opposite is, alas, not the case."

It took me a minute or two to figure out that that he was implying that I was the disease-ridden one. I thought of the Martians in H. G. Wells's *War of the Worlds*, who had all kinds of superscientific weapons but no resistance to Earthly diseases, having long disposed of all their own. The comparison didn't make the implication seem any less insulting, although it was slightly less distressing, in its way, than Josh's insistence that I only suffered from imaginary diseases.

"So," I said, eventually, "you won't give me any clothes because you're afraid that they might start some kind of plague in your world when I don't need them any more. You could always burn them—or, better still, send them back with me."

"We cannot permit any of our materials to enter your ecosphere, for fear of disruptive consequences," the monster told me, apologetically. "Nor is decontamination as simple a process as you imagine. If it were only a matter of bacteria, burning would easily suffice—but what causes us anxiety, as well as making you a vital resource in our hour of need, is your remarkable complement of protovitalistic energies."

"I have no idea what that means," I confessed. "Or any of the rest of it, really. I don't know what not-a-biotic means, or cataloguers and analysts. It's all Greek to me. I'm sorry."

"The word I used was gnotobiotic," the monster told me, spelling it out for me. "It means that my flesh is free of all biomolecular materials that do not actually belong to it, including commensal micro-organisms. A cataloguer is a humanoid life-form of relatively short stature with silver or grey colored skin and large almond-shaped eyes. Its species is one of several collecting data on the physiology and culture of the human species on the eve of its extinction. An analyst is a humanoid life-form of considerably taller stature, which usually adopts quasi-human form to communicate with human beings, although that is not its native appearance. Its species is another of those collecting data, but its methods tend to be more invasive...."

While it was talking, I recalled what the monster had said about the cataloguers and analysts being frequent liars, and thought about the way that Josh would have reacted. "How do you figure out which is the liar and which is the truth-teller," he'd have said, "when they're both accusing the other of telling lies?" He liked logical puzzles. Maybe that's why he'd once liked me.

"I'm sorry," I said, "but the explanations of the explanations aren't any clearer than the explanations themselves. On the other hand, this protovitality whatsit sounds like the sort of thing they put into antiwrinkle cream, so I might be able to follow the argument a little bit better in that instance. I'll try."

"The phrase I used was *protovitalistic energies*." the monster said, in the sort of patronizing tone that make-up consultants often adopt. "Do you know what *vitalism* means?"

"I think so," I said. "It's healthy stuff that clears out all your toxins and perks you up."

"Not in the sense of the term that I'm using," the alien replied, its voice taking on a slight tone of exasperation. That seemed odd, when I thought about it—not because I thought aliens oughtn't be able to get exasperated, but because they oughtn't to be able to express exasperation in the tone of a synthesized voice. "In your world," the monster went on, "it's a seemingly-obsolete theory of biology, which attributes the fundamental phenomenon of life to the activation of inert matter by some kind of vital force or energy."

"Oh, I see," I said. "As in *Frankenstein*, where the patchwork dead body is brought back to life by a big jolt of electricity." I'd never actually seen the movie, but I'd read the book to the kids when they were young, just as I'd read them *The War of the Worlds*. You have to make some educational compromises in the interests of encouraging a healthy attitude to reading.

"That would be one of the least plausible speculations corollary to the notion," the monster conceded, reluctantly, "but you're thinking along the right lines. If my reading of your timeline is correct, vitalistic theories were still widely held by your ancestors until quite recently, when organic chemistry made sufficiently rapid progress to reveal the actual workings of metabolic pathways—at which point it was realized that vitalism was an unnecessary hypothesis, ripe for excision by Ockham's razor."

"Josh uses a Phillips," I said.

"I'm sorry—just forget the last bit. The point is that your contemporaries have abandoned vitalism as a theory of life, because it no longer seems applicable to organisms of your sort—quite rightly, since your kind of life really can be almost entirely explained in other terms. True vitalism doesn't emerge for the first time until several hundred million years downstream of your present. As your kind of metazoan life evolves, however, all of its commensals evolve in parallel—not merely your parasitic worms, bacteria and viruses, but multifarious entities whose existence you don't even suspect yet, including the most primitive imaginable entities of nascent protovitalistic energy. Their existence is irrelevant to most creatures of your organic sort, although they play a peripheral role in maintaining the phenomena of human consciousness, but the existence of their remote descendants is extremely relevant to the kinds of life and consciousness that entities of *my* kind experience. Do you see what I'm driving at?"

"I'm not an idiot," I told it. "You're saying that I'm carrying lots of not-quite-material bugs, which are distantly related to things that you're carrying."

"That's nearly correct," the monster conceded, now contriving to sound surprised, in the supercilious manner Josh tends to put on whenever I have a good idea. "In my case, however, *carrying* gives the wrong impression. Humans often think of themselves as immaterial entities of mind or soul which merely employ bodies as vehicles. The image is little more than a plausible illusion, in the human case, although the elements of some such situation are present in your primitive version of consciousness, but evolution is indeed capable of producing organisms of that general sort. We really are compound creatures, in which entities of an energetic nature are intimately allied with fleshy hosts. Our vitalistic components are the very essence of our sensitivity and intelligence, and their versatility allows our minds to be much more flexible, versatile and powerful than yours."

"My husband says the same thing about his mind," I told the alien. "Personally, I think it's him that's a bit lacking in the soul department."

The monster sighed, as if to say: *Well, I tried*. It was sounding more and more like Josh with every minute that passed. My legs were getting restless, and I had to wriggle a bit, although I tried as hard as I could not to seem as if I were doing some kind of subtle erotic dance.

"Well, Zoe," the monster said, "that's the reason why we have to be so very careful in handling you—and also why we need to take the risk. You have lots of these primitive energy-entities inside you, whose individual properties extend across the whole of a wide spectrum. The vitalistic component of each of our subspecies is much more specialized, refined by natural selection from a very specific sector of the spectrum."

"The red part, so to speak," I said.

"I see the joke," the creature conceded, disdainfully. "Yes, if it helps you to grasp the issue, you may identify the sector of the spectrum from which my own vitalistic component comes as *the red part*. To carry the analogy further, my own subspecies is under threat from creatures of another sort, so different that it would be analogically legitimate to describe their innate energies as violet, or even ultraviolet. We have no ready-made weapons with which to fight them, but we are very familiar with the theory that might allow us to manufacture some, if only we can exploit and mobilize the right resources."

It took me a moment or two to cotton on to what it meant, although it was obvious enough. "And that's me, right?" I said. "You kidnapped me out of my nice centrally-heated bedroom, leaving my comfortable winter nightie behind, so that you could *mine* me for the raw materials of what passes for biological warfare in your world."

"That is correct," the monster told me, seeming slightly relieved that it didn't have to try to spell it out any more clearly.

"I suppose," I said, acidly, "that it wouldn't do me any good to say that I didn't want to be used like that? As a matter of principle, I mean—not just on the trivial grounds that if I had to compare you with your enemies, I'd probably find them every bit as ugly."

"You suppose correctly," it said, a trifle stiffly. "We have you, and we intend to use you, with all possible speed. If our enemies had you, they would not hesitate to do likewise. Fortunately, we have obtained access to the analysts' records of the vital point in the stream—not an easy thing to do, given the hectic activity that surrounds your pre-extinction phase."

"And instead of just taking what you needed while I was sleeping peacefully, utterly oblivious to what was happening," I said, "you thought you'd wake me up instead, so I could stand here stark naked listening to your stupid explanations before you started sticking needles in me?"

"You mistake our motives, Zoe," the monster told me. "Although the protovitalistic energies we seek are largely irrelevant to the fundamental processes of your kind of organic life, they are not entirely irrelevant to human consciousness. In order that you may serve our purpose we need you to be conscious, and fully informed. The process of abstraction does not involve needles, and will be quite painless in a physical sense—but a certain amount of mental effort on your part would be most helpful."

As you can imagine, I picked up the vital part of that sentence immediately. "What do you mean, painless *in a physical sense?*" I asked. I remembered that I'd once read the children a story about emotional vampires that fed on love, which leeched the capacity for affection and anxiety out of their victims, leaving them utterly dispassionate, devoid of hope and fear. If they expected to do that to me, I thought, they were at least ten years too late to catch any sort of tide. I'd had three children, and they'd all grown up.

"There will be no pain, Zoe," the monster said, "if you can refrain from inflicting any upon yourself. What we would like you to do, if you will, is *remember*. We would like you to review your life, as scrupulously as you can. That is the aspect of human mental activity in which the protovitalistic energies are most involved—not as instruments, but as catalysts. You will not lose any of your establish memories, I assure you, while we identify and refine what we need—nor, of course, when we subsequently erase your memory of this experience."

I thought about that for a moment or two. Eventually, I said: "So I *can* refuse to co-operate?"

"No," the monster said, brutally. "We have the means to keep you fit and well, and the means to keep you awake. I have told you what I want you to do. How easy, do you think, will it be to *avoid* doing it, given that you have so few alternatives? You have nothing to lose by co-operating, Zoe, and will go home all the sooner if you do. It's as simple as that."

Josh would have approved of the paradoxical aspect of it. If you tell someone *not* to think about an elephant, he's fond of pointing out, they can't do it, because trying not to do it is the same as doing it. However hideous the monster was, at least he was asking me, straightforwardly and not entirely impolitely, to think about the elephant—or, to be strictly accurate, about me: my life, my past, my accomplishments.

I agreed to help out as best I could; it seemed like the sensible thing to do, as well as the only thing I could do.

* * * * * *

For a long time, while I reviewed my life and loves, my labors and desires, my hopes and my dreams, nothing much happened. As promised, there were no needles, and no pain that wasn't an effect of RLS or unpleasant memories. I couldn't detect the means by which they were working on my protovitalistic energies, but as I'd never known that I had any protovitalistic energies, and had no senses that would have allowed me to discern the red, the violet and all the bits of the spectrum in between, that wasn't entirely surprising. In all probability, the bell-jar was chock full of invisible vitalistic instruments busy vivisecting my poor excuse for a soul, but all I actually felt was restless legs. Whatever means the aliens had of keeping me awake was holding the CFIDS at bay.

The other seats in the control room were sometimes full and sometimes empty, but Kitten's was always occupied. Whether it was always occupied by the same individual, I couldn't say. The monsters were presumably able to tell one another apart, but they'd all have looked alike to me even if the curved glass hadn't distorted their appearance.

They fed me, if you can call it feeding, by means of the box in the back wall of my upturned test tube. The panels did open, but only to expose other panels behind them. When I placed my hands flat on the surfaces that were normally covered up, they felt slightly warm. That was it. They weren't pumping any fluids into me, let alone giving me anything to eat, but as long as I pressed my hands against the active panels every few hours or so I didn't feel hungry and I didn't get dehydrated. I didn't feel any need to excrete anything, either, which was a tremendous mercy—I didn't even get sweaty armpits.

When I asked about it, Kitten explained that they were feeding me with something akin to the raw vitalistic energies that provided sustenance to the more sophisticated soul-things that infused their intelligent subspecies. The force couldn't nourish me directly, but it interacted with the protovitalistic energies native to my own body, which were capable of catalyzing physical processes as well as mental ones. In essence, my own protovitalistic energies were being stimulated in order to cause my body to make counter-provisions for a short period of effective starvation. It wouldn't have kept me going for very long, but it worked pretty well as long as my confinement lasted.

When I eventually got back home I'd only been gone for twenty minutes or so on the clock, but I thought that I'd been in the glass case for at least a week. That didn't make sense, because I hadn't had anything to drink, and you can't go without water for more than couple of days. On the other hand, I'd lost a couple of stone, which you can't possibly do in less than a fortnight, even if you fast—so it didn't make sense either way. At any rate, although the CFIDS came back with a vengeance from then until the end of January, I didn't put the weight back on when I started eating and drinking again. I guess that was one aspect of the experience that worked to my advantage.

I won't bore you with the details of my long trip down memory lane. What you'll be far more interested in, I imagine, is the war.

The scarlet slug-things were working to a tight deadline, because they didn't know what the enemy—the violets—might be up to while they were putting together their biological A-bomb. I never got to see one of the violets, so I have no idea what color they were, but I don't suppose for a moment that they were actually violet. I imagined them as three-eyed and lumpy, much like my captors, but for all I know they might have had five heads with six eyes each, and thirty-two legs apiece. I did ask once, but Kitten ducked the question. After that first long conversation, he became less generous with information and explanations.

I say "he" at his point, rather than "it", not because I ever discovered any evidence that our sexual categories had any equivalents in their alien biology, but because simply I'd begun to think of him as "he", maybe because of the echoes of Josh I could hear in his synthetic voice. On reflection, those echoes might have been real, in the sense that they'd actually borrowed Josh's voice for the purposes of synthesis, or they might have been purely subjective—but whatever the truth of the matter was, Kitten became "he" to me. He excused his lack of communicativeness, once the honeymoon period was over, by saying that he didn't want to distract me too much from my reminiscing. It might have been true, but I'd heard too many excuses from Josh to swallow it without a pinch of salt. He did make occasional attempts at conversation, though, presumably in the interests of trying to keep me sweet. He even gave me a few tidbits of news regarding the progress of hostilities.

"We have intelligence suggesting that the violets are working on some kind of ultimate weapon too," he said. "It's not impossible that they've got their own human in a facility not too different from this one, but we have to hope that they're working along other lines, which will prove less effective."

"What will happen to me, if they strike first?" I asked.

"You'd be sent back. We've made provisions."

"Not for my benefit, of course—just to make sure I don't fall into enemy hands," I said, to show him that I was capable of putting two and two together.

"Partly," he admitted. "There's also the matter of making sure that, however the war turns out, there's no possibility of a further disaster being precipitated by the retention of a dangerous source of infection. If our need weren't so desperate, we wouldn't be taking the risk of entertaining you at all."

I thought of telling him that it hadn't been so very entertaining, even for someone who hadn't got a TV at home, but I thought I ought to be diplomatic. After all, there was a sense in which I was humankind's ambassador to the alien nation.

I couldn't help wondering whether Kitten was telling me the whole truth, or whether he even knew it himself. The reds were obviously desperate to get their crucial blow in first, and were terrified by the prospect of being beaten to it. It seemed to me, though, that even if I were returned home with all possible speed once the red weapon was ready, that Kitten's anxieties about the possibility of a further disaster following the war's supposed end might be well-warranted. The weapon they hoped to derive from my protovitalistic energies would be used as a strike weapon, if possible, to win the war—but if things went awry, from the red viewpoint, it might end up providing a counterstrike. I couldn't help fearing that the produce of my frail flesh might end up as a doomsday weapon in a case of Mutual Assured Destruction.

You might suppose that I shouldn't really have cared about that, or anything else, except for the possibility that I might not get home—but I did care. It was a matter of principle. I remembered, too, that Kitten had said that the human race was on the brink of extinction, and that remark had reawakened all my old fears about the Cold War turning into a nuclear holocaust. That was one of the things I had to remember, to help them sort out the violet components of my protovitalistic spectrum.

Anyhow, I felt that it would be a terrible tragedy if two whole subspecies got wiped out in an orgy of mutual antipathy. No matter how ugly they were, or how alien, they were thinking and feeling beings. I don't have a clue where they came from, but wherever it was, I figured that the extinction of sentient life-forms there would be just as awful a waste as the extinction of sentient life-forms here. I asked Kitten more than once whether there was any possibility of making peace.

"None whatsoever," he told me. "Our biology isn't like yours; our struggles for existence aren't like yours. Vitalistic life doesn't have much room for compromise. Conflict is a matter of competing energies, not competing political ideologies. Yours is a very primitive form of life: slow, inefficient, horribly ugly and almost certainly an evolutionary dead-end—although we don't know a great deal about what goes on downstream—but it has its advantages."

"Ugliness," I reminded him, "is in the eye of the beholder."

"Absolutely," he said. "I have three and you have two, so yours are outvoted." His sense of humor was improving. I think he learned more than he'd anticipated by talking to me, just as I learned more than I could have anticipated in talking to him. If his hopes had been fulfilled, and his side had won the war by a clear margin, I probably wouldn't remember this, but I think the planned memory-wipe was overlooked in all the confusion.

I don't know for sure whether his side won the war or not, although it's certainly possible that what the slug-monsters in the control room were doing for the three minutes before the darkness came was their idea of a victory dance. I might have been mere minutes away from being sent home in a spirit of cheerful and slightly tearful camaraderie—but once the darkness did arrive, the automated system had to kick in. If the darkness was the first-strike weapon, I can only hope that the one I'd provided was never used in retaliation, but I suspect that mine was used first and that it was the darkness that became the counterstrike: the doomsday bomb. Kitten was right, though; the ultimate weapon the opposition had been working on was quite different from his.

The darkness didn't arrive in the manner of a light that had been switched off; it was more measured and methodical. It was as if a crowd of shadows were oozing from invisible cracks in the walls and floor of the control room: shadows that had the ability to *devour* the seemingly solid flesh of the slug-men, and which set about doing so with a certain amount of relish.

They probably screamed, but I couldn't hear them. I felt their terror and their pain, though, in a sympathetic fashion. Long winter days make me feel depressed at home, but the darkness of long winter days is nothing compared to *that* darkness, and it did more and worse than fill me with depression, even though I didn't have the right kind of biology to be devoured by it. My SAD went into an overdrive I'd never imagined that it could possibly possess.

I couldn't feel the darkness *physically*, because it was really some kind of vitalistic shadow-monster, eclipsing the energy that sustained the slug-things and swallowing their souls, but I was certainly *conscious* of the darkness, in a fashion that was far more intense than any mere awareness of what it was and what it was doing.

The slug-things weren't a pretty sight while they were alive, but that didn't mean that I could take the slightest delight in seeing them dissolved, turned inside out and consumed, or in feeling the tragedy of their annihilation.

What the darkness looked like to their unhuman eyes, and what it felt like to their other senses, I have no idea—but Kitten had told me enough about the spectrum of vitalistic energies to give me some imaginative inkling of the horror of it.

The reds had been intent on extracting a weapon from my deadly repertoire that was very specific—one that could be very carefully *aimed*, so as to be deadly to some of the life-forms of that curious world but utterly harmless to others, like an earthly virus that's deadly to pigs but utterly harmless to sheep. It was, I suppose, a good strike weapon to aim against a foe whose innate energies lay in a very different part of the vitalistic spectrum.

What the violets had done, by contrast, was to develop an all-purpose, all-devouring energy weapon that could annihilate *anything* within its ecosphere. If it had been used first, it would presumably have been targeted with great care—but if it had, in fact, been used as a counterstrike by the violets...well, as I said, perhaps I shouldn't have cared, but I did. I still do. The thought that we might still go the same way, if things get out of hand in the Middle East, doesn't make it any easier.

I'd like to think that my guys were the right side, insofar as there was anything to choose between them. I'd like to have been helping the good guys, or at least the less worse guys. I'd also like to think that the loss of the war *hadn't* led to the extinction of all the intelligent subspecies in their ecosystem. I fear, though, that the darkness claimed everything—except me. I was sent back by some kind of reflexive fail-safe mechanism, designed to make sure that I would pose no further danger to anyone in that other world.

I think about the experience a lot. It seems absurd, I know, but I think about it most when I think about leaving Josh and the possibility of getting a divorce. I know how easily divorce can turn into an all-out war whose ultimate result is Mutual Assured Destruction. I sometimes wonder whether the differences between us might just be a matter of different protovitalistic energies catalyzing our consciousness in different ways, and nothing really to do with *us* at all, even if those energies really are all that any of us has by way of a pathetic excuse for a soul—but that doesn't help either.

Anyway, I shan't be doing anything in a hurry, no matter how restless my legs become or how depressed I get.

I know now, although I didn't before, how very afraid of the dark I am.

CHAPTER NINE

LETTING THE CAT OUT

Milly and Janine both seemed rather subdued during the journey back to Salisbury. The light banter they'd exchanged on the way out had faltered. Although Milly had manifested such mood changes before, and she was the one tacitly in control of the situation, Steve couldn't help wondering, anxiously, whether Janine might have picked up some mysterious subliminal signal during the meeting to inform her that all was not well within her relationship with her best friend. When a pause developed in their conversation, Steve could not bear the silence.

"You know that old enigma about whether a tree falling in a forest makes any sound if there's no one round to hear it," he said, more-or-less randomly. "Here's another. Is a woman really naked if there isn't another human being to look at her? I mean, obviously she's got no clothes on, but is she really *naked*?"

"Have you spent the last two hours imagining Zoe naked?" Janine asked. "That's disgusting. She's old enough to be your mother."

"It's a valid philosophical question!" Steve protested.

"I didn't believe what she said about coming back two stone lighter and not putting the weight straight back on when she started eating again," Milly said. "It's never that easy—believe me, I know. I bet she's had liposuction."

"Maybe she had it without telling her husband," Steve suggested, "and had to think of a bloody good story to explain the sudden shrinkage." He knew that the suggestion was a casual breach of the AlAbAn rule that required him to refrain from suggesting that a story-teller might be telling lies. Given that he was in the privacy of his own car, however, with only his two girl-friends for an audience, he figured that no one was likely to object. Milly and Janine, however, obviously thought differently about the propriety of this particular suggestion.

"Some of us humans," Milly said, in a tone that was slightly ominous as well as obliquely accusatory, "probably have more protovitalistic energies than others."

"And some of us," Janine said, as if supplying an echo, "have probably had run-ins with those emotional vampires that leech all the affection and anxiety out of you, and leave you with stones for souls."

Steve didn't dare retaliate, in case things got out of hand. He *had* imagined Zoe naked, but it hadn't seemed like a disgusting thing to see or do. Her story had surely encouraged, if not actually required, some such imaginative effort. He'd felt sorry for her, because she was obviously stuck in a loveless marriage from which she dared not make her escape, because she felt too vulnerable to be fully exposed to the world's vicissitudes. Perhaps he shouldn't have cared, but he did. It was a matter of principle.

"Shall I drop you at home before Janine and I go on to the Chinese, Milly?" he asked, politely.

"No, that's all right," Milly replied. "I'll come and eat with you, if you don't mind. If you want to follow the usual routine I can walk home from Jan's—it's no trouble. I promise that I won't stay long. I wouldn't want to get in the way of your amatory plans."

Steve thought that was a bit rich, but there was nothing he could say.

"That wouldn't be fair," Janine said. "If we're all eating together, we should pick somewhere near your place. Does the Pheasant do food?"

"After a fashion," Milly said—causing Steve's faint heart to flutter again, since he and Milly had been into the pub in question on more than one occasion as a couple. Milly was quick enough to substitute a suggestion of her own, though. "I know a better place—an Italian called the Arlequino. They do some nice chicken dishes as well as the usual pasta and pizza—veal too if you can stand the guilt. They won't be booked up on a Thursday."

"Fine by me," Janine said.

"You'll have to give me directions," Steve told her.

Milly laughed in response to that. Janine laughed too, as usual, although she couldn't have known why Milly was laughing.

Steve wasn't looking forward to the meal, but some distraction was provided when they walked into the restaurant, because Janine and Milly spotted their friend Alison at a corner table and rushed to greet her. She was dining with a man at least ten years her senior, who seemed distinctly discomfited by the fact that his tryst had been discovered. They were just finishing their desserts.

Steve had always thought Janine and Milly an exercise in contrasts, because Janine was so slightly built and Milly so robust, but Alison provided a striking contrast with both of them. While the others had very dark hair, Alison's was quite fair, although not so bright as to qualify as blonde. Whereas Janine's features were delicately sculpted and Milly's boldly outlined, Alison's were strangely indistinct, the basic thinness of her face being compromised by rounded cheeks, and her snub nose looking as if it had strayed from another face entirely. The starkest contrast of all was, however, in her eyes. Whereas Milly and Janine had eyes as dark as their hair, Alison had pale blue eyes that would presumably have looked far brighter in sunlight than they did in the dimly-lit Arlequino.

Alison was not as distressed by the encounter as her companion seemed to be. She stood up and welcomed her friends gladly. When Janine introduced Steve as "my boyfriend, Steve", she introduced her own companion simply as "Mark".

"We've just been to AlAbAn," Milly said. "Now that Janine's a regular, you really ought to come along. "We could all travel out together in Steve's car—all you'd have to do is pop around to my place by seven." She turned to Steve to add: "Ali only lives two streets away, the other side of the Pheasant."

"It's okay by me," he said—causing Alison to look directly at him for a little longer than she had when he was introduced.

"So you're Steve," she said. "I've heard a lot about you."

"We've already done that routine, Ali," Milly said. "Janine's already assured him that she hasn't loaded us down with embarrassing details of his intimate habits, so there's no point trying to wind him up."

"I wouldn't dream of it," Alison said, smiling at Steve to emphasize that she wasn't being sarcastic.

"We have to organize another night out," Janine said. "How about Tuesday next?"

"I don't know," Alison said. "I'll figure it out—ring me tomorrow. It's great to see you, but will you excuse us now? We need to finish our coffees and get on. Maybe I'll see you Tuesday, if I can make it."

The waiter was hovering, evidently anxious to get Milly, Janine and Steve seated on the far side of the room, and they consented to be led away. By the time they'd finished studying the menus and were looking around expectantly for someone to take their orders,

Mark had paid the bill and was hurrying Alison along. Alison waved goodbye as she left, but Mark never glanced in their direction.

"No prizes for guessing why they're in such a hurry," Milly said "He's obviously married—has to get home to the wife once he's dipped his wick."

"Poor Ali," Janine said. "I wish she could find a nice single one, for a change."

"She chooses them deliberately," Milly opined. "Thinks that it's less complicated. Besides, it allows her to be ruthless when she fills us in on the stories so far. If she actually cared about them, she'd be as coy as you are."

"She cares, in her own way," Janine said. "She only gives us all the pornographic details because you gloat over them so much."

"And you don't? If she's feeding a demand, it doesn't just come from me. It's okay—you don't have to worry about letting on in front of Steve. He'll understand."

Janine was blushing. She obviously didn't want Steve to think that her tastes in gossip were seriously salacious, or to wonder whether Alison was really content to feed her appetite without getting anything in return.

"It's Alison's fault that we can't invite you to our little soirées, Steve," Milly went on, blithely. "Janine and I are paragons of virtue by comparison, with Jan being contentedly monogamous nowadays and me being practically a nun, so Ali has to play the slut or we wouldn't have anything to talk about at all. In any case, she's not as good-looking as we are, so she has to try harder—plain girls always have more sex, because they can't afford to be so picky."

"That's not fair," Janine objected, although she couldn't possibly know how unfair it really was.

"She's got very nice eyes," Steve observed. "They must really reflect the sky on a sunny day."

"Oh God!" Milly groaned. "He's been imagining *her* naked too. Don't you ever stop?"

"Ignore her, Steve," Janine said. "She's bounced back from her post-meeting *triste* and now she's delirious. What's that phrase you use, Mil? Emotional incontinence?"

The waiter finally arrived at that point to take their orders. Steve was glad of the interruption, and invited Janine to go first. Janine and Milly both ordered lemon chicken, but Steve went for the veal Marsala in spite of the fact that he knew that Janine would disapprove. Instead of allowing Janine time to comment on the evil of veal crates, however, Milly immediately reverted to their prior topic of conversation.

"I don't suffer from emotional incontinence," Milly said, as if her character had been called into question. "That's something I observe in others. I'm merely being witty and charming. For instance, Ali's emotionally incontinent, in failing to resist the slimy charms of all the office Romeos at the Town Hall—at least until she's tried them and found them wanting—and verbally incontinent too, when she tells us all about her adventures. You and I, by contrast, are always in control of our amatory affairs. How about you. Steve? Is this problem you have with imagining women naked getting out of control? Do you brag about your conquests in the staff-room?"

"I don't have enough imagination to picture women naked," Steve said, grimly. "I'm a science teacher. I certainly don't talk about my sex life in the staff-room. Every one else did, at one time, but that seems to have faded away now, mercifully."

"They've finally forgiven you for all those broken hearts, have they?" Janine put in, perhaps thinking that she was helping Steve to withstand Milly's onslaught.

"No hearts were broken," Steve insisted, gruffly. "Things just got a bit tangled last term, that's all. It's ancient history now. Can we possibly talk about something else?"

"Sure," Janine said. "At Tom Cook's, Christmas breaks are all the rage. Do you fancy one?"

"Actually," Steve said, awkwardly, "My parents expect me home for Christmas. I haven't yet plucked up the courage to disappoint them, although I keep meaning to. I'm an only child, you see."

"So are we all," Janine said. "I *never* go home for Christmas. It's okay—I wasn't thinking of the Costa del Sol, or even darkest Wales. You can get ferries over to St. Malo and Le Havre, you know."

Steve still hadn't told Milly exactly what his phobias were, in spite of the fact that she'd asked a few probing questions, but if he had, Janine would not have been aware of the fact. There was another matter of principle at stake, and Steve tried to use his facial expression to remind Janine that she'd promised not to let Milly in on their secret. She seemed to get the message. "Okay," she said. "Too boring, obviously. No more travel talk, then. Book any flash cars today, Mil?"

"A few BMWs, one Jag and one top-of-the-range Saab," Milly said. "Nothing special. I'll do better tomorrow, and even better on Saturday. Saturday's when the rank amateurs and compulsive liberty-takers come out in force. I love Saturday shifts. There's no opportunity to wind up the school run brigade, but the sheer variety is more than adequate compensation. You two will be getting together, I suppose?"

"Nothing special," Janine answered. "Multiscreen, wine bar, Chinese and home."

"Sounds special to me," Milly said, with a contrived sigh. Her sighs were almost as infectious as her laughs, and it was all that Steve could do to stop himself from echoing it.

"Love life still not going well?" Janine asked, innocently.

"Not going at all," Milly lied. "Not for want of offers, mind—but I'm not about to take up any of the colorful suggestions my punters make. What I need is a nice safe parker who respects yellow lines, always feeds his meter and always sticks close to the kerb. Not a lot of them about, these days."

"Tomorrow's a really bad day for me," Steve said, figuring that if no one else were going to steer the subject-matter on to safer ground he'd better do it himself. "Two sessions with the sixth—one a double period—and two with year eleven. We've got past optics and the digestive system, but the periodic table and circulatory system aren't much better."

"When do you get on to reproduction?" Milly asked, brutally.

"Not till January," Steve answered, calmly. "That's with the sixth. I don't have to explain it to the year elevens at all, thank God, although they're the ones most likely to provide practical demonstrations of teenage pregnancy. The circulatory system can raise problems of its own, though—especially when we get the little darlings to ascertain their own blood groups. They're a lot keener on sticking needles in one another than in themselves."

"Tell them that it's good practice for future drug-taking activities and tattoo acquisition," Milly suggested.

"The class smartarses would only argue that it's better to smoke heroin and crack than to inject it," Steve said, "and launch into elaborate discourses on the technicalities of body-piercing and the aesthetics of tattoo-placement. Mind you, the year elevens would probably be more than capable of doing all of that with even greater gruesomeness, if the curriculum provided them with an opening. At least GCSEs weed out the worst cases of extensive self-mutilation; the A level groups are much less prone to it."

"But harder to lead around by the nipples," Milly supplied, mischievously. "Which must be a pity, given that they're legal."

"No touching allowed," Steve said, wearily. "Strictly forbidden, no matter how old they are."

"Must be difficult to restrain yourself, though, on occasion," Milly followed up, relentlessly. "All those nubile young girls, hungry for a proper education. We were, weren't we, Jan?"

"I'd never dare," Steve assured them both. "They terrify me far too much. Older women are saner and safer by far—most of them, anyhow."

"I'd hate to think that you were only with me because I'm easier to deal with," Janine said.

In desperation, Steve made another stab at changing the subject. "I real Carl Jung's book about flying saucers the other week," he said. "He wrote it before the alien abduction business started, so it's mostly about sightings, but it's easy enough to see how abduction experiences could be slotted into his theory. He reckons that the entire UFO mythos is a psychological response to contemporary historical crises, in which the collective unconscious supplies the conscious mind with encoded archetypal imagery appropriate to the hopes and fears of our era. He thinks the collective unconscious is something fixed and stable, though—the product of our evolutionary heritage, which constitutes as well as containing the mythical past. I think it's a lot more malleable and changeable. I reckon that modern idea-structures like the UFO-complex are part and parcel of our attempts to remake and remold the collective unconscious—constructing the mythical future, as it were. That's what's really going on at AlAbAn meetings, I think. We're exchanging ideas of the mythical future, so that imaginative cross-fertilization can re-equip the collective unconscious with a new set of archetypal instruments."

"Did you notice that he said all that without once drawing breath?" Milly said to Janine.

"He often does that when he's desperate," Janine replied. "Learned it in the classroom, I suppose."

"Don't tell me that you haven't been reading around the subject," Steve said, to both of them. "You must have formed theories of your own regarding the stories we've been listening to. They cry out for some sort of psychological explanation—Zoe's most of all."

"I've looked up a few things on the net," Janine confessed. "There's a lot of crazy stuff out there in cyberspace, but not a lot of psychology."

"I keep my UFO books in the bedroom," Milly said. "They're almost as good as self-help manuals for reading oneself to sleep, but not as instantly effective as the *Highway Code*. Reading books about alien abductions at bedtime produces more strange dreams than theories, as you might expect. AlAbAn meetings sometimes have the same effect, but I don't think the idea of Zoe naked in a glass cage will do as much for me as it will for Steve."

"Zoe's story was interesting in terms of its biology too," Steve said, although he realized belatedly that it might have been a mistake to mention Zoe specifically, "although the idea that the course of future evolution might one day produce a simulacrum of vitalist theory isn't as easy to accept as Jim's suggestion that creationism might one day become an active philosophy instead of an idiotic way of trying to deny all the evidence of geology and paleontology. You've been going to the meetings a lot longer than we have, Milly—you must have come across lots of similar notions. After all, the members are feeding on one another's dreams, aren't they? They're borrowing ideas all the time to fit into their own stories."

"It's more or less taken for granted in the group that people are entitled to borrow anything they take a fancy to," Milly said, cruelly improvising yet another *double entendre* that would be inaudible to Janine. "It's an essential element of being a successful mutual support group."

"I must have a long talk to Walter Wainwright some time—or maybe Amelia Rockham," Steve continued, doggedly. "They've heard all the stories, going back forty years and more. They must be aware of the broad patterns. I wonder when the emphasis of the stories began to shift from space travel to time travel—some time after the Viking landers proved that Mars is lifeless, obviously. There was probably a transition phase, when the emphasis shifted from interplanetary craft to starships—but time travel's more pertinent now, as well as more convenient, if what's really going on is the gradual manufacture of a new mythical future. It needn't be conscious of course—all the borrowing, I mean. In fact, it probably makes more sense if it's almost entirely unconscious."

"It's not," Milly assured him.

"We're not supposed to be skeptical, Steve," Janine reminded him. "We're not supposed to write off people's stories as hallucinations or fabrications, let alone make up fancy theories to explain them away. Have some consideration for Milly, will you?"

"Oh, don't mind me," Milly said. "I won't let him explain away my abduction experience before I've even reported it. You can be as skeptical as you like in private, Steve—but you really shouldn't bring that kind of talk to group, and it would be too exploitative to start pumping poor Mrs. Rockham for evidence to feed your psychobabble. Walter could probably cope, but maybe you'd do better to keep it all to yourself. No need for verbal incontinence, is there?"

Steve was profoundly glad when the time eventually came to split the bill and move on. He took Milly home first, then headed for Janine's.

"You seem very edgy tonight, Steve," Janine observed. "Is something wrong?"

"Nothing at all," Steve assured her. It's just that my relaxation techniques don't seem to be working as well as I'd hoped, even on the everyday stress of work. I'm in two minds as to whether to go back to Sylvia next Tuesday for another booster session, or whether to give up on her altogether. Maybe I ought to try Prozac."

"That's a bit desperate, isn't it?"

"Is it? I read somewhere that Prozac and its generic equivalents account for nearly a third of NHS drug-spending. That's a lot of pre-scriptions, considering that it isn't actually a cure for any definable disease."

"That's only because it's so difficult to get Viagra on the NHS," Janine said. "If people could have *that* for the asking, it would probably take up more than half the drug budget. Mind you, it's ob-viously easy enough to get off-prescription, I get emails every day offering me cheap supplies—almost as many as I get offering me penis extensions."

"I just delete them," Steve said, trying not to sound overly de-fensive.

"Of course you do," Janine said. "Why would you need Viagra, when you have me? Or Prozac, come to think of it. Aren't I anti-depressant enough."

"They aren't just antidepressants," Steve told her. "They affect other brain functions too. They *might* help with my phobias."

"Milly told me that," Janine observed. "About the other effects, that is. Shall I ask her if phobia treatment is one of them? She reads a lot of pseudomedical self-help books—a hangover from her eating disorder days, I guess. She seemed fine tonight, though—a very healthy appetite, for someone with no measurable love life. I do hope she didn't throw it all up as soon as she got home. She needs to keep her strength up, in her line of work. I won't mention that they're your phobias, though—I'll just put it as a hypothetical ques-tion."

"She'll guess," Steve said, grimly. "Please don't bother."

"She was a bit hard on poor Alison, I thought," Janine went on, as Steve locked the car and followed her to the door of the house that contained her flat. "I think it's because Ali slept with one of her boy-friends once. She always assures Ali that it's all forgiven and forgotten, but I'm not sure that it is, really. Milly isn't a naturally forgiving person—that's why she's such a good traffic warden."

"What happened to the boy-friend?" Steve asked, innocently.

"Mil dumped him as soon as she found out. Never saw or spoke to him again. You have to take a firm line in such matters, don't you? You can't tolerate a boy-friend who'll sleep with your friends behind your back. No future in that at all."

In the past, Janine's boast that that no one could possibly need Viagra if they had her had always been totally justified, but the generalization faltered that night. Steve had to make his excuses and leave, hoping desperately that he would be able to do better the following night.

* * * * * * *

The situation couldn't last, of course. Steve had known that all along, and so had Milly. At first, Milly had taken some delight in it, obviously pleased to have out-competed—or at least out-maneuvered—her slightly prettier friend, but as time went by the delight ebbed away and her guilt-feelings increased in proportion. Their three-way dinner seemed to have exaggerated that process considerably; when Steve next saw Milly, on the following Monday evening, she was in a terrible mood. Steve half-expected her to say that it couldn't and mustn't go on, but she didn't. Indeed, she seemed even more resolute in the absence of the delight factor than she had while intoxication was buoying her up.

Neither of them had dared voice the thought that Janine was bound to find out eventually, because that would have forced them to discuss what would happen afterwards, but Milly was a past master at hinting and Steve was very quick on the uptake where that sort of hint was concerned, so he was as fully aware of her cognizance of the fact as she was of his. They hadn't reduced the frequency of their meetings, though; the awareness lent an extra measure of urgency to their physical relationship.

"I've got an appointment with Sylvia tomorrow evening," Steve told Milly, as they lay in bed—more by way of informing her that he wouldn't be seeing Janine than to excuse his inability to see her.

"Bully for you," Milly said, though not abrasively—the sex had taken the edge off her bad mood.

"Progress seems to have stalled," Steve explained. "With the relaxation, that is. Of course, the difference might be that the stress level at work has increased markedly, because of the pre-half-term course-work rush. It's all deadlines these days—as soon as one's past, another looms. Rhodri will be after me with heaps of scripts, wanting me do the plagiarism checks."

"The Christmas shopping season starts soon," Milly observed. "More frustration leads to more ill-advised parking, which leads to more tickets, which leads to more road rage. A vicious circle, I might get some Prozac. You can buy it on-line, you know. No point in bothering the doctor. You can get Viagra too, if you need it."

"I don't" Steve said.

"Of course not. You're young and fit—only ten years past the sexual peak that your pupils are enjoying so much. At least it's not affecting your cricket now that the season's finished."

Steve said nothing, because all the things he could think of were things he couldn't voice, like *we can't go on like this indefinitely* and *we can't keep the secret forever.*

In the event, the secret stayed kept for exactly one more week.

Steve and Milly didn't immediately realize that disaster had struck when they walked into the Pheasant on the following Monday evening to find themselves confronted yet again by Alison and her friend Mark, who were rushing through the preliminaries to yet another illicit assignation. At first it seemed that Milly had saved the day with her genius for improvisation. "Hi, Ali," she said, without hesitation. "You remember Steve. don't you—Janine's boy-friend. Janine will be along any minute. Won't you join us? It's ages since the three of us got together, and you let us down last Tuesday."

"We can't stop," Alison was quick to say, obviously unwilling to expose her date to the kind of suggestive inquisition that Milly could contrive, with or without Janine's support. "Thanks anyway."

"That's a shame," Milly said. "It would be a useful opportunity for Mark and Steve to get to know one another. Maybe, if I can rope in an escort of my own, we could all go out together one night."

"It is a shame," Alison agreed, failing to hide her insincerity. "We must do that some time. We really have to dash now, though—function at the Town Hall." She glanced at Steve, her blue eyes offering an apology, apparently signaling that her annoyance was reserved for Milly.

"He probably does function at the Town Hall," Milly said, when the other couple had left. "I hope he has a leather-topped desk. We wouldn't want Ali to get splinters in her tits, would we?"

"Considering that she's supposed to be one of your two best friends," Steve observed, as he bought the drinks, "you don't seem to like her very much."

"I love her to bits, really," Milly said. "You know how it is with old friends—insults that would be terrible if addressed to an outsider become jokey gestures of affection. She can't help being a slut any more than you can. I don't hold it against her. She makes jokes about me, too, when we're all together. We even contrive to wind Jan up occasionally, although it's not easy."

"You don't think she'll mention to Janine that she saw us together, next time she bumps into her?"

"No chance. She'll erase the encounter from her memory, because she won't want me going on about her being caught with the same married man twice over."

Milly was usually a good judge of such matters, so Steve took her word for it, and didn't spare Alison another thought until half past ten, when he and Milly were interrupted in mid-sex-session by someone hammering on the door of the flat.

"Oh fuck," Milly said, disengaging hastily and groping in the dark for her discarded underwear. "This isn't going to look good. The nosey bitch must have twigged—and she's gone and shopped us. Who'd have thought it?"

"Don't answer the door!" Steve whispered.

"Don't be an idiot," Milly said. "She doesn't need a traffic warden's eagle eye to know that your car's parked right outside the front door. Get dressed, double quick—and let me do the talking."

Steve had to admire Milly's optimism, but he knew as he pulled his clothes back on that no story in the world was going to convince Janine that there was a perfectly innocent explanation for his being in Milly's flat.

He never got a chance to find out what kind of story Milly would have improvised. As Milly herself had once observed, actions speak louder than words; when she opened the door to the flat Janine gave her an open-handed slap that knocked her off her feet.

"How could you?" Janine demanded, not even glancing at Steve but going to stand astride Milly's supine form, her righteous fury belying the obvious fact that Milly's superior strength would have allowed her to knock seven bells out of Janine if she'd cared to make a fight of it. "How in the name of God *could you?*"

Milly didn't even try to get up, let alone make a fight of it. She stayed on the floor, supporting herself on her elbows. "I don't know, Jan," she retorted, eventually. "How do *you* think I did it?"

"I knew you never really liked Alison," Janine said. "Through all those years of pretending to be her friend, I knew you didn't like her, even before she fucked your boy-friend—but I never suspected, even for a minute, that you secretly hated me. I never even suspected that you were pretending with me too. Why, Mil? For God's sake, *why?*"

"I wasn't pretending," Milly said. "Honestly. I like you more than anyone else in the world—and Ali too. I always have."

Janine seemed to be disappointed that Milly wouldn't get up, so that she could hit her again, but she wasn't the kind of girl who could kick someone in the ribs or stamp on them, so all she could do was move her fists impotently up, down and around. Finally, confronted with Milly's refusal to give her any further grounds for verbal or actual violence, she rounded on Steve, who was just checking to make sure that his fly was done up.

"If it was her you wanted," Janine said, "All you had to do was say."

Steve observed that the phrasing of this remark left no room for a safe response. He couldn't, after all, say that he hadn't wanted Milly at all, or that he had wanted both of them. His actions had already spoken, far louder than words.

"It wasn't his fault," Milly said, making a direly unconvincing show of springing heroically to his defense, on seeing that he couldn't defend himself. "I took advantage of him. I'm sorry. I was jealous of you. I always have been. I wanted him because he was yours."

"Don't flatter yourself," Janine retorted, immediately seeing through the maneuver. "You didn't need to be Helen of Troy to pull this tosser. He'd have fucked you just as readily if you'd had a wooden leg and a paper bag over your head. Of course it's his fault—and yours too. It's the kind of fault that needs one hundred per cent commitment from both parties. I never want to speak to either of you again, ever. Next time you see me in the street, look the other way—if you don't, I will."

"You don't have to be like that," Milly said. "Shit happens, right? We can still be friends."

"Shut up, Milly. Steve, you're a coward and an idiot—and this silly bitch is worse than you. You deserve one another. I hope you'll be very happy together, now that I'm out of your lives."

"Thanks, Jan," said Milly, abruptly switching from attempted mollification to sarcasm. "It won't be easy, but you can be sure that we'll do our very best." She managed not to flinch when Janine made as if to hit her again, in spite of the fact that she was still propped up on her elbows—but Janine couldn't reach Milly's face without bending down, and there were obviously limits to the extent to which she was prepared to lower herself. Instead of lashing out again, the outraged party contented herself with turning on her heel, marching out and slamming the door behind her.

Milly released a deep sigh, and got to her feet. "Well. I didn't think she'd react as badly as *that*," she said. "She might have given me a chance to explain. We've been friends forever—you'd think she owed me that."

Steve sat down on the sofa and put his head in his hands. He didn't burst into tears, though. He was just miming despair.

Milly came over and sat down beside him. "It could have been worse," she said. "At least the situation's clarified now. She'll probably come around, when she's had a chance to calm down and lick the wound, and we can all patch things up. The worse case scenario, right now, would be if I dumped you too, but I'm not going to do that. I might have lost a best friend—temporarily, I hope—and you might have lost the prettier of your two girl-friends, but we've still got each other. It's not the end of the world."

"Did you plan all this?" Steve asked.

"Don't be ridiculous," Milly replied. "Even if I'd wanted to, which I didn't, how could I have done it? I really didn't believe that Alison was smart enough to have guessed that I was lying about Janine being along in a minute, and I certainly didn't think that she'd be malicious enough to phone Janine even if she had. She owes me one, remember. I've been really nice about her fucking my boy-friend, always taking trouble to reassure her that she was forgiven, because our friendship was too precious to throw away over something so silly. I don't know how many times Janine heard me say that, but it was certainly enough to make her think twice about the appropriate response to what she just found out. I expect too much of people, you know. I always have. You're not going to turn on me as well, are you? That would be just *too much*!"

Steve observed, without any great surprise, that the question and its supplementary remark were phrased in such a way as to leave him no choice at all.

"Oh well," Milly said. "I suppose we'd better go back to bed to lick our own wounds—and whatever else seems appropriate."

* * * * * * *

It wasn't until Steve was alone again that remorse really kicked in. He had always known, of course, that the one he really wanted was Janine. Janine had been absolutely right in her description of him. He'd been a complete idiot to get involved with Milly in the first place, and an arrant coward to carry on seeing her behind Janine's back without making any attempt to correct the situation. It wasn't until he was no longer in Milly's curiously assertive presence, however, that he felt the full impact of his idiocy and coward-ice. The fact that he hadn't been able to turn on Milly—because that really would have been *too much*—only made things worse.

What he wanted now was to dump Milly and obtain Janine's forgiveness, but he couldn't, firstly because he couldn't believe for a moment that Janine would actually take him back, secondly because he couldn't do that to Milly—who obviously hadn't planned for things to turn out the way they had and was just as distressed about it as he was—and thirdly because it would make him seem like a really shallow person if he cast off a perfectly serviceable, attractive girl-friend, who was obviously willing to stick to him through thick and thin, in favor of one who no longer wanted to know him, but was slightly better-looking. As a secondary school science teacher, Steve had always prided himself on being a cultured individual, and had always been prepared to recruit the support of John Keats in support of the strict equivalence of beauty and truth in matters of the heart, but he had a sneaking suspicion that even Keats might not ap-prove of his ditching Milly purely on the grounds of her lack of deli-cate perfection.

Because the bust-up had happened on a Monday, Steve had an excuse—albeit a feeble one—to call Janine regarding the possibility of picking her up so that they could attend the Wednesday meeting of the survival course. She told him, in no uncertain terms, that she no longer had the slightest interest in going to a survival course with him, because if it should ever happen that he and she were the last man and woman on Earth, she would not wish to survive. She in-structed him never to call her again, for any reason whatsoever, in-cluding Milly's hopefully-imminent death and the end of the world as she had known it.

The wounds inflicted by this harsh exchange were still raw when Steve drove Milly out to East Grimstead on the Thursday for the AlAbAn meeting. He hadn't been able to take Milly to the sur-vival course on Wednesday, because enrolments weren't transfer-able. Unable to bear the prospect of going alone, he had abandoned the course, in spite of having paid the fee up front. He didn't want to be thought of as the kind of person who might abandon a survival course when the going got tough, but there seemed to be no alterna-tive.

Steve was astonished to find, when he followed Milly into Amelia Rockham's front room, that Janine was already there, sitting in one of the green armchairs sipping tea from a pink cup. Steve was utterly nonplussed by this discovery. He stared at Janine in amaze-ment, but Janine refused to meet his gaze.

Milly obviously felt a similar amazement. "What the hell's *she* doing here?" she whispered in Steve's ear, as they made their way to the slightly-worn Naugahyde settee on which Steve had previously sat with Janine.

Steve couldn't help wondering, briefly, whether Janine's appearance might part of some kind of Machiavellian scheme, cunningly adapted to the purpose of getting him back without losing face and putting the boot into her faithless ex-best friend into the bargain, but that seemed to be far too much to hope for. "I don't know," he replied, glad to be able to tell the truth for once.

What puzzled Steve even more than Janine's presence was the attitudes of the other people gathered in the room. He remembered only too well what had happened in the days leading up to the swearing of his oath that he would never date anyone at work again, no matter what. He'd only been going out with Tracy for a matter of months, and it had been a relatively casual thing, but when he'd split with her in order to have a whirlwind affair with Jill it was as if World War Three had suddenly broken out in the staff room. Fully eighty per cent of the other staff-members had "rallied round" Tracy, to the extent of staring at Steve and Jill as if they were green snot on a grubby handkerchief, and even the twenty per cent who were determined not to desert Jill, either because they were her special friends or because science teachers had to stick together, had made it pretty clear what they thought of Steve's wayward character. Then, of course, he'd split with Jill, and the entire staff-room had found him guilty of his war crime and sentenced him accordingly— except for Rhodri Jenkins, whose position as deputy head compelled him to keep lines of communication open.

There was nothing like that at AlAbAn. The other members of the support group obviously felt that their responsibility to be caring and sympathetic extended far beyond matters of alien abduction. There were no disapproving stares, no curled lips, no snide whispers. Everyone was exactly as polite to Steve and Milly as they were to Janine. The only people in the room whose expressions gave the slightest evidence that a major shift in intimate relations had taken place were Steve and Milly. Even Janine seemed serenely comfortable in her green armchair, chatting away to Amelia Rockham as if she had never been anything but unattached, until Walter Wainwright had completed the formalities and it was time for the one of the members to relate an experience.

This time, it was "Danny". He'd attended the previous three meetings, having joined the group not long after Steve, and had apparently been a lot quicker than Steve to decide that this was as safe an environment in which to tell all as he was ever likely to find.

CHAPTER TEN

ERRAND OF MERCY

This happened a fair while ago but I never tried to talk about it before. I've lived most of my life over the other side of the plain, in Warminster, so I grew up with UFO talk. When I was a kid, I reckon I was just about the only one in my class who'd never seen one and didn't have an idea about them. I wasn't even one of those smartarse skeptics who lectured people about optical illusions; I just didn't take part.

I went through my twenties the same way, never giving much of a thought to the fact that I was living in the world's number one UFO hotspot. I suppose you might think it ironic that almost as soon as I took a step up in the business—I'm a plumber by trade—and moved to Salisbury, I was taken. Not that I remembered it at the time, mind; I'm one of those people who got the memory back much later, in a series of disjointed flashbacks that had to be pieced together like a jigsaw before I got a grip on the whole thing.

It might be have been more sensible, I suppose, just to accept that my mind had made most of it up in an attempt to make sense of a couple of meaningless dream-images. I thought so for a long time, but lately...well, let's just say that it's been on my mind quite a bit while I've been fixing taps and installing boilers, and I figured that maybe the time had come to get it out in the open. It's not that I want to be rid of it, even if I could, but...well, I know that most of you are veterans at this lark, so you probably understand what I mean better than I do.

At any rate, it happened, one dark and moonless night. I woke up for no reason I could figure, went to the window and opened it wide. It was a senseless thing to do, given than it was mid-January. The blast of cold air set me shivering madly, but the tractor beam grabbed me almost immediately. Rumor has it that most people see lights, but I couldn't see anything. It was pitch dark, and I just moved into the heart of the darkness, as if I were being swallowed by a black hole. I must have blacked out myself—for a matter of minutes, I thought, when I first began to remember, or maybe days, although I've now concluded that it might well have been years, or even centuries.

That might seem ridiculous, I guess, but having heard what some of you have said about being put back into your beds after a matter of minutes even though you'd lived through weeks while you were gone, I've given the matter much deeper consideration. If you can spend a week on an alien starship and then get returned a few seconds after you were taken, there can't be any reason, in principle, why you couldn't be away for much longer and still get back in good time. I didn't age much while I was away—not to any extent I could detect—but I reckon the aliens might be able to fix that too, with their advanced medical techniques. They certainly fixed me up well and properly in other ways.

When I woke up, I was in a space-suit. I call it a space-suit, even though I was never actually required to wear it in outer space, because calling it a diving-suit would be even more absurd. It might be better to call it a cold-suit, but that wouldn't give you much of a visual image, whereas calling it a space-suit will put the right sort of picture into your heads. In any case, although I can't actually be sure that the surface where they put me to work was completely airless, any air it had must have been very thin indeed, and I'm pretty sure that it was *extremely* cold.

I don't know much about the way the suit was kitted out internally, but it must have had mechanisms for supplying food and water, presumably intravenously, as well as air, and some provision for soaking up various bodily wastes. At the end of every shift the aliens would change all the various canisters strapped to my back and sides, but I never got out of the suit, even when I got into my hammock to sleep.

There was nothing much else to do apart from work and sleep. There was nothing to stop the workers talking to one another, although we had to touch helmets to make ourselves heard, but I never found another one who could speak English. Although our visors allowed us to see out easily enough, it wasn't so easy to look through two of them to see into the interior of another helmet, but I figured out soon enough that my co-workers weren't even human. They were all built on the same model—two legs, two arms, six feet tall, give or take a couple of feet—but when it came to faces it was like a crowd scene in some TV sci-fi series. The alien slave-drivers wore suits too, and we could see as much of their faces as we could of one another's. They didn't look particular nasty—no fangs or anything of that sort—but they weren't handsome and they certainly weren't friendly. They didn't fraternize with the unhired help.

Some of you have had experiences in which the aliens took the trouble to explain to you what they were doing, but they probably only do that if they need to. The ones that kidnapped me didn't go in for explanations, although they could synthesize English well enough to give out orders via some kind of microphone in the suit's helmet. From the moment I went to bed that first night to the moment I got up the next morning, maybe ten or a hundred years later, I never had a genuine conversation with another living soul. I certainly tried to engage my suit, or whoever was transmitting to its speaker, in meaningful dialogue, but it was hopeless. I asked a million questions but none was ever answered.

"Where am I?" I'd say.

MOVE FORWARD, the suit would say.

"What is it that you want me to do?" I'd asked, when I wanted to create the illusion that we were communicating like normal people—but I knew that when it replied, telling me where to go or what sort of action I had to perform, it was just issuing a command. If I didn't do as I was told, it would repeat the order once, and then it would use *the whip*.

I always thought of it as *the whip*, although I guess it must have been some kind of electrical device to stimulate the pain centre in my brain. Whatever it was, I learned very quickly to do as I was told without any undue delay.

When I say that I was gone maybe ten or a hundred years, I don't mean that I was conscious of working thousands or tens of thousands of shifts. My best guess is that I worked a couple of hundred, maybe ten hours apiece. Allowing for sleep time, that probably means that I was actually on-site for about half a year—but I had to be taken there, you see, and brought back. My guess is that the journeys took a long time. I don't have any idea where we were, but it certainly didn't look like the Earth we know and love. My theory is that when I was taken I was put into some kind of suspended animation chamber, maybe frozen down to within a couple of degrees of absolute zero, so that I could be shipped to another system, maybe ten or twenty light-years away—but that's just a guess. The suit never told me where I was, or why we were doing what we were doing, or why the people who needed to get it done had to raid a dozen or a hundred different worlds to get their slave labor when they could have got the whole crew from just one.

That's all it was: just slave labor, sheer drudgery. Most of you might have been taken because the aliens wanted to study you, or extract something precious from your biochemistry, or whatever, but they only wanted me for the strength of my arms. They didn't even want me to do any plumbing. Maybe they also wanted my patience, and picked me because I was the kind of person who could be patient, laboring in poor light, all alone.

Not many people could have gone through what I went through, I suspect, without going completely crazy from the isolation. I'm not claiming to be absolutely sane myself, but I'm not claiming, either, that any difficulty I might have in forming relationships of late is due to having being sentenced to six months to a year of hard labor on another world, without ever being able to exchange two meaningful words with another living soul. All I'm saying is that I came through it in better shape than some people would have. I did my time. I survived.

Sorry, I'm rambling a bit. What you want to know is what the place was like and what I had to do there.

Well, it wasn't what you might call a picturesque environment, but it could have been worse. The planetary surface was very uneven—a mess of crags and ditches—but there weren't many sharp edges. It was mostly rock, in various shades of grey, with a liberal topping of white ice, but there were streaks and splashes of rust-red color. In addition to that, there were the plants, which were almost all silver while they were closed, although the colored edges of their folded-up petals often showed through in streaks and whorls. There didn't seem to be any liquids on the surface, but it was obvious that it hadn't always been that way. All the ice must once have been liquid, and there must have been wind and rain to erode the rocks and hollow out rivers—but that must have been a long time before. Now, everything was still and fixed and seemingly dead—except for the plants and a few very tiny things that could scuttle or wriggle around in the hollows and crannies.

The plants weren't numerous enough to form clumps, let alone forests. Sometimes I had to walk fifteen or twenty miles in the course of a shift to collect enough to fill a hamper. They weren't so rare, though, that I ever failed to get my quota, even when the elevator took me to one of the less promising outlets and the directions the suit gave me took me into barren territory.

By day, the plants opened up, unfolding their leaves to catch the sunlight. For that reason, we worked mainly at night, when they closed themselves up into ovoids or warped cubes. They weren't easy to gather even then, because their stems were hard to break, but they were brittle enough to snap if you chopped them hard enough in exactly the right spot. There was a knack to it, which was one of the few things the suits couldn't communicate directly. Whoever was controlling the whip had to be lenient for a week or two while I got the hang of it. Eventually, though, it got so I could crack the stems first time, without causing any supplementary damage.

Mostly, I used a tool that was like a cross between a sickle and a crowbar. Occasionally, I was given something different for another job, but most of us—the slaves, that is—were schooled in the use of a single implement. The ones who worked down below had a variety of different ones, including some that looked far more suited to a plumber's specialist skills, but those of us trained for surface work didn't do much else but gather plants.

Most of the plants were structured like angular lettuces, with lots of layers of leaves, but the leaves were more like metal than flesh—flexible, the way a spring is flexible, but not soft. Whatever color they wore on the surfaces that caught the light, the undersides of the leaves were always paler and shinier, which is why they looked silvery when they were furled up. The light-gathering surfaces had a mat finish; some were so dark as to be literally black, but most were dark red or dark green. Blues and purples were uncommon, but not unknown. Sometimes you'd find a mixture of colors in a single specimen, just as you'd occasionally find a more complex shape, but most of them were all one color, variegated in slightly differing shades, and fairly symmetrical in shape. When we worked by day, while the petals were fully opened, the suit would usually instruct me to look for specimens of a particular shape or color, which would have been harder to spot by night, but it didn't seem to me that the aliens counted any of them more precious than the rest. I think they were just trying to make sure that they got a more-or-less balanced selection down below.

Down below is where we sent or took our harvests when we'd filled our hampers. That was what the whole operation was about: taking plants from the surface into caverns deep beneath the surface, through artificial shafts. There were shafts designed to carry elevators and trains as well as pedestrian traffic, and shafts packed with all manner of machines deeper down. Down below, most of the work was done by machines, although the aliens still needed slaves with hands and legs to undertake trickier tasks and trickier journeys.

I didn't spend much time down below—three shifts out of four I didn't spend any time at all there except for the journeys from and to the dormitory—so I'm sure that I only got to see a tiny fraction of the aliens' below-surface operations, but I saw enough to be sure that they were re-settling the plants in crop-fields a long way beneath the surface, near enough to the core of the planet for me to be able to sense a difference in gravity. The caverns were artificially lit, but they seemed to require hundreds of glaring electric bulbs to provide the kind of energy that was provided on the surface by the sun.

Why were the aliens doing it? Well, they certainly didn't see fit to tell me, but I eventually figured it out, with the aid of the plants.

The plants didn't talk back when I talked to them any more than the aliens did, and I can't even say for sure whether they had thoughts as well as feelings, but I'm perfectly sure about the feelings. I didn't imagine them.

It wouldn't have been surprising, I suppose, if I had started having delusions born of isolation, but I didn't invent the plants' feelings, or my growing sensitivity to them. It didn't happen immediately, but I hadn't been laboring all that long when I first began to realize that I could sense the plants' pain when their stems were broken, just as surely as I could sense the lighter gravity when I was down in the caverns. Once I was convinced that it *was* their pain that I was feeling—which felt quite different from the pain of the whip, even though I knew that it was the same *to them*—I began to sense their other feelings too. I never sensed a thought—not, at any rate, any thought that I could translate into words—but that only helped to convince me that my sensitivity was real. If it had been a delusion conjured up in answer to loneliness, I'd surely have imagined that they could talk to me as well as communicate their feelings.

There wasn't any significant difference, so far as I could tell, between the way the plants felt pain and the way I felt it, even though their pain didn't feel the same to me as my own pain did. I guess pain doesn't vary much from one species to another—not, at least, the kind of pain that's associated with a sharp break. The other feelings did differ, though, not just from my feelings but between plants of different shapes and different colors. I can't say that I could identify all the feelings, but I could feel the differences between them.

I translated those differences into shades of human feeling, although I'm pretty sure that plant feelings must be different from human feelings. Pain must be pain, whoever and whatever you are, but all the other emotions entities can feel must surely be different. Not that I'm saying that plants don't love one another, you understand, or don't feel fear and anxiety and regret—but I figure that plant love is likely to be markedly different in kind and texture from human love, and plant anxiety from human anxiety. I figure, too, that there must be some plant emotions that are utterly alien to human sensation, and vice versa. I translated their feelings into human love, anxiety and so on, because that was the only vocabulary of emotion I had, but I'm pretty sure that there were differences and distinctions that I couldn't catch, which didn't apply to pain in anything like the same degree.

If the familiar plants that surround us—Wiltshire plants, I mean—were able to feel, they'd probably feel just as differently from those alien plants as they would from us. Most of the plants we know disperse their pollen on atmospheric winds, or employ insect vectors, which rely on that same atmosphere to sustain their flight. Their fertilized seeds likewise tend to rely on the movement of wind, water or animals to discover and reach new places in which to grow. All their sensuality must be bound up in those processes, reflective of their particular uncertainties. On that alien world there was no wind to speak of and very little in the way of animal life, none of which could fly; that world's plants had to use different methods to introduce their pollen to one another and dispatch their seeds to colonize new ground.

On the inhospitable surface of that terrible world, the plants had to be far more ingenious than the flora of Wiltshire to secure their own fortunes. The only vectors they could employ were creatures that walked or wriggled, and the essential unreliability of the native animal life was reflected in the fact that many native plants produced pollen and seeds that were capable of doing their own wriggling and walking. The entities themselves were mostly too small to be seen with the naked eye—let alone eyes that were trapped inside a space-suit's helmet, peering through a thick visor—but the feelings associated with those entities were different. Once I was empathically tuned in, I could sense that whole aspect of their experience.

The empathy in question wasn't *my* talent, of course—try as I might, now that I'm back on home ground, I can't get more than the faintest emanation of plant sensibility—but the alien plants must have been powerful empathic transmitters. Obviously, they needed that ability for some existential reason of their own that our plants haven't yet discovered. Maybe some day, in the distant future, when Earthly plants become sentient and intelligent, they'll be powerful empaths too—but as yet, they aren't.

I really needed that empathy, while I was so far away from home, working as a slave, even though the extent to which I had it was so pathetically limited. I suppose that I was no more than an eavesdropper on the plants' emotional intercourse, but I needed that murmur of emotional gossip. It wouldn't be correct to call it music, but what it did to me inside was something akin to what music can do. Music, you see, is the nearest thing to a method of empathic broadcasting that humans have yet devised, and there's a sense in which the sum of all the empathic broadcasts on the surface of that weird world added up to a kind of orchestral harmony. Maybe that's what people are trying to signify when they talk about the harmony of the spheres, although I don't know how they'd know about it, because there isn't any harmony in any sphere near here, at present.

I don't actually *need* that kind of empathy now, of course—not *here*—but I miss it anyway. Maybe, if I had it still, I'd be a slightly better and happier person than I actually am. I listen to music all the time, but it's not the same—just an echo, too blurred even to be thought of as distant. I guess the empathic broadcasts of alien worlds don't reach as far as Earth—or haven't yet. If they only travel at the speed of light, maybe they will, eventually.

If I could only sense the feelings of Earthly plants...but if Earthly plants have feelings, they don't have the same ability to transmit those feelings that the plants of that other world have...or *had*....

Sorry, I'm getting confused again. I must try to keep things in better order. What you want to know next, I suppose, is what the empathic sensations eventually added up to. What was it that I learned to feel as I went about my work on the surface and made occasional trips into the depths? What translation did I make of the plants' sensibility and sensuality?

For a start, they were sad. Sadness was the backcloth, or the subsoil, of the plants' emotional experience; it touched everything else they felt, including their joy and their ecstasy—and they did, occasionally, have moments of joy and ecstasy, although my presence as a not-so-grim reaper inevitably inhibited them in that respect.

I thought at first that it might be my reaping work that was generating the sadness—that what was making them feel sad was the fact that some huge clodhopping alien in a rubber suit was coming to chop them off at the stem and carry them off into the bowels of the planet—but I realized soon enough that I was wrong. Once the fear of anticipation and the pain of the actual severance had come and gone, they weren't unduly disturbed to be stuck in the hamper or dispatched into the core of the planet. They didn't seem to dislike the beds to which they were transplanted, set down so that they could generate new roots. Indeed, once they began to put down their new roots, they began to feel what I translated as gratitude as well as contentment...but all permanently tinged with sadness.

My second thought was that maybe they were sad on my be-half—that they were receiving and reflecting, perhaps in amplified fashion, my own feelings as a slave laborer light-years away from home—but that was just narcissism on my part. They probably could sense my feelings, more easily and more accurately that I could sense theirs, but they were no mere echo-chambers. The sadness was theirs, and theirs alone, even though I could sense it too. It was a regretful and fatalistic kind of sadness—the kind of sadness that relates to a long life-history rather than ephemeral events.

They weren't short-lived, those plants—I think they probably lived for tens of thousands of years—but there was something in their sadness that went beyond mere individualism, even on that sort of time-scale. Theirs was the mournfulness of something vast and enduring; their equivalent of Earth's Gaia was much more coherent than Earth's, and much more stable. Theirs was the sadness of some-thing close to eternity, something that felt with a depth that I could hardly begin to contemplate.

Eventually, I figured out that they were sad because their world was dying. I don't just mean that their Gaia-equivalent was *fading away*, because the mass of everything living was gradually and in-exorably diminishing following the drastic thinning of its atmos-phere and the drastic cooling of its surface. I mean that it was ap-proaching some kind of apocalyptic event—something that would finish off what remained of life on the surface at a single brutal stroke, once and for all.

That was the purpose of the whole operation, you see. We slaves had been pressed into service because time was of the es-sence. What we were doing was transplanting living things from the surface into deep artificial caverns, in the hope that they might be able to survive the coming catastrophe. What we were doing was assisting in the construction of some kind of ultimate storm-shelter or nuclear bunker. The alien slave-masters weren't native to the world, of course, any more than we were: they were on an *errand of mercy*, trying to save that world's Gaia-equivalent from extinction, to win it a few thousand million further years of existence, and of feeling, if not of thought.

That's why the sadness on which I eavesdropped was such a special kind of sadness, alleviated but never wholly displaced by so many other strains of emotional music. I don't know why the aliens didn't explain that to us, rather than just working us as slaves; maybe they'd tried asking for volunteers and got nowhere, and had decided in desperation that the end justified the means. At least they didn't work us to death. They must have driven a lot of us crazy, but they sent us home again when we'd done our bit, not much older or worn-out than when they'd first picked us up.

I don't know for sure, because I could only sense feelings, not thoughts, but I think the planet's sun was due to explode, or at least undergo some dramatic metamorphosis, into a white dwarf or a red giant. What the plants were sad about was the impending end of life on the surface—life that had been around for billions of years. Set against that background of sadness, though, they had an awareness that there was still a good chance that life would go on, deep inside the world, insulated from all outer effects by miles and miles of solid rock, for hundreds of millions of years more. It wouldn't be the same—how could it be?—and it would only postpone the inevitable ultimate end, but it was something.

The plants couldn't have survived on their own. There were no native life-forms capable of hollowing out caverns miles beneath the surface, and lighting them with the aid of thermal energy radiating from the molten core. Maybe there never had been, or maybe they'd died out, or maybe they'd simply gone away. Maybe—just maybe— it was the remote descendants of earlier natives that had come back on their errand of mercy, bringing their legions of slaves to do the drudge-work that they weren't prepared to do themselves.

I knew full well that I'd never have gone if they'd asked me. I knew full well that I'd have been terrified of the prospect, and that I'd have hated the work, even though I'm just a plumber here. I can't even say, with my hand on my heart, that I'm glad that I went. I certainly didn't enjoy it while I was there. It was hard, thankless, and unutterably boring...and yet, I don't think the time was wasted. I wouldn't do it again, but I'm not sorry that I did it once. I learned a new kind of sadness, with all manner of subtle qualifications, and I think I'm a little richer for that, and maybe a little less sad myself than I otherwise might have been.

I haven't made a great success of my life, I suppose, but that's not because of anything the aliens did to me, and I'm certainly no worse off than I would have been if I'd never been taken. I know now, though, that any sadness I might have felt—might still feel— about not having made a great success of my life, isn't a big deal, compared with the kind of sadness that the consciousness of a whole world might feel, confronted by a sun about to explode, even while knowing that it's not alone, and that it might have a little time yet, thanks to the kindness and courtesy of strangers.

It wasn't just the sadness, though, and I don't want to leave you with the impression that it was. I don't know what to call the other thing, or how to give an impression of it, but there *was* something else that was almost ever-present in the emotions of the plants: a kind of *desire*. I don't mean the kind of desire that's associated with everyday propagation and reproduction—the longing to pollinate and be pollinated, the yearning that every adult organism has to produce fruitful seed, and the yearning that every fruitful seed has to grow into an adult. They had all that, of course, with all its petty delights and disappointments, all its petty jealousies and triumphs, all its petty fantasies and releases...but they had something else, something more.

They had, I think, a sense of their own *becoming*, not in the individual sense that we have, but in a grander sense that applied to their whole community, if not to their whole Gaia-equivalent. I suppose that some such hyperconsciousness must be a natural corollary of empathic communication. At any rate, they had some sense of where they were bound...or, at least, where they were *aiming* for. It would be wrong to say that it was what they *wanted*, or even that it was a condition they would settle for, if only it were practicable, but it was something of which they dreamed, something that attracted them.

They dreamed of being stone. They dreamed of being a kind of matter that they were not—a kind of matter invulnerable to the fate that awaited them. They dreamed of being free from the threat of death.

They knew, if they knew anything at all, that it was impossible. They knew, if they knew anything at all, that they couldn't undergo that kind of metamorphosis, even to escape the destruction or transmogrification of their sun. They were more metallic by far than the kinds of plants we know, but they were still organic in their innermost being, and couldn't turn to stone by means of any other process than petrifaction, which is itself a kind of death.

Even if they weren't the kinds of creatures who could think and know, they *felt* the impossibility of their dream—that I know, because I felt it too, and I *am* the kind of creature who can think and feel, even though I'm only a plumber and haven't made a great success of my life. I felt the impossibility of their dream, but I also felt its attraction, its seduction, its tantalization. Maybe, at the end of the day, it was just another shade or facet of their sadness, or maybe a shade or facet of their anxiety, but I don't think so, I think it was something different, something better.

I couldn't bring it back, of course, any more than I could bring back their particular kind of sadness. I do remember it, though, as more than just the knowledge that something once happened to me, more than just a mere matter of fact. I don't think about it much while I'm at work—which, God knows, isn't slave labor, no matter how tedious it sometimes seems—but when I'm at home, on my own, thinking and feeling that it really might be nice to have someone to talk to, I put some music on, and I listen...and, in the nicest possible way, I dream about turning to stone.

You might think that if you were to dream that, it would seem like a nightmare, and maybe you're right. I can't speak for you—but I *can* speak for those alien plants, on that alien world, somewhere in the lonely depths of space. I can assure you, on their behalf and on mine, that it isn't a nightmare at all the way *we* dream it. Maybe it's more than a little sad, but it's a good kind of sadness. It's comforting—more comfortable in their way of feeling, and mine, than any idea of heavenly bliss could ever be.

When the lights finally go out in their underworld, because the core of their planet has cooled, and the outer surface has been sterilized by the explosion of their sun, they'll still be dreaming, impracticably and impossibly, of somehow turning into stone without ceasing to be themselves in the process, or losing the ability to feel their own inwardly-generated and uncannily communicated emotions.

For that reason, if for no other, they still have something to live and die for, and always will.

CHAPTER ELEVEN

HAVING SECOND THOUGHTS

When the meeting broke up, Steve thought that it was only polite to offer Janine a lift home, but she turned him down. That didn't surprise him overmuch, but the reason she gave left him flabbergasted.

"I don't need to trouble you," she said, "Walter's giving me a lift."

Steve hadn't been under any illusion that Walter Wainwright actually lived with Amelia Rockham, even though he still suspected that they must have had some kind of a fling some time in the dim and distant past—doubtless before he had been born, and probably before there'd ever been a Mr. Rockham or a Mrs. Wainwright—but that knowledge had somehow never translated into the idea of Walter Wainwright getting into a car and driving home, let alone the idea that he might offer Janine a lift.

Steve wondered, momentarily, whether he ought to revert to his first impression and reclassify Walter as an old lech, but he couldn't do it. He had seen and heard enough of the old man by now to be certain that Walter's charm was genuine, in spite of its quaintness, and his caring attitude sincere. If Walter was giving Janine lifts to and from AlAbAn meetings, his motives had to be as pure as the driven snow.

Milly wasn't too pleased about Steve making the offer to Janine. "You mustn't rub salt in the wound, Steve," she said, carefully not specifying whose wound she was talking about.

"I just thought she might tell us what she was doing here," Steve said, lamely. If the truth didn't always seem so lame, he thought, he wouldn't be forced to tell so many lies.

"Isn't it obvious?" Milly said, knowing full well that it obviously wasn't.

"Go on, then," Steve said, as he unlocked his own car and opened the driver's door. "Explain it to me."

Milly waited until she'd got into the front passenger seat—Janine's seat, as it had previously been—and buckled her seat-belt before saying: "She wants to hear our stories. She probably intends to keep on coming until she hears them, but she'll get bored eventually if we decide to wait it out. She wants to know why fate brought you and me together, instead of you and her. She wants to know why there's such a powerful bond between us, and why neither of us could ever be happy with anyone else—but she'll never really understand it."

"Oh," Steve said. "Is *that* why?" It hadn't been what he'd expected to hear. He didn't believe for a minute that it was true, or that Milly thought that it was true. He switched the car stereo on as he pulled away from the kerb, but the music didn't start him dreaming of turning to stone. In a way, he thought, it might have been better if it had. He had a sneaking suspicion that there might be a powerful dose of sadness waiting around the corner, which would affect his coming night of passion almost as much as the bleak weeks to come. He tried to put on a brave face, though, for Milly's sake.

"Danny's wrong, of course," he said, "to take it for granted that he was on another planet. He didn't need all that improvisation about suspended animation. He was time-traveling, just like all the others. He just went further downstream than anyone else who's told their story in recent weeks, to a time when the Earth's ecosphere is in decay. He was—will be—moving the essential components of the ecosphere into a safe haven in anticipation of some dramatic cosmic event. The sun won't be a G-type star forever, you see. When it runs short of its basic fuel—hydrogen, that is—its fusion reaction will become more complex, producing heavier elements. There's a critical point at which the whole process will undergo a qualitative change, and the sun will swell up explosively to become a red giant for a while. I think the time-travelers who borrowed Danny were—will be—preparing the Earth's ecosphere to survive that event, in preparation for a new flourish thereafter: a kind of evolutionary Indian summer."

"I thought you were convinced that all our experiences are being produced by the collective unconscious," Milly said. "Just dreams, manufactured in response to contemporary crises."

"Oh, I am," Steve said. "I wasn't speaking literally. Well, in a way, I suppose I was—but I was speaking figuratively as well. Like the rest of us, Danny's involved in the collective unconscious's construction of a mythical future. We live in an age of science, though, so the mythical future has to be responsible—at least to some degree—to what we can now anticipate about the inevitabilities of the actual future. In constructing its delusionary experiences of displacement, the collective consciousness is maintaining as much fidelity as it can to rational plausibility. Danny may be only a plumber, and must have made a mistake in assuming that he was space-traveling rather than time-traveling, but he's obviously in closer touch with the *zeitgeist* than he knows. If the mythical future is to perform its proper function within our imagination, it has to be built on sound foundations. If we're to be effectively consoled as the consciousness of our own immediate extinction becomes more widespread and we pass through the denial phase of our reaction, then we need to know that life will go on, recurring in all its myriad forms no matter what future catastrophes overtake it—even the transfiguration of the sun. I only hope that we can learn to take sufficient consolation from that sort of knowledge before our own eco-catastrophe really puts the screws on. If we can't...."

He stopped, figuring that the train of thought required further reflection before it could be sensibly carried forward. Milly was the kind of girl who read herself to sleep with pop psychology books, though, and she knew well enough which phase followed denial in the typical sequence of reactions to bad news.

"If we can't," she said, "we're going to see anger on an unprecedented scale. If we can't learn to accept our destiny, shrug our shoulders and say *shit happens*, we're going to turn on one another with a kind of savagery the world has never seen before. It might have its entertaining aspects, though, don't you think? Speaking from my own experience, road rage can provide some amusing spectacles, provided that you're not on the immediate receiving end of it. Rage on the Road of Ages, as it approaches the abyss, will certainly be melodramatic."

Steve thought about the abyss in question, but only briefly. "The problem is, he said, "that we will be on the receiving end of it, soon enough if not immediately."

"I know," Milly told him. "But I also know that it's unavoidable. There's nothing anyone can do about it—not even the collective unconscious, armed with a brand new vision of the mythical future. AlAbAn doesn't have that kind of clout, even among its own members. It's relentlessly placid, but you can't imagine for a moment that people like Zoe and Danny have actually solved any of their personal problems by virtue of having had their experiences, let alone that they're now equipped to look forward to the end of the world with equanimity."

"No, I suppose I can't" Steve admitted. "My theory obviously needs further modification. I really do need to sort that out, if I'm to make sense of my own story."

"It doesn't actually have to *make sense*," Milly told him. "Sometimes, stories work better if they don't. A little mystery does no harm."

"*My* story has to make sense to *me*, if I'm to tell it," Steve said. "That's the kind of guy I am."

"You don't really know what kind of person you are, Steve," Milly said. "That's your trouble. You could be happy, you know, if you wanted to be. You could be *contented*. But you always insist on complicating things. You have to learn to let go, Steve. Janine's history, and AlAbAn's just a matter of people telling it like it was, and not worrying overmuch about what it might have meant in some great scheme of things. It's you and me now, and we'd both be better off if you could accept that and make the best of it."

"You might be more contented yourself," Steve riposted, recklessly "if you weren't feeling guiltier with every day that passes about having stolen your best friend's boy-friend and ruined your friendship in the process. But you can't help feeling guilty, and complaining about my lack of contentment is really just a way of regretting your own. You can't help it, any more than I can. I'm really not the only one in this car who suffers from emotional incontinence, am I?"

"If you could be happy, I could be happy," Milly insisted. "It's not your fault, I know. You can't help it—but it really would be better for everyone if you *could* help it. Lord knows, I'm not perfect, but I really do think that I restrain my innate tendency to emotional incontinence a little better than you do. I'm not the one who has phobias so painful that he can't even bear to talk about them."

"I was coping with those," Steve said, "until all this blew up. I was making steady progress. I'll be able to make progress again, in time. It just takes time."

"Of course it does," she replied, in a soothing tone. "That's why I can't bear to see you prolonging your turmoil. If you could just accept things as they are, count your blessings and restore your inner harmony, you'd be able to get on with the work of making yourself a better person, in full control of your fear and lust alike. I'm trying to help you, Steve, but you're not really helping yourself just now."

"No," Steve had to admit, "I'm not. I do need to keep working on that. I'm not like Danny, though—I wouldn't want to turn to stone in order to get away from the pressure. I *like* lust, even though it gets me into trouble sometimes. I like getting carried away occasionally. Obviously, I don't like getting panic attacks, especially when they stop me doing things that other people do routinely, but you were right when you said before that underneath the subjective element of dread, it's just an excitation of the nervous system. I ought to be able to moderate or renegotiate that excitement, if only I could master the trick of it. That's all it requires, really—a trick, a technique. Relaxation can only provide a partial solution, just as repression can only provide a partial explanation, but that doesn't really matter. The point is to find something—anything—that works *for me*. The trouble with self-help manuals and psychological theories is that they have to generalize, while the problems individual people have are often highly idiosyncratic. Advice and therapy can't deal with the *unique*. That's one of the good things about AlAbAn, I think. It allows people to express the uniqueness of their predicaments, the idiosyncratic aspects of their personality that can't be shoehorned into conventional explanations—but it only provides a means of expression. It doesn't provide answers, or practical solutions."

"Draw breath, Steve," Milly said, with a sigh. "You have to stop occasionally to draw breath, or one of your flights of fancy will choke you some day."

"Sorry," Steve said, through gritted teeth.

Milly picked up on his resentment and was instantly repentant. "No," she said, "don't be. I'm a cow. I ought to be pleased that you're able to relax to that extent, to let yourself get carried away. I ought to be pleased that I can lend you an ear, and I ought to try harder to keep up with your runaway trains of thought. I need to do that, don't I, if we're ever to be content with one another, and put the unfortunate origins of our relationship behind us? You're right— I'm as guilty as you are. If this is to work, I need to get a better grip on my own emotional incontinence. I can do that. It's what I'm supposed to be good at—and I'll pause to draw breath now, in case I'm the one who ends up choking on my own cataract of words." She tried to laugh.

Steve tried to copy the laugh, even though it wasn't one of the infectious kind. Outside, it had started to rain. He switched the windscreen wipers on, and their slow rhythmic thrum combined with the beat of the music on the radio to form an exotic and strangely hypnotic alloy.

Relax, Steve instructed himself. *Relax, and let things flow. Give it time, and it will all work out, one way or another. Only give it time, and all the wounds in the world will heal.*

Unfortunately, he couldn't convince himself of that.

* * * * * * *

Steve made yet another appointment to see Sylvia Joyce the following Tuesday. She welcomed him as she always did, glad to have a regular client but slightly frustrated by the fact that she wasn't being permitted to manage his treatment as she wished.

"I gather that it's not going well," she observed, sympathetically, as he slumped down on her couch. Steve sensed a certain smugness behind the commiseration.

"It *was* going very well," he said. "I was much more relaxed at work, and the time seemed ripe to move on from the quotidian to the exceptional, and make some serious inroads into my problem with bridges and heights. Then things went a bit pear-shaped in my love life, and the everyday stress went through the roof again."

"Well, these things happen," Sylvia told him, unnecessarily. "You have to put them behind you and move on. Would you like to tell me what happened?"

"Emotional incontinence," Steve said, curtly. "I was perfectly happy with my girl-friend—*really* happy, for once in my life—but I ended up in bed with someone else. When my girl-friend found out, she dumped me. I'm still with the other girl, Milly, but she suspects that I'd rather be with Janine and she feels guilty because Janine was her friend, so it's hardly an ideal relationship. It's a complete mess, really."

"Are you asking for my advice about that?" Sylvia queried, hopefully.

"No, that's all right," Steve said. "I can call myself a stupid idiot—I don't really need you to do that for me. I know how stupid it is to say that I just *ended up in bed with someone else*, when I know perfectly well that it's something I chose to do, even though I knew it could only lead to disaster, simply because it put an extra notch on my bedhead, another name in my little black book."

"Why did you want to see me today, then?" the therapist asked.

"Because I'm having second thoughts about the regression thing," Steve admitted. "I think I might need to go a bit deeper after all." He tried not to look at Sylvia's broad smile of triumph, but couldn't help it.

"That's excellent," she said. "I really think we might make some progress, if we can get to the real root of the problem."

"I don't think the problem has a *real root*," Steve said, "and I think that's a major aspect of its problematic quality. I think it has an imaginary root—and is, in essence, an imaginary problem."

"Calling it imaginary won't make it go away, Steve. It's a real problem, with a real root."

"Let's not get sidetracked into matters of definition," Steve said. "The point is that I need you to do what you did before, and take me back to the abduction experience. I've tried to do it by myself, but I can't. If you can help me get over that difficulty, it would be useful—if you could make a tape, maybe, that could take me back to it without your actually having to be present."

"I'm not sure that would be a good idea, Steve, even if it could be done. If you're trying to induce panic attacks in yourself, it's probably a good idea to have someone else present. In any case, I'm not sure that the abduction experience is the target we should be aiming for—that's an expression of your problem rather than a causative factor. We need to go further back in time, to your childhood."

"I can see why you're making that assumption, Sylvia," Steve said, "but I have my own ideas about what's going on here, and I'm not so sure that the answer doesn't lie further *forward* in time. You were right about AlAbAn helping me to come to terms with the abduction experience, and I think you're also right to assume that it might help me to tell the story of my experience to the group. In order to do that, though, I need to get a firmer grip on it—to remember more of it, if that's the way you want to put it, although I'm beginning to think that remembering is only part of it, and not the more important part. Either way, I need to revisit it—and for that, it seems, I need your help. So, please will you regress me again, to the point at which I began to freak out last time? I'm sure I can handle it better now—at least, I'll do my very best. It will help. I'm sure of it."

Perversely, Sylvia no longer seemed at all sure that she wanted to regress him again. Perhaps, Steve thought, she didn't like the manner in which her authority was being challenged. She wanted to be the one in charge, not some mere instrument of *his* plan.

"You seem a little confused, Steve," she observed.

"Much more than a little," he said. "But I'm trying to resolve things. I did think, just for a moment or two, that perhaps I didn't need to get to grips with my problems any more. They'd only come to seem urgently inconvenient because I'd started going out with a travel agent, and now the travel agent in question has dumped me because of my affair, the fear of flying and the fear of bridges no longer seem so desperately relevant. Milly might not want to travel far, and even if she does, I might not feel the same pressure to fall in with her wishes. Indeed, the idea that my inability to travel might prove to be a breaking-point in our relationship doesn't seem to be a particularly horrific prospect. I think I could walk away from Milly, provided I had an adequate excuse, far more easily than I could ever have walked away from Janine. On the other hand, I'm well aware that both those arguments show me up as something of a coward, and that it really would be better to get to grips with my phobias, even though the immediate spur is no longer there. I thought of trying Prozac too, but that just seemed to be another form of cowardice. At any rate, I want to try this first." He took a deep breath.

"Your abduction experience can't possibly be the cause of your phobias, Steve," Sylvia reiterated, stubbornly. "It's just another symptom. It would be a mistake to concentrate on it too intently, when we might get a lot closer to the cause by looking further back."

"As I said," Steve told her, doggedly sticking to his guns, "I understand why you would make that assumption, but I think there's another possibility. I need to revisit the abduction experience, if only to prepare myself properly for letting it out at AlAbAn, and obtaining the kind of support that Walter Wainwright and his cronies can provide."

"That might be a step in the right direction," Sylvia conceded. "You approve of AlAbAn, then? You really are getting some benefit from it?"

Figuring that the therapist' office was one place that he didn't have to observe the AlAbAn code of practice, Steve felt free to cut loose "They're all totally crazy, of course," he said. "Every last one of them is deluded as to the nature and significance of their experiences. But yes, I do approve of AlAbAn, and yes, I really am getting some benefit out of the meetings."

"I don't understand," Sylvia confessed.

"Yes, you do," Steve said. "You know perfectly well that none of them has actually been abducted by aliens, any more than you or I have. Their experiences are products of their unconscious minds, which concoct and conjure up their supposed experiences in response to some inner tension, failing or yearning. All so-called experiences that come up by that sort of route, with or without the assistance of hypnosis—all the buried memories of child-abuse, all the past lives, and so on—are eruptions of raw dream-stuff that our unconscious minds shape into hollow imitations of real experience. You know that, but you also know that the experiences are no less valuable because of it. You know that it's a good thing—a healthy thing, in its way—and that people really can get some benefit from it, in terms of self-knowledge and self-understanding. That's why you sent me to AlAbAn in the first place, and that's why I'm here now, wanting your help to make the most of the opportunity"

"I keep an open mind about the reality of all my clients' experiences," Sylvia told him, sternly. "I don't pass arbitrary judgments of the sort you just did."

"They have the same policy at AlAbAn," Steve said. "I can see the point of that, too, just as I can understand why it's so very difficult for me simply to dump Milly and go to Janine on bended knees, pleading for her to take me back. I'm even beginning to understand, I think, why I have so much difficulty walking or driving across bridges, even when I want or need to get to the other side. But that's the sort of crap I need to cut, the sort of confusion I need to clarify. I need to see the AlAbAn stories for what they really are, and my own story for what *it* really is. That's why I have to go back to it. Are you going to help me or not—we haven't much time left, if we're going to do it today?"

Sylvia opened her mouth, probably to say that perhaps it might be better to leave the regression until the following week, when more time would be available—but she thought better of it. She closed her mouth again, paused for thought, then said: "If that's what you want, I'm prepared to try it."

Without any further ado, she began her relaxation routine. Steve fell in with it readily enough, obeying all her softly-spoken but imperious instructions. He wasn't entirely sure that he would be able to recover the false memory, even with Sylvia's help, now that he was so determined in his conception of its falsehood, but he figured that such adventures in fantasy might require two participants, just like the other adventures in fantasy that had landed him in so much trouble.

He relaxed, and gradually drifted off into the altered state of consciousness that some people thought of, rightly or wrongly, as a trance. For a moment or two, he even forgot what it was that he had been trying to do....

Then he was back on the time-ship again, watching the world end, from a situation so very, very high above the dark and dismal planet that it was literally unbearable....

* * * * * * *

ALIEN ABDUCTION, BY BRIAN STABLEFORD * 167

When Steve went round to Milly's flat that night so that she could demonstrate another of her talents by cooking for them both, she was eager to learn the outcome of his session. He had confessed the nature of his phobias to her, and the ways in which they tended to manifest themselves, in order to raise her to another kind of equality with Janine, even before he had told her that he had made an appointment with the hypnotherapist. She was avid to know what progress he had made; it was as if she hoped that the difficulties he and she were experiencing in their relationship might be cleared away with all the rest of his troubles, leaving the two of them secure in serene harmony, utterly content with one another for ever more.

"It wasn't so bad," Steve told her. "I didn't actually turn grey, apparently. Because my carotid arteries didn't tighten up, I didn't faint—it's very difficult to faint when you're lying down, because gravity doesn't hinder the blood-supply to the brain. I did the cold sweat, mind, and the rapid breathing. Sylvia had to make me breathe into a paper bag until the carbon dioxide build-up activated the reflex that sucks more air into the lungs. I felt sick, but I didn't throw up. All in all, pretty average."

"But you did get back aboard the spaceship? You saw whatever terrible thing it was that kicked off the phobic response?"

"Oh yes. I imagined myself back aboard the time-ship, and I looked out of the window. I saw the vertiginous drop. More importantly, I saw what was going on at the other end of it. I also picked up something substantial from a preliminary phase, before the window opened up, so I now have a pretty good idea what happened before the moment of abject terror as well as afterwards. I think I can start to piece it all together now, and I think I can convince myself that the panic wasn't warranted—or was at least excusable as a melodramatic device—because the story has a happy ending. Given time, I think I can get the whole story together for telling at AlAbAn. Not next Thursday, mind...maybe in December. January at the latest. Do you think you might be ready to tell your story by then?"

"Yes," she said. "When you're ready to tell yours, I'll be ready to tell mine. That goes without saying. There's a bond between us— I always knew that. Even before the first time I met you, when Jan told me that she had a boy-friend who wanted to see what an AlAbAn meeting was like and could give me a lift in his car, I knew we'd get on. I know it sounds silly, but I knew that we were fated to be together."

Steve couldn't help remembering the way Sylvia Joyce had taunted him with the quote from *Hamlet*. Milly was trying too hard, as if to convince herself—and when she did that, it was often a prelude to a complete change of mood.

"Is that when you decided to steal me?" Steve asked, keeping his voice neutral. "Before you'd even met me?"

Milly shook her head. "No," she said. "You know I didn't decide any such thing. You know I was just borrowing you, when I got the chance—when Janine gave us the chance. She did *give us the chance*, you know, when she told you to take me to the meeting while she was in Brighton. I think she knew what would happen. Subconsciously, I think she knew that she had to bring us together, because she knew we had a bond. She knew we were right for one another."

"You may be partly right about her giving us the chance," Steve said, soberly. "But she didn't tell me to go to the meeting with you while she was away on her training course because she wanted to see whether I'd cheat on her, and she certainly didn't want me to. She *never* expected us to sleep with one another, because she trusted both of us—you as well as, and as much as, me. What she *did* expect, I think—and what she wanted—was for us to talk to one another, and maybe tell one another our stories. She thought it might help us both, if we could help one another to get our abduction experiences out into the open. She was trying to help us both—you *and* me—because she was our friend. She wanted to help us both move on. She's the kind of person who's very keen on people *moving on*. Why else would she have become a travel agent?"

"There's no point in continuing to take her side, Steve," Milly told him, petulantly. "You're supposed to be on *my* side. I'm your girl-friend now. We have to make this work, or we'll both lose everything."

"We'll do what we have to," Steve said. "We'll tell our stories when we can, and see where it goes from there."

"I suppose I ought to be grateful that you don't want to leap up next Thursday and get it all off your chest," Milly said. "At least we'll be together while you're taking your time—and we'll have that time, too, to make things better. With any luck, Janine will get bored waiting and stop coming to meetings."

Steve wasn't entirely sure, in his own mind, why he needed more time to sort his story out. He couldn't quite see why he couldn't just stand up at the next AlAbAn meeting and tell the assembled crowd what his mind had dredged up, with the aid of Sylvia's prompting, even if they might think that it was a load of unripe bullshit. He was, after all, no stranger to that situation. He was a science teacher in the second best comprehensive in Salisbury, ninety per cent of whose pupils took it for granted that everything teachers said was bullshit, even if they needed to memorize it to get them through their exams. Even so, he really did want to get his story *straight*. He really did want to get it *right*, so that he, at least, would know that it wasn't *entirely* bullshit.

He hoped, although he certainly wasn't going to say so to Milly, that Janine would have the patience to stick around until then. He knew that his story wouldn't help her to understand his betrayal of her trust, let alone encourage her to forgive it, but he still wanted her to hear it, when it was complete. He wanted her to have that unique insight into his dreams, anxieties and hopes, and into the mythical future to which they were both party, even though they were apart.

For all these tangled reasons, when Walter Wainwright called for volunteers at the following Thursday's AlAbAn meeting, Steve and Milly stayed glued to the seat of the antique Naugahyde settee, feeling the pressure of Janine' gaze even though she was conspicuously ignoring them, while some doddering old man Steve had never seen before—who introduced himself as "Neville"—got up to tell a tale that he had obviously told before, maybe a dozen times over.

CHAPTER TWELVE

A PASSION FOR PRINT

I haven't been to group in quite some time and I don't see any familiar faces—except, of course, for Amelia and Walter. That's reassuring, in a way, because it gives me reason to hope that I won't be boring anyone too much—except, of course, for poor Amelia and Walter. I suspect that I've been a bit of a bore all my life—my late wife, Jenny, told me often enough that I wasn't the brightest spark in the fire—but I don't mean to be and I don't relish the reputation, so I hope that the younger people here will be able to find something in my story that's a little bit interesting, even though it isn't nearly as melodramatic as some of the tales you'll have heard.

There was nothing unusual about the way I was taken, except that I was taken from my car rather than my bedroom. This was way back in the early 1960s, so I was still in my early twenties—it was seven years before I met Jenny—and I'd only just got my driving license after finishing teacher training and getting my first proper job teaching general science at a grammar school in Warminster. I didn't really have any need to be out so late, but I liked driving in the dark, when the roads were quiet, so I was doing it for its own sake rather than having any pressing need to get from A to B. I don't remember parking, but the car was safely parked when the aliens put me back into it, so I suppose they must have had some way of hypnotizing me into pulling over, putting the handbrake on and switching the engine off before I got out of the car and stepped into the tractor beam.

I don't know how long I was on the ship, and I only have brief flashbacks to tell me what they did to me there. I remember them lifting my eyeballs out of their sockets, one by one, and placing them on my cheeks while they ran needles into my optic nerves and my cerebral cortex, but I suppose that's the sort of thing that's bound to stick in one's memory, even when lesser events dissolve into forgetfulness. It sounds horrible, I know, but even though I wasn't under a general anesthetic I couldn't feel any pain or any horror; it's only in retrospect that the thought of it makes me wince.

I doubt that I was on the operating table for much longer than a couple of hours, and I doubt that I spent more than twelve hours on the ship in total. When I woke up in my car I'd only been gone twenty minutes, so I naturally assumed, at first, that I'd fallen asleep at the wheel and dreamed the whole thing—it wasn't until I started attending AlAbAn meetings that I realized how easy it is for the aliens to play tricks with time.

I drove home, at least half-convinced that I'd had a dream, perfectly prepared to forget the whole thing. Lots of people do, according to Walter—but they're the ones who can just get on with their lives as if nothing at all had happened. I wasn't able to do that. My life had changed completely, although it took a few days for me to realize that fact, and much longer than that for me to figure out why.

The next day, as soon as school was over, I drove to the central library in Salisbury. I went into the reference section, pulled half a dozen books off the shelves, sat down and began to read.

When I say "read", though, I don't actually mean *read*. What I actually did was turn the pages and look at each one in turn. I took time to do it—I actually scanned the pages rather than merely glancing at them, maybe for three or four seconds each—but I didn't actually register anything consciously. I was just about aware of what it was that I was reading, in the sense that I knew whether it was algebra, poetry or some sportsman's biography, but I only got the vaguest impression of the content. I was turning the pages too quickly; my brain couldn't take in the information at that sort of pace. I couldn't slow down, though, any more than I could stop. I didn't leave the library until it closed at eight-thirty, by which time I was tired and starving.

I had to catch up with my marking the next day, but that only took an hour or so. Back in those days we didn't have anything like the kind of paperwork to cope with that teachers have nowadays, so there were no lesson-plans to prepare or any nonsense of that sort. By five-thirty I was back in the library, and I didn't leave until it closed. On Saturday I was in there all day, and I spent Sunday being very grateful that the library didn't open on Sundays.

I knew something was wrong with me, of course, but I jumped to the conclusion that I had suddenly developed an obsessive-compulsive personality disorder. I tried to book an appointment with a psychiatrist, but with school and my library work there wasn't a suitable gap in my calendar, so I had to try to tackle it myself. I tried to stop myself going to the library. I tried to stop myself turning the pages at that hideously metronomic pace. I tried to pick out books that I wanted to read instead of the ones to which I was drawn. In every instance, I felt sick—not nauseous in the strict sense that I wanted to vomit, but just plain *horrid*. After a week or so of fighting it, I gave in. I was distressed and depressed, and my work at school was beginning to suffer, but I couldn't let up. I was trapped.

And that's when I met Amelia for the first time.

She wasn't Amelia Rockham in those days; she was still Amelia Jennings. She was a little younger than me, but she'd qualified as a librarian at exactly the same time as I'd qualified as a teacher, and the junior position at the central library was her first job. I'd noticed her, of course, on my way in and out, and sometimes from the corner of my eye while I was working, and I'd seen the puzzled way she'd looked at me—which was understandable, given that I must have seemed a total madman. When she came over and sat down in the chair at seven forty-five on a quiet Monday evening I nearly broke out into a cold sweat for dread of what she might say.

"You seem to have quite a passion for print," she observed.

I think I managed to mutter "Yes." I was in the grip of a passion all right, but I wasn't sure that print was the target of it, or that the passion was really *mine* in the strictest sense of the word.

"I won't disturb you, then," she said. "I just wanted to thank you."

I couldn't look up, but I managed to say "Why's that?" without stammering.

"You always put the books back in the right places," she said. "No matter how many you pile up when you come in, you always put them back exactly where they came from."

"It's no trouble," I assured her.

"I thought at first you were studying to go on some TV quiz show," she said, "or maybe that you were some kind of performer, like the Memory Man in that old Hitchcock film—*The Thirty-Nine Steps*, I think it was—but you're a teacher, aren't you, over at Warminster Grammar?"

"How did you know that?" I asked, still not looking up.

"Pupils get around," she said. "Some of them even come into libraries occasionally. I don't mean to be presumptuous, but it occurred to me that you might find this helpful, if your passion for print will allow it."

She got up and went away then, but she left a little piece of paper on the table with an address, a day and a time written on it. I suppose I should have spoken to her again as I left but I was too embarrassed to do anything but nod. She smiled, but didn't say anything.

There was no AlAbAn in those days, but there were meetings of self-styled UFO investigators—including, luckily for me, meetings that took place after eight o'clock in the evening. The piece of paper Amelia had given me was the time and place of such a meeting, hosted by someone named Walter Wainwright.

My first impulse was to feel insulted, and to avoid it like the plague—but in the end, I went to the meeting. Amelia was there, of course—and to tell you the truth, that was the only reason I stayed, and certainly the only reason I went back the following week. That was odd, in a way, because she didn't say much more to me than *hello* on either occasion, and certainly didn't give any outward sign that she was attracted to me. I suppose I was just being optimistic, or just appreciating the fact that I was somewhere other than the library or school. However paradoxical it might sound, I felt *safe*, simply because I was among strangers, with nothing at stake if they found out about my obsessive-compulsive disorder.

I didn't feel safe at school. I'd begun to take my lunch-breaks in the school library, eating sandwiches while scanning pages, and rumors had begun to circulate there about my *unnatural* passion for print.

All the talk at the UFO investigation meetings was about sightings and newspaper reports—there was nothing about abductions in those days. I thought the people in the group were just exotic train-spotters. I didn't really have an opinion on the stuff they were talking about, even though I was working in Warminster, not far from Cley Hill, where a lot of the sightings had been made. I didn't really care one way or the other. All the speculation about what the riders of the alien spaceships might want with us, and why they didn't just land their flying saucers outside the Houses of Parliament and ask to see Harold Macmillan, seemed like so much hot air—but it was comfortable hot air, and I was content to drink it in while hoping to catch Amelia's eye, hoping that she might smile at me again, hoping that she might make the move that would take our relationship to some further stage.

I couldn't make any sort of move myself, of course, because I was too embarrassed about being crazy. I was probably a fool to think that she might, given that every time she was on shift while I was in the library it must have seemed to her that I was deliberately ignoring her, putting her in second place behind my absurd passion for print

It was at the fifth investigators' group meeting I attended that Amelia made a move of sorts, but it wasn't at all what I'd expected. It was during a run-of-the-mill discussion about what the UFO people might want, when she suddenly piped up. She didn't even glance in my direction, but I knew that she was really talking to me and not to the others.

"They're studying us," she said. "They've come here to find out what we're all about. Maybe they'll make contact eventually, and maybe they won't, but they want to find out everything they can before they even think about doing that. They're not going to be able to do it just by watching us, of course, or by monitoring our radio and TV broadcasts. They need more detail and more depth. They need to study our books, our libraries. They can't just turn up in a library themselves, of course—but what they could do, if they were clever enough, would be to recruit humans so serve as their eyes, to do their reading for them.

"They'd need more than eyes, mind; they'd also need brains to interpret what the eyes see, though not necessarily consciously. They'd need to plant their bugs in the cerebral cortex as well as the optic nerves—but they wouldn't need all that many surrogate observers, provided that they were willing to take their time with the project: two or three in Britain, maybe, the same in France and Germany, half a dozen in America, Russia and China. There are a lot of books in the world, but they wouldn't have to read them all, and the more they read the more they'd be able to refine their search. A few dozen people working for a couple of years—five at the most—would enable them to learn pretty much all that they'd need to know about the human race."

There were objections, of course, and questions, and further elaborations of the hypothesis—that was the kind of group it was—but I virtually stopped listening when Amelia finished speaking, because I knew that she was right. I knew that she'd guessed what had been done to me, just by watching me night after night, plowing through all those books without really being conscious of what I was reading. Because she was a member of Walter's group as well as a librarian, she'd been able to deduce what had happened to me, and she'd wanted to let me know, to reassure me that I wasn't mad. She'd even taken the trouble to try to reassure me that it would probably be a temporary thing, and that I'd eventually get to the end of it, and come out the other side.

She didn't expect me to say anything to the meeting, and I didn't. When I offered to drive her home afterwards she refused, explaining politely that one of the others always gave her a lift. She said she'd see me at the library the next day—as, of course, she did, although we weren't able to have much of a conversation. I did try to talk to her after closing time, on that occasion. I even plucked up enough courage to ask her to go for a drink with me, but she had other things to do. I figured out pretty quickly that there wasn't any chance of establishing an intimate relationship with her—not any longer, at any rate—but that only made it all the more remarkable that she'd reached out a helping hand, to let me know what I needed to know and to help me remember what I needed to remember.

That was when I accepted that it hadn't been a dream, that night in the car, and that I really had been appropriated and adapted by the UFO people as an instrument for the absorption of human knowledge...and human folly too. I wasn't just reading encyclopedias and textbooks, you see—I was reading all kinds of stuff. The only thing they let strictly alone was the fiction section. I read literary criticism and I read poetry, but I didn't read novels of any sort, let alone science fiction. I guess the bugs they'd planted in two dozen exemplary human brains could tell them everything about human character they might have learned from Henry James and Virginia Woolf, and more. They certainly didn't need any education when it came to aliens and spaceships.

I suppose I had fallen in love with Amelia, after a fashion, even though there wasn't really any present in our relationship, let alone any future—but I was young, and those sorts of things pass, even for people who aren't bogged down in obsessive-compulsive disorders. Nowadays, I suppose, if I'd turned up at her library every day except Sunday, and gone along to her UFO-group meetings once a fortnight, people might have accused me of stalking her, but we didn't have stalkers back in the sixties, so nobody said anything derogatory about that particular aspect of my passion.

Once I knew what was happening to me, the reading business became a little less distressing, although it didn't get any less burdensome. Although the aliens allowed me time to do my job, they weren't overly concerned about how well I did it; although I scraped by, it was obvious to me, the head and all my colleagues, that scraping by was what I was doing.

I often wondered how much better I might have been as a teacher if I hadn't labored under that crippling handicap during the crucial formative years of my career. Sometimes I think that I could have been really good, really successful—but I didn't have the chance. I didn't lose my job, but I didn't make progress either. In the end, I had to leave the grammar because I knew that everyone else knew that I wasn't as good as I ought to be, and wasn't making any progress. I ended up in one of the new so-called comprehensives in Swindon, although I always thought of it was a jumped-up secondary modern, where second-rate teachers were perennially engaged in the hopeless task of trying to teach third-rate kids the exact extent of their hopelessness. The aliens had let me go by then, but...that's not what concerns us here at AlAbAn, is it? What you want to hear is what I learned about the aliens while they had me under their spell: what I deduced about the nature and purpose of their enquiry.

First of all, I think I can say with a reasonable degree of certainty that they didn't see eye to eye with one another. They were in competition, even conflict. I could tell, by the way they made me take the books off the shelves and put them in order for reading, that I was following several different agendas simultaneously, all of them bidding for priority within the limited time available. I must have been like the radio telescope at Jodrell Bank, with dozens of different astronomers trying to book time on me, wanting to point me in a hundred different directions to study different phenomena—pulsars, quasars, supernovas and so on. It wasn't just the fact that there were different academic specialists among the alien scientists, but that the different specialists all thought that their route to understanding was the best one and deserved greater priority. You get the same thing in schools, where teachers in different subjects each think that their own subject gives a special insight into the working of the universe or the human mind—at least, you get that in grammar schools, where the teachers actually pretend to care....

Secondly—although this is more tentative, as well as weirder—I think they have a mathematics and a physics that are different in kind from ours. That may not make sense, but maybe the fact that it doesn't make sense says more about the limitations of the human imagination than we'd probably like to believe. At any rate, for as long as they were using me, the aliens kept making me pick out textbooks in pure and applied maths, and they can't just have been measuring the extent of our progress. If what we know about maths and physics were mere objective knowledge—a simple recognition of the way logic works and the way the universe is put together—they could have found out how far we'd got by looking at a handful of textbooks. The fact that I had to keep on looking at more and more books of that sort suggests to me that there was a puzzle there: that there was something distinctively human about our maths and our physics, with which the aliens had trouble getting to grips. I suspect that it wasn't just simpler than theirs but qualitatively different, maybe because their senses reveal things to them that ours don't.

Thirdly, I think they have a particular fascination with human games and sports. Again, you might think that reading a few rule-books would tell them all they needed to know, and that a couple of journalistic accounts and autobiographies would have filled in the psychological margin easily enough. In fact, I read almost as many books about games and sports as I did about chemistry, biology, politics and war—not just one edition of Wisden or Timeform's *Racehorses of the Year*, but twenty, not just one biography of a chess grandmaster or one guide-book to playing poker, but dozens. Is that, I wonder, because they're games and sports fanatics them-selves, or because they don't play games and sports at all? I don't know exactly what interest they have in that aspect of our experi-ence, but it's considerable—and maybe it makes their total lack of interest in fiction even more remarkable.

I might, of course, have been a specialist instrument. Maybe I just happened to be the reader assigned to maths and sports, while there was some other poor soul sitting in a library in Manchester or Edinburgh who was spending his entire time reading Mickey Spil-lane, Barbara Cartland and Iris Murdoch, or plowing through end-less histories of the Napoleonic wars and the Third Reich. Who can tell? I tried to ask Amelia, of course, but it was so difficult to get time with her alone. I might have brought it up in the UFO investi-gators' meetings, but I could never bring myself to tell them my story, in case they didn't believe me. Can you imagine what it would have been like to reveal my secrets to a bunch of losers who were considered to be certifiable lunatics by most of their fellows, and have them deride it as madness? Of course you can—and that's why AlAbAn is such a wonderful thing, and why we all owe Walter such a tremendous debt for moving on from that first group, starting up a much more useful one, and keeping it going all these years.

By the time AlAbAn grew out of the ashes of the old UFO-spotters group, of course, the aliens had let me go. They only used me for four years, and then they released me. I don't think they'd found out all they wanted or needed to know, but they released me anyway. I don't think I'd outlived my usefulness, either, although I have to admit that I was a bit of a wreck by then. I don't think they were being kind—but they *were* being reasonable. They figured that I'd done my bit, and was entitled to my freedom. It was someone else's turn to take up the burden of an empty passion for print.

I remember going to the library the first night I didn't have to, not out of habit or because I didn't know what else to do with myself, but because I wanted to see Amelia, I wanted to stand at the issue-desk and look her in the eyes. I wanted her to see me as I really was, free at last from my affliction—and I wanted to thank her properly, for the help she'd given me in getting through it. That was the night I saw the engagement ring on her finger, sparkling in the harsh and unrelenting gleam of the neon striplights.

"I'm better now," I told her. "I won't be coming here any more."

"It won't be the same without you," she replied.

"I *could* come here if I wanted to," I told her. "If I had a reason to come, I could come."

"Have you a reason?" she asked.

"Is that an engagement ring?" I asked.

"Yes it is," she said. "I'm getting married in the spring."

"To Walter Wainwright?" I asked.

"No," she said, "It's not anyone at the UFO group. In fact, my fiancé doesn't entirely approve of the UFO group. I might give that a rest for a while."

"Me too," I said. "It isn't really my sort of thing. They aren't really my kind of people. I'm glad you told me about it, though. It helped me. *You* helped me. I'm very grateful for that."

"You're welcome," she said. "It's a librarian's job to help people with their research. I like to help when I can—and you always put the books back exactly where they came from. There are plenty of people who don't."

I reached out my hand then, and she shook it. I saw her again, of course, now and again, even before AlAbAn was formed, but I never really *saw* her. I never really *took her in*. It was rather like the reading I did while the aliens had me—not just with Amelia but with other people too. I saw them, but I didn't take them in. I didn't register them properly. I didn't *read* them, or get any benefit from them, or react to them in any kind of meaningful way. It wasn't passion I was short of, but I wasn't really capable of owning my passions then. Getting your freedom back is only part of the process of self-liberation, you see—you have to learn to use it. That took some time.

Teaching wasn't a problem—not the kind of teaching I was doing by then, at any rate. Setting up a private life to fill all the time that I was no longer spending in the library was something else. I did manage it in the end, though. I met Jenny; I took possession of my passion; we got married; I met Walter again; I joined AlAbAn; I finally told my story. That was a liberation too, of sorts. As you all know perfectly well, though, you're never entirely free of the aliens once they've had you, even if they haven't planted bugs in your eyes and your brain. Sometimes, you have to tell your story a second time, and a third...and even when you can give the meetings a rest for a while, you can't let them alone forever. Once the aliens have turned you into an obsessive-compulsive personality, you can't help repeating yourself, never letting go of one ritual without taking up another.

I lost my passion for print, mind. That was one passion I didn't manage to turn into a possession or begin to master. In fact, I developed something of an allergy to text—not a physical allergy, like hay fever, but a mental allergy, a kind of late-onset dyslexia. I don't mean that I couldn't read; I could read perfectly well when I had to, but the only reading I could do was *functional* reading. I could look things up when I needed to, read forms and street-signs and mark the kids' work, but I couldn't read for the sake of *interest*. I couldn't read fiction, or biographies, or maths and science books, and I certainly couldn't read anything remotely to do with sports and games. I couldn't concentrate. I couldn't take the meaning in. It made me feel sick—not in the sense that I wanted to vomit, but in the sense that my flesh would rebel against the dominion of my mind.

Jenny could never accuse me of having a passion for print. Throughout our marriage I couldn't even read a newspaper. I watched the TV news instead, but that only encouraged her to think that I was boring. I never told her my story. I never took her to an AlAbAn meeting. I wanted to keep all that away from her, because I didn't want her to worry about the fact that I still had alien bugs in my eyes and my brain. She might have worried, you see, that the aliens were still using me, even though they weren't forcing me to consume print any more. She might have thought that they were using me to study *her*, as intimately and minutely as any human being could be studied. I didn't want that. I think I might have been a little bit anxious about it myself—she often complained, poor dear, that I didn't pay enough attention to her, that we were never quite intimate enough, no matter how much we loved one another.

If the aliens *had* still been using me, I think they'd have made more varied use of me. I'd have traveled far more, and been a lot more sociable. If the aliens had wanted to use me as a direct observer, as well as a reader, they'd surely have given me more equipment. They'd have given me more zest for life, more curiosity, more skill in observation. I'm fairly sure that they really did let me go, that they really were being discreet in not interfering too much with the pattern of my life. It was in their interests, I suppose, that I didn't attract too much attention to myself, but I don't believe they were only thinking of themselves.

I might have made more of my life, of course, if they'd never taken me in the first place. If I'd had a chance to get better at my job, I might not have come to hate it quite as much, but it's not a good idea to blame all one's misfortunes on others. We have to take responsibility for ourselves, and if we don't make as much of our freedom as we can, when we get it, we have only ourselves to blame. I can't complain. If only I'd made more of my opportunities, or even taken in a little more of what I read while the aliens' passion for print had me in its grip, and worked around it a little more skillfully, who knows what I might have been able to accomplish?

When I finally got to hear the story of Amelia's abduction, I realized that she'd coped with it much better—although, in fairness, it was a more exciting experience than mine. Most of the stories I've heard at AlAbAn, come to think of it, have been more exciting than mine—but we can't all undertake odysseys to the remoter regions of space and time, can we? Some of us are picked to work at home, and that's our lot. Some of us get cancer, like poor Jenny, and die.

If the aliens want to take me again, for some other purpose, they're very welcome. My eyes aren't what they used to be, but I'm in pretty good condition otherwise, for my age, and they have the technology to fix us up if they want to. I'd really like to find out more about them, if I can—not just by means of all the stories people bring to AlAbAn, fascinating as they are, but in a more intimate sense. If they really can and do live with a different mathematics, even if the differences are far more abstruse than two and two making five, I'd be interested to try and get a grip on that, if only for a moment. It would be really something, I think, to be able to make an imaginative leap like that. I've tried—God knows, I've tried—but I've never been able to do it.

I often go driving at night, even when I've nowhere to go—and sometimes, even when I do have somewhere to go, like tonight, it's the drive rather than the destination that draws me out. Once the aliens have got into your head, you never can settle for conventional destinations, conventional motives or conventional passions.

CHAPTER THIRTEEN

MAKING SLOW PROGRESS

As he and Milly drove back to Salisbury after listening to Neville's story, Steve couldn't help thinking about Janine sitting in the passenger seat of Walter Wainwright's car, perhaps taking Walter into her confidence regarding her troubles, and telling him things that she'd never told Steve. He didn't suppose for a moment that Walter Wainwright would make a pass at her, or that she would be anything less than scandalized if he did, but the notion that they might be in the process of building some kind of intimate relationship, however Platonic, troubled him anyway. Janine, after all, didn't really *belong* at AlAbAn; she was only there in order to exact some strange kind of fee from Steve and Milly by listening to their stories, and disapproving of their togetherness in the meantime. Walter Wainwright surely ought to disapprove of that, and certainly ought not to be assisting in such a malign project.

"It's hard to think of poor old Amelia once having had a stalker," he said to Milly, to break a silence that was on the point of becoming awkward.

"No, it's not," Milly said, continuing a habit she'd lately developed of contradicting Steve's harmless conversational remarks. "She must have been quite pretty back in 1962, or whenever, and even if she hadn't been, men were no different then than they are now. A public library's the sort of place that attracts weirdoes—mercifully."

"Why mercifully?" Steve asked.

"If they weren't attracted off the streets," Milly stated, confidently, "they'd all be stalking female traffic wardens."

"Except for the ones hanging around the schools," Steve said, reflectively. "Mind you, the perverts peering in through the railings are harmless by comparison with the sex-bombs who are already inside. Hell hath no more demonic temptress like a year eleven siren with a crush. Poor Neville must have found himself on the wrong end of one of those from time to time."

"He was safely married for most of his career," Milly observed. "Whereas you're single, and still the right side of thirty. The little harpies probably see you as a legitimate target—just as the aliens did."

Steve knew that the last remark was the first cast in a fishing expedition, but he wasn't about to rise to the bait. "It must be much worse for you," he said, dryly. "*Everybody* thinks that traffic wardens are legitimate targets, from pervs with a passion for women in uniform to road rage sufferers armed with machetes."

"I'm just glad that you fit into the former category, darling," she said. "Mind you, if you'd met some of the traffic wardens I've met, you might lose your passion for women in uniform."

"If you'd met some of the school kids I'd met," Steve countered, "you'd know that I'd lost it long ago."

She looked at him sideways then, and he could see the temptation in her eyes. What she wanted to ask, by way of a casual joke, was: *Well, if it's not the uniform you're kinky for, what are you doing with me?*—but she didn't dare. She seemed far less confident now of the destiny that she had hitherto credited with responsibility for their relationship—a relationship that was far from having attained a stage at which remarks like that could pass automatically as jokes. Steve couldn't see any prospect of getting to that sort of stage any time soon, if ever, and he suspected that Milly couldn't either. At present, there were far too many meaningless things he couldn't bring himself to say to her, even when wit or curiosity prompted him, just as there were too many things she couldn't bring herself to say to him, even when the conversational flow or the logic of a situation licensed them.

Moving back to safer conversational ground, Steve said: "I think Neville's still after Amelia, you know. She's a widow now, and he's a widower, so he must figure he's in with a chance again—but good old Walter is still around to confuse the situation, just as he was always around in the old days. There *is* something between Walter and Amelia, I'm convinced—and probably always has been, even though they both married other people. Maybe they were abducted together. Has there ever been an account of a double abduction, in the time that you've been attending meetings?"

"No," Milly said. "It's always been one at a time. Mind you, I've never heard Walter's own story, or Amelia's. According to your theory, there couldn't be any double abductions, could there? If it's all a matter of private dreams reflecting the uniqueness of the individual, no one could ever share an abduction experience with anyone else, even if they had the most intimate relationship in the world."

"Maybe not," Steve conceded. "There'd be no barrier, of course, to someone including another person in their own abduction experience, but there's no way that the other person could have the same experience. Unless, of course...." He trailed off.

"I wish you wouldn't do that, Steve," Milly said. "It's all very well wanting to think your ideas through before offering them up for my sagacious judgment, but leaving your sentences dangling like that is annoying as well as untidy."

"Sorry," Steve said. "What I was thinking was that maybe, in certain circumstances, one person might be so keen to forge a bond with another person that they'd actually appropriate the other person's experience, and confirm—maybe even sincerely believe—that they'd experienced it too."

"Are we talking about Walter and Amelia or about you and me?" Milly asked, immediately.

"I was just thinking," Steve said. "Hypothetically."

"Is the reason you won't tell me any details of your experience because you don't want me to have the chance of appropriating it for my own selfish ends?" Milly persisted. "Do you think I'm planning to adopt you as a character into my experience?

"No," Steve said. "That would be absurd. We both know perfectly well that we began formulating our experiences before we'd met, so it would be blatantly anachronistic for either of us to include the other in our stories. Mine's a solo flight, just like all the rest."

"So's mine," Milly conceded, a trifle reluctantly. Steve guessed that she was wondering whether that concession further weakened her argument regarding the existence of some mysterious bond between the two of them, which might somehow justify their having done the dirty on Janine.

"It would be interesting, though," Steve said, attempting to defuse the tension filling the car, "to know what did go on between Walter and Amelia, if anything. Why didn't they get together, I wonder, if they had so much in common? It's pretty obvious why Neville couldn't come between them—but if Amelia was as attractive as she probably was, and Walter as handsome as he probably was, you'd think they'd have made an ideal couple."

At least, he didn't add, *it's impossible to imagine Walter screwing Amelia's best friend behind her back.* As soon as the thought was formed, though, he couldn't help contradicting himself, and thinking that maybe it *was* possible, given that Walter might have taken an entire lifetime to reach his present state of grace, and might have been just as wild and wayward in his youth as any other young man handsome enough to obtain easy opportunities to screw around. Maybe, Steve couldn't help thinking, that was why Walter was taking such a sympathetic interest in Janine's plight.

Milly had obviously been following a different but equally embittered train of thought. "I'd have thought you'd have been rooting for Neville rather than Walter," she said, "After all, you and he are bound to have a natural *rapport*, being birds of a feather."

Steve knew that he was supposed to protest against the implication that he could ever be driven to the kind of stalking behavior that Neville had exhibited, so that Milly could tell him, hypocritically, that she'd only meant that they were both science teachers. He decided not to give her the satisfaction. "I never quite had his passion for print, alas," he said. "I did used to read a fair bit, once, but I couldn't keep it up when other distractions took over. One of the reasons I did science at school was because there was less homework reading involved than there would have been in history or English."

"You read Jung's book on flying saucers only the other week," Milly pointed out.

"That's different. That was research. I've always been prepared to do *functional* reading, to investigate facts and theories. I just can't get *into* books the way you can. I could never plough through *Atlas Shrugged* or *Star Maker*."

"What Neville was doing was *purely* functional research," Milly reminded him. "He couldn't get into the books either, and he certainly never imbibed the central message of *Atlas Shrugged*. Birds of a feather, as I said. Maybe the aliens figured that you'd be more useful to them as a serial seducer of innocent maidens—maybe you're their instrument for researching sexual relationships. Not in the sense that you're a Kama Sutran experimenter, of course—more in the sense that you're obliged to run the gamut of all the tangled emotions that sex can whip up. Maybe your emotional incontinence is down to a microchip in your grey matter—just one more information-stream for the aliens to mop up at their leisure."

"Right," Steve said. "Neville did the theory of maths and sports, I'm doing the practicals on sex and unreasoning terror, Jill's doing female hysteria and the tactics of guerilla warfare in the staff-room, and every other science teacher in the country has another little subset of specialties. Walter and Amelia, meanwhile, are studying the side-effects and after-effects of the investigative process—the aliens' equivalent of Her Majesty's Inspectorate of Schools. You're doing practical sex from the female viewpoint, and the ethics of parking. It all makes perfect sense."

"I ought to be able to laugh at that, oughtn't I?" Milly said, with unexpected sobriety. "I ought to be able to do one of those giggles that used to make other people giggle—even you, once upon a time—but I can't. I've lost my giggle. I can see the joke, but I just don't find it funny any more. I've fucked everything up, haven't I, Steve? I wanted you, and I stole you, and now you're no use to me. You're like one of the fruits in the Bible—the ones that grow by the Dead Sea, which look luscious on the outside, but only taste of ashes when you bite into them. I've fucked things up for you, too, and for Janine. It could have been perfect between you and Janine, but I fucked it up, and now everything tastes of ashes for all of us."

Steve had seen a great many of Milly's abrupt changes of mood, but had not yet become wholly accustomed to them, and certainly hadn't learned how to react to them. This seemed to be one instance, though, when duty called him to take the sting out of her self-accusatory hail.

"It wasn't you," Steve said, almost wishing that he believed it. "It was me. I was the one who did the fucking up. It's my fault, not yours. I spoiled your friendship with Janine, just as I spoiled my own relationship with her, and just as I'm now in the process of spoiling my relationship with you. I wish I could say that I couldn't help it, but I'm sure that I could have done, and still could, if only I could have figured out the trick of it, or begun to master the technique. I'm the one with the emotional incontinence, remember—the one who lets his nervous excitement drive him, instead of owning it and controlling it. I'm the one to blame."

Milly sighed deeply. The car moved through Alderbury, which seemed sleepier than ever now that the November nights had begun to turn cold at last, keeping sensible people indoors. After a pause, she said: "Well, that helped, didn't it?"

"Not really," Steve said.

"At least we feel like comforting one another now," she said, "instead of sniping. Shall we go straight home instead of stopping off for food. I've got some eggs in the fridge—I could make us an omelet. Unless you'd rather get something delivered."

Steve assured her that an omelet would be fine. It was, too; Milly had some ham and tomatoes to put in the omelets, and enough bread to make toast on the side.

While they were eating, Milly said: "If I were a liar, I *could* imagine myself trying to appropriate your abduction experience, trying to squeeze myself into its content one way or another, or to squeeze you into mine as a spear-carrier, but I'm not. I'll just have to stick to what I can remember, although it's not as neat a tale as Zoe's or Neville's. I'll do mine first, if you like—you're very welcome to borrow from it if you want, but I don't suppose you'll find anything in it you want or need. At the end of the day, we're both still alone, aren't we?"

"No, we're not," Steve said. "We fly solo in our alien abductions because we're all unique, not because we're alone. We all share the same collective unconscious, and the same mythical future, although our conscious minds sometimes rebel against both. Even though we're flying solo, there's a sense in which we're all in it together, all collaborating on the work of revision and refinement—not just the people who attend AlAbAn meetings, but everyone, and not just everyone who's alive now, but all the people of the past who helped to build and shape the collective unconscious we inherited...and maybe, in a sense, all the people and non-people of the futures of which we catch glimpses in our dreams. Maybe there *is* such a thing as time travel, but we've mistaken its nature, because we always tend to think in terms of machines and gadgets, of ships and string and sealing-wax...."

"And whether pigs have wings," she finished for him, disregarding the boiling sea. "They don't."

"Not yet," Steve agreed. "But they will, in the fullness of time."

She laughed at that, quite spontaneously, and he laughed too. She put out her hand. He took it in his own, and squeezed.

"I'm sorry that I accused you of being like Neville," Milly said. "You're not. He's the exact opposite: the very model of emotional constipation."

"An equally uncomfortable affliction, I dare say," Steve said. "Our attitudes to education do appear to be fairly similar, though. He didn't seem to regard it as a vocation either."

"A sense of vocation isn't given to everyone," Milly told him. "There's no need to feel bad about that. Those of us who do have a sense of vocation have no particular reason to feel proud of it. After all, what's so saintly about a compulsion to punish people who park their phallic symbols in the wrong places."

Steve managed to laugh at that, quite spontaneously, although he suspected that it would only have made him wince a week—or even an hour—earlier. Maybe, he thought, the corner had been turned. Maybe, from now on, things would get better, and the path of slow progress would be resumed.

Things did get better, but very slowly. Things got better at school, too, and not just because the relaxation techniques that Sylvia Joyce had taught Steve were once again taking some of the sting out of the stresses of teaching and marking. His fellow teachers had begun to stop treating him like a leper, and were on the brink of admitting him back into the fringes of their community. On the Monday after the AlAbAn meeting, Tracy condescended to say hello to him when the two of them happened to meet in the corridor, and once that fact was known to everyone else—having been carried at the speed of light by the school grapevine—it threw the door wide open to the inevitability of his eventual rehabilitation.

"Are you still doing that survival course at the tech?" Rhodri Jenkins asked him, idly, on the Wednesday lunch-time, while the deputy head was fishing for spare bodies to play minder between four and half past five.

Steve was tempted to lie, but couldn't quite bring himself to do it. "No," he admitted.

"You can do computer club again, then," the Welshman said, oozing satisfaction at the unexpected windfall. "You'll get your reward in Heaven, as well as in your pay packet. I thought you were doing the course with that travel agent of yours, in preparation for the disintegration of society, so that you could become the new Adam and Eve."

"That's off," Steve admitted. "I'm going out with someone else now." He considered the possibility of attempting to get out of computer club supervision by inventing a date with Milly, but the truth was that Milly was visiting her parents in Bath, having been summoned home by her mother to discuss some unspecified impending crisis. She'd be catching a three o'clock train after doing an early shift. He decided to let the matter lie, and collect the moral credit due to him for helping the deputy head out of a hole.

"Well, at least you're not shitting on your own doorstep any more," the Welshman commented. "What does this one do for a living?"

"She's a traffic warden."

"Sleeping with the enemy, eh? Had to bribe her to stop her giving you a ticket, I suppose? Got a face like a horse and an arse to match, I dare say."

"Actually, she's very good looking, in a slightly Junoesque sort of way" Steve said. "You're right about having to seduce her to escape the ticket, though. It's lucky I've got the face of an Adonis."

There was no way his fit of honesty was going to extend as far as letting on to the deputy head that he had met Milly as a result of attending meetings of Alien Abductees Anonymous—that would be almost as suicidal as admitting to a chronic fear of flying, heights and bridges.

"Very lucky, I dare say," Jenkins said. "Will you be trying the same trick next time some butch motorcycle cop flags you down for speeding on the motorway?"

"That only happens on old American TV shows, Rhodri," Steve told him. "We've got speed cameras on motorway bridges now—it's all automatic."

"I know that, boyo. I was just making a point, in my subtle Cymric fashion, about the double-edged nature of your armor against adversity. I suppose I was trying to steer the conversation around to a point where I could gently warn you, without seeming too deputy-head-like, not to take reckless advantage of the fact that you've been provisionally readmitted to the human race, female-staff-wise. I'd prefer it if you could stay in everyone's good books from now on—it makes my job much easier."

"That's Welsh subtlety, is it?" Steve remarked. "I'd hate to see you try to drop a leaden hint."

"You'll certainly know it when it lands on your toe," Rhodri said, with an approving chuckle. "Glad to see you so cheerful, too. Is that the return ticket from Coventry or is it the traffic warden confirming everything they say about women in uniform?"

"It's just my sunny nature," Steve assured him, "and the fact that the sixth-formers have put blood and lymph behind them and got on to the nervous system. Tingling neurons are fun—and brains make everybody think."

He *was* in a tolerably good mood, though, considering that there were still two days to go until the weekend; he survived computer club without losing his serenity and went home, having already caught up with his marking, to cook himself a substantial plateful of sausages and chips, delete all the spam from his email inbox and spend a lazy evening catching up with postings on YouTube—which he did in perfect safety, there being no blurred cliffhanger climaxes on view.

Steve couldn't help wondering, occasionally, what Janine might be doing, now that she was no longer being educated in survival techniques, but he didn't let the thought torment him too much. He didn't have bad dreams either, when he finally went to bed.

* * * * * * *

Steve spent the following Wednesday evening—the one before the next AlAbAn meeting—at Milly's flat. The vague plan they had both had in mind for the evening was a Marks & Spencer's ready-made meal hot out of the microwave, with a bottle of Merlot, a cursory chat about the various hassles of the day—in which Milly's abusive road-users would beat Steve's abusive kids hands down, as usual—and then sex, before Steve went back home so that they could both spread themselves out to sleep instead of jostling for position in the inadequate space available in Milly's single bed. As things turned out, however, the agenda somehow got turned around, so that they had the sex first, and then lay in bed, mildly exhausted but unable to sleep, for an hour or so before Milly could pluck up the energy to switch on the microwave and pull a couple of plates out of the cupboard.

Steve knew that it wasn't really lust that had dragged them into bed ahead of the other items on the agenda. Even though their relationship had become less strained since the evening when Neville had told his story, Milly had not got over feeling guilty about having stolen her best friend's boyfriend, nor had Steve stopped regretting that he had been a culpable accessory to the crime. They both missed Janine, who was still refusing to speak to either of them, although they had both tried to reinstitute contact. Steve knew that Milly was only pretending that her lust was urgent in order to cover up her other feelings, just as he'd earlier pretended that the urgency of his own lust excused what he'd done. He still didn't need Viagra, though; he appreciated every opportunity that presented itself to lose himself in that kind of emotional incontinence.

It wasn't just the timetable of their evening that was turned on its head. Instead of exploiting their easiest conversational resource while they were eating, by laying into the horrific habits of pupils and drivers with their usual sadistic glee, they were somehow drawn to tackle the most difficult. They returned, for the first time since the aftermath of the previous meeting, to the topic of their untold stories—not to give away any actual details, but to resume discussion of the necessity of getting around to telling them.

"I don't want to keep putting it off any longer," Steve said. "When I said that I wouldn't be ready till January, it was just cowardice speaking."

"You can talk," Milly said. "I've probably been to more meetings without spilling the beans than anyone else in this history of the organization, even if it has been going since before I was born. *That*'s cowardice." Steve observed, though, that although there was shame in her voice, there was a certain perverse pride too. "I'm not sure why I've been such a coward," Milly went on. "In a way, it's not like me at all. It only took me three weeks to confess everything at the Eating Disorders Group. I suppose I was a lot better at vomiting things up in those days. Maybe, if I hadn't got that straightened out...."

"It has nothing to do with that," Steve said. "It's a totally different matter. You were just waiting for the right moment. I can understand that—but I don't want to put it off any longer. I've got what I needed from Sylvia Joyce, and I don't have any real excuses left. I'm certainly not going to wait for Janine to get bored and go away. That really would be cowardice. Tomorrow, when Walter calls for volunteers, my hand is going up."

"Mine too," Milly said. "We'll let Walter decide which of us goes first."

Steve frowned slightly at that, because he knew that Milly must know, just as well as he did, what would happen if Milly and Steve both volunteered to tell their stories. Walter would be certain to give priority to Milly, partly because of the length of time she'd been in the group and partly because his old-fashioned politeness would oblige him to operate on the principle of Ladies First.

"You don't have to do that, Mil," Steve said. "I don't mind going first, if you'd rather."

"Why would I rather you went first?" Milly countered.

"No reason," Steve said, "but if you did...I wouldn't want to push you into something you're not quite ready to do."

"I know that," Milly said. "Nor would I." She didn't repeat what Steve had said about not waiting until Janine had stopped attending meetings, but it was obvious that something of the sort was on her mind. If Milly's tiny kitchenette had been large enough to contain a metaphorical elephant as well as the breakfast-bar at which they were eating, Janine would have certainly filled the role, even though she was a good deal slimmer than Milly now that Milly was eating regularly and hardly ever throwing up at all.

"Would you rather go first?" Steve asked.

"You've only been coming for a few weeks," Milly observed, instead of answering. "That's normal. There are some who want to get it over with as quickly as possible and blurt it out at the first opportunity, but most wait to see how things go and hear a few stories, so that they can reassure themselves that their own experience isn't going to sound significantly sillier than anyone else's, and that the listeners are going to treat them with extra-thick kid gloves. That's only sensible—but I was convinced of all that nine months ago, and I still haven't put up my hand. That's silly. If I keep on this way,

Walter will get even more suspicious. He probably thinks I'm some kind of snoop, doing research for a book or something."

"*Alien Abduction: The Wiltshire Revelations*," Steve suggested. "You've read all about Roswell, now read all about East Grimstead. If anyone's inviting suspicion of that sort, it's more likely to be me than you. I'm a science teacher, after all—I'm supposed to have a vested interest in debunking."

"As a science teacher, though," Milly pointed out, "you're not expected to be literate. Science teaching isn't what it used to be back in dear old Neville's day, is it?" She paused for a moment, and then said: "You aren't, are you? Thinking of writing a book, I mean. You'll have to change all the names—including yours."

"No, I'm not," Steve said. "You'd be a useful mine of information if I were, I suppose, after all those meetings—but if I wanted to do the job properly, I'd have to con Walter or Amelia into telling me all. I couldn't bring myself to do that. That would require true journalism cynicism, which I don't have."

"Think of all the stories they must have heard, though, in almost forty years!" Milly said. "If only they'd kept some kind of record—what an archive that would be! Maybe they have. Maybe Walter's insistence on not writing minutes is just a bluff, and as soon as he gets home every Thursday night he whips out his fountain-pen and writes down every word. Maybe Amelia's got a hidden mike somewhere in the sitting-room, and a cupboard full of tapes. I can't believe it, though. If they're not honest, nobody is. They're honest, I'm sure of it."

"And we should try to follow their good example," Steve said. "Whichever of us goes first, I think we're both ready, I hope I'm ready, at any rate. For someone who suffers from emotional incontinence, you know, I can be quite hesitant at times."

"Whenever you have to cross a bridge, for instance," Milly supplied. Steve didn't take it as an insult. He took it as a jokey casual remark.

"And whenever I need to be regressed," Steve added. "I have to take myself in hand, don't I? I have to grit my teeth and get on with it."

"Me too," Milly said. "As I said earlier, let's both throw caution to the winds, and let Walter decide. He might pick you. Maybe it would be better if I did go first, though—I might have to spend more time in Bath over the next few weeks. It's not impossible that I might even have to miss an AlAbAn meeting or two, if things go from bad to worse."

"Why, what's up?" Steve asked.

"Probably nothing—but Dad seems to have had a mini-stroke, and Mum's terrified that he's working up to a big one. He's had high blood-pressure for ages, but he hates taking his beta-blockers. He says they take all the zest out of life. When she nags him, it only makes him dig his heels in. She thinks he'll listen to me, but she's wrong. Just because I'm his darling daughter doesn't mean that he's going to take my advice—quite the reverse, in fact. Anyway, nothing terrible has happened yet, but I thought I'd best warn you that it might. We'll be in the run-up to Christmas soon, and that always piles on the stress within the family."

"Mine are the same," Steve admitted, "although Dad's as fit as a fiddle. They'll be badgering me to go home, I dare say, but I'm going to put my foot down and say that I can't go. I won't say that I intend spending it with you—they'd just start nagging me to bring you with me."

"Whereas my lot will want me all to themselves, and would react with horror if I said that I wanted to bring a guest. Still, we'll cross that bridge when we come to it—if it's not too high or wide."

"Metaphorical bridges," he assured her, "are no trouble at all."

He meant it at the time, but he couldn't help remembering it wryly when the moment came the following evening, and neither he nor Milly raised a hand. In the event, the only person who moved a muscle, after an unusually protracted pregnant pause, was a woman who looked to be in her early thirties, who introduced herself as "Megan".

CHAPTER FOURTEEN

THE PURPOSE OF LIFE

I was one of the lucky ones, in the sense that the ones who abducted me took the trouble to explain what they were doing, and to reassure me that I'd be perfectly safe.

I did spend some waking time on an operating table, but I wasn't shackled and there were no needles or unbearably bright lights. I don't even remember the worms—they'd done that while I was still asleep—although it did make me feel sick when the android told me about them. I think I'm right in calling him an android, although he might have been a robot—I've never been entirely clear about the difference between them. Anyhow, he was the spitting image of Michelangelo's statue of David, right down to the delicate marble complexion and the...well, let's just say that although they'd animated him, they hadn't given him any clothes to wear.

I never saw the aliens themselves—just the David they'd built to act as a go-between, to explain what they were going to do to me, and why. I think he was telling me the truth, though; if the aliens had wanted to be dishonest, they wouldn't have let David tell me about the worms.

It's a cliché, I know, but the first thing I said when I woke up was: "Where am I?"

David was already standing there, waiting beside the operating table. The lighting was soft, so it wasn't immediately obvious that he was a statue, especially as he was able to move and talk, but he couldn't exactly pass for human either.

"You're in a research facility," he said. "We need your help. We're sorry that we couldn't ask nicely, but there are very powerful reasons why we have to be extremely discreet. We'll have to play some slight tricks with your memory, I'm afraid, before we send you home, but we will send you home, safe and sound. In the meantime, you'll have quite an adventure. If you can get into the right frame of mind, you'll find it very interesting. If you remember it at all, you'll remember it as a dream. Whether you remember it will probably depend on how good you are at remembering dreams; some people are, and some aren't. It won't be a horrible nightmare, though—nothing that will leave you with post-traumatic stress syndrome."

"You're just a puppet, aren't you?" I said. "You're fronting for aliens who are so horrible to look at they don't think I could bear it."

"The fact that you've jumped to that conclusion suggests that you could certainly bear it," he said. "We're not *that* horrible—but we're a long way from human. That's why we had to recruit you, I'm afraid. We can't set up an immediate mind-link with the subjects in whom we're interested. We could do the necessary preliminaries step-by-step, but as we've already done the laborious groundwork on the human species, it's a great deal less time-consuming to use you as an intermediary, exploiting the basic physiological similarity between you to transpose the subject's mental experiences into your brain, and read it off from there."

"I don't understand," I said, pulling out another one from the cliché-supermarket.

"I apologize for my incompetence," David said. "All we want you to do is to lie down in a bed, quietly, and go to sleep. In the bed next to you there will be another person, who looks very similar to you—I don't just mean that she looks human, but that she looks *like you*. The resemblance is really quite uncanny, considering that she's from eight hundred million years downstream. In the fullness of time, all kinds of fragmentary patterns repeat, some more often than others. We're interested in that process of repetition, of course, but we're even more interested in the slight variations.

"What we want to do is to make a record of this other person's mind—her memories, her life-story. In time, we could tune our apparatus to do that directly, feeding information from neuroworms embedded in her brain into our own multiplexus, but it would take a long time and we'd probably need to analyze a couple of hundred subjects to make the basic calibrations. Fortunately, we've already been working on humans for the best part of a subcentury, and we have an abundant supply of expert neuroworms, which can read off the contents of a human brain with no difficulty at all—especially humans we've already decanted—so...."

"Hang on," I said. "What do you mean, *already decanted*."

"You've been here before, Megan. You probably don't remember it, except maybe as a distant dream. That knowledge should help to reassure you that you won't come to any harm. This time won't be very much different from the last, and it will probably leave no more trace in your memory. This time, though, you'll be working for us rather than serving as a subject yourself. It's an oversimplification, but in essence, you'll be reading the subject's mind and we'll be reading yours, because it's a lot easier to set up that kind of indirect link than it would be to set up a direct one."

"And what are *neuroworms*?" I wanted to know.

"Wireless telepathy is fiendishly difficult, exceedingly vague, and frequently unreliable," David told me. "Good mind-reading requires actual neuronal connections. Inorganic wires are almost as inept as no wires at all. We use biological connectors—artificial neuronal constructs. They're not really *worms*, but the resemblance encourages the terminology."

"And you're going to stick these worm-things into my brain?"

"We already have. Please don't be alarmed. You can't feel a thing, because there's nothing to feel. We did it while you were unconscious because you might have found it mildly disturbing to feel them going up your nose, but there wasn't any pain and there won't be. We'll connect them to the subject's apparatus through your ear, so you won't be able to see anything unpleasant."

I have to admit that it was because I didn't want to think too much about brainworms dangling out of my nose and my ears that my next question was: "Why?"

"We're scientists, Megan. We study climax communities—the whole sequence, or as much of it as we can access. Upstream is mostly easy, but downstream is a different matter, because the boomerang effect doesn't work both ways and the time police are more restrictive there. We're trying to make sense of the sequence. We're trying to discover whether there's any direction to Earthly evolution—whether it has any kind of long-term objective or purpose, or whether it's just a series of arbitrary explosions of adaptive radiation, in which self-conscious intelligence is merely an occasional and entirely haphazard by-product."

I didn't understand much of that, either, but it would have been a waste of time to say so. "That's why you took me the first time?" I said, trying to stick to what I did half-understand. "You were learning about humans. And because you've already learned about humans, you think you can use me again, to help you learn about some other almost-human race that's evolved somewhere else."

"Very good, Megan. You've got it. It's some*when* else rather than some*where*, but that's a trivial difference."

"So when I asked *where am I*, I should have asked *when am I*?"

"Not exactly. You're still in a research facility. Actually, the when of here and now's a little difficult to specify in calendrical terms. I'm afraid there's no point my trying to explain the subtleties of the relativity of space-time and matter to a human. The eight hundred million years separating you from your apparent twin is measurable, though. In one sense, that's trivial too, because even complex entities are bound to be replicated, given time enough, and DNA's possibilities aren't by any means endless, but in another sense...we really don't know yet whether there's an underlying pattern, or whether there are only pseudopatterns generated by the play of chaos. Then again, in one sense we have all the time in eternity to play with, but in another, we're in something of a hurry. We're going to move you now, and get you hooked up. I hope that I've told you enough for you to make sense of your experience, because making sense of it is what we need you to do. Either way, we'll chat again before we send you home."

Having said that, without giving me a chance to ask another silly question, he reached out a marble hand and touched me on the forehead.

The hand wasn't cold, but it wasn't soft either. There was no pain, but it put me out like a light, and when I woke up again....

* * * * * * *

Actually, I suppose I *didn't* wake up again. In all probability, I hadn't even woken up once.

I never actually saw my supposed twin from eight hundred million years in the future, although I saw through her eyes, so I don't know how exact our facial resemblance was. There were no mirrors in her world, and there was nothing in her memories about ever having paused beside a still pool to stare into it, wonderingly, in order to contemplate her own reflection. She was no narcissist. Nor, in spite of what David had said and the aliens who'd made him might have thought, was she any mere echo, of me or of humankind.

Her name was Lili, although the syllables didn't have any resonance of meaning in her world akin to the resonances they carry in ours. They had no flower called a lily, and they'd certainly never had a Marlene Dietrich droning away while standing under a fake lamp-post.

I can't possibly describe the experience I shared with Lili in terms of the order in which the information came to me. I suppose, given that time and experience are linear—or seem that way to us—the impressions must have arrived in sequence, but the sequence didn't become meaningful until I could rearrange the bits and string them together in a way that made sense, and that meant reconstructing them into a very different linearity—into a *life-story*. It was her memories that I was exploring and storing, and memories have an innate chronological order of their own, which is very different from the order in which they're likely to present themselves to an adult mind, whether it's awake or asleep. That chronological order is the one I had to recapture for the aliens, and for you.

Maybe it would have been far less chaotic if we'd both been awake, subjecting our trains of thought to the discipline of consciousness—but if we'd been awake, we'd also have been distracted by the flux of sensory input. Given that we were both asleep, I suppose there's a possibility that it was all some kind of crazy dream, from beginning to end—her dream, or mine, or some lunatic collaboration between us—but I don't believe that it was. I think the neuroworms connecting her grey matter with mine were able to impose a discipline of their own, to make her remember and to help me to take her memories aboard in my own brain, sort them out and organize them coherently, and store them as if they were memories of another life I'd lived, alongside or instead of my own.

I sometimes wonder, now, if the aliens who'd made David—or others like and unlike them—had done something similar with other humans they'd analyzed and catalogued, and whether those other twice-used humans might be able to recover those other lives in their own dreams, or under hypnosis...and whether, if so, the human race that exists here and now might be a kind of reservoir of neuroworm-decanted memories of other lives in other times, not just from eight hundred million years in the future but from other parts of the sequence, other parts of the pattern...but you can speculate about that for yourselves, just as easily as I can. What you want to hear is what I found out about Lili, reorganized into a coherent narrative of a life half-lived, and a destiny still expected.

I think the aliens might have made a mistake, based on superficial appearances, when they jumped to the conclusion that Lili and I really were alike, and that the future race to which she belonged really was as close to human as the complex chromosomal play of DNA is ever likely to produce again. Even though they had their own elaborate neuroworm technology, the aliens may not have suspected what kind of creature Lili really was. They might have assumed, because she looked like me outside, that she'd be like me inside, where it really counted.

But she wasn't.

Her flesh wasn't her own. Even her brain and its resident mind weren't her own—not really. Even her memories weren't *entirely* hers.

That other human race, which will evolve eight hundred million years from now, will be self-conscious, like us. It will be intelligent, like us—but it won't be free. It will be a subject species, a kind of domestic animal. It will be a manufactured product rather than the culmination of a process of natural selection, created by selective breeding and direct biological engineering so that its individuals might serve as hosts for indwelling parasites. Those parasites will look like giant worms, living in the gut of the future human race like hookworms or tapeworms in a human gut, but the comparison will end there. It might be more accurate to say that they'll be like snails, *wearing* human beings the way snails wear shells.

Lili was born with the parasite inside her, but she didn't know it was there at first. It had been put into her mother when her mother was about half way through her pregnancy, snaking its way up into the womb where Lili was as yet no more than an embryo and making its way into her half-formed intestines. It was very tiny then, just like Lili; it grew along with Lili, but Lili didn't find out that it was there for quite some time. She still didn't know it was there when she learned to talk, and began to learn all the other things she needed to know in order to live within her tribe. Her parents could have told her, and older children could have told her—but they didn't. There was a time for her to learn the truth, and a time for her to be innocent.

Lili's tribe lived by the sea, in a region whose climate seemed placidly sub-tropical to me. They were basically fisher-folk. They had a few vegetable-patches scratched out above the high-tide line, in which they grew various kinds of tubers. They also sent expeditions to harvest the natural produce of the savannah that stretched inland from where they lived—all vegetable produce; they weren't hunters, even though there were vast hordes of herbivores on the savannah. It was the sea that provided the basic elements of their diet, though.

They ate fish, but they ate shellfish and seaweed in greater abundance. They had primitive boats, made of hides stretched over wooden frames, but most of their food-gathering was done at low tide; they studied the phases of the moon very attentively, because their most abundant harvests were achieved when the moon was full or new, when the influences of sun and moon combined to produce the highest and lowest tides.

They had ovens, where they baked pots as well as cooking food, using wood for fuel. They did a certain amount of metal-working, but they were basically stone-and-ceramic technologists. Metal blades were very precious, and used with great care. The tools they used most frequently were pounding tools for breaking the shells of mollusks and crushing seaweed into pulp.

They seemed to be a happy and contented tribe. They led secure lives, even though the savannah had more than its fair share of dangerous predators—not just mammals, birds and reptiles, but monsters unknown in our world. They did suffer occasional losses to those predators, which occasionally raided their villages by night, but when they went foraging on the savannah they were guarded; they were also guarded in their homes by day and by night, although they rarely saw their guardians They were secure in their contentment because they were *protected*, watched over and defended by the most jealous of all the monsters that stalked the savannah. Sometimes, their guardians failed in their protective duty, but not often.

Lili was happy and contented too, and not just while she was innocent. When she learned about the thing that lived inside her, it changed her conception of herself and her species, but it didn't terrify her. Why should it? Everyone had one—everyone, at least, who was under the age of forty. When a host reached forty or thereabouts, the parasite moved on to the next phase of its life-cycle. It wasn't really a worm, you see; it was a larva. It was only a parasite for part of its life. After that...well, its adult phase is difficult to describe, but you need to get past the idea of caterpillars turning into butterflies, or even into dragonflies. *These* monsters were a whole other order of being.

They were beautiful, in their way—textured like marble—but they were also incredibly hideous. They had more than twenty senses, and organs to suit, and they had all the kinds of limbs you can imagine, with some to spare. They started off quite small, but there was a lot to eat on that savannah—the Earth will have a lot more biomass then than it does now—and they kept growing for centuries, if they survived that long. They were the top predators, but they weren't short of rivals. They also had parasites of their own, and things could get pretty rough between themselves, especially in the mating season. One reason why they had so many limbs was that so many of them were modified as weapons. When they competed for mates, they didn't hold back; Lili had seen several such contests, albeit from a safe distance.

By the time Lili was half way to adulthood she knew that every meal she ate was feeding a larva as well as herself, that when she grew fat it wasn't really her growing fat, but the larva inside her. She knew, too, that when she was old enough to marry, she and her husband would both be feeding larvae, and that when she fell pregnant, she would be feeding the larva as well as her own infant, before and after the unborn infant acquired a parasite of its own. None of that seemed horrible to her. She was cheerful. She was contented. She was secure.

She learned to fish, and to cook, and to gather the produce of the savannah. She learned to sing, to play games, to flirt and be courted. She learned to love the monsters that protected her, always on her side because she was carrying one of their young. She learned all the knowledge of her tribe, and all its folklore. She learned what I'll call its religion, for want of a better word, although it was really just a matter of biology. She learned the reason for her existence. Her tribe didn't have the sort of god that our tribes and nations have always had to make do with, because they didn't need that kind of god. They knew where they came from, and what the purpose of their existence was.

I'm telling you this more in the manner of a lecture than a story, because that's the way I eventually organized the information, but you need to remember that it wasn't told to me as a lecture, I *remembered* it all, haphazard bit by haphazard bit, and while I pieced it all together I pieced it together as a life that *I'd lived*. I remembered it as a happy life, a beautiful life, a life worth living. All the while, there was something else in me—another set of memories, another life, another intelligence—that couldn't look at and live in Lili's memories in quite the same way as Lili, but while I was there, giving Michelangelo's David a helping brain, I *was* Lili, and her memories were as much mine as my own, and they were happy, serene, idyllic.

Hers was a childhood like none that was ever possible for any human of our kind, Hers was an adolescence that was never possible for any girl of our sort. Hers was a young adulthood that was...well, you get the picture. She wasn't yet thirty when she was taken by the time-traveling aliens, and put to bed so that I could read her mind. She'd had two children of her own, and expected to have one or two more.

As I said, though, her mind wasn't really her own—not entirely. The larva lived in her gut—which isn't, technically speaking, inside the body's flesh at all—but it put out feelers. By feelers I don't mean the kind of antennae that insects wear on their heads. I mean *real feelers*: natural neuroworms. The larva didn't just share her meals; it shared her thoughts, and it used her brain to think thoughts of its own.

While Lili learned, the Lili-larva learned, and some of what the larva had to learn was what any larva of its kind needed to know in order to comprehend and continue its own life-trajectory. It learned those things, in large measure, the same way Lili learned about matters beyond the immediately practical: from speech and story, exemplary dramatization and educational exposition. Its primary education came, for the most part, out of the mouths of human beings, who had to carry the heritage of their parasite species in their myths and memories as well as their own. Some of it, though, came from the mouths of monsters. The monsters had mouths as well as everything else—including mouths that could formulate human speech.

The Lili-larva was happy too, while it was a larva. It knew that it had sterner challenges ahead, when it became an adult, but while it was a larva its larvahood was comfortable, protected, idyllic. The Lili-larva took part in Lili's games, Lili's thoughts, Lili's own happiness...just as I did.

The adults of Lili's species worked hard while they were under forty, not just on their own behalf but on their larvae's behalf. Sometimes, they even did work for the monsters. They loved work. They derived a great deal of pleasure from it—perhaps, though not necessarily, because they had neuroworms sticking into the pleasure-centers in their hind-brains, which rewarded them every time they did anything to further their purpose in life, to serve the monsters. After forty or thereabouts, they didn't work any more. After forty, they were fattened up to be eaten. Sometimes the adult monsters that emerged from the pupae formed by the larvae they'd nurtured took part in the feast. Sometimes they didn't. They didn't have any particular sentimentality about that kind of relationship.

I can't tell whether the adults who were eaten, when they reached the age of forty-two or forty-three, enjoyed being eaten. Maybe they did and maybe they didn't. I know, though, that Lili was looking forward to being eaten—that she regarded it as a privilege to be treasured and devoutly desired, an entirely appropriate consummation of the purpose of her existence. She hadn't the slightest desire to avoid being eaten. The pseudohumans of eight hundred million years hence will know that they must die, but they won't experience any *angst* in consequence. They'll love being alive, while they're working for their larvae and their children, and for the monsters that made them, but they won't mind the thought of dying in the least. Lili didn't, at any rate...not, at least, while she was lying on that bed in that research establishment somewhen inexpressible, dreaming the dreams that I was translating for the aliens who had made Michelangelo's David.

Afterwards, when they sent her home...I don't know anything about that, do I? But I wonder, sometimes, if she'll remember, just a little, or if she'll dream, sometimes, about another set of memories, another life, another existence: an existence that's only cheerful *sometimes*, only contented *rarely*, and not idyllic at all, in sum. She couldn't see anything horrible in her parasite, or in the monsters that would eat her one day—if one of their rivals caught her first—but she might have been able to see something horrible in the fragments of me that slipped into her brain while her neuroworm-borne fragments slipped into me. She might have been able to find something horrible in the mere possibility of a creature that looked like her but had no awareness of the purpose of her life, no awareness of why she existed or where she was bound.

Maybe, I sometimes tell myself, that wouldn't make Lili miserable at all, Maybe it would make her even happier, to know that she might be like that but wasn't, Maybe it would just make her value her own happiness a little more. After all, I can't say that it's made me any happier to have shared her bliss, her joy, her contentedness. If anything, it's only added to the burden of my own uncertainties, my own self-dissatisfaction. It would be too cruel, don't you think, if every meeting of minds only served to make both the participants more miserable than they were before? I'd like to think that Lili went back home, eight hundred million years in the future, no worse off for her abduction, and perhaps a little better.

Not that I have any complaints myself, you understand. There's more to life than happiness, isn't there? Perhaps, if I've learned anything, I've learned that even happiness can be horrible, and that what people ought to be searching for isn't happiness at all, or the purpose of life, but a different kind of reward. So I wonder, now, whether I ought to be searching for something else, if only for a different kind of happiness that's *earned*, through understanding. I sometimes wonder, now, whether we might be the unluckiest intelligent species that will ever inherit or inhabit the Earth, simply because we're the first, with no others to look back on and take inspiration from, and not the least vestige of an emergent pattern to contemplate.

I wonder other things, too—darker things. I can't help myself. I'm *almost sure* that the aliens were wrong, and that Lili and I only looked alike on the outside, while being utterly different on the inside, but I can't be sure, can I? Maybe, I sometimes can't help thinking, it's me that was mistaken, and the whole human race along with me. I know that we don't have huge larvae in our guts that are destined to turn into monsters with far more senses and limbs and mouths than any sensible creature could ever need—but that doesn't necessarily mean, does it, that our flesh and our brains and our minds are entirely our own; that there aren't things living inside us that aren't really *us*, even though anatomists think they are, and which use our brains for thinking their own thoughts, dreaming their own dreams. If they're never apart from us, physically, I suppose there's a sense in which they'd be part of us by definition...but still, if they had their own thoughts, their own dreams, their own *happiness*....

We know, you see—all of you must know it as well as I do—that our brains are capable of entertaining other lives, other memories, other beings. Maybe they're all put there by neuroworms, or some equivalent technology, but nature has its own technologies, doesn't it? What human and alien artifice can produce by design, DNA can usually produce by natural selection, given time and the right challenge. We're already full of nature's neuroworms. How can we be sure that they're all really *us*, and that none of them are conduits to alien experience? It's unlikely, I know—but once you've been an instrument in an alien investigation, eight hundred million years downstream and somewhen unspecifiable, you can't help wondering.

I can't, anyway.

I loved Lili. I loved being with her, and I loved *her*. I loved her childhood, her adolescence, her children, her Lili-larva. I loved her happiness. I still treasure her happiness, whenever I can obtain a glimpse of it. I'm glad I haven't forgotten her—although I did, for a while, and it wasn't easy to piece her back together again, fragment by fragment, dredging her up from my dreams, sorting her out, and making her coherent—but I'd done it once and I did it again, and I take immense satisfaction in that. Michelangelo's David would be proud of me, I think, and the aliens and monsters too. I'd like to think that it helps to prove that we humans aren't quite as pathetic, incompetent and wretched as we might seem, within the great scheme of things, to creatures who can see that scheme, and are making headway in understanding it.

I'd like to think that some day, eight hundred million years from now, Lili will catch an occasional fugitive glimpse of me, in the deepest recesses of her dream-memory. I'd like to think, too, that she might contrive to be just a little bit happy that I was once alive. I know that she won't have any particular reason to be happy about that, but why shouldn't she? We'll be together for a little while, after all, and togetherness is good, isn't it?

Even we think that togetherness is good—and we don't have any reason to think so that's anywhere near as good as Lili's, do we?

CHAPTER FIFTEEN

CLEARING UP MISCONCEPTIONS

"I thought you were going to put your hand up," Milly said, when Steve put the car in gear and pulled away, with his eyes on the rear-view mirror, in which he could see Walter Wainwright politely opening the passenger door of his Renault Megane for Janine. Steve hadn't done that for Milly, and had never done it for Janine in all the time they'd been going out—not even in the first flush of sheer infatuation.

"I think I would have put my hand up if you'd put yours up," Steve said—honestly, so far as he could tell. "I only hesitated—but then, when you didn't put your hand up, I got stuck in the hesitation. I suppose you got caught in the same sort of trap."

"No, I just chickened out," Milly said, appropriating the petty virtue of admitting her fault frankly.

"I'm sorry," Steve said, defensively.

"It's okay," Milly replied, claiming the additional petty virtue of generosity. "I was supposed to go first—that was the deal. When I didn't put my hand up, you must have thought I was pulling a fast one on you. And it wasn't just me, was it? You were thinking about Janine, too. Even though you're with me now, you're always looking at her."

"Given that we sit side-by-side while she always plonks herself down in the green armchair," Steve said, his defensiveness edging towards paranoia "that's a simple matter of geometry. Should I complain because *you*'re always looking in her direction instead of turning your head through ninety degrees to stare at me?"

"Women are allowed to look at one another," Milly said. "It's a completely different emotional experience. Anyway, I'll have another go next time—at putting my hand up, I mean—whether you do or not, I mean. I *am* ready. I wish I *had* done it today, then I wouldn't have to follow Megan. Her story was much better than mine. I know that the group's the most supportive support group anyone could ever hope to find, but my story's not nearly as good as most. I've tried to dress it up with philosophizing, the way Megan did, but I'm no good at that sort of thing, and I can't alter the actual events, can I? That would be cheating. It's just my luck to have an experience that wasn't as *neat*, or *pretty* or *delicate* as other people's. On the other hand, that's me all over—bloody typical."

She stopped then, quite abruptly. Out of the corner of his eye, Steve saw her blush. He'd never seen her blush before; three years' experience as a traffic warden had rendered her pretty much embarrassment-proof. He realized that she thought she'd revealed too much of herself, not merely in what she'd just said but in her failure to volunteer to tell her story. It was, he thought, the failure of her resolve that she was condemning as "bloody typical", as well as all the respects in which she thought that she couldn't quite measure up to Janine.

"Mine lacks literary polish too," he said, trying to help her out. "Megan obviously did a lot of work on hers before she ever showed her face at AlAbAn, and people like Arthur and Neville have honed theirs by continual repetition. There's a sense, of course, in which they're all simply *made up*, but there's a more important sense in which they're not, in which they really are *given* to us, as they are, on a take-it-or-leave-it basis. It *would* be cheating to switch things around or invent things in the interests of more dramatic tension or smoother development. No matter how mad we all are, there's a profound method in our madness. The collective unconscious isn't the kind of thing that has motives or makes purposive plans, but there's still a sense in which we're instrumental. We have parts to play.

For once, Milly was prepared to join in. "Megan's right," she said. "We're not entirely ourselves. We might not have huge worms inside us, wearing us like smart cockleshells, but there are still things in us that aren't really *us*—things we can't command and can't control. Emotional incontinence."

"I think it might go further than that," Steve said, reflectively. "The limited empire of reason is part of the human condition. The bits of our minds that we think of as *us* have always had to battle against impulses from elsewhere—animal spirits, the passions, the *id*, whatever you want to call them—but this is something different."

"*This?*" Milly echoed, not quite getting his drift.

"Alien abduction," he said. "AlAbAn. The way our stories intersect and overlap. Something else is going on."

"Of course it is," Milly said, with a wry smile. "We're being abducted by inquisitive aliens—probed and analyzed and put to work on all kinds of weird tasks in other times, and maybe on other planets. No wonder we're not quite ourselves. We're probably infested with all kinds of escaped neuroworms from a multitude of future eras, whose cross-breeding will produce even more monstrous varieties. Maybe that's why we're about to become extinct. It probably has nothing to do with global warming and the release of all that trapped methane—we're going to be eaten up by parasitic worms from the great swamps that sprawl all over the time-stream. Now *that*'s a better story by far than the one in my experience. If only I could work that into a tale to tell...."

"Maybe that's why they're so interested in us," Steve said, going with the flow. "Maybe we're not just the first manifestation of Earthly intelligence. Maybe we're also the first species to have been destroyed by time-traveling researchers. I have to teach the second-year A-level students about Heisenberg's Uncertainty Principle. I don't really understand it myself, but what it boils down to, so far as I can see, is that the act of observation affects that which is being observed. In physics, that comes about because very tiny things are very sensitive to the interference that any process of observation involves, but there's a similar problem affecting the observation of entities that are aware of being observed. The time-travelers may be changing us simply by virtue of all the ways in which they're trying to observe us—including turning some of us into instruments of self-observation. Maybe it's not just us; maybe the same thing will recur all along the time-stream, with every species that becomes interesting being warped and then obliterated by the interest it attracts. You're right, Mil; that's a much better tale than the one I dredged up from my so-called recovered memory. If we could make a story out of that—or *two* stories, to tell at consecutive meetings...."

"It would be cheating," Milly finished for him.

"Yes, it would," Steve agreed.

"Not that...," she began and then stopped.

"Not that we can claim the moral high ground," Steve finished for her, "when it comes to cheating on our friends and lovers."

Milly was blushing again, but Steve kept his eyes on the road. "See," he said, after a slight pause. "Wireless telepathy isn't all *that* difficult. We need to get the tales we have out into the open, don't we? In one sense, we have all the time in the world, but in another...we don't. I'll make you a definite promise. I *will* put my hand up next week—*and* the next. If you go first, I'll be right behind you, and if you change your mind again...then I'll lead the way."

"I won't change my mind again," she said. "I'm really not that sort of person."

He knew that she wasn't telling the exact truth, but he also knew why she'd said it. She was reminding him, in what was supposed be a subtle fashion, that he *was* that kind of person, and couldn't deny it.

"It's a definite promise," he repeated. "No going back. We might not be any happier afterwards, mind—but maybe there are more important things than happiness."

Milly didn't reply to that—but then, Milly didn't know what a big thing it was for him to make that concession, even if she did suspect that he was thinking about Janine, and not so much about happiness as sexiness. In his heart of hearts, though, Steve couldn't help wondering whether, once he and Milly had both got their secrets out into the open, it might somehow become easier to trade Milly in for Janine than it was just at present, when they all had so much to hide.

They had just reached the outskirts of Salisbury when Milly suddenly grabbed at her coat pocket. Steve didn't understand what she was doing, at first; then he realized that she must have switched off her mobile's ring-tone so that it wouldn't disturb the AlAbAn meeting, but had left the vibrate function activated in case someone wanted to get through to her urgently.

"Hello, Mummy?" Milly said, when she had got the phone out and had read the name of the caller from the display. "No.... Oh.... Yes.... No.... Yes...first thing in the morning. I promise. Yes."

"Bad news?" Steve asked, as she let the hand holding the phone fall back into her lap.

"Daddy's had another stroke," Milly said. "He's just been taken into hospital. He might die."

"Oh," Steve said. "I'm sorry."

"It's not your fault," she said.

* * * * * * *

Steve and Milly had had plans for Friday and Saturday evenings, but they all became redundant when Milly had to take the train to Bath first thing Friday morning, not knowing when she'd be able to return. Steve was able to gladden Rhodri Jenkins' heart and rake up extra moral credit by actually volunteering to stay on after hours on Friday afternoon. He set out to follow exactly the same schedule thereafter as he'd followed on the Wednesday, except that he bought fish and chips instead of cooking for himself. He'd barely settled down at his PC desk and picked up his headphones, however, when his doorbell rang.

Steve couldn't help feeling a flutter of hope that maybe it was Janine, who had decided at last that they really ought to have a serious talk, and see if they could patch things up. When he opened the door, though, that faint flicker of hope turned instantly to ashes. It wasn't Janine; it was her friend Alison.

Alison was dripping wet, because it was raining heavily outside. She had no umbrella and she was bare-headed. Her raincoat was soaked, and so was her almost-blonde hair, which seemed almost grey in the dull light. Her blue eyes weren't bright at present; they too seemed almost grey, in harmony with her dismal attitude.

Steve froze, holding the door defensively, as if he were facing a charity-collector or a pair of neatly-dressed Mormons.

"Is Milly here?" Alison asked.

"No," Steve said, bluntly.

"Oh," Alison said. "Only, I've been round to her place, and she's not there. Janine said that she might be here."

That cleared up the mystery of how Alison had found out his address—as a schoolteacher, of course, Steve wasn't listed in the telephone directory—but it still left a lot of questions unanswered, none of which Steve dared ask.

"Well, she isn't," Steve said. He realized, though, that the brusqueness of his tone, which was only significant of his own embarrassment, might suggest to Alison that he might be lying, and that Milly might have sent him to the door with instructions to deny that she was there when she really was. It was for that reason that he added: "She had to go to Bath. Her father had a stroke. I don't know when she'll be back."

"Oh," Alison said, again. "Right. I left her a voicemail, you know, ages ago—twice, just in case she deleted it without listening to it the first time. She still won't return my calls. I don't want it to end like this. I don't suppose, by any chance, that you'd be willing to have a word with her?"

"About what?" Steve said, utterly confused.

"About the situation. It's unfair. You must see that. It really wasn't my fault."

"What wasn't?" Steve asked, helplessly.

He watched comprehension dawn on Alison's face. "She hasn't told you, has she?" she said. "She hasn't told you what actually happened?"

"I have no idea that you're talking about," Steve confessed.

"I didn't shop her to Janine," Alison said. "Not deliberately. It was an accident. I had no idea you and she were together, that night in the Pheasant. I had no reason to doubt that Janine would be along any minute, and if I had thought something was going on, I wouldn't have phoned Jan to tell her. In fact, when Janine phoned me half an hour later, I automatically assumed that she was phoning from the Pheasant, because Milly had told her that she'd seen me, and that we'd talked again about getting together for one of our nights out because I'd had to rule out the previous Tuesday. I assumed that Milly was there with her. I didn't mean to let the cat out of the bag. I didn't know there was a cat *in* the bag, and if I had, I wouldn't have let it out—but I didn't, so I did, by accident. It wasn't my fault. It really wasn't. Milly won't listen, though. She blames me. Did she tell you about the letter?"

Steve shook his head, dumbly.

Alison shook hers, because she was on the brink of tears—an impression assisted by the raindrops clinging to her slightly puffy cheeks. "Look," she said, "Can I come in? I can't talk about the letter on your doorstep. It's too...can I come in?"

Steve opened the door fully and stepped aside. Alison came in, and sat down on the settee. Steve pulled one of the dining chairs away from the table and perched on it awkwardly, keeping the bulk of the coffee-table between them. This was, after all, Alison the Slut, who had a dark history of screwing Milly's boy-friends. She didn't look much like a scheming temptress at the moment, however—not with her wet hair plastered to her skull and the collar of her blouse soaking wet—and Steve believed everything she'd said about the way in which Janine had found out, entirely accidentally, that he and Milly had been together in the pub on that fateful night.

"Would you like a cup of tea?" Steve asked, because that was the sort of thing people were supposed to ask when other people came into their homes.

"No thanks," Alison replied. "Milly wrote a letter to the Town Hall—addressed to the Town Clerk, of all people, although it got passed around quite a bit. It was about me and Mark, and a few other people working for the council I'd previously had relationships with. It gave details. Luckily, most of the details were false, because I'd embroidered the tales I'd told Janine and Milly, and that made most of the rest potentially deniable. The allegations were dismissed as malicious or unprovable, so no formal action was contemplated, let alone taken. I haven't lost my job, and neither has Mark—but even so, it was extremely embarrassing. It got back to Mark's wife...and one or two of the other wives too, all of whom believe that there's no smoke without fire. You can't imagine what it's like to become the Scarlet Woman of Salisbury throughout the local government system."

Steve thought briefly about Tracy and Jill and practically being sent to Coventry, but he realized that the comparison must be rather pale. Alison worked at the hub of the civic community, along with hundreds of other local government officials and God only knew what else, in actual corridors of power. He really couldn't imagine what it would be like to be cast as the Scarlet Woman of Salisbury in circumstances like those; being cast as the Roaring Boy of the city's second best comp obviously didn't come close.

"I know she wrote the letter before she heard my voicemail," Alison said, "and wouldn't have done it if she'd realized, but even so...she could have given me a chance to explain. I know there was the other thing, which was all my fault, but I don't know how my times I've apologized for that, and she's always said that she'd forgiven me, and that we'd moved on. I really didn't think that she still hated me for that—but even if she did, she really could have given me a chance to explain before doing *that*. And now she won't return my calls. She won't even let me *try* to make it right."

"Oh," was all Steve could say. Alison had not, in fact, burst into tears, but she still looked as if she might. He had no idea what to do in a situation of this sort, so he stayed silent.

"I'm sorry," Alison said. "You must think we're all completely mad—all three of us. Didn't bargain for this sort of palaver, I imagine, when you first started dating Janine."

"No," Steve admitted.

"We aren't like this really," Alison said, regretfully. "We weren't like it when we were at school. You don't teach at our old place, do you—you're at the other one?"

Steve nodded.

"Still," Alison went on, "You must know what it's like—the kind of friendships schoolgirls form, and try to hold together when their schooldays come to an end. There was a bigger group of us at school, of course, but we three were always the core of it. When we decided not to go away to university—which was a sort of mutual decision, in a way, and a perverse one, given that Milly, at least, was certainly university material—we got tighter. I suppose we got tighter still when Milly's parents moved to Bath and she stayed, apparently staying *with us* rather than just *behind*. She was the one who was most insistent on us staying friends then, although Jan had never got on with her parents, so she needed the unholy trinity too. So did I. I think I always needed it most, even though I didn't have that kind of practical reason. I was always the hanger-on, not as pretty as them. I always had to work harder to be part of it—to entertain them. It was as if they were two queens and I was the court jester. Sometimes, it was as if I were doing things on their behalf. Janine and Milly talked incessantly about losing their virginity, but I was the one who did it first. They talked incessantly abut screwing this teacher or that, but I was the only one who did it at all. Half the things I did, I only did so I could tell *them* about it, because it amused them so much—and then Milly puts it all in a bloody letter to the Town Clerk! If only I hadn't made up all those gory details! If only I hadn't done the things I did do, in order to have some gory details to embroider! You can see, can't you, why it's all so bloody *unfair*?"

Steve contrived a hesitant nod.

"Don't look so frightened, Steve," Alison said, with only a slight harshness in her voice. "You're in no moral danger. Jan did suggest, when she gave me your address, that if I found you on your own I could get my own back on Milly by doing *my thing* again, but she really wanted me to get *her* own back, and she didn't *really* want that. It would be too much, even for me—and it's not really *my thing* at all. I'm really not that sort of person. I mean, it's one thing to get carried away in a reckless moment, and screw someone else's boyfriend without giving a thought to the possible consequences, but it would be something else entirely to *plan* something like that, wouldn't it?" She waited for Steve to nod again before adding: "So you're quite safe. I won't throw myself at you. Okay?"

"I understand," Steve said. "I'm sorry—I didn't know about all of this. It's taken me by surprise. I suppose Milly didn't want to confess to me that she'd made a mistake, and didn't think it would matter if she let me carry on thinking that her original conclusions were justified. She wouldn't have told me about the letter anyway, I don't think...and, to tell you the truth, I'm not so sure I needed or wanted to know about that."

"I'm sorry," Alison said. "I really did come here looking for Mil, not to make trouble. It might be best, on reflection, if you don't tell her I called. I'll ask Jan to let me know when she comes back from Bath, and keep on trying her at her flat until I find her there—preferably on her own. Jan will know when she comes back, won't she? I know they're not talking to one another, but Jan still sees her at that UFO group they go to, doesn't she?"

"Yes," Steve said. "But it only meets once a fortnight."

"Well, maybe Jan will start returning Mil's calls, and they'll begin patching things up. Then, maybe, we can get the whole thing patched up. I suppose it shouldn't matter, really, now that we're all grown women with our own jobs and our own lives. We should all have our own boy-friends too, I suppose, but Mil seems to have the monopoly for the moment. If we could just get one each, and stop borrowing one another's...sorry, that's a bit undiplomatic, isn't it?"

"Don't mind me," Steve said. "I'm sorry for my part in causing you all such distress. If I hadn't slept with Milly behind Janine's back, you wouldn't be in difficulties either, so I suppose I'm as much to blame for your troubles as Milly is...more, even."

"You weren't to know," Alison assured him. "The roots of the problem go back a long way. You were just a catalyst. You just did what men do. You disappointed Jan, mind—she thought you might be better than that."

"I don't know why," Steve said. "She knew my track record. I never have been any better."

"Fair enough," Alison said. "What she probably really thought was that she was special enough to break your pattern and keep you in line. She's always been the prettiest one of the three, you see— she probably assumed that what had happened to Milly could never happen to her. I love her dearly, but she's always had that hint of smugness about her. That's why she's so terribly broken up about it."

"Is she?" Steve said, genuinely surprised.

"Oh yes. She won't thank me for letting you know, but she's taken it very hard. Not because you're anything extra special, per- haps—more because she lost out to Milly. It won't last forever. It can't, because she needs us as much as we need her. The fact that she's seeing so much of her parents will be a constant reminder of that. In the end, she'll have to patch it up with Mil, and Mil will have to patch it up with me, because we're still best friends, in spite—or perhaps because—of the fact that we're all so jealous of one another. At least, I hope we'll patch it up."

"And what about me?" Steve asked.

"Pardon?"

"What happens to me, when you all get back together and patch it up?"

"God knows," she said. "What do you want to happen to you?"

Steve couldn't answer that one without betraying someone, so he said nothing.

"It's not my problem," Alison told him. "I've got enough of my own, and I'm certainly not going to add yours to my list as well as Jan's and Mil's. If it's any help, Jan really does want you back— desperately, even—but I'm not sure that she'd be willing to take you back. I don't know how much pride she has, but it's a lot more than I've got. What Milly wants, I don't know—she won't return my calls. What do *you* want?"

There was still nothing Steve could say, so he said it.

"You don't know," Alison said, on his behalf. "Or, if you do, you daren't say. Don't worry about it. It's not your fault. You just happened to fall into the whirlpool. Being abducted by aliens is a breeze compared with getting caught up in this sort of maelstrom, I dare say."

Steve could see that Alison was no longer on the brink of tears, even though the rain hadn't quite evaporated from her face; indeed, she seemed to be growing more robust by the minute, drawing strength from the knowledge that he was in a predicament as awkward as her own.

"You've never been abducted, then?" Steve said, knowing how feeble the remark was as a riposte.

"I get abducted by aliens all the time," she replied, trying to contrive a laugh but not succeeding. "I'm the group slut, remember: the Scarlet Woman of Salisbury. Aliens are always probing me in uncomfortable places. Mil used to pester us to go to AlAbAn meetings with her, in the beginning, but Jan thought it was too silly, and I thought it was unnecessary. I used our girls' nights out as my confessionals, you see. I never believed for a moment that Milly really believed she'd been abducted, but I could never figure out why she was going to the meetings. You probably understand that a lot better than I do."

"I think so," Steve said. "Actually, I don't believe for a moment that I was physically transported into the distant future by a time-traveling spaceship armed with a tractor beam—but that's not the point. The point is that the experiences are real, even if they're just a particular kind of hallucination. Milly's not lying, and it's not some kind of game she's playing with Janine and you. Something really did happen to her, and it really did disturb her, even if she never left her nice warm bed."

"Right," Alison said. "Maybe I ought to start coming to the meetings, now that Jan's a regular. It might help us get back together and settle our differences. What do you think?" While she was speaking she stood up, obviously having decided that it was time to go. Because she'd never so much as unbuckled the belt of her raincoat, there were no further preparations to be made.

"It's up to you," Steve said, standing up in his turn. "I don't have an opinion, one way or the other." He walked her to the door of the flat, and opened it for her.

"Thanks for listening," she said, hesitating on the threshold. "You did me a real favor—I needed to talk to someone, to get it all out in the open. I could hardly spill the beans to anyone at work."

"You're welcome," Steve said.

"You can tell Mil whatever you like," Alison added, "or nothing at all."

"We don't have anything to hide, do we?" Steve said.

For the first time, Alison smiled. "No," she said, "we don't. Nothing at all. Not so much as a single wicked thought. You'd almost think that we were the kind of people who could learn from our past mistakes. Thanks again."

"You're welcome," Steve repeated, automatically. Instead of going back to his PC, though, he went back to the settee and sat down, carefully avoiding the slight damp patch left by Alison's coat-clad backside.

He couldn't help wondering what might have happened had he made the first move that Alison had so ostentatiously refrained from making—maybe by making a heroic effort to comfort her when she'd almost been in tears—even though there had never been the slightest possibility that he might have done anything of the sort, in this or any other universe. He had, at the end of the day, proved to be better than *that*.

* * * * * * *

Milly phoned later that evening to say that she'd be in Bath all weekend and perhaps most of the following week. Her father was still in the Intensive Care Unit, because he couldn't breathe unaided, but he was stable at present. If he managed to recover sufficient control of his muscles in the wake to the stroke to breathe unaided again, there was a chance that he might also be able to talk again, and live some sort of a conscious life—but if he didn't, he might relapse into a permanent vegetative state. Only time would tell—and even the best possible outcome, it seemed, would not restore him to anything that would pass for a normal life. It was unlikely in the extreme that he'd ever be able to walk again, or feed himself.

Steve didn't mention Alison's visit. It didn't seem to be the kind of thing that he ought to try to explain on the phone, especially when Milly's father was lying at death's door.

The situation eventually extended throughout the entire week. Steve spoke to Milly every evening on the phone—which seemed to emphasize the fact that he was suspended in a kind of existential limbo, always at a loose end, playing internet poker or surfing. He did three stints of after-school supervision on Monday, Wednesday and Thursday, but when he volunteered again on the Friday Rhodri Jenkins actually turned him down.

"Have to share the burden, boyo," the deputy head explained. "Can't get into a situation where the shirkers can get way with it because the suckers are willing to do all the work. Can't get too dependent on you, either, as you'll doubtless be making up for lost time when your girl-friend finally gets back—although it's beginning to look as if that might not be before the end of term. Don't go getting up to any mischief in the meantime, mind. It's high time you settled down, and a traffic warden's exactly the kind of woman you need to keep you in line."

In spite of this instruction, Steve attempted to call Janine that night, for the first time in three weeks, thinking that she had probably seen Alison since the previous Friday, and that Alison might have put in a good word for him, in the cause of getting all the warring factions together to settle their various differences. Janine refused to talk to him, and told him, not for the first time, never to call her again. Evidently her pride still had the upper hand in its ongoing contest with her desperation.

By the time Saturday night rolled around, Steve was feeling seriously restless. He'd spent the afternoon betting on the exchanges, but he'd ended up thirty pounds down and exceeded his self-imposed limit for the week. He knew that he had to resist the temptation to think that he *had* to go on line to win it back at poker, because that was the way to addiction. He was well up to date in checking out the other websites on his favorites list, and he couldn't face the thought of an evening watching television, even though his ability to cope with cliffhangers had been recently tested, and not found wanting. He didn't dare try to call Janine again so soon after his last knock-back, and also rejected the possibility of trying to discover Alison's phone number, after only a few moments' consideration.

Eventually, Steve looked Walter Wainwright up in the phone book and rang him to ask if he could have a quiet word in private about AlAbAn rules and etiquette, as he was planning to volunteer to tell his story the following Thursday.

"I'm very busy, Steve," Walter said, apologetically, "especially with it being quiz night at the Royal Oak. I haven't missed one of those in twenty years. The quiz doesn't start till eight, though, so I suppose we could have a quiet drink beforehand, if that would be convenient for you."

"I don't have anything else to do," Steve assured him. "Where is the Royal Oak, exactly?"

It wasn't until Walter told him that the Royal Oak was in Codford St. Mary that Steve remembered having been there once before, when Janine had reluctantly taken him to meet her parents, who lived in Codford St. Peter. That didn't prepare him, though, for the shock of walking into the pub's lounge at five past seven and running straight into Janine, who was carrying a pint of lager in one hand and two gin-and-tonics in the other. Steve almost ducked, but it was obviously her father's lager, and Janine wasn't the kind of girl to use someone else's pint to make a futile gesture.

"Are you stalking me, you slimy bastard?" she demanded hotly.

"Actually," Steve said, in his best martyred tone, "I'm meeting Walter Wainwright." In the meantime, he put two and two together, and realized that the reason Walter was giving Janine lifts to AlA-bAn meetings probably had something to do with him knowing her parents, as he'd mentioned more than once when Janine started going to the meetings. Presumably, that acquaintance was not unconnected with Walter's twenty years' experience of quiz nights in the Royal Oak. Steve also realized that Janine was so short of something to do on a Saturday night now that she'd dumped him that she was volunteering for her Dad's pub quiz team, in spite of the fact hat she didn't get on with her parents at all.

Steve found Walter without further ado, and asked him what he was drinking. He returned from the crowded bar with a whisky and water for Walter and a glass of Shiraz for himself. "The reason I wanted to talk to you," he said, without further ado, "is that I've formulated a theory that might help to explain what's really going on in people's abduction experiences, and I wondered if it would be within the rules to present it to the group along with my own experience."

"You aren't the first person to have a theory, by any means," Walter told him, dolefully, "and you wouldn't be the first to tell the group all about it, if that's what you want to do. I'm always reluctant to tell people that there are things they shouldn't say, because we're a support group, and we want people to feel free to say whatever they need to say—but you're a teacher, so I'm sure you can see that there's a slight problem...well, of course you can, or you wouldn't be here now, would you? The thing is that, in order for us to support you, as fully as we'd like, we do need you to show a little reciprocity. If you were to start using other people's experiences as fodder for your theories, you see, that might not seem very supportive to them. They might feel that their experiences were being questioned, or even undermined, and that's not what AlAbAn is all about. Theorizing your own experience is perfectly fine—the search for explanations is always part and parcel of coming to terms with the experience, but it might be polite if you stuck to your own experience, and didn't involve anyone else's."

"I take your point," Steve said. "But not being able to make generalizations is a bit restrictive, given that making generalizations is what theorizing is all about. I probably won't need to refer to anyone else's story in a specific sense, but I will have to refer to the general themes that keep cropping up."

"What sort of general themes?" Walter asked.

"Well, the fact that all the stories I've heard are interpretable in terms of the aliens being time-travelers rather than space travelers, and the fact that, if you look at them collectively, they do add up to a vague image of what the future will be like: a long series of adaptive radiations, producing very different kinds of climax communities, punctuated by large-scale extinction-events."

"You haven't been coming to the group very long, Steve—just since the beginning of September, if I remember rightly, and we're only at the beginning of December. I'm not sure that you ought, as a good scientist, to be generalizing on the basis of such a small sample."

"Fair comment," Steve said. "I'd love to have a broader perspective, if you'd care to share your own observations with me. It wouldn't necessarily harm my theory, though, to find out that the time travel theme is fairly recent and fairly localized, because the sort of process I'm envisaging is a dynamic one. It would be entirely expectable, for instance, that all experiences of alien sightings and excursions would have been interpreted in terms of space travel back in the 1960s, because that was the dominant idea of the day—a key notion in our attempt to interpret our situation in the universe and our prospects for the future. Things are different now—the idea that we can see the future as the pioneering of new frontiers in space is more-or-less dead and buried, and all our calculations regarding future social progress have been confused and confounded by global warming and the unfolding ecocatastrophe. It's not surprising, in those historical circumstances, that we should be interpreting our abduction experiences—and, more importantly *sharing* our abduction experiences—with the aid of different hypothetical reference-points. Do you see what I'm driving at?"

"Oh yes," Walter said, earnestly. "I may be an old fool, but I'm not an idiot. I've read Jung too, you know—and a lot of books you probably haven't. I've heard other theories, remember. They come and they go. That's not what AlAbAn is *for*, Steve. AlAbAn's purpose is to lend support to people who have these experiences, who couldn't get that support from anywhere else—not from their families, or their workmates, or their friends. It's for people to tell their stories in a non-skeptical environment, where no one will laugh at them or accuse them of deluding themselves. I don't want to violate that principle here and now by questioning your theory or suggesting that you shouldn't have a theory. I'm delighted that you've found that means of getting to grips with your own experience, and you have my full support in extrapolating it as far as you can and as far as you need to. I don't want to censor what you might want to say to the meeting, be it next Thursday or some time in the new year. All I'm asking you to do is think about it, and try to make sure that you're continuing to offer us the kind of support you want and expect from us. We're not scientific investigators, and we're not educators—we're just a group of friends, trying to help one another out. If I've learned one thing in forty years of chairing the local branch of AlAbAn, it's that we all have to come to terms with our own experiences in our own way."

"We're all unique," Steve said. "Yes, that's part and parcel of my theory. Even though we're all unique, though, we're also all parts of something greater. AlAbAn is a collective as well as a set of individuals. The communication aspect is important."

"Yes it is," Walter said. "It's very important. That's why we have to be so careful. That's why we have to be supportive, and non-judgmental, and accept one another for exactly what we are, instead of trying to fit one another's experiences into our own way of seeing. I think you know well enough what can happen to a group of friends when that kind of supportiveness breaks down."

Steve started slightly at that, although he realized that he had no call to be surprised. Even if Janine hadn't taken Walter Wainwright into her confidence by telling him everything, the old man wasn't blind, and he was certainly no fool.

"You must have formed general impressions of your own," Steve said, "in more than forty years. You must have ideas of your own as to what's really going on."

"Of course I have," the old man agreed. "I even used to formulate theories, once upon a time. Then I gave it up—not just for the reasons I've just given you, but for another. You might not be as sympathetic to that one, given that you're a teacher, but I'll tell you anyway. Theorizing is, in essence, a matter of telling other people what to think, telling them how to interpret their own experiences. Even if the theories are right—in fact, especially if the theories are right—they don't like it. They resent it. Even if they need it, the way your pupils need the substance of the national curriculum, not just in order to pass their exams but to function as thinking individuals, they still resent it.

"Running AlAbAn and its predecessors has taught me that people like listening to stories. They're prepared to be interested in things that happened to another person, and sometimes become quite enthusiastic to know what happened next. Because of that, they're prepared to take an interest in how what happened made the story-teller feel, and sometimes in what it made the story-teller think—but mostly, they just want to know what happened next. What they're not interested in, and won't thank a story-teller for, is telling them how it's supposed to make them feel, and what it's supposed to make them think. When I realized that, I made my own decision as to what was important, and what my groups could actually do for people—people like you, Milly and Janine.

"I want to give people space and time to come to terms with their own experiences in their own way, whatever that might be. I've been lucky enough to find other people to help me do that—especially Amelia. I've been friends with Amelia for more than fifty years. I'd like to think that we'd both been lucky in that respect, and that we'd shared our luck with our other friends. It's up to you, Steve. You can say anything you want to at the meeting. All I ask is that you think about it first—about all our mutual friends, even the absent ones, and whether you can support them as well as supplying your own needs. It's not easy, sometimes, as you well know."

"I get it," Steve said. "Thanks, Walter—I think that's what I needed to hear. At any rate, it's a judgment worthy of Solomon, and I certainly don't think that you're an old fool. I never did. I think they're setting up for the quiz now, so I'd better leave you to it. Thanks for slotting me in."

"Actually," Walter said, "you could return the favor if you've nothing better to do. We're a man short tonight. Our history specialist had to go into hospital for a hernia operation."

"I'm a science teacher," Steve said apologetically.

"I know," Walter told him. "We rarely get science questions, unfortunately, but it doesn't much matter. We rarely win, even when we're at full strength. Our combined ages usually add up to far more than three hundred, which is a lot of experience, but our memories aren't what they used to be and we've lost touch with modern fashions in just about everything. If you can bear the thought of spending Saturday night with four old men, we'll be glad of your company as well as your input—unless, of course, you'd feel happier teamed with people of your own age. There are always a few strays around to form up new teams, and you might do better playing against us than for us. The prizes aren't up to much, though."

Steve looked around, to watch the other teams forming up. Janine, he observed, was the only young person in a team of older people, although her father and his three companions weren't nearly as old as Walter and the other old men who were shuffling over to join him now that he'd signaled them to do so.

"They won't let you on to that team, I'm afraid," Walter said, following the direction of Steve's forlorn gaze. "They're frequent winners, so there's always a queue to join them. It put one or two noses out of joint, I can tell you, when Janine got in ahead of their regular reserves—but family always counts for more than convention, and rightly so. She pulls her weight, mind—very good on geography, I understand. We get a lot of geography questions, since the budget airlines made foreign tourism so cheap. Not our forte, alas—Stan and Keith haven't been out of the country since they came back from National Service in the Far East in the fifties. Different generations, different attitudes."

"I don't travel abroad myself," Steve admitted, "but if you'll have me, I'm in. Maybe we'll get an unexpected glut of science questions and give Janine's Dad a run for his money."

No such glut materialized, alas, and Walter's team came a poor seventh in spite of Steve's heroic assistance in the well-trodden field of popular culture. Unfortunately, the Royal Oak had no shortage of experts in that area, whose knowledge of television shows was far greater than Steve's. He was able to take some comfort, though, from the fact that Janine's father's team hadn't won either, perhaps because their new star player had been distracted by the necessity of looking daggers at Steve all night.

Milly phoned him, as usual, on Sunday afternoon. "I phoned three times last night," she said, "but you had your mobile switched off."

"I had to," Steve explained. "Rules of the game. I went to see Walter Wainwright to check up on lines I might be in danger of crossing if I tell my story on Thursday, and got drafted into playing for his team in his local pub quiz. No ring-tones allowed."

"Would that be the quiz night at the Royal Oak in Codford, by any chance?" Milly asked, her suddenly-icy tone seeming to freeze the phone in Steve's hand. "The one that Janine's father always wins?"

"He only came third last night," Steve said, feebly. He waited for the deadly question, but it never came; Milly, it seemed, already knew—or was prepared to take it for granted—that Janine must have been there.

"I just wanted to ask Walter about group protocol," Steve insisted. "I thought, with your father being at death's door, that you might not make it Thursday and I'd have to do my thing instead, as I'd sworn on oath." He figured out a moment too late why that had been an extremely unwise thing to have thought, let alone said.

"You mean," Milly said, "that you were planning to tell your story *while I wasn't there?*"

Steve's explanations, which had to do with promises made and anxieties formed and a general tendency to thoughtlessness, stuck in his throat, while Milly added; "Well, you don't have to worry. Dad's still stable, and seems likely to remain that way for some time to come. Come hell or high water, I'll be there."

She kept her promise, although Steve didn't see her until she phoned after school had packed up on Thursday to tell him to pick her up at the railway station at seven. Their conversation on the way out to East Grimstead was entirely dominated by the subject of her father's health and her mother's response to its deterioration. Steve couldn't help noticing that Milly seemed to be suffering more considerably than was strictly necessary in sympathy with her parents; she didn't seem to be herself at all.

"You're in no condition to tell your story," he observed, as he parked the Citroen, although he knew there was some risk in saying so. "Far better to let me go first."

"It's just talking," Milly replied. "I can do talking. I don't have panic attacks when I relive my experience." When Steve opened his mouth to reply, she immediately added: "Just leave it, will you. Let's get inside. I'm dying for a cup of tea and a biscuit."

She seemed to be telling the truth—at least, once they were inside, she paid far more attention to her tea and biscuits than she paid to Steve, or anyone else.

When the time came for Walter Wainwright to call for volunteers to tell a story, they both stuck up their hands immediately, as agreed. As expected, Walter chose Milly.

CHAPTER SIXTEEN

ROAD RAGE INCIDENT

I've been coming here a long time and I want to apologize for having taken so long to tell you my story. I've known for a long time that it's no more bizarre than most other people's stories, and that you'd be perfectly polite about it, but I just wasn't ready. There were times when I thought I'd never be ready, but I think I am now. I think I can tell it without fainting or breaking down in tears. The memory of nearly being eaten by six different sorts of dinosaurs, shot dead by leering lizards with comic-book blasters and blotted out by shadows from the other side of time, all in the space of a couple of hours, doesn't seem nearly as frightening now I've done a few shifts as a traffic warden in school run territory.

As far as I can tell, the whole thing was a chapter of accidents. I think it was supposed to be a standard abduction—the little guys with the silvery skin and the almond-shaped eyes had me strapped down to an operating table when I woke up, and they were standing around me with the usual assortment of giant hypodermics and probes.

One of them was already leaning forward with a face-mask to give me another dose of anesthetic gas, and if he'd completed the action I dare say I'd have been out for the count until I woke up next morning feeling slightly nauseous and wondering whether I'd had a bad dream. He didn't manage to get the mask over my nose and mouth, though, before there was an almighty bang and the whole ship lurched.

The little guys went down like so many skittles. I suppose they must have been screaming in pain and howling in anger, although they sounded more like a flock of seagulls arguing over the last sardine, with a few rusty buzz-saws thrown in for good measure.

The lurch was only the beginning. I don't know whether flying saucers are supposed to be able to loop the loop, but the little guys certainly weren't ready for it when it happened—and after doing a further somersault we started spinning and swaying like crazy, tilting every which way. The aliens were tumbling like dice, but I was okay because I was securely strapped down—or sometimes up, and more often sideways than either. My head was spinning even worse than the ship, of course, and I blacked out a couple of times from vertigo and the after-effects of the anesthetic, but I've been to Alton Towers more than once, so my stomach's had a chance to get used to roller-coasters.

Everything settled down for a moment or two, and some of the aliens began to pick themselves up off what was now the floor—they were obviously tougher than they looked—but then there was another crash and off we went again, spinning and cartwheeling worse than the first time. This time, when we finally came to a stop, the ship was upside-down, and only a couple of the little guys were still capable of getting to their feet.

They didn't pay any attention to me, hanging upside-down in my straps. The ones who could still move quickly scuttled out of the room, and the ones who could only move slowly crawled after them at their own pace. The three they left behind weren't moving at all.

All of the restraints had held, and it took me several minutes to work my right hand free, but I managed to slip it out eventually. I was able to work the other waist-strap loose then, but I didn't actually unfasten it until I'd loosened the ankle-straps and the strap on my left wrist as well. Then, very carefully, I extracted myself from the restraints and let myself down. I didn't pay any attention to the injured aliens—I just wanted to get out of the crashed spaceship before its nuclear reactors exploded, or whatever.

It wasn't easy to find my way around, with the corridor and all the doors being upside-down, and some of them being more than a little caved in. The fact that none of it was really built for human-sized people didn't help. In the end, I managed to find a great gash in the side of the ship. I was a little thinner in those days, because I still had a problem with food and my self-image and so on, and I just about managed to squeeze out. I was so intent on the business of *getting* out that I didn't really take much notice of what was outside until I was actually *out*. I suppose I'd been subconsciously expecting Salisbury Plain, or maybe the New Forest, but what I found certainly wasn't anywhere in Wiltshire or its neighboring counties.

The first thing that hit me was the heat; it was like stepping into a sauna—and by that I mean that it was humid, sweltering heat. It wasn't actually raining, although the sky was solid with murky cloud, but it was as if the air were saturated with steam. There was enough vapor around, at any rate, to cut visibility to twenty or thirty yards, even where there were gaps in the trees. I say trees, but they weren't the sort of trees you see in Wiltshire. Some of them looked a bit like coconut palms, but most of them looked like giant ferns or monstrous cannabis plants. It wasn't just the serrated leaves that brought cannabis plants to mind—the air reeked with all kinds of nasty perfumes, some of which only had to be inhaled to send me as high as a kite. That's what it felt like, anyhow, as I tried to stagger away from the crashed saucer.

I was very conscious, as I made my escape, of having bare legs and no shoes; the hospital gown I'd been wearing on the operating table, and was still wearing, seemed extremely flimsy. Staggering wasn't easy, because we hadn't come down on dry land. The water I was wading through was ankle- to knee-deep, but it was clogged with all kinds of thick weed. I looked around right away for something that could pass for an island, but the first one I saw didn't look very inviting at all, because there were half a dozen of the silver-skinned aliens taking cover there. They all had guns and they were all shooting into the mist, at something I couldn't see.

I was glad that they were shooting in the opposite direction to me, but I figured that towards them definitely wasn't the direction to go. I started to make my way around the body of the stricken saucer, looking to get even further away from the guys with the guns. That was when the first dinosaur stuck its head out of the water and tried to sink its teeth into me.

When I say it was a dinosaur, I'm speaking approximately. I didn't know where I was, and I couldn't be sure that I hadn't been transported to some alien world, so it could have been some entirely alien life-form, but the moment I saw it I thought: *dinosaur*. It might not have been a dinosaur in the pedantic sense. Maybe it was some fairly distant and modestly-sized relative of a plesiosaur, but I don't really care much more now than I cared then.

Looking back now, I'm just grateful that it only had a head the size of a football, and fangs no worse than the average rottweiler. Its neck was flexible, but not so clever that I couldn't dodge its lunge. If I'd run into one of the ones that looked like a souped-up crocodile at that particular moment I wouldn't have lived to see all the rest, but as things were, I managed to duck under the head's thrust, and managed to get far enough out of range thereafter that its second attempt missed by a yard. Its body was under the water, and must have been impeded by the weed, because it didn't come after me.

I managed to get into the open before the thing with wings tried to take my head off—some kind of pterosaur, I guess it was—and I managed to shin up one of the things that looked more like a tree than most of its neighbors before the snaky thing came writhing over the giant-sized lily-pads. I didn't even see the crocodile-thing until I was six feet up the spiny trunk and comfortably out of reach of its snapping teeth. It waited at the bottom of the tree, though, just in case.

I took a moment to relax once I was clear of the things in the water, but I soon found out that I wasn't safe. What passed for the plant's trunk was like a vast fir-cone, maybe ten or twelve feet in diameter. There was no shortage of footholds, but I wasn't the only one that found them convenient. I don't know what to call the thing that swarmed around it and tried to bite through my leg, but I was profoundly glad when it took a bullet in the belly and fell into the crocodile's waiting jaws. At least, I was profoundly glad until I figured out that the bullet had actually been meant for me.

When the second bullet thudded into the woody stuff next to my head I tried to move around the plant, to get the thickness of the bole between me and the invisible shooter. I managed that, and then thought about going up into the crown—but when I saw the eyes and teeth that were waiting for me up there I calculated that I'd be better off on the ground, trying to put as many tree-trunks between me and the crashed saucer as possible. That meant that I had to avoid the crocodile, but it was busy with its meal, and obviously didn't want to leave meat that was safely dead in order to chase meat that might escape.

I managed to steer a course that avoided much of the water, and covered at least twenty yards without anything horrid getting within a foot of taking a bite out of me. My feet were stabbed by thorns and bruised by stones, but I never paused—until I ran straight into another bunch of shooters, who seemed very anxious to get to the party while there was still some sport to be had. If they hadn't been wearing clothes—uniforms, it seemed to me—and carrying guns they might have passed for native wildlife, because they looked like bipedal lizards, not so very different from those velociraptor things in *Jurassic Park*, but the guns they had were ray guns straight out of some other sci-fi movie, and one of them took a pot-shot at me as soon as he caught sight of me. I was lucky that it missed by at least a yard, because if I'd been as close to the trunk it hit as I'd been to the one that the bullet had splintered a couple of minutes earlier I'd have been knocked flat by the blast and scorched by the gout of flame it emitted. As it was, I was able to keep running, in yet another new direction,

I think they could have shot me in the back if they'd really wanted to, so I guess, in retrospect, that the screaming-match they started might have been the rest of the gang telling the one that had fired at me that I wasn't an approved target. I didn't have thought to spare for such niceties at the time, though; I just wanted to find some place—any place—where I'd be safe enough for a minute or so to try to get my breath back. Hauling that humid atmosphere in and out of my lungs was like trying to breathe soup, and the fact that I was so high by then that I was half-convinced that I could fly really wasn't helping.

Another crocodile tried to grab my foot as I splashed through the shallows, and I had to duck under another diving pterosaur, but the crocodile only had short legs and the pterosaur was a glider rather than a true flier, so neither of them came back for a second bite. I reached another spur of dry land, where there was just about enough space to move about under the giant fern-fronds, and the only things trying to bite me, for the moment, were mosquitoes. I had already begun to look around for something that might qualify as a better refuge when the mortar-shell fell and exploded, and there was suddenly flying debris everywhere. This time I *was* knocked flat, and more than a little scorched.

In what passed for normal circumstances in that awful place, I wouldn't have been able to lie helpless for as much as a minute without six different local scavengers gathering to bicker about which bit of me each of them was going to get to eat, but a bomb had just gone off. Now, I'm free to wonder whether it was the first bomb that had ever gone off on the surface of the Earth, but I wasn't sure at that moment whether I was on Earth or not. In any case, things were definitely not normal.

It took a full five minutes for the scavengers to arrive, and when they arrived they certainly weren't local. I could have believed that there were things like massive upright-walking locusts living along-side dinosaurs, but not upright-walking locusts carrying bazookas and machine-guns. There were ten of them. They seemed to be arguing just as much as the locals would have, but I had no idea why. They might have been arguing about which of them would get to eat me, shoot me or rape me, for all I knew; I didn't have a clue. All that I did know—and there was no doubt about it whatsoever—was that they were hopping, blazing, foot-stamping, tantrum-throwing mad.

I kept my head down long after I was capable of sitting up, hoping that when they finally started blasting they'd blast one another instead of me. They probably would have, if it had come to that. Instead, it was the lizards in uniform that started blasting them, and when the locusts opened fire themselves, it was the lizards they aimed at.

It was quite some firefight, while it lasted, although it didn't involve any more mortar rounds. Five of the ten insect-people went down, various bits of their upper bodies and heads having been boiled, seared or fried by the lizards' ray guns. I've no idea how many casualties the lizards took, nor have I any idea what had happened to the silver-skinned dwarfs, or which side they might have been on if they'd still been within shooting-range. If the lizards weren't wiped out, though, they must have beaten a hasty retreat, because I was alone with five of the locusts when silence finally fell.

It was authentic silence. When I'd first emerged from the crashed saucer, before the shooting had started, there had been a sonic background of buzzings, whistlings, and squawkings, but there was no buzzing, whistling or squawking now. The firefight had sent every animal and insect for half a mile around stampeding away from us.

The silence didn't last, though. The locusts started arguing again—not quite as vociferously as before, but nastily enough. Their voices were high-pitched and full of whistling sounds, and they made my eardrums ache. I was convinced by then, though, that they weren't about to shoot, eat or rape me. Whatever sort of bone of contention I'd become, it evidently wasn't one that required them to rend me limb from limb right away.

For the first time, I had a moment to think—or would have had, if it hadn't been for the dope I'd breathed in and the whistling in my ears, either one of which would have made it difficult to string two thoughts together to make a train. Somehow, though, I managed to think that what was happening was *all wrong*. Whoever these various sets of monsters were, and whatever beef they had with one another, they shouldn't have been shooting up the neighborhood. Like everyone else, I'd heard the story about what might happen to future history if a time-traveler accidentally stood on a Jurassic butterfly—and here were these guys crashing spaceships and lobbing bombs at one another.

I guess I wasn't the only one to think that. I'd just got around to wondering whether the history-changing potential of their recklessness might be what the big argument was about when the shadows came, and the locusts really freaked out.

I call them shadows, because they were black and didn't seem to be made of anything. They weren't so much *there* as conspicuously *not there*, if that makes any sense at all: just weird flickering patches of *absence* moving through the interstices of the material world.

If each individual shadow was a separate entity, there were probably a dozen or so converging on the locusts, but they might all have been different aspects of the same entity—perhaps two-dimensional cross-sections of the multitudinous limbs of some ten-dimensional creature cutting through our three-dimensional space. Maybe the locusts knew what the shadows were, and maybe they didn't—but they knew enough to know that their guns and bazookas were useless now. They never fired a shot—just ran like hell.

They were very fast, but running was just as futile as shooting would have been. The shadows chased them down, and...well, I don't exactly know what they did. Maybe they devoured the locusts, maybe they just pulled them out of our space and into some other dimension. Either way, whenever a shadow caught a locust, it flowed all around it, and the locust was gone—utterly annihilated, it seemed.

One, two, three, four, five—all gone, in less time than it took me to count.

Then they came for me.

Actually, they came for the dead bodies first. They cleaned up the patch of ground like the charwomen from hell—one quick flick of the shadow-duster, and everything was gone: body-parts, ichor-stains, shell-cases. Broken ferns became whole again; burned leaves were healed. It was like time winding back, but only for a second or two. Once the bodies were gone and everything else was on its way back to the condition it had been in before, the shadows settled on me—more than one of them, I think.

* * * * * * *

I thought that I was dead. I thought, in fact, that I had been an-nihilated as utterly as the locusts.

Strangely enough, I continued thinking that I was dead for quite some time. I actually continued to think that I was *experiencing non-existence*, and if Descartes himself had come along to tell me that it was a contradiction in terms, I'd have told him that unless and until he'd actually been there and done it, he ought to keep his medita-tions to himself.

It wasn't just that I thought I wasn't; it was that I actually thought that *because* I thought I wasn't, I wasn't. I know *that* doesn't make sense—not now—but it did at the time...except, I suspect, that I wasn't *at the time* at all, and that was what the trouble was. I was out of time, or beyond time, or in a special sort of darkness where nothing was possible but things still were.

I had been high on that dope-laden atmosphere, but I wasn't high any more. I had been in pain, from half a hundred bruises and several superficial burns, but I wasn't any more. I wasn't...*anything*, and yet, after what might have been a split second or a billion years, I came back into the light, back into space, and back into time.

I was back on the operating table—the same operating table I'd been on before, so far as I could tell—but I wasn't strapped down. The straps were still there, loosened or unfastened as they had been when I'd wriggled out of them, but I wasn't in them. There was no sign of the little silver-skinned guys with the almond-shaped eyes, or any of their scary equipment. There was no one there but the shadows—who were still very conspicuous by their apparent absence, like holes in reality.

When I first sat up there seemed to be at least forty of them, but by the time I'd dangled my legs over the side of the table—which was the right way up now—there was only one.

Then there were none—except that something had stepped out of the final shadow, which certainly wasn't the entity that had cast it. It was a human woman. She looked like me—enough like me, in fact, to suggest that I'd served as a model, though not so nearly identical as to seem unduly creepy. She was wearing a traffic-warden's uniform just like mine—except, of course, that I wasn't wearing mine. I wished that I was, instead of the hospital gown. It was a very clean hospital gown, though—there wasn't a trace of blood or ichor on it.

"Thanks," I said. "Assuming, that is, that you just rescued me from Jurassic Hell, and don't have any plans to eat, shoot or rape me."

"Technically," she said, "it was late Triassic Hell, about two hundred and seventeen million years upstream of your pick-up point. Thank you for not losing your mind."

"At a guess," I said, "that's down to you too. You seem to have cleaned me up so well, inside and out, that I'm a good deal better now than I ever was before."

"That'll be temporary, I'm afraid," my approximate doppelgänger told me. "You might be able to hold on to some of it, if you're lucky, but time and the flesh will take their toll. You do deserve congratulation, though—you really could have come apart completely."

"I've been to Alton Towers more than once," I told her. "Rides terrify me, but it's the kind of terror I can tolerate. Are you taking me home?"

"Yes. We'll put you back as close as possible to your point of abduction. You might lose thirty minutes, maybe an hour, but no one will have noticed that you were gone."

I nearly said that they could have put me back a whole week later without anyone noticing or caring that I was gone, but I managed to stop myself. "What about the others?" I asked. "The lizards, the locusts and the midgets with the creepy eyes? Do they get to go home, or have they been sent to the naughty chair?"

She frowned slightly at that. "They won't be going home," she said. Rightly or wrongly, I took that to mean that appearances hadn't been deceptive, and that they really had been annihilated.

"So what are you?" I asked. "The time police? Every time someone stamps on a butterfly back at the dawn of time, you arrive to tidy up?"

"Yes," she said. I got the impression that she wasn't being *entirely* straight with me—but I also had a sneaking suspicion that she'd somehow put the question into my mind, purely in order that she could say "yes" when I asked it.

"But I get to go home because I'm innocent? I was just unlucky to be aboard the alien spaceship, getting probed without my consent, when whatever happened, happened?"

"Yes," she said, again.

"This is silly," I told her.

"Yes," she said, again—and then, just to break the pattern, she added: "It *is* silly—but it's not pointless. There's a reason for doing it this way."

I think I was supposed to ask what the reason was, or make another lucky guess at it, but time and the flesh were beginning to take their toll, and I was feeling more like myself—my *real* self, alas.

"What do those little idiots think they're playing at?" I asked, instead. "Why are they always snatching people out of their cozy beds and mucking about with them? If they've come all the way from Alpha bloody Centauri, why don't they just make contact and engage us in a mature dialogue like sensible unhuman beings?"

"If they really had come from Alpha Centauri they probably would," she said, with a slight sigh. "As things are, they daren't. Even minimal contact is a risk—if your species weren't on the very brink of extinction, they wouldn't risk it."

"Because it's not just Triassic butterflies you're worried about, is it?" I guessed. "Discreet as they are, in their own inefficient fashion, they're still risking the shadows by interfering with the twenty-first century."

"Yes."

"Don't start that again. They're *all* risking the shadows—the locusts, the lizards, and any number of others. They're all being as discreet as possible...but even so, they're all getting in one another's way. Why?"

"Some times attract more travelers than others. Your time is the hottest spot of all."

"Are humans really that interesting?"

"Not in themselves—but you were the first to reach that level of self-conscious intelligence and technical expertise, and you killed yourselves off with such amazing alacrity. That narrows the window of opportunity to researchers, you see, and generates unusual traffic density."

"I see," I said. "It's not so bad if they all obey the rules of the road and the parking restrictions, and show a little patience when things get sticky—but when frustrations build up, it only takes one little bump to set them off."

"Yes," she said, blatantly ignoring my previous complaint. Some people let uniforms go to their heads, and become unreasonably officious while wearing them, but I don't believe that she was that sort of person. Like me, she was doing her best.

"Not such a little bump, though, to bounce them two hundred million years," I observed. "Or is two hundred million years just a blink of Brahma's eye in the context of the great *kalpa*?"

"Yes," she said, again—but again she relented, and added: "There is a logic to it, although it's no more obvious to them than it is to you. There's a reason for the traffic, just as there's a reason for the rules. Dark matter holds the galaxies together, for now, and dark time protects the integrity of cause-and-effect, for now."

"For now?" I echoed.

"Obviously, *for now*. That's what *now* is."

"But there won't always be a now?"

"Of course there'll always be a now—but it's not as simple as that. There'll always be a then, too, but there'll also be an eternal if, just as there always has been. In the fullness of time...." She paused.

"Go on," I said, "In the fullness of time...what?"

"That," she said, as she turned back into a shadow, "is the question."

I couldn't resist saying: "I thought *to be or not to be* was the question," even though I was talking to nothing. I don't often get the chance to think of lines like that, and it was disappointing not to have been able to get it out on time. I had to imagine her reply—which was, of course, "Yes, of course."

I told myself that I'd been dreaming, but I didn't believe it. I also told myself to hang on tight to the dream I hadn't been dreaming, just in case I could bring back a little of that other self, in spite of the pressure of time and the flesh, and welcome it into my soul forever. I tried...and if nothing else, I remembered.

I think I did a little more than that, and maybe just thinking that was enough, because I've hardly thrown up more than half a dozen times since then, and even though I've put on a little weight, I don't feel bad about it. I don't feel bad about being hungry, and I don't feel bad about eating—not often, anyhow. I think I'm cured, or very nearly, and if I had to go a little bit crazy in order to get to that point in my life, I don't mind, so long as it's the kind of craziness that doesn't hurt me, or anyone else.

I did what I could to check, by the way, and so far as I can tell from the surviving fossil evidence—which is *extremely* limited—I really was in the late Triassic, and it really was the way it looks in those overcrowded pictures in the books they sell to kids, with all the species the artist can depict crammed into every double-page spread. The place really was *teeming* with life, and the pace really was as hectic as I've tried to make it seem.

The world really was young then, and full of vigor. Life has mellowed since—*all* of life. It's become more mature, more refined, more measured...not so much, I suspect, because we've all evolved, as because the atmosphere isn't full of psychotropic perfumes any more. We can't get high as easily nowadays; our nervous systems aren't in such a state of perpetual jangling excitement.

Maybe, however implausible it seems, it was the time police's drug squad that put the whole era off-limits to time-travelers. I'm not so sure that my estimates of possibility and plausibility can be trusted now, though, any more than they could when I was cleaner than clean. I could easily believe that the whole thing was a dream, and a dream that didn't really make sense, if it weren't for the fact that if it *were* a dream, I'd have to take responsibility for it, and try to figure out what my subconscious was trying to tell me—whereas, if it were real, as I assume it was, it was just something that happened to me, and by not killing me, made me stronger.

I hope that I can still hang on to that assumption, now that I've let the story out and exposed it to the cold light of public scrutiny, but I think I'm ready, at last, to take that chance. If it all evaporates, it evaporates, but I hope it won't. I hope it will continue to be real, and true—and to help me, if I need that kind of help, to be me.

CHAPTER SEVENTEEN

USING TWISTED LOGIC

Milly's bad mood was not lifted by the welcoming response that her story received. Sensing her need for additional support, the members tried even harder than usual to put her at her ease, but she seemed unable to respond.

As soon as they were alone in the car, Milly let out the mother of all sighs. Steve estimated that it must have beaten her previous personal best by several cubic centimeters of exhalation, but even that didn't seem to bring her any relief.

"I'm sorry," she said. It seemed more like an expression of bitterness than genuine apology, and it made Steve feel even more uncomfortable than he already was. He wanted to make her feel better, but had no idea how.

"It's okay," he said, tentatively, and he steered westwards. "I know it's a bad time. I'm the one who should apologize. I should be able to offer you more comfort, more support."

"Do you even know what I'm apologizing for?" Milly asked, scathingly.

"Probably not," Steve admitted. "It doesn't matter. You don't have to apologize for anything. Not to me."

"We're not in the meeting any more," she said. "You don't have to follow the rules now that it's just you and me. If I'd wanted that kind of support twenty-four seven, I'd have picked someone from the group for a boy-friend."

"You did," Steve pointed out.

She sighed again at that. "So I did," she agreed. "What I was apologizing for, by the way—what I thought I *ought* to apologize for—is the lousiness of my story. I don't know why it was so lousy, given that it's the only one I've heard in months that had dinosaurs in it, and ray guns, and anything that a reasonable person might call action, but I have to admit that it was lousy. It was upside-down, for one thing. The conversation bit should have come before the action, not after. After is always bound to be an anticlimax. Nobody else's subconscious makes that kind of mistake—I bet yours didn't."

"It wasn't lousy," Steve said, without responding to the final remark. "In fact, I found it extremely interesting, and tantalizingly puzzling, too."

"Well," she said, sourly, "I'm glad it provided fodder for your theories. Did I mention that I have to go back to Bath tomorrow?"

"Not specifically," Steve said, "but I assumed it."

"I suppose I shouldn't have left—Mum certainly thought so. Dad doesn't know anything about it, thank God, but Mum *needs me*, so she says. She doesn't. She just disapproves of me deserting what she thinks of as my post. She doesn't believe I came back for the meeting. She thinks I'm such a nymphomaniac that I couldn't stand another night without getting shagged senseless. She has no idea—not that you can't shag me to your heart's content, mind, given that I don't know when we'll find another opportunity, but I hope you'll forgive me if my brain's not fully engaged."

"We don't have to do anything if you don't want to," Steve said.

"If we don't," she said, ominously, "I'll only worry about what you've been getting up to while I was away. Not that I have any unique claim on you, obviously. You're free to make your own arrangements while the cat's away."

"Contrary to popular belief," Steve said, nettled by her tone, "I'm not a sex addict. I haven't done anything untoward while you've been away. I didn't exchange two words with Janine at that stupid quiz night, and I didn't make a pass at your friend Alison when she came looking for you."

"Alison came looking for me?" Milly sounded astonished, but her tone didn't freeze up the way it had when Steve had mentioned the Royal Oak.

"Yes. She want to make things right. She told me what really happened."

"And you believed her?"

"Yes, I did. You really ought to talk to her, Milly. I know you don't really think that she's lying about letting the cat out of the bag accidentally. I think you're just ashamed about the letter you wrote."

"She told you about that too?" Milly said, carefully keeping her tone as neutral as possible.

"Yes."

"You must have had quite a chat. Did you really turn her down when she ripped her clothes off and begged you to screw her?"

"She didn't. She never even took her raincoat off. We just talked."

"You liked her, didn't you?" Milly said, accusingly. "She got round you. Did she cry? Did she tell you what a beast I've always been to her, and how Janine's always lorded it over her because she's so plain? Did she make you feel sorry for her?"

"As it happens," Steve admitted, "I did quite like her, although she didn't go out of her way to play on my sympathies. I think you like her too, in spite of the fact that the jokey insults got way out of hand for a while. For what it's worth, I think you should make up with her."

"Well, I suppose you might as well fuck her too," Milly said, after a pause, her voice recovering its bitter taint. "Then you'll have the unholy hat-trick to your credit. Maybe we can all make up, and you can have us all in perpetuity. It's every man's dream, isn't it, to have his own private harem? Secret of the universe: men are polygamous, women monogamous. Evolution's little joke—no wonder we're scheduled for early extinction. Does Janine know that Alison's been crying on your shoulder."

"Janine gave her my address," Steve said.

"*Of course* she did," Milly said, striking her forehead in a mock-melodramatic fashion. "She sent her round to pay me back, didn't she? She wouldn't lower herself to get her own knickers dirty, so she sent Ali the Slut. Perfect. You really should have gone along with it, you know. I'm not much good to you, for the time being, and you'll need to get your end away somewhere, won't you? Abstinence isn't really your thing, is it? We don't want you being driven to distraction by all that juicy jailbait up at the comp, do we?"

"Don't be like that, Milly," Steve said. "I thought we were past that stage. Walter Wainwright gave me a long lecture last Saturday on the benefits of friends supporting one another unquestioningly, refraining from judgment or skepticism. Actually, he talked a lot of sense. If you and Janine and Alison could fix things up between yourselves...."

"Oh, shut up, Steve! It's easy enough for Walter Wainwright to talk sense, now that he's way past the age of competition. I bet it wasn't so easy when he, Amelia and Neville were locked in passionate complications, with or without their respective spouses. You do realize, I suppose, that if Janine, Alison and I were to repair our three-way friendship, the price of peace might be that none of us would ever have anything further to do with you, this side of the end of the world?"

"The thought had crossed my mind," Steve admitted.

"And then you thought that maybe you'd be better off without us—good riddance to the whole unholy trinity?"

"No," Steve said.

"Just me, then. You want me to make it up with Alison so that you and Janine can get back together?"

"No," Steve said, a little less certainly than before. He expected more bile in response to his uncertainty, but Milly fell silent. She stared out of the window in the passenger door, although there was little enough to be seen. The stretch of road along which they were traveling had no street-lights.

After a three-minute pause, Milly pulled herself together again, and repeated: "I'm sorry."

"What for?" Steve asked, cautiously

"For everything. Being such a cow. Taking it out on you. It wouldn't be fair, even if you'd done something, but you haven't. I let things get on top of me. Dad, leaving to come back here, the meeting...everything."

"It's not your fault," Steve said. "The situation with your Dad's about as bad as such situations get. It's bound to take its toll."

"No reason why it should take its toll on you too," she said. "I'm not actually trying to drive you away, you know, whatever it looks like. You're all I've got—the best thing I've got, at any rate. I'm sorry I wasn't as pleased to see you as I should have been, and that I'm still spiky now. I can't help it."

"It's okay," he said, inadequately. Then, desperate to find something to say that might ease the situation, he said: "Your story really was interesting. You might not care any more about my theory than Walter or the rest of the group, but it's important to me, and your story fit in very nicely. It raises some very pertinent questions, which I need to think about before I do my party piece in a fortnight's time. God, it'll be nearly Christmas then—it's the day school breaks up. I haven't given Christmas a single thought. I must tell Mum that I absolutely can't go home this year, or she'll be buying food in for me and including me in all her silly plans."

"I can't think about that yet," Milly said, flatly. "I can't make any plans at all, although I'll try to be here for the meeting. Tell me about these pertinent questions that you'll have to think about. I probably need the distraction."

"Okay," Steve said, hoping that his relief at being beckoned back to safer ground wasn't too obvious. "I can't help wondering why the time police wiped out everyone except you—why they felt it necessary to put you, and you alone, back where you belonged in the time-stream."

"I wasn't involved in the actual incident," Milly reminded him. "I was just an innocent bystander, caught up in it by accident. I didn't break any laws. That's what the shadow-lady said."

"That would be one possible explanation," Steve conceded.

"Do you have a better one?"

"I don't know."

"But you think there's something wrong with hers—I mean mine?"

"Not necessarily," Steve said. "But I'm not so sure that time police can afford to be as interested in matters of guilt and innocence as a dutiful traffic warden. If their job is to maintain the integrity of the time-stream, why weren't they just as concerned to make sure that the lizards and the insects got safely back to where they belonged as they were to take care of you?"

Milly thought about that for a few moments, then said: "Maybe they did get safely home. I just saw them vanish—I don't know for sure that they weren't sent back, although the shadow-lady said they weren't. Then again, maybe time-travelers don't *belong* in the sense that abductees do, Maybe, once they've abstracted themselves from the time-stream in order to skip through some other dimension from one time to another, they've already broken the chains of true causation."

"Both perfectly plausible hypotheses," Steve conceded. "I wonder whether there's something else at work, though—something your time-traveling traffic warden was trying to explain when she said that there's an *eternal if* confusing the fact that there'll always be a now and a then. Do you remember Jim's deer? There may be forces at work deliberately disrupting the time-stream as well as forces repairing it. Maybe those were involved in what happened to you."

"Except that in your theory, nothing *actually* happened to me at all," Milly said, her tone changing again as she lost the ability to lose herself in what seemed to her to be an idle flight of fancy. "Or to Jim, or Megan, or anybody else. It's all just dreaming."

"Not *just* dreaming," Steve said, trying to prolong the intermission in her suffering.

"*Un*just dreaming, then," she said, with a brief flash of her customary wit. "The collective unconscious trying to remake itself, and fucking us over while it does it, by feeding us all kinds of pseudoreality tripe. I'm sorry, Steve, I know you're only trying to help—to save me from thinking about Dad, or about Janine and Alison, for that matter—but it isn't working."

"It's okay," Steve said, again. "No need to apologize. Not your fault." He gripped the steering-wheel a little harder, glad that the lights of the city center were now in view, as well as the reddish pall that always hung over the city on cloudy nights, like a hazy umbrella.

Milly sighed again. "There's no soothing me tonight, I'm afraid," she said. "Too tightly wound to unwind. Sometimes, I think I might never unwind again. You ought to be thankful, really, that I'm only here for the one night. I can do one night, I think—but I'd be a really lousy lay these days if we were together all the time, and that would be a really bad move, relationship-wise. I'll do my level best not to go away again leaving you glad that I've gone, desperate to find a replacement before I come back. You must have had much easier girl-friends than me in your time."

"One or two," Steve agreed, figuring that there wasn't too much risk in admitting it, "but there are worse things in life than not being easy."

"I hope so," Milly said, with yet another sigh. "I wish Dad had chosen a better time to hover between life and death. It would be a lot more convenient all round if he'd just make up his mind. And please don't tell me that his mind probably isn't in a fit condition for making itself up—I do realize that."

"If it turns out that you can't get back a week next Thursday," Steve said, as he slowed the car down and looked or a parking-spot, "shall I tell my story in your absence, or do you want me to wait until the new year? I can tell you tonight, in private, if you like, so you won't need to worry about it at all."

"I'll try to get back," Milly said. "If not, I'll tell you when the time comes. I've done mine properly, and it'll be best if you can do yours the same way. Then Janine can do hers, if she wants to."

"Janine isn't an abductee," Steve said, as he pulled the hand-brake on. "She's only coming to hear your story and mine—to get some weird sort of closure."

"No, she's not," Milly told him. "I thought she was, but that was before I talked to her. She says she kept on coming because she'd begun to remember. That's the only reason. She says she's not trying to pay us back for betraying her, however much we deserve it—not in that way, at any rate. I still have my suspicions about her sending Ali round to see you, but I think she's telling the truth about the meetings."

"You've talked to her?" Steve repeated, wonderingly, with his hand frozen on the door-handle. "I thought she wasn't talking to either of us. When? Why didn't you tell me before?"

"Yesterday. We talked on the phone. She couldn't bring herself to blank me, because I wanted to tell her about Dad. She didn't want to talk about anything else—she certainly didn't tell me that she'd seen you at the Royal Oak's quiz night, or that she'd given Alison your address—but she did want to tell me that she wasn't coming to meetings just to upset us. By the way, in case it gets back to you by some other route, I really did tell her that she could have you back if she wanted you."

Steve felt as if the head of a claw-hammer had thudded into his heart, although he didn't know exactly why. He clutched the door-handle even harder, but didn't attempt to turn it in order to open the door. "What did she say?" he asked.

"She said she doesn't."

Even Steve, who would never have considered himself a good judge of the subtler nuances of female conversation, knew what a world of difference there was between "She said she doesn't" and "She doesn't".

"I'm not some piece of carrion that you two can quarrel over like a pair of stroppy scavengers," he complained.

"Of course you are," Milly retorted, although there was no trace of bitterness in her tone now. "But we're not going to fight. We're going to try to be better than that, if we can. I don't think she means it when she says she doesn't want you back. I think she might take you back, if you went about it the right way."

Which is what? Steve thought—but he didn't say it, because it would have been ungentlemanly. On the other hand, he didn't immediately leap to say that Milly was the only one he wanted, and the only one he ever would want. He knew that she wouldn't believe him. He finally opened the car door, and got out. Milly got out too, and looked both ways before crossing the road.

Steve followed her. He knew that he didn't dare ask whether she really would simply allow Janine to take him back, if that turned out to be what he and Janine both wanted, and if they went about it the right way—but he dared to think that it might be possible.

He had completely lost track of Milly's mood, now, and had no idea what was going on between them. He followed her meekly up the stairs to the front door of her flat, and then paused on the threshold, not entirely certain that he was about to be welcomed in. She held the door open for him, though, and closed it behind him.

"Home sweet home," she murmured.

"Would you rather I went back to my place?" Steve asked.

"No," she said. "unless *you* want to, of course."

"No," he said.

"That's settled, then," she said. "For now. Tomorrow is another day, as the book says."

"I honestly don't know what you're trying to say," Steve confessed, as she took his coat and hung it up on the rack.

Milly headed for the bathroom, but she paused long enough to turn round and say: "Maybe Dad's stroke has put things in a different perspective. I just want to like myself a little better than I've been able to of late, while I've been the kind of person who'd hijack her best friend's boy-friend while her friend was away on a training course. All I'm saying, Steve, is that you don't owe me anything. You certainly don't have to stay with me, if you'd rather be with someone else."

She disappeared then, without giving him a chance to reply, and didn't reappear for quite some time, after various sounds of running water. When she emerged again, she had taken off her make-up and was wearing the kind of expression that forbade him to take up the thread of the conversation where it had been left dangling, demanding that he let the matter lie and start anew. He had to use the bathroom himself, so that was easy enough to do. When he came out again she was in the kitchenette, making a cup of hot chocolate.

"My experience was very different from yours," Steve said, out of the blue, "but once you've heard it, you might understand me a little bit better."

"Are we talking about abductions again?" Milly asked, rhetorically, keeping her tone conspicuously light. "I suppose I ought to look forward to it, then—even though we both seem to have been working thus far on the principle that people might like us better, and maybe even love us more, if they didn't understand us at all."

* * * * * * *

Steve drove Milly back to the railway station early the next morning, and then drove to school, where he found Friday far less taxing than he usually did. Afterwards, he drove out along the A30 to the far side of Wilton, then turned round and came back again. He suffered no ill-effects at all—which was a small triumph, but a significant one.

"One step at a time," he murmured, when he got back to his own flat. "Nullify the symptoms, and there'll be no need for a cure."

The next day, after doing his shopping, he took his courage in both hands and drove to Southampton, where there were much bigger bridges to be found. He went back and forth across the stretch that broadened the Test into Southampton Water no less than four times, then stopped off for a late lunch in the new national park. He wasn't about to tackle the Clifton Suspension Bridge just yet, but he felt that he was getting on top of the situation.

Milly called at four to report that there was no further change in her father's condition, but Steve didn't tell her what he'd been doing. She didn't drag out the conversation for long, but before hanging up she said; "I called Ali, by the way. We're on track to make up. I promised I'd have a drink with her next time I'm in Salisbury, so that we can sort it all out."

"That's good," Steve said.

"I called Jan again, too. She was at her parents' place, so we couldn't really talk, but I think she might come along—to meet with Ali and me, that is."

"Even better," Steve said, automatically, although he remembered what Milly had said on Thursday night about the price of the three girls restoring their relationship might be that none of them would ever talk to him again.

"Maybe you can come too," Milly concluded.

"Maybe," Steve agreed. There was nothing thereafter but a few conventional exchanges of gestures of affection.

Although he wasn't planning to go out, Steve took a shower, as was his habit on Saturday evenings. He was just wondering whether to spend an hour on the Internet before making himself some dinner when the phone rang again. He didn't recognize the caller's number.

"Hello?" he said, warily. He was always paranoid about the possibility that the year elevens might somehow have got hold of his number, so he never surrendered his name to unknown callers.

"Steve? It's Alison—Janine's friend."

"Oh," Steve said. "Hi."

"I just wanted to thank you for talking to Milly. She said you'd told her I called round and you'd advised her to make up. I've just had a long chat with her."

"That's okay," Steve said. "It was nothing, really. Milly told me you'd talked."

"Did she tell you that she talked to Janine, too, and that we might all get together when she's next in Salisbury."

"Yes, she did," Steve said.

"Did she tell you that she suggested that I might ask you to have a drink with me in the Pheasant tonight?" Alison went on.

Steve looked at the phone quizzically. "No, she didn't," he said, speaking very carefully. "Why would she do that?"

"You can probably think of as many reasons as I can," Alison told him, "but the one she gave me was that if we're going to have a big summit conference to decide whether we can still be friends, and if you're included, then perhaps you and I should get to know one another first. That probably seems as unlikely to you as it does to me, but I'm not lying. If you don't want to, that's fine, but I figured that if I'm being put to the test, I ought not to duck out."

"You think *you're* being tested?" Steve said, skeptically.

"Of course. You too, probably, but me definitely, and perhaps primarily. I told her I'd been round to your place looking for her, and that you'd let me come in, but she said she already knew. I told her nothing happened, but she said she already knew that too. I think she thinks that the only way to be sure that nothing will happen in future is to set up the experiment and see. It's a bit convoluted, I know, but that's the way Milly's mind tends to work. Straight as a corkscrew—in the nicest possible way, of course."

"I'd noticed that," Steve said. "In the nicest possible way, of course. So, the idea is that you and I meet up, and nothing happens—which will prove to Milly that it's possible for her to keep on being friends with you, and that it's not yet time to give me the elbow."

"That's the idea," Alison confirmed. "Her idea, remember. When I mentioned the possibility to Janine, though, she told me to go ahead. I'm not entirely sure what she expects. If you feel that you're being pushed around, by all means say no. I'd be off the hook, because I could say that I'd tried."

"I don't know whether I'd be off the hook or not," Steve admitted. "I don't know what Milly expects me to do."

After a slight pause, Alison said; "You don't actually have to treat it as a puzzle to be solved. If it helps you make up your mind, you're not in any moral danger. Believe me, this is not Milly's nightmare version of Alison the Slut talking. It's Alison the Chastened, who's having a *really* tough time at work just now, and doesn't even have a pub quiz to go to. A quiet drink with someone I don't have to impress, entertain or drop my knickers for would be a real godsend."

"Okay," Steve said, not entirely sorry to have been put in a position in which he couldn't really refuse without seeming churlishly ungallant. "Shall I meet you in there at half past seven?"

"Fine," she said.

She was ten minutes late, but that was only to be expected. She wouldn't have wanted to take the risk of getting there ahead of him and standing there on her own. She asked for a glass of red wine, and he told the bartender to make it two. They retired to a corner opposite the one in which she and Mark had surprised Milly and him, on the fateful night when the proverbial cat had escaped from the bag—as it had been bound to do, eventually.

"I like it here," Alison explained. "No plasma screen to bring in the football crowd, and no video jukebox. Not the sort of place to attract hen parties, thank God. A bit too convenient for the Town Hall, maybe, but if I'm seen, it's no bad thing for me to be seen with someone who doesn't work there."

"I'm more likely to start whispers going than you are," Steve reminded her. "The regulars are bound to have seen me here with Milly. It probably isn't a secret that she's in Bath, nursing her sick father."

"Is she nursing him?"

"Not literally—but you know how rumors go. I'm sorry you've been having a tough time at work. I know what that's like. I've only just been let out of Coventry at school, although my crimes were committed way back in June and July."

"You're lucky," she said. "Mine extended over every month in the calendar, and not just this year. Never again, though. You always think you can get away with it forever, until..." She passed her forefinger over her throat.

"Never again," he agreed, raising his glass as if the phrase were a toast.

"Actually," she said, "it wouldn't do me any harm at all to be seen with you. You're a substantial cut above my previous best, let alone my average, looks-wise."

"Are you fishing for compliments?" he asked.

"Don't be daft. I'm under no illusions about my ability to compete with Milly and Janine. You must have a hard time at school, if teenage girls are anything like what they were in my day."

"Not as bad as all that," he told her. "There's safety in numbers, I think. One girl with a crush might turn into a stalker, but when there are four or five...."

"Or forty or fifty."

"...they're too busy comparing notes and competing for attention to cause any serious difficulties."

"And besides which," Alison supplied, "you must get quite a kick out of basking in all that adolescent admiration."

"I'm just a science teacher, not a singer in a boy-band or some football player. At the end of the day, that fact that I'm still fairly young and fit can't compensate for the fact that I'm just one more bullshit-spouting bastard they have to call *sir*."

"False modesty is just vanity in disguise," she told him. "If I'd had a teacher like you when I was fifteen, I'd have wet my knickers dreaming about you, even if I'd known that you were terrified of flying and went to a support group of alien abductees."

Steve gave her a hard stare while he worked out that the former item of information must have come from Janine rather than Milly. "Well," he said, eventually, "we're supposed to be getting to know one another, aren't we? I'd prefer it if you didn't keep mentioning knickers, though—it's a bit provocative."

"Sorry," she said. "If I tell you my life story, though, it won't be easy to avoid it. Except that that's not *me*, really. It's just someone I invented, and now have to put away. Perhaps we should make a deal—I'll tell you about the real me, if you'll tell me about the real you. That way, we won't overexcite one another, and we'll both know something that Janine and Milly don't."

"Okay," he said. So that was what they did, for the remainder of the evening, until Steve walked Alison home, and said goodnight without so much as giving her a peck on the cheek. She said thank you for that, and probably meant it. Then he walked back to his own place, and put his relaxation CD on to play while he lulled himself to sleep.

* * * * * * *

Milly's father continued not dying throughout the following week, although Milly returned to Salisbury on the Wednesday evening, having finally persuaded her mother that she couldn't afford to continue missing work. She spent Wednesday night with Steve, but told him that she was going to have to do overtime in the office on Friday, Saturday, Monday and Tuesday in order to make up some of her lost income. On Sunday, she'd arranged to meet Janine and Alison—but Janine had insisted that he not be invited.

"Alison and I had a long chat last Saturday," he told her. "Just to get to know one another."

"I know," she said.

"Did we pass the test, then?"

"What test?" she said, disingenuously. "I think she's forgiven me for writing that letter. She says she has, but she might just be saying it and not really mean it."

"I think she means it," Steve said.

"Of course you do—but I've known her a lot longer than you have, and I've seen her turn over new leaves before. Anyhow, we can get together late Saturday, if you want, and maybe have a proper date on Wednesday. I'm sorry it's a bit thin, as sex-schedules go."

"It's fine," he assured her. "I might drive up to Reading on Saturday, and visit Caversham. Next Wednesday's out, though—it's the school Christmas party and I can't get out of it. The sixth-formers are included, so it's more a matter of acting as a policeman than having fun, or I'd invite you along. I can see you afterwards, though, if you like—at your place or mine."

"Reading will be hellishly crowded the Saturday before Christmas," she reminded him. "Be careful not to overdo it—you don't want any setbacks before Thursday. I suppose I could switch my overtime from Tuesday to Wednesday, if that would help."

"It wouldn't," he said. "I've got an appointment with Sylvia—I'll need the booster even if things go well in Reading, because of Thursday. I could do Monday, though."

"I'm firmly committed then," she said. "No matter—can't be helped. Saturday and Wednesday nights at my place will be fine, no matter how late. You can pick me up on Thursday at the usual time."

Steve was careful on the Saturday, and contrived to go over Reading Bridge as well as Caversham Bridge in a moderately relaxed state of mind, before braving the Christmas crowds in the Oracle. He bought presents for Alison and Janine as well as Milly, although he hadn't the slightest idea whether any of them would be considered appropriate, let alone welcome. He had a session with Sylvia Joyce on the Tuesday, which went well, although he played safe by refusing her offer to regress him. The school Christmas party went as well as could be expected, in spite of all the mistletoe and the extreme determination of his sixth-form groups to explore the limits of permissible misbehavior.

"You look nervous," Milly said, when Steve picked her up to drive her to the meeting at which he was due to reveal all about the recovered memory whose exhumation Sylvia Joyce had begun. "You don't have anything to be scared of, you know. Compared to a class of fifteen-year-olds, the AlAbAn crowd must be the easiest audience imaginable."

"It's not like doing a science lesson, though," Steve said. "All that comes straight out of the textbook. This is different."

Steve had spoken to Milly on the phone several times since she'd met with Alison and Janine on the Sunday, as well as hooking up with her on the Wednesday night, but she hadn't said a word about the outcome of the big discussion, and she didn't say anything about it while they drove to East Grimstead. She was more even-tempered by far than she'd been a fortnight before, but she still couldn't pass for cheerful. Steve couldn't help feeling that he was being gradually edged out of the relationship, in the process of being discarded by slow degrees. He'd been tempted more than once to call Alison and ask her what had happened at the meeting, but he hadn't dared. Milly would undoubtedly have regarded it as going behind her back.

"I broke my personal record for booking four-by-fours this week," Milly remarked, as they turned left in Alderbury. "I hadn't been away very long, but the school run scum had already got used to taking liberties. I wrote so many tickets my wrist got sore. If I were paid on a commission basis I'd have made up all my lost income."

"Is your vendetta against gas-guzzling vehicles, or women with small children?" Steve asked, indicating by his tone that it was a joke rather an accusation.

"Both," Milly told him, not taking the least offence. "I'm against all emitters of toxic substances, whether liquid, solid or gaseous. By the way, did you know that the council are thinking of introducing a parking permit system for your street? I had to review the paperwork on Tuesday evening"

"I got a leaflet through my letter-box," Steve said. "It won't make any difference to me. If I need a permit, I'll get one. I've never parked illegally in my life. I'm a teacher, after all—I have to set an example, just like you."

"Yes we do," Milly said. "That's why I've never learned to drive—so I'll never be tempted to add to the world's burden of exhaust fumes. Before you jump on me for collaborating in your sin, remember that you'd be making the journey anyway."

"It would be a slightly shorter journey if I didn't call for you," Steve pointed out, and threw caution to the winds by adding: "Mind you, it was a considerably longer journey when I used to pick Janine up as well, so I suppose you can take credit for reducing the margin—although I suppose we ought to factor Walter Wainwright's detour into the equation too. The arithmetic of virtue's quite complicated, when you really get down to it, isn't it? Sometimes, it almost gives one a sense of relief to remember that the ecosphere's fucked and the whole human race is doomed to imminent extinction."

"Doomed we may be," Milly countered, "but in the meantime, the rules still apply. People can't just park wherever they want to, no matter what sort of excuses they have. People have to have consideration for other people, no matter how fucked up the atmosphere is."

Steve had no idea whether she was really talking about parking, or about people screwing other people's boy-friends and girl-friends, or both. "I know," he said, anyway, as he found a legal parking-spot within easy walking distance of Amelia Rockham's cottage. "I wouldn't want it any other way."

As they walked into the meeting together, Steve tried to compose himself, or at least to persuade himself that he wasn't undertaking a metaphorical walk to the scaffold. He was amazed to see, when he got inside, that Janine wasn't alone in the green armchair. Alison was perched on one of the arms, with her arm outstretched along the back, behind Janine's head.

Alison nodded a friendly greeting, which seemed to take in both Steve and Milly. They both nodded back, and Steve even risked a glance that attempted to inform Janine that she was included in the greeting too. Janine didn't nod back, but her gaze wasn't hostile, or even coldly indifferent.

"There you are," Milly whispered in his ear, as they settled into their familiar settee. "One more supportive skeptic to add to your audience. That's what I call pulling power."

CHAPTER EIGHTEEN

A CAN OF WORMS

I wanted to tell you about my theory as well as my experience, but I talked it over with Walter, and he gave me some good advice. He assured me that I certainly wouldn't be the first person to have brought a theory to the group, and that the group would be just as tolerant and supportive of the theory as they are of unembellished stories, but he suggested that it might be polite not to use my interpretations of other people's stories as evidence for my theory. He's right about that, so I'll be as discreet as I can, but when it comes to my own experience, it's impossible to separate the process of remembering from the process of interpretation, so I'm afraid you'll find that every aspect of what I have to tell you is shot through with my ongoing attempts to understand what it means.

There's one more thing I ought to say, because I know that none of you would ever be so impolite as to say it, even though you've every right to think it. How, you might think, can you possibly take a man seriously as a theorist of the time-stream and the universe, when you have manifest proof before your eyes that he can't even manage his own love life with a modicum of intelligence or decency? If it were just a theory in physics, of course, that wouldn't matter—just because Isaac Newton was paranoid, it doesn't mean that the theory of gravity is a paranoid theory—but my theory isn't like that. My theory is a theory that's intimately bound up with such matters as intelligence and decency, and you might be quite right to suspect it of being no more than a pretentious kind of special pleading answering to my own feelings of inadequacy. On the other hand, that might be its greatest strength rather than a fatal weakness—you'll have to make your own minds up about that.

My experience began a few months ago, when I consulted a hypnotherapist about certain phobias I have, to do with flying and heights. I'd always had the phobias, but I'd never consulted anyone about them before, because I'd always taken the view that I could live within their limits. I'd always told myself that the simplest response to a fear of flying is not to fly, and the simplest response to a fear of heights is not to go to the upper floors of tall buildings, especially ones that have open atria or glass-sided lifts. Bridges are a problem too, but it's a matter of degree. Wiltshire, mercifully, isn't replete with wide rivers, and if it ever becomes absolutely necessary to go to Wales one day, I can always go via Gloucester. What prompted me to get help wasn't the day-to-day difficulty of living with my fears but the fact that I'd got a new girlfriend, who was a travel agent. I'm a schoolteacher myself, and most of the people I'd previously had relationships with, after leaving university, were also teachers. There'd never been any particular pressure to go on foreign holidays—but a travel agent is in an ideal position to get ultra-cheap deals, and the first option on deals that are simply too good to miss. I knew the matter was going to come up eventually.

I didn't expect that the therapist would be able to cure me, but I'd been told that she could teach me relaxation techniques that just might allow me to get through a short-haul flight without overdosing on tranquilizers. That's all I actually wanted, but Sylvia—that's the therapist—suggested that if I could figure out the psychological origins of the phobias, I might do even better.

"I don't know about that," I said. "We might be opening a can of worms." She had a jokey response all ready for that one, though. "Better a can of worms than a can't," she said.

I eventually gave in, and gave her permission to trawl through some of my memories, just to demonstrate the method. She found a trauma easily enough—but the memory wasn't from early childhood, and the nightmare it recalled couldn't possibly have caused phobias I'd already had for years. At first, in fact, I thought that it was just a perfectly ordinary nightmare that had been *produced* by my phobias, which my conscious mind had sensibly repressed, dutifully refusing me access to a disturbing and utterly unreal experience.

I don't believe that Sylvia suggested that I come to AlAbAn because she thought that the recovered memory might be real. Although she couldn't give me any specific information, I'm pretty sure that she's sent other people here in similar circumstances, for exactly the same reason: to help them see that such experiences aren't unique, as a preparatory stage in being able to entertain them more hospitably, to analyze them, and figure out what they're trying to tell us. I probably wouldn't have come if I hadn't mentioned the existence of the group to my new girl-friend, as a kind of joke. She'd already heard of it, because one of her friends had been coming here regularly for months, and between the two of us, we worked up curiosity enough to take a look. As you know, we kept coming back thereafter.

Sylvia will probably be pleased by the outcome of her suggestion, because she'll think that everything has gone to plan: that I've completed the de-repression of my nightmare, and pieced it together so that I can relive it and relate it, delivering it up for analysis in the hope that it might give us the clue that will lead us to the *real* traumatic experience that generated my phobias. Well, maybe it will—but that's not where it led me when I was able to piece it together, in the light of the other stories I heard relived and related in this room. It led me to something much more important than an understanding of my own petty failings and foibles—because I realized that it wasn't just *my* nightmare, and that it wasn't just a lurid transfiguration of my own anxieties.

In accordance with the rules, I make no judgment about the nature of anyone else's experience, but, speaking for myself, I'm quite certain that I was never actually taken out of my bed and transported into an alien vessel. My experience was subjective—but that doesn't mean that it wasn't real, or that it wasn't an authentic revelation. It *was* real, and it *was* an authentic revelation; the only point at issue is whether it only reveals something about my twisted mind, or whether it also reveals something about the nature of the universe and the time-stream...or, indeed, whether every vision that reveals something about any individual's mind, however twisted, also reveals something about the nature of the universe and the time-stream.

What I dreamed, in summary, is this. I dreamed that I was taken aboard an alien vessel, by means of a mechanism that convention calls a "tractor beam", although I learned in the course of my dream that the term is slightly misleading. I dreamed that I was being subjected to some kind of examination there, without any explanation, and would have been returned to the course of my life none the wiser, if the aliens' plans hadn't been interrupted. In my case, though, the interruption wasn't caused by some kind of weird transtemporal traffic accident, or a scheme that went awry. It was a summons—some kind of mayday call, to which they had to respond, even though I was aboard and surplus to requirements. That was when the aliens thought it necessary for one of them to put on human form, and adopt the human language, in order to explain to me why they could no longer simply opt out of my memory.

In my dream, the mentor appointed to talk me through the adventure took on the appearance of a portrait of Edgar Allan Poe, with which most of you are probably familiar. I have no idea why; I'd surely have been more inclined to trust him if he'd pretended to be Charles Darwin or Albert Einstein, both of whose portraits were far more familiar to me than Poe's, but Poe was who he decided to pretend to be.

"Where are we going?" I asked him, when the vessel set off. It had no portholes, and I didn't feel any sensation of acceleration, as I would have if it had been heading out of the Earth's gravity-well, but I knew we were moving without quite knowing how I knew. It was as if some sixth sense, which I'd never had occasion to use before, had suddenly come into play—and as if my brain, even though it had no previous experience of the exercise of that sense, was pre-adapted by evolution to recognize its input.

"Three and a half billion years downstream," Poe told me. "Where no time-traveler from our era has been before—not, at least, any who returned to tell the tale. So far as I know, no ordinary tourist or business-traveler from any other era known to us has ever been that far downstream, until now."

"How come it's possible to go now, if it's never been possible before?" I asked."

"The darktimers only had to open the way, apparently. We didn't know that, although we always suspected. We could never tell whether the asymmetry in the boomerang effect was an aspect of the laws of physics or an aspect of the darktimers' interference—assuming there's any meaningful difference between the two. I'm afraid your language and your understanding have built-in limitations that are making this attempted explanation very confusing. *Darktimers* isn't actually a helpful term—but then, even *before* and *now*, not to mention *then* and *but*, have their inconveniences in this particular context."

"I can see how the reality of time travel would throw terms like *now, then* and *before* into a certain confusion," I admitted. "Once the future has to be redefined as *downstream*, the implication inevitably arises that the whole river has its own simultaneous pseudo-presence, while time-ships move back and forth along it through the infinite sequence of individual moments."

"Spoken like a practiced schoolteacher," Poe said, not meaning it entirely as a insult. "If you're lucky, that talent for jargonmongering might stand you in good stead wherever—or whenever—we're going."

"But the fact that the time-ships can move back and forth, even within whatever limits you're trying to imply by speaking of a *boomerang effect*, carries all sorts of further implications," I said. "Popular physics in the twenty-first century had begun to think of time travel in a slightly different way, with every jump instituting a new history, contained in its own alternative universe, avoiding paradoxes by reckless multiplication of new realities. The idea that time-travelers can move back and forth within a single time-stream suggests that the stream must be protected in some way against history-changing actions—-that there must be some kind of mechanism for maintaining the integrity of the temporal fabric, whether one envisages it as a natural healing process or as a corps of policemen. Is that what you mean by *darktimers*?"

"Not exactly—it's a good deal more complicated than that. Yes, the stream is self-healing, to a degree. Yes, there are time police—so many agencies, in fact, that liaison between them is a bureaucratic nightmare—but the darktimers are an order of magnitude further back in the chain of ultimate causality...or ultimate connectivity, if *cause* is too loaded a term."

"Is it?"

"Of course it is. The problem is that connectivity's not much better. Don't punish yourself too much for being simple-minded—you can't help it. Humankind was the first in the known sequence, after all: the alpha of self-conscious intelligence. In a sense, of course, the whole pattern must have been innate in the Vendian worms, or the archetypal cyanobacteria, or the geometry of DNA—but in another, you humans were just like those predecessors: alphabet soup, waiting for some higher intelligence to come along and consider you as an anagram."

"You're talking in riddles," I pointed out.

"I know. There's no other way. I can't even promise you that what you'll get to witness is any kind of solution rather than one more layer of complication in the riddle, but it will probably be spectacular, and that's not to be underestimated. You'll repress all this at first, of course—that's the way your defensive mental reflexes are programmed—but you'll probably recover the memory soon enough. Now that our original plan's been superseded, I suspect that the experience you're about to have won't be the kind that can rest content in Lethean darkness."

"Will my phobias be cured when it all bubbles up again?" I asked.

"No," he said. "I'd hang on to the phobias, if I were you. Flying's dangerous, and so are sheer drops. Only an idiot crosses bridges every time he comes to one; you should always think twice about that sort of thing. Do you really want to waste time talking about your phobias? When we get to where we're going I'll be fearfully busy. Any questions you want answered, you'd better ask now—I probably won't be able to put the answers into terms you can understand, but if we try hard, we might make a little progress."

"This ship isn't really a ship, is it?" I said. "I don't believe that time travel is a matter of shifting material objects at all. I suspect that the only things you can transmit into the past are hallucinatory experiences—but you are *transmitting* aspects of those experiences, aren't you? They're not entirely spontaneous."

"If you only want to ask rhetorical questions," Poe said, "I might as well leave now. Matter is another of those treacherous terms. If matter is the possibility of sensation, this ship is certainly material, and so am I. Give me a lever long enough...but let's not get ahead of ourselves. You can't know much about the kind of relativity theory that accommodates matter as well as space and time, but you know about dark matter. You know that baryonic matter only accounts for a tenth of the mass of the universe, yes?"

"Yes," I said.

"So you can get some sort of grasp on the analogy of *dark time*—the notion that the way we baryonic entities perceive time and its transactions is similarly fragmentary. It's not something your maths can cope with, but that's a limitation in your maths, not in the fabric of reality. You can attribute some sort of meaning, however shadowy, to the notion of dark time?"

"I suppose so."

"Good—and you're familiar with the cosmological anthropic principle?"

"Yes. If any of the fundamental constants—the empirical content of the laws of physics—were slightly different, then the universe of baryonic matter wouldn't be able to give rise to life. Some people interpret that to mean that the universe of baryonic matter must have been designed to accommodate life. Others think it's a trivial observation, because if the universe weren't able to contain life, there'd be no one around to make the observation. You're making a point about the *darktimers*, aren't you? Some of you think that there are intelligent entities in the dark matter sector of the universe, who designed the universe of baryonic matter actively and purposively, and some of you don't—and dark time just adds a further dimension to the problem."

"There's the schoolteacher again. Do you have any questions that aren't rhetorical, or have you made up your mind about everything?"

"Is the human race really going to become extinct by the end of the twenty-first century?"

"No. A few scattered groups will hang on until the twenty-second, along with the rats and mice. But yes, you're doomed. So are the hundreds of other intelligent species that future adaptive radiations will produce, though, including all the ones that acquire the ability to travel in time, all the ones that develop technologies of emortality and all the ecosystems that contrive to cultivate holistic intelligence. We're all in the same boat, existentially speaking—but we don't die alone. Even the species that don't develop time-travel are contactees. We're all in the same boat, dreaming the same fundamental dream of the eternal Phoenix. We're all connected. We all contribute."

"What about the species that develop space travel?" I asked. "They don't need to die. They can go on forever, at least in theory."

"Space travel is impractical," he told me. "Not impossible, just impractical. It's really a plant-intelligence thing rather than an animal one, although it requires collaboration—we have the hands, but they have the patience. While the stream runs in its present course, communication across interstellar distances is problematic. Yes, in a manner of speaking, starfaring species don't have to die out—but they do have to change, and profoundly. Maybe the dream we're all dreaming extends much further than anyone can tell, but while we can't tell, how meaningful can the extension be? If space travel's a matter of particular interest to you, watch out for the big guns—but you'll have to watch, now, and make up your own mind. I've got a strong suspicion as to what it is you'll see, but I don't know anything for sure, and I don't know how long it will take. At any rate, I have to go. We all have to answer to the call, except for accidental passengers like you. I can't honestly say that you've used your conversational opportunities as wisely as you might have, but you know your own interests best, and you are only human. Good luck."

He vanished then, without bothering to use a door—but he opened a window before he left, so that I could witness the task that all the time-machines ever manufactured, in three and a half billion years of my future history, had been summoned to that juncture in the time-stream to accomplish.

* * * * * *

It goes without saying, I suppose, that when Edgar Allan Poe opened the window, I froze with absolute terror. "Panic attack" doesn't even begin to describe it. If he hadn't switched off the simulated gravity as he left, I'd have collapsed on the floor, but I wasn't able to do that: I had no alternative but to float, motionless, unable even to turn away.

I was looking down at the Earth's surface through hundreds of miles of empty space, from orbit; I could see an entire hemisphere, three-quarters sunlit, albeit dimly.

The terror never went away, although it ebbed slightly as I grew more accustomed to the perspective. Everything I saw was filtered through that emotional veil, saturated with panic. And yet, there was nothing actually terrifying in what I saw; that dreadful vertigo was *in me*, a product of my viewpoint, and there was no real reason for it at all. Cosmonauts looking down from Mir don't feel it. They find the view exhilarating and inspiring. I ought to have been able to do the same, but in order to describe it to you now I have to make an effort *not* to remember, to concentrate on the words and not the memory itself. That's where being a schoolteacher comes in handy.

I wouldn't have recognized the Earth if I hadn't known that's what it was. There was no blue ocean, no white clouds. The surface seemed entirely solid, mottled in various dark hues, unblurred by any intervening atmosphere. It looked lifeless, although I know now that it wasn't. I know now that millions of laborers recruited from various past eras had been pressed into service to transplant the greater part of its surviving ecosphere into artificially-lit subterranean caverns.

At first, I thought that there was some kind of vaporous shell surrounding the planet, blocking out some of the sunlight. While I watched, it grew thicker, darkening the plant' surface even further. I realized gradually that the specks making up the shell weren't as tiny as I'd first thought. They were spaceships—or, to be strictly accurate, time-ships. There were billions of them, and more were arriving with every second that passed. The shell never became solid, because the ships never came close enough together to form an uninterrupted mass, but the far side of it seemed quite opaque from where I was floating.

I couldn't *see* the tractor beams come into play; they were invisible. I was conscious of their engagement, though, thanks to that sixth sense which registers travel through time. Tractor beams aren't just invisible ropes, you see; they don't only operate in space. They're temporal technology themselves; they move things by exploiting the relativity of matter and time, which Poe hadn't even tried to explain to me. They weren't actually *pulling* the Earth out of its orbit in any simple sense; they were using the combined force of the engines that gave them ability to travel through time to modify Earth's mass in such a way that it began to draw away of its own accord, and to accelerate as it did so.

I couldn't judge the trajectory or the velocity of the Earth's movement very well, but I knew that it was moving away from the sun, and that it was moving through time as well as space in hurrying to its new location. It was *hurrying*, because time was very much of the essence. There were good reasons why time-traffic into that era had been so severely restricted, and why it still was. The time-ships had only gathered momentarily, and were only able to use their innate technology briefly.

For a moment or two, I wondered whether the time-ships might be converting the Earth into a huge starship, and whether the shell might reformulate itself as some kind of big gun—you'll remember that Poe had mentioned big guns—to fire the planet out of the system towards a new and younger sun. That wouldn't have been impossible, but it was impractical, even given the combined power of every time-machine that had ever existed in the sporadic history of Earthly intelligence.

What the armada of timeships actually did, during the brief interval in which it functioned as a coordinated whole, was to maneuver the Earth into a new orbit, somewhere out beyond the present orbit of Saturn—an orbit that wasn't empty even before they replaced the Earth within it, but became a good deal fuller thereafter.

In subjective and shipboard terms, the whole experience took no longer than a few minutes—maybe far less, allowing for the effects of terror on my subjective perception of duration—but the vessel was traveling through time as well as space, and my guess is that millions or tens of millions of years elapsed *outside*, while the solar system was reconfigured by the time armada.

They didn't move much else from the inner reaches of the system—a few hundred asteroids, maybe, and half a dozen Jovian and Saturnian satellites. They left the gas-giants themselves, along with Mercury, Venus and Mars, to be swallowed and digested by the new unimproved sun. There was a lot of traffic in the other direction, though. They left Uranus and Neptune where they were, with all their satellites in tow, but they hastened back and forth between Earth's new orbit and trans-Neptunian space like huge swarms of bees, transporting iceballs from the Kuiper Belt and the Oort Cloud, not just by the hundred but by the thousand, and placing them in the

Earth's new orbit like a vast string of pearls. It took hardly any time at all—as a matter of necessity.

In the early days of the solar system's formation, before the sun had fully condensed and the planets coalesced, the temperature in its outer reaches had been moderately balmy. I don't know whether that's when life actually began, or whether the Arrhenius spores were already there, suspended in the mix of supernoval debris that constituted the heavier elements, but that was when our system's life first awoke, long before taking up residence on Earth and giving birth to the Vendian worms.

There was a lot of life lying dormant in the iceballs of the Kuiper Belt and the Oort Cloud, which had been waiting for a long time to have its day. It was nothing complicated—perhaps nothing more sophisticated than a primal bacterium—but it was life nevertheless, ready to be taken over by the Ultimate Worms. The Ultimate Worms were the worms who didn't know the meaning of the word "can't", although they certainly had a keen sense of the practicality of things, and they were perfectly ready to allow that cometary life to begin its own multiple evolutions of self-conscious intelligence.

I saw the Pearly Ring take its place as the next venue in the story of solar evolution. I saw the Earth take pride of place within it, ready to be gifted with a new atmosphere and new oceans, in anticipation of the flowering of the sun.

I saw the sun explode, if that's the right word for it, and I saw the wreckage of the explosion settle once again as a red giant star: the perfect light-source for the purpose-designed Pearly Ring. I saw the Ultimate Can-Do Worms begin the next phase of their work, extending their mastery of metamorphosis to the limits of their imagination, and stretching those limits all the while. I kept an eye out for the big guns, as Poe had advised me to do, and eventually caught a glimpse of them, although I might have missed them if I hadn't been on the look-out, given the distance from which I had to watch, the near-blindness of my continuing panic, and the fact that the whole process was over almost as soon as it had begun.

As Poe had said, space travel is, essentially and fundamentally, a plant-intelligence thing. It was the Worldplants, blossoming in some of the meatier ice-balls, forever singing their empathic rhapsodies in anticipation of the climacteric symphony of the vegetal Omega Point, which took on the burden of sending seeds, spores and pupae into the great dark surrounding the system. That ammunition vanished beyond the practicality of further communication almost as soon as they were fired, but it wasn't wasted. The seeds, spores and chrysalides weren't equipped with any kind of bio-rocket, because rockets are essentially short-term methods of propulsion. They were given such impulse-velocity as the plants' big guns could contrive, and left to make their way thereafter with only time-twisting technology to help them on their way. But they were dispatched in millions, now that the solar system finally had biomass to spare, at least for a little while.

My immediate hosts were never called upon to go into the darkness themselves. Our work was done in and around the Pearly Ring, with lightning rapidity. I saw the new worlds of the Ring in birth, but I saw them from a distance, through a veil of dread, and there's nothing I can say about the societies that were born on the reawakened Earth and its thousand neighbors. I have to suppose that they were Utopian, but I might be wrong about that. It's possible, I suppose, that they were worlds full of terror, communities entirely motivated by blind, sourceless panic and desperation. It's possible—but I don't believe it. I don't believe it, because the Ultimate Worms didn't just have the legacy of a lousy six hundred million years of post-Vendian evolution and a few tens of thousands years of human intelligence to draw upon. They had the legacy of four billion years of natural selection, thousands of intelligent species, the great symphony of plant intelligence and all the potential of time-travel technology to draw on—more dreams than we could ever imagine.

I believe that theirs was a true creationist enterprise, guided by wisdom and wit, justice and decency, even though I only saw it for a moment before the assembled time-ships had to disperse again and boomerang back to their multitudinous points of origin, and even though my senses were distorted by irrational, all-consuming fear.

* * * * * * *

Now, you might think that what I've just described couldn't possibly have happened, or that I can't possibly believe that it did, given that I've stated my firm conviction that time travel isn't a matter of transmitting material objects at all. There's a sense in which UFOs are subjective products, reflections of the collective unconscious—which don't, therefore, have the power to move grains of sand or mountains, let alone plutons and planets—but that's not so. Time travel, you see, *is* real, even if the only thing that can really be transported back through time is imagery and ideas. *Minds* can travel through time, twisting it as they go, and it's that twisting that produces the actual propulsive power to move worlds. Although I saw what I saw as a vast armada of vessels plying tractor beams, that was just a way of seeing it, a means by which it became the possibility of sensation.

Human psychotherapists tend to have a rather one-dimensional view of the collective unconscious. They tend to think of it as something built up within the recesses of the brain by the legacy of evolution: the product of past causes, whose contents constitute and contain the mythic past. They tend to think of it as something massive and virtually unchangeable, to which we conscious human beings have to adapt if we want to rest easy in the privacy of our own thoughts and desires. But even Carl Jung didn't have imagination enough to see beyond the obvious. Because time travel *is* possible, if only for images and ideas, the collective unconscious is actually something that we're all in the process of making, day by day and century by century, whose making will continue for at least another three and a half billion years, and probably much longer.

For us humans, located at the very beginning of True History and constituting the first real flexing of the Phoenix's wings, experience of the collective unconscious often is shackled and bound by the chains of the mythic past. The mythic future was always there in embryo, though, and humankind is now becoming pregnant within it, too late to do much with it ourselves before it we become extinct, but not too late to make a contribution, and maybe a crucial contribution, to the heritage of transtemporal consciousness to come. Even those of us who are terrified by any and every glimpse we might obtain into the vast abyss of time can see it as something in the making, something to which we can make a significant and lasting contribution, even though we're doomed. There is, after all, a sense in which we'll still be here, and still be accessible to transtemporal sensation, in dreams if not to the sense of touch, *long* after we're gone.

I don't know whether faith can move mountains; I suspect not. But I do know now that dreams can move planets, and relocate them when the sun swells up like an intoxicated balloon. I do know that, even though the billions of time-ships that I saw were in my mind and not in outer space, they could still play tricks with time, and that the relativity of matter and time allowed them actually to move the world, and take it to the next phase of the Phoenix's evolution.

If the Worms that Could had been the worms that couldn't, life would still have gone on; some of the iceballs would have melted in the glow of the red giant, and the great story would have picked up new momentum, in time—but that won't be necessary. The collective unconscious will be able to do the trick, provided that it's nurtured properly, and doesn't try to do too much too soon.

Maybe there aren't many people on Earth who know that, as yet—but we know it, because we've been told the stories and shown the sketchy outlines of the pattern. We can tell.

We've opened the Can of Worms, and we don't have to be disgusted by what we see, no matter how terrifying it might be, because we understand—don't we?—that a can of worms is infinitely better than a can't.

CHAPTER NINETEEN

HEARING THE VOICE OF SANITY

As Milly had often said, the East Grimstead branch of AlAbAn was a very supportive support group. Walter Wainwright thanked Steve very kindly once he had taken his seat again—feeling only slightly queasy, thanks to his new-found mastery of the art of relaxation. Everyone else in the group agreed that his sketchy theory about the workings of the collective unconscious, and the contribution that AlAbAn was making to it—even though the end of the world as its members knew it was pretty much at hand—had given them a lot of food for thought, which they would try their very best to digest. No one thanked him personally for casting new light on their own experiences, but no one cast a shadow of doubt on anything he'd said or challenged the coherency of his own narrative.

As they were on their way out to the car, though, he said to Milly: "I should have written it down. It was too rushed, too unbalanced, too crowded. I could have done better. I should have taken more time to prepare a lesson-plan. It isn't as if I haven't had practice, and time to figure out my own weaknesses in that respect "

"Don't beat yourself up about it," Milly said. Then, pausing *en route* and turning to face him, she said: "You know don't you, that I'd never ask you to go on a foreign holiday, or to drive across the Severn Bridge, or to go up the bell-tower in Salisbury Cathedral—and I wouldn't be disappointed in you, either. I wouldn't be compromising my own ambitions."

"No," Steve said, "I didn't know."

"Well, you do now," she said. After another pause, she added: "But I don't suppose it's enough, is it?"

"It's more than enough," Steve assured her. "The catch is that it doesn't quite solve the problem, does it? We both still feel badly about Janine. That wouldn't last forever, though. If we were to give it time...if we were able to give it time...."

He was floundering, and would probably have trailed off anyway even if he hadn't been interrupted, but Milly had already turned away because Alison was running to catch up with them.

"Sorry," Alison, said. "I know it's a bit of a cheek, Steve, but you couldn't possibly give me a lift back to town, could you? Mr. Wainwright's already got two other passengers as well as Janine, and I feel a bit uncomfortable crushed in the back seat with those morose old men. If you'd rather I didn't, it's okay."

"No, that's all right," Milly said. "We've plenty of room in our back seat, haven't we, Steve?"

"Yes," Steve said, not quite sure when the Citroen's back seat had become "ours", or whether it was really Milly's prerogative to decide who was entitled to sit in it.

Once they were all aboard, Milly turned to Steve, blatantly ignoring Alison, and said: "We don't have to come to the next meeting, Steve. We've told our stories now. We don't ever have to come again, if we don't want to."

"Of course we do," Steve said. "Telling the stories doesn't solve anything, in itself. That's why people like Neville—he's one of your morose old man, Alison—have to keep coming back, telling them over and over again, worrying away at the underlying problems. To solve the problems, you have to be able to learn, not just from the stories themselves, but from the underlying patterns and the underlying meanings. We have to figure out how we ought to fit into the universe and one another's lives. If Janine's begun to remember, I want to hear what she's remembered—but it's not just her. I want to hear all the other stories too. Don't you?"

"I suppose so," Milly said. "I'm the one who's been coming for ages, after all. It was my thing before it was anyone else's, and I suppose it's still my thing now that everyone else has joined in. Did you enjoy it, Ali? Oh, sorry!"

The exclamation that interrupted Alison's reply was caused by the fact that Milly's phone was vibrating in her pocket again. She pulled it out and said; "Yes, Mummy, I can talk." Then her attitude changed. Had it not been so dark in the car, Steve knew, he and Alison would have been able to see her turn pale. He didn't need the confirmation of Milly's muttered curse to know that her unconscious father had just given up the unequal struggle to maintain his terminally-damaged body.

Steve kept his eyes firmly on the road while the brief telephone conversation continued to its inevitable end. Alison never made a sound. Neither of them spoke when Milly put the phone away; they waited for a signal.

Milly didn't break into tears. She swore several times more, under her breath, and then said: "I suppose he'd have thought, if he were still capable of thinking, that he'd be saving us trouble, ducking out with four days still to go till Christmas. He wasn't to know that I'd be in Salisbury, desperately trying to fix things up with my boy-friend by planning to have a private Christmas with him, tomorrow, before having to go back to look after Mum—a private Christmas for which I've already bought all the food, all of which will spoil and go to waste while I'm away...along with the relationship, in all probability. He didn't mean to inconvenience anyone by not taking his bloody tablets, and he doesn't now. It's just bad luck."

"I didn't know...," Steve began.

"I know you didn't know," Milly said. "I was just about to tell you. No point, now. Shit happens, as Janine's so fond of saying, Things get spoiled. Sometimes it's somebody's fault—mine as often as anyone else's—and sometimes it's not. Let's just hope there's a bloody train, and that you can get me to the station in time to catch it."

"No," Steve said, feeling that it was now time to be assertive. "I'll drop Alison off, and then I'll drive you to your flat. While you're packing, I'll load the food you bought for tomorrow into the boot—given that we're well into the hours of darkness on the longest night of the year, it'll be better than a fridge. Then I'll drive you to Bath. Tomorrow, I'll cook the food. It'll probably see me through weekend, but none of it will spoil and nothing will go to waste. I promise you—nothing will spoil and nothing will go to waste. Okay?"

"I get it," Milly said. "Double meanings and all. Thanks. Have you ever driven to Bath before?"

"No," Steve said, "but that's of no consequence. I'll take the most direct route and I'll cross any bridges I happen to meet on the way without a moment's hesitation. I've been practicing."

"At least it's the right side of the Avon Gorge," Milly said.

"It wouldn't matter," Steve said, doggedly, although he knew that it was probably a lie. "I will get you to where you need to be. You'll have to direct me to your place though, Alison. I don't know where it is."

"I'll tell you which way to go when we get to town," Alison assured him. "It's only a couple of streets away from Mil's, so you won't lose any time."

"I might not be able to get back until the new year," Milly remarked. "This isn't the best time of year for arranging a funeral."

"It's okay," Steve said. "When it's all done, we can start over. There'll still be time enough before the end of the world to gather a few rosebuds where and when we may, and even make merry once the mourning's done."

"You certainly know how to cheer a girl up, Steve," Milly said, dourly. "Don't you think that we ought to dedicate ourselves to doing something useful, maybe in the desperate attempt to preserve the ecosphere, rather than investing our precious remaining moments in mere pleasure-seeking."

"It's not mere," Steve told her. "That's the whole point of my theory—although you only glimpsed the barest shadow of it tonight. Our pleasure-seeking isn't just the jetsam of contemporary consciousness, of no significance whatsoever in the scheme of things. Because time travel exists, even if it's just a matter of mind, *everything counts*."

"And what if time travel doesn't exist?" Milly asked. "What if it's all just a tissue of fanciful lies?"

"If time travel doesn't exist *yet*," Steve said, "we, or someone like us, will have to invent it. It's okay, Milly. We can afford to be patient. We, and they, have all the time in the world."

* * * * * * *

By the time Steve had fulfilled his promises to Milly and driven back to Salisbury from Bath it was three o'clock in the morning. He unloaded the car as quietly as he could, and then went to bed, physically and emotionally exhausted. He slept until eleven; the one convenient aspect of Milly's father's timing was that term had ended the day before and he had no need to get up for school.

After waking up, Steve made a careful inventory of the various materials he had removed from Milly's refrigerator, so that he could amend his own weekend shopping list. Then he drove to the supermarket in order to lay in supplies of his own for what was promising to be a very peculiar Christmas. He knew that if he cared to phone his mother and tell her that his own plans had been rudely disrupted, and that he could make it home after all, he'd be welcomed like the prodigal son he had never actually contrived to be, but he hadn't the least inclination to do so.

At three o'clock, Alison phoned him. "It's a bit of a cheek, I know," she said, "but I couldn't help overhearing, last night, that you'll be cooking more food tonight than you can eat. I wondered if

I could possibly be of any help—with the cooking as well as the eating, that is. You wouldn't be in any moral danger."

"Why do you keep saying that?" Steve asked. "Even when I only had Milly's uncharitable description of you to go on, I wouldn't have made any such assumption. Now I've met the real you, I certainly wouldn't make that assumption, so there's no need to go out of your way to dispel it."

"Sorry," Alison said. "I suppose it's just that if I'd ever done anything like this before, I *would* be working on that assumption, and I'd probably be able to assume that the person I was calling would be working on it too. I suppose I'm really talking to myself, not you. Is that a no, then?"

"You'd be very welcome to help me make inroads into Milly's turkey crown and vegetable mountain," Steve said. "You don't have to help with the cooking, though. Will it be all right if I cook for seven?"

"Absolutely. Can I come over a little earlier? You don't have to let me help, but I could pester you with unnecessary conversation and make the job more difficult."

"As you please," Steve said.

When Milly phoned him at four Steve told her that he had invited Alison round to help him eat the surplus food—and for that purpose alone—and apologized for not having asked her permission first. Milly said that it was perfectly all right, that he didn't need her permission, and that she was glad that her food wouldn't be going to waste.

Alison arrived at half past five, clutching a bottle of Australian Shiraz, and proceeded to delight him with conversation while he shuttled back and forth between his kitchen and the front room, where he'd set up his dining-table.

"Milly never got a chance to tell me what went on at your peace talks on Sunday," he said—not entirely honestly. "Did it go well? Is harmony in the process of being restored?"

"That depends what would count as harmony," Alison said. "Milly said sorry about the letter, formally, and I forgave her, formally—after which she assumed that the matter was done and dusted, although I can't quite remember her adopting the same attitude when the situation was reversed. After that, it was pretty much the Milly and Janine show, with me being expected to serve as referee and mediator. They seem to have patched things up, after a fashion, as they always have when they've fallen out in the past, but they can't really settle it until they've decided what to do about you—which they can't really do on their own, although they certainly tried. I gathered while eavesdropping from the back seat of your car on Thursday that Milly had begun to take tentative steps in the direction of involving you in a settlement, but that's obviously been postponed. It's not really my business, mercifully—although they might try to use me as a referee and mediator, once they're convinced that I won't make any pathetic attempts to grab you for myself. I don't want to play mediator, though—mostly because I don't think there's any satisfactory solution to the problem."

"Oh," Steve said. He'd just about reached the same conclusion himself, but he was slightly disappointed to hear it so casually confirmed.

"From their point of view, that is, not yours," Alison added, perhaps misunderstanding the import of his *oh*. "All you'll have to do, once Janine's wounded pride has relented to the point of letting her dismiss your fling with Milly as *shit happens*, is make your choice. Everyone assumes that you'll choose Janine, although we all know that you're way too soft-hearted to put the boot into Milly callously, especially with her Dad just having died and all. The future scenario everyone envisages, I think, is that the awkwardness will drag on for a bit longer—maybe a few more weeks—until you and Milly have completed the job of making yourselves and one another thoroughly miserable. Then she'll consent to be sent packing, with a great show of mutual reluctance, and you'll be free to get back with Janine, miserably at first but eventually...well, who knows? Milly and Janine might have to part then, but at least they'll be able to part as friends rather than enemies, and it will make them both feel better."

Steve could only stare, dumbfounded.

"Sorry," Alison said. "I know that laying it out like that won't help cut short the trouble and pain—but that *is* how it will go, if we three witches have read the future rightly. Did you have some other scenario in mind, perhaps? Better tell me, if you did, so I can do my humble best to steer things in that direction. You do have the choice, you know—and at the end of the day, it would be stupid to stay with Milly just because you couldn't bear to make yourself look bad by dumping her. Make a song and dance about it, by all means, but don't cut off your nose to spite your face."

"Actually," Steve said, "I'd got the impression that Milly and Janine were building up to the decision that their friendship was too precious to waste over some mere bloke, and that it would be me who would be expelled from the sacred circle."

"They'll probably try to convince themselves of that while they're in the process of making up," Alison admitted, "but it'll never go the distance. At the end of the day, they're just a couple of girls, whose one experiment with lesbianism in their teens only helped to confirm that all three of us are irredeemably straight. You qualify as a real prize, even for Janine. You probably think that you have nothing much to recommend you apart from your pretty-boy looks—being a newly qualified none-too-bright teacher in the second best comprehensive in Salisbury hardly qualifies as potential for a glittering career, and the fear of flying's a bit of a drawback—but you're also quite a nice bloke, which most good lookers aren't, and you're a bit of a romantic in your own way, which is quite sweet, and you're relaxed enough around women to be good company whether you're sleeping with them or not...and I don't think you quite realize quite how much of an asset the looks are. Trust me, Steve—you *will* have the choice. You'll get Janine, even if it means—as it might—that Janine and Milly will have to go their separate ways. They'll contrive to make that as gracious as possible, if it comes to it, so it won't rankle too much. They'd be able to manage that even without my help."

"What about you?" Steve asked, figuring that it was the safest question on offer. "Will you be able to carry on being friends with both of them, if they do split, or will you have to choose?"

"Oh, it seems to me that I can't possibly carry on being friends with either of them—but I'll try to negotiate a parting on good terms too, so that it doesn't rankle."

"Why can't you carry on being friends with them?" Steve asked.

"I could give you a bullshit reason if I wanted to, but as I'm the real me just now, I might as well just admit that they're too good-looking. I can't compete. If I continue hanging around with them, and craving their approval, I'll always be the loser of the group of three—the court jester, there for their amusement and to carry the bags. I don't want to do that any more. I know it doesn't reflect well on me to say that from now on I only want to swim in pools where the other fish are no bigger than I am, but I'm twenty-six years old. I have to start making serious preparations for some kind of future. If I'm going to reinvent myself properly, I'll have to get away from Jan and Mil and all the baggage we carry—but I'll have to do it in a moderately dignified way. Like Jan and Mil, we'll need to part as friends rather than enemies, with all outstanding debts settled. It won't be easy, but I think I can do it. We'll need at least one more coven-meeting to achieve it, but we'll need one anyway, because we still have your fate to decide."

"You just said that I'll get to decide my own fate," Steve pointed out.

"Of course you will," Alison told him, "but Jan and Mill will still have to pretend that they decided it for you, between themselves. That's an absolute must, so far as saving face is concerned. Fortunately, you're the kind of bloke who'll let them. I only wish...."

Before Alison could voice her only wish, the doorbell rang. Steve glanced at his wristwatch, and saw that it was half past six—just about time to get serious with the vegetables. His eyes met Alison's, which showed the same hesitant suspicion as his own. He went to the door and opened it. Janine was standing on the threshold, clutching a bottle of oaky claret.

"I know I should have called," Janine said, as she moved past Steve, "but I thought it might be less awkward if I just...." She stopped as she caught sight of Alison.

"I guess you had the same thought as me," Alison said, in a tone far less sprightly than the one in which she'd just been showing off her cleverness to Steve.

For a moment or two, it looked as if Janine might not take off her coat, but then she did. Evidently, she meant business—although Steve was far from certain exactly what that business might be.

"When did Milly ring you?" Steve asked.

Janine looked at him, apparently not quite sure how to answer.

"Milly rang you, didn't she?" Steve said. "To tell you that I was cooking the food she'd bought for dinner *à deux*, and to suggest that this might be a good opportunity to begin patching things up. What time did she call?"

"About four-thirty, I guess," Janine said. "She was sorry for leaving it so late, she said, but things had been a bit hectic in the family home. I'm sorry too—obviously, I ought to have given you more notice."

"I'll go, if you like," Alison said, speaking to Janine.

"No," Steve said. "You mustn't."

"Well," Alison said, "given that I've helped you so much with the cooking...shall I put the veg on now? I can put in a little extra—there's plenty in reserve. If that's okay with you, Jan."

"Of course," Janine said. "I wouldn't dream of trying to send you away. I should have remembered that Steve gave you a lift home last night—you must have been in the car when Milly got the news. She didn't tell me that she'd invited you too. I suppose she thought it would help us all if we were both here."

"There's time to do some mashed potatoes too," Alison said. "Just in case there's not enough roast for three. Don't move a muscle, Steve—entertain your other guest while I see to it." She vanished into the kitchen, but stuck her head out again a moment later to say: "Oh, by the way, Jan, there's nothing going on. I've already explained to Steve why I could never sleep with him, in the unlikely event of his ever being desperate enough to ask me. He understands, and he's fine with it."

When Alison had vanished for a second time, Janine said: "She never changes. I suppose you're surprised to see me."

"Very," Steve admitted.

"Milly and I had a long talk on Sunday. Alison helped us out. We decided that things had to be settled, to spare us all any more pain. I just wanted you to know that I'm okay with the situation. I was hurt, but I'm better now. You're with Milly now, and that's okay. I think it might be possible for us all to be friends, if we're mature and sensible about it."

"Right," Steve said. "That would be good."

"And Milly needs support from all of us just now," Janine went on. "We have to put her first. She's always been a bit fragile, you know, since she had the bulimia. She seems all right now, but the fact that she's been a regular at AlAbAn for a year and more is an indicator that she never quite got back to normal."

"You and I are regulars at AlAbAn now," Steve pointed out. "We've all had our experiences."

"Well, I'd be the last person to claim to be completely normal," Janine said, insincerely, "and you've had your troubles too—but Milly's the one who's in the firing line at present. We have to figure out how best to help her. I'm glad Ali's here. It'll give us all a chance to compare notes. You and I will have to put our differences aside."

Steve wasn't sure that he'd had any differences to put aside, even before Alison had given him her version of the likely future scenario towards which everyone was supposed to be working. He wasn't exactly sure why Milly had rung Janine immediately after he'd told her about Alison coming round to eat up the spare food, but he could see well enough why Alison thought that Milly's mind was as straight as a corkscrew, in the nicest possible way. He had no idea how straight Janine's mind was at present.

"Well, I'm glad you came," Steve said. "It means that I can give you both your presents, in case I don't see you again before Monday.

Alison's head reappeared round the kitchen doorway with suspicious alacrity. "You bought me a present?" she said.

"You bought us *both* presents?" Janine said. "I didn't buy you one."

"Me neither," said Alison.

"Oh, they're nothing special," Steve assured them both. "I happened to be in Reading last Saturday, and there's a Natural World shop in the mall there. I like the shop—it's a little bit trinkety, but it's the kind of place in which a secondary school science teacher feels perfectly at home. You'll have to forgive me if the presents are a million miles away from anything you actually wanted."

He fetched the packages from the cupboard, and handed them over. Alison came back into the sitting-room so that she and Janine could compare gifts.

"It's a rock," Janine observed, when she'd unwrapped hers. "I think it's broken."

"It's split in two so you can move the two halves apart and look inside," Steve said.

Janine did that, and looked suitably surprised by the mass of crystals inside the seemingly-unprepossessing ovoid, arranged in layers around a central cavity.

"It's a geode," Steve explained. He could have gone on, but Alison intervened.

"I've got a rock too," she said. "Shaped like a snail."

"It's an ammonite," Steve said. "I used to hunt fossils down on the Dorset coast when I was a kid, with my Dad—that was probably a major factor in my choice of career. I never found one as big or as neatly-formed as that one, though. It's about a hundred million years old, give or take twenty million. Those crystals have been locked up inside the geode far longer, unseen by human or any other kind of eye. I'm sorry they're not posh jewelry, but I've always thought that it's nice to have something on the mantelpiece to remind us how old the world is, and how small our troubles—or humankind's troubles—are, in the context of geological time."

"Jesus," Alison said. "You really are a romantic, aren't you, in your own weird way?"

"You used to hunt fossils along the Dorset cliffs?" Janine said. "How on Earth did you manage that?"

"You hunt for fossils at the bottom of the cliffs, not the top," Steve told her. "I never, ever, went near the upper edges. I've always been a bottom-of-the-cliff sort of person, since earliest childhood."

"What did you get Milly?" Alison asked.

Steve was too smart to be caught out by that one. He shook his head, mysteriously. "I'd better see to those vegetables," he said, as he beat a hasty retreat to the kitchen, leaving Alison and Janine to compare trophies and replan their tactics for the next few moves in their convoluted game.

* * * * * * *

Milly's father's funeral was arranged for the following Wednesday—the day after Boxing Day. Steve wanted to go, in order to lend Milly his moral support, and offered to drive Janine and Alison, but Milly said on Boxing Day that she'd prefer it if they didn't, because none of them had actually known her father, even though Alison and Janine might remember having met him when they were children. The funeral, she said, was essentially a family occasion. This gave Steve the impression that Milly didn't think that his moral support, and that of Janine and Alison, was worth anywhere near as much as he and they did.

"Have you seen much of Janine and Alison since Friday?" Milly asked, in all apparent innocence. It was a question she hadn't asked before, although they'd talked on the phone every day—and Steve hadn't volunteered the relevant information.

"We've got together a couple of times," Steve said. "Nothing to worry about—Alison was always there to act as chaperone."

"I wasn't worried," Milly told him. "You don't need to be chaperoned, and neither does Jan. Alison might, mind. She's the double-dyed slut."

"That's unfair," Steve told her.

"I know," Milly replied. "It's just part of our relationship—you wouldn't understand. Watch out that she doesn't pull the wool over your eyes. I love her dearly, and I'm truly sorry that I wrote that wretched letter, but she's a sly one."

"When will you get back to Salisbury?" Steve asked.

"I'm not absolutely sure. Because of the holiday I haven't missed out on that much work, so it's difficult to resist Mum's insistence that I have to stay till the weekend. Probably Sunday, I guess, although I'll try to get away before—I'll see you that evening. I'm back at work on Monday, of course. If you want to see Janine again, that's fine—with or without a chaperone."

"Is that that you want?" Steve asked.

"I'm thinking about what you might want," Milly said. "From my point of view, mind, you're probably safer with Jan than hanging around at a loose end. It sounds awful, I now, but I think I can trust her morals better than she was able to trust mine—and if I can't, I'd hardly be in a position to complain, would I?"

Steve related this conversation to Alison on the Friday, when they met up for a drink in the Pheasant, without a chaperone.

"She's right, I suppose," Alison said. "I am a sly one. It doesn't make any difference, though, does it? Everything's working to plan. Jan is preparing the ground to take you back and Milly's preparing to hand you over. It'll take time, but you'll get there in the end."

"According to you, it was supposed to be my decision," Steve reminded her.

"Yes, of course—but that's the decision you'll make, isn't it? We're all anticipating the same future here. It's because it *is* your decision that we know how things are bound to turn out. Milly's just accepting the inevitable, and saving as much face as possible."

"But why is everyone taking it for granted that I prefer Janine?" Steve asked. "Nobody's actually asked me."

"Actually, I did ask you," Alison reminded him. "You didn't answer, but I took that as tacit confirmation. Jan's the best-looking, even without taking into account your predilection for doll-like delicacy. If someone had a particular liking for tall women in uniform, that might narrow her advantage over Milly, but no one's under any illusions here. Milly tried flat-out competition with Janine, back in her bulimic days, but she had to admit in the end that it was pointless. Jan wins—that's just the way it goes. Shit happens. We've been friends long enough to know that."

"Do you think all men are that shallow, or just me? Do you really think that it always comes down to looks, and nothing else."

"It's all men, in my experience," Alison told him, "and yes, alas, it always does seem to come down to looks. Beauty is the bottom line. Always has been, always will be. *Beauty is truth, truth beauty—that is all ye know on earth, and all ye need to know.* That's Keats."

"I'm familiar with the quotation," Steve admitted, feeling somewhat caught out, although she couldn't have known that he'd used it himself to make the same cynical point he was now trying to blunt.

"Well, that's the long and the short of it. In spite of the special pleading of pulp romantic fiction, from *Jane Eyre* on, the looker always gets the guy she wants—permanently, if she wants him permanently—and as many other guys, on a temporary basis, as she fancies along the way. It was a bit different, I suppose, back in Keats' day, when girls weren't allowed to be sluts. When everyone had to pretend to be a virgin, even lookers were only entitled to grab one and stick to him, so everyone lower down the scale could pick a fresh one from the remaining pool, but it's not like that any more.

These days, lookers can sample to their heart's content. Can you honestly put your hand on your heart and contradict me?"

"There isn't just one linear scale of beauty," Steve said, defiantly. "Different people are attractive in different ways, and different people have different tastes. Plenty of men might prefer Milly to Janine, or you to either of them."

"In your dreams—or mine, more likely. It works the other way too, Steve. Didn't you always win, in competition with your male friends, in the days when you weren't such a loner?"

"I'm not a loner," Steve protested, although it was certainly true that he hadn't restarted hanging out with people from work since he'd got his return ticket from Coventry, rarely saw anyone from the cricket club during the winter months, and knew perfectly well that internet poker didn't count as authentic social interaction.

"But you don't have friends the way Janine, Milly and I are friends, do you?"

"No, thank God," Steve riposted. "I wouldn't need enemies, would I?"

"Don't be like that," Alison said. "I'm not getting at you— certainly not trying to hurt you. If I'm getting at anyone, it's myself. You're right, too—with friends like Janine and Milly, I certainly don't need enemies. I mustn't give you the wrong impression about that, either. They're not my enemies, and there've been plenty of times when I really needed them. It's easy for me to slag them off while I'm out with you, all smug because it makes me look good in envious eyes—but when things go wrong, they provide a safety net for which I've often had cause to be thankful."

"I still think you're oversimplifying," Steve said. "If I do get back with Janine, it won't be just because of her looks. I'm really not that shallow."

"And I'm really not trying to pick a fight," she said. "I'll take it as a compliment that you care enough about what I think to disagree with me."

Steve smiled wryly at that. "Oh, I care," he said. "I'd begun to rely on you as the voice of sanity in a deeply confusing and disturbing world. I suppose you're right, and I'm only protesting because I'd like you to think better of me than you do, even though I don't deserve it."

"Now you're trying to make me feel guilty. That's not fair—I'm too easy a target...and I wish that wasn't true in more ways than one, although it obviously is."

"I wish you wouldn't run yourself down like that," Steve said.

"Why? So you can pretend that I'm more attractive than I am, so that you needn't be ashamed to be seen with me."

Steve didn't reply to that.

"Okay," Alison said. "That was stupid, and unfair, and made me out to be a liar when I said I wasn't getting at you. I really was trying to be the voice of sanity, but it's harder than I thought. Obviously, I'll need more practice before I can perfect *that* act. Now I'm babbling. Janine would have been—will be—*so* much more controlled."

Steve frowned. "What do you mean, *will be*?" he asked.

"Just a guess," she said. "I thought tonight might be a practice run for the unchaperoned outing you didn't quite have the confidence to tackle yet. I thought you might have asked me out on my own because you weren't quite ready to ask Janine out on her own, and I couldn't help feeling a little bit resentful about it. Tell me I'm wrong, and I'll take your word for it."

Steve knew that telling her she was wrong wasn't going to sound at all convincing, given the circumstances, "You're too clever for your own good," he said, instead. "and too paranoid by half. You're my voice of sanity, remember?"

"So I am," Alison said, probably agreeing to all three propositions. "I've spoiled things now, haven't I? You won't ask me to do this again."

"If I were as shallow as you think I am," Steve said, "I probably wouldn't—but I'm deep enough to know what the voice of sanity is worth, and you do seem to need more practice. Are you coming to AlAbAn on Thursday?"

"Wouldn't miss it for the world," she aid. "It's Janine's turn to tell her story. I missed Milly's, unfortunately, but there's no way I'm going to miss Jan's. I'd quite like to hear your theory, too."

"No, you wouldn't," he said. "Walter Wainwright explained why people don't like listening to other people's theories, and I've just learned by experience exactly what he meant. I'm a teacher, so I'm supposed to be thankful for any education that comes my way, and I'm trying to be—but there's no reason why I should inflict my theory of alien abductions on you."

"Okay," she said. "So what happens next?"

After a long pause, and knowing that it was probably a stupid thing to do, Steve said: "What do you really think of me, Alison?"

"Really and truly?" she said. "No matter how much it might hurt?"

"Really and truly," he said. "No matter how much it might hurt." He was assuming, of course, that she meant that it might hurt him.

"I fancy you more than anyone else I've ever fancied in my life," she said, "and part of me wants to take full advantage of this brief window of opportunity to get you into my bed, if only for one night—but the other part knows that it's just your fortuitous looks and your accidental charm that attracts me, and that if I did trick you into the occasional bout of side-dish sex, thanks to my uniquely winning combination of slyness and sluttiness, it would only break my heart all the more violently in two every time you moved on again, whether it was to Janine, or Milly, or someone else entirely. So I'm not going to, no matter how much I presently might want to cling to you for as long as we both might live and bear all your children. It's all about saving face, you see. Even I can do that, though I haven't much to save."

"Well," he said, after another suitable pause. "That's sanity, I guess."

"And you see right through it, don't you? You don't think for a minute I could keep it up. You think that if you keep on calling, it's only a matter of time before you'd catch me in a weak moment, and that once you'd broken my resolution you could have me any time you wanted, no matter what you might do in between times."

Steve suspected that might be true, but he honestly didn't think he was the kind of person who would behave like that, once it had been described to him in such brutal terms.

* * * * * * *

Steve had his final appointment with Sylvia Joyce on the following Tuesday, at which he informed her that he'd related his abduction experience to the AlAbAn meeting before Christmas, and felt a little better for it. He also told her that he was coping much better with bridges, although he still got slight heebie-jeebies if he pictured the Avon Gorge in his mind's eye and couldn't yet know what might happen if he should attempt to board a plane.

"We really should try another regression," the hypnotherapist told him. "Now that you've pieced together the abduction experience and brought it out into the open, we ought to be easily able to go deeper, to discover what lies beneath and behind it."

"Nothing lies behind and beneath it," Steve said. "It was a nightmare generated by my phobias. If you repeat the trick, you'll probably find others—or produce others. I really and truly believe that there is no moment of trauma whose magical revelation will explain my phobias or whose abreaction will cure them. My phobias are just some random physiological accident that I have to learn to get along with as best I can. I've got enough to worry about without adding more supposedly-paranormal experiences to the list. I don't want to start conjuring up imaginary childhood traumas, let alone exploring hypothetical past lives or making contact with the dead."

"Why don't you want to make contact with the dead, Steve?" the therapist asked, seizing on his throwaway remark like a hawk pouncing on an unwary shrew.

"Because I don't. I have way too much trouble with the living," Steve informed her.

"What do you mean by that, exactly?" Sylvia came back, inevitably.

"I mean," Steve said, taking a very deep breath, in the expectation that he would need it, "that the girl-friend I had when I started this farce cast me aside like a worn-out sock because I slept with one of her best friends, and wouldn't speak to me for weeks, but now looks as if she might condescend to get back together, provided I do penance for the sin for as long as we're together. The said best friend hadn't been my replacement girlfriend for much more than a fortnight when she started having acute pangs of guilt ill-befitting a traffic warden, and my attempts to help her work through said guilt pangs came to little or nothing, partly because she was distracted by her father's terminal illness and sudden death and partly because she seems to have decided that she actually wants to give me back to my former girlfriend, in order that she can feel magnanimous. In the meantime, their other best friend has started playing mind-games with me of a kind I've never encountered before, and I have no idea how I ought to deal with it, or whether I can deal with it without inflicting a mortal wound on her, or me, or either or both of her friends. I'll be back in the bear-pit with year eleven in a matter of days, on the long and lonely trail to GCSEs, with increasing coursework anxiety adding an extra layer of insanity to all the customary hormonal turmoil, until the exams finally bring the cauldron to boiling-point. My hypnotherapist, who was only supposed to be teaching me relaxation techniques so that I might be able to get on a plane one day without excessive chemical assistance, wants to delve into my psyche to see if there's anything in there nastier than what she's already excavated. To cap it all, I can no longer do my shopping in Sainsbury's without looking pityingly at all the other poor sods pushing their carts, blissfully ignorant of the fact that the human race will be extinct before the end of the century, except for a few scattered groups who'll make it into the twenty-second before the methane chokes them or they cook in their own rancid juices. Why, on top of all that, would I want to see dead people?"

"Do you think you might be depressed, Steve?" the hypnotherapist asked, tenderly.

"Of course I'm depressed. Anyone who was in my situation and wasn't depressed would be off his head. If it wasn't for...." He stopped, realizing that he'd let her get one up on him again.

"If it wasn't for what, Steve?" she asked, beaming.

"That's the worst thing of all," he told her. "If it wasn't for bloody AlAbAn, I'd have no bloody support at all. How pathetic is that?"

"It's not pathetic," she assured him.

"But they're all completely crazy!" Steve protested. "And I've joined in!" He stopped again, knowing that he'd tied himself in knots. Hadn't he spent the last few weeks figuring out a theory to explain why the AlAbAn members weren't crazy at all, but were in fact enlightened souls who had actually contrived to find a precious glimmer of light in the darkness of the imminent future? Hadn't he *almost* persuaded himself to believe it? And wasn't he still hoping, bizarrely, that AlAbAn or his theory might somehow provide a means of sorting out his frustratingly tangled relationships with Janine, Milly and Alison?

"Look," he said, not giving Sylvia time to needle him again. "Can we just do the relaxation thing one last time, okay? No regressions—let's just mobilize some inner calm, if there's any left to mobilize. If there is, I'm going to need every last little bit of it on Thursday night, if Janine gets to tell her story and I have to drive all three of the scheming witches back to Salisbury afterwards. That could be the big crunch, when it all gets sorted, one way or another."

"Fine," the hypnotherapist said. "You're the client. It's your privilege, and your choice."

CHAPTER TWENTY

THE WRATH OF DARK TIME

It would be nice to think that it was all just a dream, but I'm not the kind of person who can take refuge in that kind of cowardly intellectualizing. It was every bit as real as this room, and *he* was every bit as real as any of the people sitting in it, even though I somehow contrived to forget about him for almost ten years. I only started to remember when I began coming to these meetings, and realized that some of the things that people were talking about were already familiar to me.

I wasn't abducted; I just met a time-traveler. It happened in December when I was in year eleven at school, still living with my parents in Codford, although I couldn't wait to get away. I used to go walking a lot, even in winter—although the winters were getting mild by then—on the plain or the Ridgeway, sometimes going as far as Gravely Wood and back. It was on the Ridgeway that I ran into him, one Sunday afternoon. He didn't seem to belong there; he was wearing a business suit and light shoes, and he was wearing sunglasses—the reflective kind they call mirrorshades—even though the sky was grey and overcast.

There were usually plenty of people around at that time, even in December—it's a popular weekend walk—and it's usually quite safe, but I realized when he stepped into my path that there was no one visible behind him. When I looked round, I saw that there was no one behind me either. He was tall, and, although he didn't seem particularly muscular, I knew that I wouldn't have the slightest chance of outrunning him or fighting him off, if he turned out to be a rapist.

"I'm terribly sorry to bother you, Miss," he said, "but I wonder if you could possibly help me. I've suffered a malfunction, and I can't fix it by myself."

"What kind of malfunction?" I asked. I thought he might be using the word euphemistically, and that he might want me to do something nasty.

"It's my right eye," he said. "To be strictly accurate, it's the socket. I have the necessary tools to put it right, and I even have a mirror, but I can't see into the socket clearly enough with the mirror to perform the operation. Even if I wedge the mirror securely to free up both hands, I can't clear the contacts, let alone realign them. While the contacts aren't working properly I can't get back into my...car. The lock has an iris-recognition system, you see. It's a little too secure, in the circumstances."

Although the Ridgeway's just a footpath, with hedges to either side, people ride motorbikes there, and joyriders sometimes tear up and down it in stolen cars, but he certainly didn't look like a joyrider. Nor could I see any sign of a car in the vicinity.

I looked round again, but there was still no one in sight. "What car?" I said, eventually.

"It's not really a car," he confessed. "But then, it's certainly more like a car than a ship. I wouldn't have mentioned it, but...well, if you agree to help me, you'll find out soon enough what I am. The last thing I want to do is frighten you, because you'll need a steady hand if you're to be of any help, but it's not going to be easy to avoid causing you a certain amount of alarm, so I might as well get it over with. I'm a humanoid robot from the distant future, and my car is a time machine. Usually, the things my makers build are very well-designed, but human simulacra are rather problematic—because, in all fairness, *humans* aren't very well-designed. Natural selection does tend to fudge things somewhat, especially in eras as primitive as this one. Mine's a creationist era, of course—but for purposes of remote prehistorical research my makers have to produce simulacra, which requires a certain amount of awkward improvisation."

"Show me," I said, trying hard not to shiver.

He took off his mirrorshades, and then he took out his right eye. It wasn't on a stalk—it just came right out. He knelt down so that I could see inside. The back wall of the eyeball was covered in electronic circuitry, and so was the inside of the socket, but there were some tiny specks of grit on the back wall, which seemed to have scarred the circuitry.

"Can you see what the problem is?" he asked.

"Yes," I said, and reported what I could see.

"If they'd equipped me with a proper conjunctiva, it wouldn't have happened," he said, with a sigh. "It would have made switching eye units more difficult, and it would have run up the budget. They'll just say that it was my fault, though, for letting the grit get back there."

The robot produced a toolkit from his pocket, and showed me the things inside. They were considerably more complicated than your average screwdriver.

"I've threaded needles in my time," I told him, "and helped Dad put together the occasional Ikea flatpack, but I think this is out of my league."

"I'll tell you exactly what to do," he assured me. "All you need is good eyesight, a steady hand and plenty of patience."

"Famous last words," I said, "but I'll give it a go."

It wasn't nearly as easy as he'd tried to make it sound, of course. In fact, it was fiendishly difficult. It took me the best part of an hour just to figure out how to hold the necessary tools and how to work their controls. While I worked, though, we talked. At the time, I thought he was just naturally garrulous, or pretending to be chatty to put me at my ease. I figured that he probably didn't get many opportunities for relaxed conversation, and none at all to talk about himself.

"My makers tried to use local materials, you see," he said, apologetically, as he tried to explain how it came about that he'd gone wrong, "in the interests of accurate simulation, they said. No nanotech at all—for fear of accidental contamination, they said. I'd have been a lot more expensive, of course if they'd coughed up for state-of-the-art instead of cutting so many corners. If I were the client, I wouldn't even have taken delivery—but they don't really care, you see. If there were a serious malfunction, my internal alarm would go off; they'd send a self-destruct command back and I'd disintegrate into my component atoms. Technically, I suppose, I should have notified them of the problem, so they could decide whether or not to do that anyway, but it seemed so trivial—and just because I'm a robot, it doesn't mean that I don't have any appetite for continued existence. You people have reasonably good hands, considering that they were practically the first ones on the evolutionary market."

"Exactly how distant is this future you're from?" I asked.

"About five billion years—a few hundred million after the crucial contact."

"Contact with aliens, you mean?"

"In a manner of speaking. The system has been in contact with what you'd call aliens for a lot longer, but the conversations are very slow, and tend to be utterly uninteresting—mostly empty social ritual, if you ask me, although no one ever does. The *crucial* contact was contact with the hyperbaryonic intelligences...except, of course, that they can only contact us by making baryonic simulacra—simulacra not so very unlike me, in principle, although they're crafted to a much higher standard. *They* never suffer from bad contacts—not in the literal sense, anyway."

"What's a hyperbaryonic intelligence?" I asked.

"I'm sorry—I assumed that you'd understand. According to my files, twenty-first century humans have figured out that the kind of matter you and the stars are made out of—baryonic matter—only accounts for a tenth of the mass of the universe, and that galaxies are held together by the gravitational pull of their companionate hyperbaryonic matter. Perhaps I should have said *dark matter*."

"I'm still at school," I explained. "If I stay on, which I probably won't, I'll do English, History and French A levels—no science."

"Right," he said. "That's good, in a way. It reduces the possibility of information-contamination, in case the memory-wipe doesn't work. The apparatus works perfectly with more advanced brains, but I think there's some sort of glitch in the native software of the human cerebrum that makes it difficult to synergize with the resident censor. I envy you that—my memory is all too easily wiped. Sorry—I was explaining hyperbaryonic intelligences, wasn't I? Before the crucial contact, my makers' ancestors had no idea what might be going on in dark matter, in spite of all the probing devices they developed once they got an elementary grip on the principles of matter/time relativity and the technology of time travel. Some people thought that dark matter was essentially inert, like some sort of anchor holding the baryonic universe in place, while some thought that it was essentially reactive, capable of responses to stimuli but not of initiation. At the other extreme, some thought that godlike HI's had actually designed the BU in order to create conditions conducive to the evolution of life and intelligence, maybe just as some sort of game, or maybe as a means to some mysterious end. The latter group were quite excited when the contact came, because they thought they'd be able to find out what the BU's purpose was, and what its eventual fate would be."

"And did they?"

"In a manner of speaking. It was a bit of a disappointment, for those that believed what they were told. Some didn't of course. Personally, I can't imagine why the HI's would lie about it, but that may be a robot thing—everyone makes jokes about robots having no imagination, although I can't imagine why. After all, we never make jokes about the Ultimate Worms and the Worldplants having *too much* imagination, although it seems to me that one could make out a very reasonable case for it, given the TT agenda."

The abbreviations were becoming annoying, but I hadn't time to ask for clarifications. I had more substantial matters to attend to. "I think that's got rid of all the grit," I said, "Repairing the damage isn't going to be so easy, though."

"I'll talk you through it," he assured me. "It' all color-coded in there—but you'll have to be very careful, You'll need *this* now." He selected out a new instrument.

It took some time for me to figure out how to restore the scarred circuitry, but I began to see the pattern eventually, and was able to get on with it.

"What was so disappointing about the crucial contact?" I asked.

"Well, it turns out that the BU is just a...well, the diplomatic way of putting it is *by-product*...of processes ongoing in dark matter. It wasn't purposively created at all, let alone intelligently designed."

"What's the undiplomatic way of putting it?" I asked.

"I could have used the word *excreta*," he said, swiftly adding: "It's not the sort of word I like to use, and I know that it seems even more revolting to a human than it does to a robot. Most future intelligences, mind—even those a mere few hundred million years upstream of humankind—don't regard their excreta with the kind of disgust that we do, but that's one of the few things robots and humans have in common. There's no reason at all to suppose that the HI's are in the slightest degree disgusted by baryonic matter, or what occurs within it."

"On the other hand," I said, "there's at least a possibility that they might think of us—not just you and me, but all these other baryonic intelligences-yet-to-be—as bacteria swarming in their shit."

He actually winced at that—which was pretty stupid, considering that I was trying to do delicate work inside his eye-socket. No obvious damage was done, but it didn't help the time problem. Not that time seemed to be all that much of a problem—in the two hours I'd been working on him the sky hadn't got any darker. I couldn't see the sun behind the clouds, but I got the impression that it hadn't moved a millimeter—and there still hadn't been a soul in sight, in either direction, since the instant I first saw the robot.

"Sorry about the indelicacy," I said. "So what message did the HI's' simulacra bring from the great beyond?"

"Well, if you believe them—and I, personally, can't imagine why anyone wouldn't—they have problems of their own. My makers' ancestors had grown accustomed to thinking of dark time as a kind of regulating factor—something that prevents time travel from generating paradoxes and messing up the continuity of cause and effect so badly that the time-stream breaks up into an infinite rain of droplets. They'd always perceived dark matter in much the same way, as something holding galaxies together and facilitating the origin and evolution of life. The HI's, not unnaturally, have a very different point of view. They'd only just reached the point in their own evolution when they could begin to manipulate dark time in a manner analogous to the way my makers manipulate calendrical time—except that they don't have any analogous hyperforce to assist their own time police in protecting them against paradoxicality. They wanted—needed, in their view—to make certain adjustments to the hyperbaryonic universe in order to secure it against transtemporal disruption."

Even though I didn't know the first thing about science, I thought I could see what he was driving at—and where the argument was heading.

"And whatever the hyperbaryonic intelligences—the HI's—want or need to do," I guessed, "will have a knock-on effect on *our* universe—the BU, as you call it. The...by-products...will *get flushed?*"

He didn't wince that time, but I could sense the effort he had to make to hold still. "They assured my makers' ancestors that they weren't talking about annihilation, or even destruction," he said, "but they weren't talking about trivial change either. They didn't issue any ultimata, though; they expressed a willingness to listen to our views, and suggested that some sort of cooperative endeavor might be in order."

I thought about that for a moment or two, then said: "The HI's need your help, don't they?"

"Opinions are divided about that, too," the robot said, with a slight sigh. "The way the HI's tell it, it's more like offering us a golden opportunity—but yes, without being unduly cynical, they probably wouldn't be trying to sell us on the idea if they didn't need our active input. Anyway, that's where the system is at when I come from—the Worms and the Worldplants are trying to decide whether to do what the HI's want us to do.

"Can't you just hop into your time machines and go ask your descendants what you did?" I asked. "Or, better still, just ask the time-travelers from your own future."

"That's another controversial issue," he admitted. "Some of the makers think that the fact that they can't move any further downstream, and can't identify any time-travelers from the future, implies that the decision must have been made one way—others argue the opposite, or any of several other variants, including the obvious one that the time-travelers from further downstream have concealed themselves very cleverly in order to make the decision for us. The TT agenda has become *really* complicated of late."

I no longer had to ask; *TT* obviously stood for time travel. "Well, I said, "at least you still have the time and inclination to drop in on your remotest ancestors once in a while, to check up on the dexterity of our primal hands. How am I doing?"

"In all honesty," he said, "not as well as I'd hoped. I might be in real trouble here, if you can't get it right."

"I'm doing my best," I told him, a trifle testily. "I've got the pattern in my head—the spirit is willing but the fingers tend to fumble.

"I'm sorry," he said. "Keep trying. Take your time."

"So why *are* you here?" I asked. "If the world five billion years hence has such big decisions on its plate, why is it still sending spy-robots back to the dear old twenty-first century, which must have been very thoroughly researched by time-travelers from your distant past?"

"There's always more to learn," he assured me. "This is a fascinating era: the first brief flowering of intelligence."

"How brief?" I asked, sharply, wondering whether the effects of the millennium bug might be worse than anyone had anticipated."

"Don't worry, Janine," he said. "You'll have time to grow up, and do whatever you want with your life. The Crash won't begin until you're quite old, by your standards. The one thing that can be said for clathrate-release as a means of extinction is that it's very quick."

"How do you know my name?" I demanded.

"Didn't you tell me, Miss? Did I forget to introduce myself, too? I'm so sorry. I don't actually have a name, but you can call me Steve."

"That doesn't actually answer my question," I pointed out. "You were waiting for me, weren't you—for *me*, I mean, not just any passing stranger. You already knew who I was. You've been watching me in the course of your research—and you're going to carry on doing it, aren't you? You already know about my future, don't you?"

"I've seen a little of it," he confessed. "Yes, I was looking for you, because I had some reason to believe that you'd be more likely to help me than most of your kind, and that your helping me wouldn't create any causative ripples powerful enough to attract the time police or bring down the wrath of dark time. Please don't ask me what that reason is, because I can't tell you. Memory wipes are far from infallible, and there are certain items of information I daren't risk. Chatting about far-future possibilities is one thing; giving relevant life-chance information is another. *Don't worry* is about as far as I can go. I'm sorry. I think you've almost got it. Careful, now...."

He had to pause the conversation again to give me more detailed instructions. The next ten minutes tested my good eyesight, my steady hand and my patience to the full.

"Okay," he said, eventually. "I think that's solved the problem. Hold on."

He put his eye back in, blinked a few times, and then took out a little mirror so that he could study his iris carefully. "Great," he said. "That should do the trick. Thank you very much."

He turned away, as if to go into the bushes hedging the road

"Hang on," I said. "Is that all I get—thank you very much."

"I can't give you anything else," he said. "Ripples of causality, remember? Time police, wrath of dark time, etcetera. When I told you not to worry, because you'd have time to grow up and live your life to the full, I only meant that your civilization won't collapse for another sixty years or so, and that I've caught a few glimpses of your future self while pottering around in the temporal neighborhood. I might be the only one here who's in danger of being disintegrated into my component atoms, but that doesn't mean that there couldn't be consequences for you."

"So you can't take me for a little ride in your time machine? Not far—Tudor England maybe...a glimpse of Shakespeare at work, or Henry VIII screwing one of his six wives?"

He was free to wince now, and took full advantage. "No," he said, shortly.

"Okay," I said. "No gifts, no trips in time, no hints about key decisions in my future career—but you said yourself that chat about the distant future is safe enough. At least tell me what the hyperbaryonic intelligences want to do with the material universe, and what kind of help they need from baryonic time-travelers."

"It's rather complicated," he said, sternly, as if to advise me not to worry my pretty little non-scientific head about it. "What it comes down to, though, is that they want to do some sort of time-stream-spanning matter-exchange, converting a lot of dark matter into baryonic matter and *vice versa*, not just downstream of the contact point but upstream too. In effect, they want to modify the evolution of the galaxy—not so greatly, though, that it can't comfortably contain the entire historical sequence of our systemic life. So they say, at least. According to them, most conscious entities won't even notice the exchange, and those who do will be able to benefit from it. As I said before, they present it as a golden opportunity, not just for my makers but everyone else—but they would, wouldn't they? If they need our help, that is."

"If they want to make more baryonic matter" I said, "why don't they just fill in some of the gaps between the galaxies? There's a lot of unused space out there. If they have to maintain the proportion of the different sorts of matter, though, I suppose they'd have to obliterate the galaxies if they did that—and if they do need our help...."

"They say that they want to keep everything *in place*," the robot said. "Dark matter is locally concentrated too, and the HI's that have made contact are from our own cluster—they're in contact with others, apparently, but their transgalactic conversations make our interstellar ones seem lightning fast. What they seem to have in mind is a process of galactic metamorphosis, extending across time from BB to OP. That's Big Bang and Omega Point, if you hadn't realized."

I hadn't, but I didn't make any comment.

"My makers' ancestors once called a convocation of all the time machines downstream of the solar metamorphosis in order to move the Earth and formulate the Pearly Ring," Steve the robot continued, "but this would be a bigger job, and a more delicate one, rebuilding the connections between our present and the *very* remote past, modifying all points in between. The HI's say that it could be a big improvement, if we all play our cards right. There's a lot of talk of sewing the cosmic strings into a hypercosmic web, building empires in the cosmic dust and binding all the intelligences that ever lived into an eternal ecstatic hypostatic hypertime, but that may be just sales patter, all high-flown rhetoric and empty promises. The way I see it, if they don't need our help, they must need our capitulation— and by *ours* I mean everyone's, from the source of the time-stream to its outflow into whatever great ocean of fulfillment or chaos ultimately awaits us. At any rate, my makers aren't so sure. I honestly don't know what they'll do."

"What difference would it make to us?" I asked. "I mean human beings, not you and me."

"In all probability, nothing perceptible to your senses or your science," he said, as if that somehow amounted to good news.

"You're fairly primitive, after all, even if you do have glimmerings of intelligence and purpose."

"It couldn't save us from imminent extinction, then?"

"Of course not. The evolutionary sequence will remain virtually untouched; the alterations will work at a much subtler level—or so the HI's say. The Ultimate Worms and Worldplants are by no means united in believing them, and their own hyperphysicists aren't much help, because they have no idea what the HI's might or might not be able to do with and within dark matter, or how much trouble they might be in if they did nothing at all, or how much trouble we might eventually be in, whatever might be done or not done."

"I suppose it comes down to a matter of trust," I said, after thinking it over. "I was tempted to run like hell when I first saw you, you know, in case you were a rapist or an exhibitionist, but I thought better of it."

He winced again at the word *rapist*. I have to confess that I took a certain satisfaction in being able to make him do that, even though he wasn't really a male of the merely human species.

I'd followed him through the hedge while we were still talking, although I'd collected a few scratches doing it. He stopped suddenly, and leaned forward as if to look at something hovering in mid-air that was too tiny for me to see. Suddenly, his time machine wasn't invisible any more. He was right; it did look a little more like a car than a ship, although it bore as much resemblance to the average Ford or BMW as a wheelbarrow does to a bulldozer. I regretted not being able to take a ride in it. He sighed with relief when the door swung open in response to a quick squint.

"Goodbye, Janine," he said, "and good luck."

"You too," I said. "I hope your shoddy workmanship holds up at least as well as mine—and if your makers should ever happen to ask you for the human position on the transtemporal-galactic-metamorphosis thing, tell them to remember the most useful item of advice to be formulated in the course of the entire twentieth century."

I could tell by the way he looked at me that he was expecting to have to wince again, but he gave in anyway. "Which is?" he asked.

"Shit happens," I replied.

He winced on cue, as if he were suffering from some kind of crazy phobia—and then he got into his driving-seat, closed the door behind him, and vanished.

I hadn't noticed that the air had been utterly still, but I felt the wind that reasserted its force in the wake of his departure. I heard voices coming from the path as other walkers resumed their progress along it.

I was quite a way from home, so I had plenty of time to mull over what I'd learned while I waited for the memory-wipe to kick in—which must have happened, eventually, because I know that I didn't remember anything out of the ordinary having happened by the time I got home. I don't think I'd ever have remembered it if I hadn't started coming to AlAbAn, but I think I've got it all back now—including the second thoughts I had while I was walking home.

While I'd actually been talking to the robot he'd seemed very plausible, but once he was gone I was surprised by my own complacency, and how matter-of-factly I'd dealt with it. He must, I thought, have done something undetectable to put me at my ease, which had not only stopped me from being frightened or overwhelmed by the enormity of what was happening, but had also given me a very relaxed attitude to what he'd told me. Once he was gone, I began to wonder whether it might have been a pack of lies—and even whether he might never have been in need of repair at all. After all, I didn't really have a clue what I'd been doing, or how—the only thing I could be sure of was that he hadn't been able to do it himself. Maybe, I thought, I'd actually been disabling some kind of slave-circuit, setting him free from the command of his masters—which might, of course, have been a good thing to do, although it might conceivably have freed him to wreak untold havoc and evil in the past and future alike.

I couldn't help remembering that story that people are so fond of citing, about the time-traveler who steps on a butterfly way back in the Cretaceous, and comes back to find his own time changed for the worse. Maybe I thought, the same principle applies to helpful actions as to destructive ones. Maybe, even if I *had* just made some tiny repair, what I'd done might echo down the ages, causing all sorts of unexpected ripples of causality, without any guarantee that my altruism would be replicated in good results. Maybe, I thought, my tiny good deed might be the source of vast misfortunes, because the universe doesn't bother to balance its moral account-books, or simply doesn't care.

Maybe, I thought, the essential generosity of my gesture would be just as likely to bring down the wrath of dark time as some mean trick would have done—and not only to bring that wrath down on me, or Steve the robot, but on the whole world that will be hanging in the balance when the hyperbaryonic intelligences need the help of an armada of time machines and the capitulation of every intelligent entity that ever live or ever will live, to swap the galaxy's existing baryonic matter for a whole new crock of excreta—a job that must mean more, even to vast intelligences like them, than fiddling with the processing capacity of their sewage-farm. Was it possible, I wondered—was it even conceivable?—that what I had done might somehow influence the decision that the baryonic beings of the future solar system had to make?

Obviously, I'll never know, unless the robot Steve appears beside my deathbed just before I pop my clogs, to let me know how the fullness of time will work out—or has worked out, given that the present we're living in now could just as easily be the one *after* they changed the past as the one before. Then again, maybe my telling the story here and now will be the infinitesimal shift in the pattern, whose ripples will extend forever. Who can tell?

As I said, I don't have any fancy theories—but I can't help wondering whether AlAbAn itself is evidence that the changes the hyperbaryonic intelligences wanted to make are actually in the process of happening, day by day and week by week, in the twentieth century as well as every other point in the time-stream, and that what we do here, every second Thursday, as the memory-wipes fade away and we become free to speak at last, is part and parcel of the fulfillment of one of those high-flown promises the robot mentioned: the binding of all the intelligences that ever lived into an eternal ecstatic hypostatic hypertime.

Obviously, AlAbAn meetings aren't at all ecstatic in themselves, any more than they're eternal or located in some indefinable hypertime, but it's just about possible—isn't it?—or just about conceivable, at any rate, that they're part and parcel of our particular link to eventual enlightenment, our particular location in the great story of Earthly life, Earthly intelligence, and Earthly endeavor.

If nothing else, I think, our stories serve to remind us that our own petty difficulties—by which I mean the imminent extinction of the species as well as our pathetic inability to organize our wretched love-lives with any semblance of art or decency—aren't of much significance in the larger scheme of things. Life goes on regardless, in spite of the wrath of dark time, and the undeniable fact that shit happens.

CHAPTER TWENTY-ONE

SEARCHING FOR THE MEANING

Afterwards, Janine and Alison came over to the settee where Steve and Milly were sitting, not holding hands.

"Could you possibly give us a lift home, Steve?" Janine said. "Walter has to stay late and doesn't know when he'll be able to get away. Apparently, he and Amelia have something they need to sort out with Neville."

"Really?" Steve said. "Good for them. I hope it works out without any of them getting hurt."

"Don't be silly, Steve," Milly said. "Nobody's in danger of getting hurt. Yes, Janine, of course we'll give you both a lift."

Steve still wasn't sure that Milly ought to be granting requests of that sort on his behalf—and he was glad to see that Janine frowned too—but he made no complaint. "Great story, by the way," he said to Janine. "A nice sequel to mine."

"I think what you meant to say," Janine said, only a little frostily, "is that your story was a good introduction to mine."

"I suppose it's understandable that you might think that that was what I meant," Steve conceded, unrobotically, as he led the way along the pavement to the place where he'd parked the Citroen. "Maybe I did—I've been a little confused of late about that sort of thing, and others. Shall we stop off for something to eat, in that Italian where the four of us all came together for the first time, as a celebration of old times? Arlequino, wasn't it?"

"Steve's very big on celebrations of old times," Alison put in. "He gave me an ammonite for Christmas. Janine got a geode."

"I got an electronic mini-planetarium, which can show you the disposition of the stars in the night sky on any date, past or future, from any geographical viewpoint," Milly revealed. "It can also do the history of the universe from its beginning to its heat death—BB to OP, as Janine would probably put it—in fast forward, or in reverse. I told him that a diamond bracelet would have done the job much more effectively, but he couldn't see it. His many girl-friends haven't yet completed his education in such matters."

"It's the thought that counts," Steve said, and suddenly found himself the focal point of three quasi-medusal stares. "Well, it is," he added, defensively.

"The old year is dead and gone," Janine said. "If we're all to move forward, we have to start afresh."

"If only we mere mortals could turn back time." Steve said, as he reached the car and unlocked it, "and remake the past as well as the future, as hyperbaryonic intelligences apparently think they can. Those who can avoid or administer the wrath of dark time don't know how lucky they are."

"Yes they do," Janine told him, taking hold of the handle of the rear nearside door. "Anyway, mere mortals can't even remake the future *knowingly*—they just have to hope they've stamped on the right butterflies."

"We can do a little better that that, surely," Alison put in, "The limits of possibility are sometimes a bit narrow, and the consequences of our actions are sometimes difficult to calculate, but we're not helpless victims of fate." She still had her hands in her pockets, and there seemed to be some unspoken compact between the four of them that no one else would open their door until she too reached for a handle.

"Even those of us who've been taken on trips in time, and have some extra knowledge of the future," Milly said, "don't really have the power to change it. Knowing that the human race is going to become extinct in the next century doesn't help us to avoid that destiny."

"Maybe, if everybody were able to believe it," Steve said, "we *could* change it. Maybe, as more and more people do realize it, we *are* changing it."

"I don't think so," Janine said. "The thing about our experiences is that we only learn the trivial things, never enough to make a difference. The robot wasn't able to tell me anything that would enable me to change anything in my own future."

"Your robot did give you one hint about your future destiny, though, didn't he, Janine?" Steve said. Before he went on to the next sentence Alison took her right hand out of her pocket and opened the rear off-side door. Reflexively mirroring her action, Steve opened his own door as he went on: "He told you to call him Steve, because he knew that the name would have some significance in time to come. He called himself after *me*. You don't need me to tell you how significant that is, and would be, even if you'd just been dreaming, and hadn't met a time-traveling robot from the far future at all—which, of course, you had been and didn't."

"That's breaking the rules, Steve," Milly told him, as she got into the front passenger seat and reached for her seat-belt. "It's un-diplomatic, impolite and bang out of order. Anyway, you've got it backwards. If Janine was just dreaming, she must have called the robot Steve because she sees *you* as something of a robot. The whole thing must be symbolic."

"The thought had occurred to me," Steve admitted. He paused, as he fastened his own seat-belt, turned the key in the ignition, put the car into gear and let off the handbrake; then he continued: "I'm not a robot, though. I've always been fully conscious of what I've done, and I take full responsibility. I know that I don't deserve either one of you, and neither of you deserves to be stuck with a shit like me. That all goes without saying. The wrath of dark time has been churning in my soul for weeks, if not forever, and I'm probably due for imminent annihilation in the shape of some year eleven houri who'll persuade me to throw caution to the winds and commit career suicide—but won't it be better to have lived and loved than never to have lived at all? Even if I could turn back time, I suppose I wouldn't want to be rid of either one of you—but please don't cook me and carve me up just yet. At least wait until I've driven poor Alison home. She's not really a part of this, you know.

"Yes she is," Milly said, as she put her seat-belt on.

"I'm doing my level best to be," Alison said, doing likewise.

"I suppose we could get a pizza," Janine said, in her turn.

"I suppose we could," Milly agreed, "but it wouldn't be like old times."

"Who cares?" Alison said. "It's just food."

"The trouble with you, Steve," Janine opined, "is that you have all the wrong phobias. You focus all your anxiety on silly things so you can avoid being frightened of the things that really ought to frighten you—and you'll never get over your petty terrors until you realize that, and put yourself in order."

"Thanks for the advice," Steve said, as he turned the key in the ignition. The engine didn't start.

"You're probably right, Jan," Milly said. "I used to be anxious myself, about the silliest things, but I think I'm all right now."

"I'm a little better balanced myself than I used to be," Janine admitted. "There aren't any easy answers, but it's remarkable what you can accomplish, sometimes, with a keen eye, a steady hand, and a lot of patience."

"And a little goodwill," Milly put in.

"And a little goodwill," Janine agreed.

The car started at the second attempt, and moved off.

"You see, Steve," Alison put in. "It's always been a double act, with me as a spare part: two queens and a court jester. Ever since we were kids, it's been Janine and Milly, plus poor Alison. They've cut you up and shared you between them, like slices of a pizza, and made a great song and dance about it all. Now they're going to let you choose between them, or *make* you choose, because that's the way they play the game."

"Don't mind Ali," Milly said. "She's just jealous."

"It hurts because it's the truth," Alison said. "Although I am just jealous."

"What happened to that little goodwill you mentioned just now?" Steve asked, fully expecting to be told to shut up by at least two voices in chorus—but no such command was forthcoming. Even the wrath of dark time seemed to have let up in its churning within the secret spaces of his soul, at least for the moment." *Things are going to work out*, he told himself. *One way or another, things are going to work out*. The Citroen was already moving out of the clustered lights of East Grimstead into the ribbon of darkness that separated the village from its larger companion.

"You mustn't mind any of us, Steve," Janine told him, after a suitable pause. "It's the way things are when we're all together. We snipe at one another constantly. It's all in fun, although it sometimes doesn't seem that way to people who get caught in the rapid cross-fire. Just think of us as the three witches from *Macbeth*, cackling on the blasted heath—it's all hubble bubble, with no real substance. Is it going to be your turn next, Ali? Are you going to tell a story to the group?"

"No," Alison said. "That's one game I'm not going to play. I'm a bit too down-to-earth for all that."

"It's not a game, Ali," Milly said. "I've always tried to tell you that, but you won't believe it. Janine understands now, though. It's only a matter of time before you get involved too—you'll get hooked, just like the rest of us."

"Oh, I'm hooked," Alison said. "Well and truly—no doubt about it. Hooked and landed, lying breathless on the bank, waiting to see if I'll be thrown back or have my head bashed in. I don't see myself as a witch, though. I've always thought on more extravagant lines—you two are more like goddesses, although I'm not sure that I can fit into that particular metaphor, and Steve is a poor substitute for Paris in any case. However we fantasize it, though, I can't wait to see how it all comes out—and the fate of the universe too, of course."

"That's pretty cut and dried," Janine said. "The robot told me everything I needed to know."

"He only told you the decision that had to be made," Alison reminded her. "He didn't tell you what his makers decided."

"No," Janine admitted, "but it was pretty obvious. They agreed. What alternative did they have?"

"You know," Milly said, "on reflection, I think that my abduction experience helped to cure me of my eating disorder. It helped me to be more content with who I am, to stop trying to change myself into something I wasn't. I'm still reaping the benefits of that. If you're lucky, Steve, your own experience might help you come to terms with your phobias. If you can keep revisiting it in your head, you might find that you can get past the panic once and for all."

"That would be good," Steve said, "but I'm not holding my breath." The Citroen had passed through West Grimstead now, and was on another dark stretch of road that would last until Alderbury. He kept his eyes peeled for deer, although he'd never seen one hereabouts before. He knew that foxes could cause problems too, if a driver weren't sufficiently alert to the possibility of their unexpected appearance.

"And that's why it's not a game, Ali" Milly said. "Tell her, Steve—she might believe it if she hears it from you."

"It's not a game, Alison," Steve said. "Not from my point of view."

"Nor mine," Janine put in.

"I guess I'm outvoted, then," Alison replied, agreeably. "I shouldn't have suggested otherwise, should I? Not supportive enough—against the rules of the game."

"She's always been like that," Milly said. "She always has an answer for everything."

"And it's always the same one," Alison said. "*Remember, thou art mortal*. That's AlAbAn's answer too, isn't it? All men are mortal, and so is humankind itself—but we mustn't despair. The court still has its jester, and the Red Death isn't scheduled to spoil the feast until midnight. The jester is me, by the way, if anyone was having difficulty following the metaphor. The Red Death is methane."

"I thought I was the thane," Steve said. "Oh, sorry, no—in your metaphor, we're in Arcadia, not Scotland, and I'm a poor substitute for Paris, because I hand out ammonites, geodes and planetaria instead of golden apples. At least you got one each."

Milly laughed, dutifully but infectiously. Janine and Steve joined in.

"This *is* a bit like old times," Janine conceded. "All friends again, able to laugh."

"You know what I think?" Alison said, as Steve turned the corner and steered northwest. "I think we ought to get those pizzas to go, and carry all the boxes back to somebody's flat—preferably someone who has some booze in—where we can all sit down, and Steve can tell us what it all means: the secret of time travel; the mythical future; the key to success. You can tell us all that, can't you, Steve? What the future holds, what so much ado on the brink of our extinction is really all about, and where we fit in?"

"I could," Steve said, "but you wouldn't want to listen."

"That's fine by me," Janine said, responding to the first part of Alison's suggestion. "Milly's the one who ought to decide, though. If you've made plans, Mil, you mustn't let us disrupt them."

"That's all right," Milly said. "I'm cool with it—just so long as the car is legally parked, wherever we end up."

"May I suggest my place?" Steve said. "It's a bit ungallant, I know, but if we get something to drink with the pizza, I won't be able to drive afterwards. I really could do with a drink, and I've got a few bottles of red in my rack. You can all share a cab to your various homes afterwards."

"All?" Milly queried.

"All those who decide to go home, I mean," Steve said. "Is that okay?"

"Fine by me," Alison said.

"Okay," Janine said."

"Agreed," said Milly.

"My place it is," Steve said, confidently enough.

* * * * * * *

It didn't take long to get the pizzas made up and baked, and it only required a further few minutes to drive to Steve's flat. Milly linked arms with Janine and drew her to the settee, while Alison took the armchair. Steve didn't bother to grab a dining-chair; once he'd fished out a couple of bottles and taken the corkscrew from his desk drawer he sat on the rug in front of the gas fire, positioning himself discreetly to one side so that he didn't block the radiant heat. The boxes were opened.

"Okay, Steve," Milly said. "You can do the schoolteacher thing if you really must, and tell us how Jan's experience fits into your theory. We'll try not to behave the way we used to back in school, when we wasted our opportunities for worldly progress in order to pretend that we were above all that. We understand, now that we're all on various career ladders, how unwise it was not to listen to our teachers, pass our exams and learn to live well. Should we observe strict AlAbAn rules?"

"That's not necessary," Steve told them. "I'm supposed to be a scientist, of sorts. I'm supposed to be able to accept challenges and welcome skeptical criticism, and to modify my hypotheses accordingly."

"Don't worry, Steve," Janine said. "We'll be supportive. I know that I haven't been, of late, but I've forgiven you now—and Milly too, of course. Ali's been forgiven too. All's well that ends well."

It hasn't ended yet, Steve thought, but he didn't dare say anything about fat ladies singing, so he started the lesson instead.

"I have to teach the sixth-formers about Heisenberg's Uncertainty Principle," he said, "although I'm not sure I understand it completely myself. I do it the conventional way, by telling them about Schrödinger's cat. The cat in question is sealed in box with a deadly weapon, whose trigger is operated by a device sensitive to an event that's subject to quantum uncertainty—an event we can only express mathematically as a set of probabilities, because we can't recover enough information to give a more definite answer. The thought-experiment asks us to consider the existential status of the cat when we don't know whether the trigger has been activated or not. The common sense view is that the cat is either alive or dead, but we don't know which. The so-called Copenhagen interpretation of quantum mechanics, on the other hand, asks us to accept that the cat is neither dead nor alive, but caught in a state of uncertainty—until someone opens the box and looks, at which point the uncertainty disappears under the pressure of observation."

"It's the cat I feel sorry for," Alison murmured. Milly and Janine put their fingers to their lips.

It was at that moment that Steve realized how pointless it would be to continue with the lecture, instead of just cutting to the chase and telling them what they actually wanted to know—but he was the host, and it was his wine they were drinking.

"When I first heard the story," Steve said, "it was the cat I felt sorry for, too. How would it feel, I wondered, to be caught in a state of uncertainty, not being able to know whether it was alive or dead? If I'd asked my teacher, of course—which I never did—he'd only have said that, within the parameters of the thought-experiment, the cat can't be capable of feeling or knowing anything, because if it could, it would be an observer, and the uncertainty would collapse—but that's a cop-out. I just kept on wondering: How would it feel, to live in a state of irresolvable uncertainty? What would it be like to live in an unfixed reality, to be conscious and inquisitive, even though the world is fundamentally unstable, unmade, unknowable?"

"I feel like that all the time," Alison whispered.

"Then I realized," Steve went on, "that that's pretty much how I feel all the time. Which seemed odd, because I'd already taken aboard the scientific point of view, from which the world works by cause and effect, and in which everything happens because it has to, and everything is predictable, if only you can know enough about the logic of its situation. After all, Heisenberg's Uncertainty Principle isn't supposed to apply to the sorts of things we can see, and the sort of thing we are. We aren't supposed to have experiences that don't make sense, which are both real and not real. We aren't supposed to be trapped in a situation where we don't know what anything means, or whether it means anything at all."

"He must be quite good at his job," Janine whispered to Milly. "I hadn't realized that, never having seen him in action."

"When I started going to AlAbAn, though," Steve said, "it seemed to me that there might be a way to make sense of it, or at least a way for me to think about it. If there is such a thing as time travel, you see—even if the only things that can travel in time are ideas and images, and even if they travel subconsciously, only reflected in the conscious mind indirectly—then the world *is* fundamentally uncertain. *Now* isn't just the passive product of the past, cursed with inevitability by the tyrannical work of cause and effect. *Now* is something forever on the brink of metamorphosis, always subject to arbitrary shifts occasioned by the detritus of time travel, no matter how hard time-travelers try, no matter how many agencies of time police there are to keep them in line, and no matter what kinds of forces are at work in the unimaginable darkness outside the time-stream. Even if there were no rogue elements working to the opposite end—which there inevitably are—it would still be the case that every *now* there ever was, is, or will be is vulnerable, unstable and unsafe. Even if everything else could be brought under the umbrella of true causation, there'd still be other possibilities lurking in dark matter, or somewhere beyond."

"I take it back," Janine murmured. "No wonder they hate him at school, if he's always that pretentious."

"I can't speak for anyone else," Steve continued, "but that's what I've got out of AlAbAn: an explanation of sorts for my sensation of uncertainty, my consciousness of not quite knowing what or where or when or who or why I am, or how to find out. I agree with Janine's robotic Steve that the most sensible way to understand the kinds of entities that might be responsible for that uncertainty is not to credit them with too much purpose—or, at least, not to credit them with purposes that involve me. From the conscious point of view, whatever feeds into or emerges from the unconscious mind is essentially alien. At the end of the day, it isn't controlling us, or instructing us, or begging us to go in a particular direction; it's just shit that's happening."

Janine raised her glass, as if in salute.

"Maybe the hyperbaryonic entities, whatever they may be," Steve plugged on, "really can change the universe, changing its past along with its future, pitching the universe into a perpetual state of uncertainty, setting it to hover between alternative possibilities of conformation. Maybe, in order for that to be the state of universal affairs—for that *always to have been* the state of universal affairs, the hyperbaryonic intelligences do need our help, or our capitulation. Maybe, from their point of view—though not from ours—that's what self-conscious intelligence is *for*. Maybe, collectively if not individually, and unconsciously if not consciously, all the intelligent entities that ever lived, or ever will live, or ever might live, have a part to play in deciding what the ultimate outcome of the hyperbaryonic mass-exchange will be."

Milly reached out to clink her glass with Janine's, sharing a silent toast.

"Maybe plant intelligence has a better sense of its own part than animal intelligence," Steve continued, "because it's sedentary and contemplative, and patient in its sexuality. Maybe what the limited empathic capacity of the human mind can only construe as a dream of turning into stone could be better expressed as a desire for ecstatic hypostasis, or a vegetal Omega Point, or some other ineffectually-clutching verbal formula. Maybe we poor primitive humans can never be more than the merest of catalysts to the ongoing and eternal metamorphosis—but even if that were the case, it might be something of which to be proud. Even if there merely happened to be something accidentally contained in our blood and being that's vital; even if it were only in some crude protovitalistic sense that it's significant, still we'd be making our contribution to the evolution of the eternal Phoenix. If what the robot said is true, it's not just *future* evolution that's important, because time and change aren't simply linear processes. There's *another* dimension in which change can occur, a sort of *sideways* time, in which it's not merely the shape of things to come that's eternally uncertain but *now* and *then*. Everything in the great universal symphony of matter in motion is subject to the eternal *if*."

"If only," Alison said, not clinking her glass with anyone's.

"At any rate," Steve said, "that's pretty much the way I do feel, even though mathematics and physics aren't much help to me in describing or measuring it—and I think, on due reflection, that that's probably the best of all the possible states that a person or a universe might be in. In fact, I suspect that's the only kind of universe in which it would be possible to be a person. It's not necessary to feel sorry for Schrödinger's cat, because it's the state of uncertainty—the awareness of the fact that the entire time-stream is in a state of flux—that makes choice possible. A world without choice would be mechanical—not intolerable, because there'd be no conscious entities in it to find it intolerable, because there wouldn't be any selective pressure favoring the evolution of consciousness—but still mechanical, subject to true causation. Uncertainty isn't what makes the world go round, but it's what allows us to be aware of its movement."

"It's getting boring, Steve," Milly told him.

Steve ignored her. "I think that's why all the time-travelers we dream about are so interested in us, so keen to study and measure us. They're not just interested in us because we were the first, but because we might not be here forever. They're anxious to explore and explain our *now* because they suspect, or know, that next time they come back in time to look at us, we might have been profoundly changed. That's why the time police were so insistent on returning Milly to her point of origin, while being so careless of the fate of her abductors. It makes no difference, by the way, if all I'm talking about is dreams, because dreams are the most important thing there are, precisely because their meaning isn't already built into them, awaiting excavation and realization. The meaning of dreams is potential and provocative, awaiting interpretation and transfiguration by the imagination. That's what imagination is for, and why it's the way it is."

"It's all bullshit, though, isn't it?" Janine said. "You can't change the past, or the present. You can learn to live with it, and accept it for what it is, and move on—but you can't change it."

"You can't be conscious of past change," Steve told her, "but that doesn't mean that the past can't change or be changed. It's conceivable—perhaps inevitable—that we wake up every morning to a new world, which only seems always to have been the way it seems now. If so, we're always playing our parts, albeit unconsciously, in the remaking of that past, and hence in the remaking of ourselves, both in the present and in terms of our future potential."

"It's just bullshit," Janine insisted. "Even if it were true, it wouldn't change anything in regard to the way we live our lives."

"It might," Steve said, "if we were better able to make use of the potential inherent in our unconscious minds—in our dreams and in our faculty of imagination. If it's true, we probably are becoming better able to live our lives the way we'd like to live them, as the pattern of the time-stream shifts. If it's true, we probably do wake up every morning to a slightly better history that the one we had before—because the best of all possible worlds is a world in which that kind of progress would be possible. We all woke up this morning in a world in which the unfolding ecocatastrophe will put our entire species out of its misery in a matter of a hundred years—but the possibility might be open to us, if we can only forge the will, to extend that hundred years, bit by bit, into a thousand, or the thousand into...well, who can tell what the final span of the time-stream might be, when all the intelligences that will ever live, or might ever have lived before, have exerted their collective will to its maximum effect? Always assuming, that is, that they ever permit finality to creep in. If the animal intelligences have their way, maybe the vegetal Omega Point will just be a pipe-dream."

"I think you mean pie in the sky," Milly said, and giggled.

"If time travel ever will exist," Steve said, frowning, "whatever form it might take, then there's a sense in which we're not doomed, individually or collectively. From the viewpoint of future time-travelers, we'll *always* be here, and *now*...but we'll always be different, every time-trip, as the margin of uncertainty unwinds in hyper-time. We'll always be actively remaking ourselves and our world, always uniquely interesting. Every one of us will die, sooner or later, but, simply by virtue of having lived at all, we'll all have had the chance to explore an infinite range of personal possibilities and potential lives—not in the sense that we can live them one by one in linear series, but in the sense that we're always in a state of uncertainty, always hovering between them, always in transition. Who, in their right minds, would want to live any other way? And who, even if it's all bullshit, wouldn't want to be able to imagine it? It's the ultimate good news, after all: we do have a choice; our choices matter; we're only as limited as our imagination.

"I already knew *that*," Milly said.

"So did I," Janine added, "and I always knew that it was bull-shit."

"What do you think, Alison?" Steve asked.

"As a virtual AlAbAn virgin," Alison replied, "I don't have any basis on which to judge." Her glass was empty.

"I think we ought to revert to AlAbAn rules now," Milly said, draining her own glass. "Let's be supportive, and thank Steve for all his mental effort. Okay, Jan?"

"Fair enough," Janine said. "It's all food for thought, after all. Who am I to condemn it as bullshit? I'm on your side, Steve. Good for you. Way to go, etcetera."

"We ought to be thinking of calling that cab now," Alison put in, "if we're all going home. *Are* we all going home?"

"It's Steve's flat." Milly said. "It's his prerogative to decide whether or not to invite one of us to stay the night—and, if so, which of us to invite."

"I'm tired," Steve said, "And I've got a heavy day at work to-morrow with it being a Friday. If any of you had expectations, I'm sorry."

"You're procrastinating, Steve," Janine pointed out. "You'll still have to decide which of us to call next time you pick up the phone. You might like to give us a clue as to who it might be. We can't live with the present state of uncertainty forever, and I'm sure Milly doesn't want to continue being your girl-friend by default."

While Janine was speaking, Alison took out her phone and started thumbing in a number.

"But that's exactly what I've been trying to tell you," Steve said. "We should *welcome* states of uncertainty. If we didn't have uncertainty, we really would be existentially trapped by the inexora-ble grind of true causation."

"We want you to make up your mind, Steve," Janine said. "Do you want Milly, or do you want to try to patch things up with me, and maybe get back to where we were before? We want to know which of us you're going to call—given that you're lucky enough to have the choice again."

Janine had to speak a little more loudly than usual to make her-self heard, because Alison—who was still pretending to be the re-lentless voice of sanity in a mad world—was placing the order for the cab.

"I don't know," Steve said, not entirely truthfully. "Things might look different in the morning, when a whole new world will seem new-born. As I said, I'm tired. I'm sure I'll be able to make a more sensible choice when I've slept on it."

"He already admitted that he doesn't deserve either one of you," Alison said, putting her phone away again. "If you want my advice, I think you should both refuse to take any more of his calls, and move on. Chalk it up to experience, plenty more fish in the sea, etcetera. The taxi will only be five minutes, by the way—no queue tonight. We ought to go outside and wait on the pavement. We shouldn't wait for the driver to honk his horn and disturb the whole street."

"Well, thanks for listening to me," Steve said. "It's good to be able to put these things in shape and get them out into the open. It's been very helpful."

He watched Janine and Milly lock gazes for a few seconds, before they turned to look at Alison. They gave every impression of having turned to her merely to respond to her suggestion, but Steve thought that there was something slightly quizzical in the way they looked at her.

"You're right," Janine said, setting down her empty glass at last, "It's getting late."

"There'll be plenty of time to work things out," Milly agreed. "In the end, it will all be settled, one way or the other."

"Or not," Alison said, as she opened the door of the flat and held it open for her friends. She glanced back at Steve, and said: "Jan's right, you know. Any connection, literal or metaphorical, between all that bullshit you just came out with and the mundane business of everyday life is entirely imaginary."

"So is everything else that constitutes mental life," Steve said, "and sometimes makes it worthwhile."

Janine and Milly said "Goodnight, Steve" in chorus, neither one of them apparently being prepared, in the circumstances, to add a supplementary expression of affection.

"Any time you need to hear the voice of sanity," Alison said, "you know where you can find someone willing to fake it. Thanks for the lift—and the rest."

"You're welcome," Steve said. "All of you."

EPILOGUE

WHAT HAPPENED NEXT

In February 2009 Steve married his long-time girl-fried, Alison, at Salisbury's central Registry Office. It was a small-scale affair, and they had no need of bridesmaids. They honeymooned in Wales; they didn't need to take the long way round in driving there, even though the direct route required them to pay a toll.

Alison stuck by Steve loyally thereafter—even though he didn't always duck, when prettier women than her recklessly threw themselves at him, and his own looks eventually faded into mediocrity—and she fulfilled her ambition of bearing all his children.

Eventually, long after Rhodri Jenkins had retired, and some little while after he had given up playing cricket—without ever getting a hat trick or scoring a century—Steve was promoted to deputy head. By the time he wrote his one and only book, *Alien Abduction: The Wiltshire Revelations*, the events it described seemed to belong to a distant and confused past, when he had been quite a different person.

Even though he never quite made it to the top of his profession, or over the Clifton Suspension Bridge, Steve was satisfied that his was a happy ending to a rewarding life-story.

The human species did not become extinct in the early twenty-second century, perhaps due to the subversion of the logic of its situation by the retrospective intervention of the hyperbaryonic intelligences in the flux of the time-stream, and perhaps not. The species did, however, become extinct eventually, as was inevitable.

The consequences of humankind's slightly-protracted lifespan were not entirely insignificant, but they were barely noticeable to most of their intelligent successors; that particular element of the Great Unfinished Transfiguration made little or no difference to the metahistory of time travel or the ultimate formulation of the Cosmic Collective Unconscious.

No final version of the time-stream was ever concluded by any kind of Ultimate Consensus; in that context, there could be no such thing as a happy ending—but the everlasting uncertainty was, in its own exotic fashion, glorious.

ABOUT THE AUTHOR

BRIAN STABLEFORD was born in Yorkshire in 1948. He taught at the University of Reading for several years, but is now a full-time writer. He has written many science fiction and fantasy novels, including *The Empire of Fear*, *The Werewolves of London*, *Year Zero*, *The Curse of the Coral Bride*, and *The Stones of Camelot*. Collections of his short stories include *Sexual Chemistry: Sardonic Tales of the Genetic Revolution, Designer Genes: Tales of the Biotech Revolution*, and *Sheena and Other Gothic Tales*. He has written numerous nonfiction books, including *Scientific Romance in Britain, 1890-1950, Glorious Perversity: The Decline and Fall of Literary Decadence*, and *Science Fact and Science Fiction: An Encyclopedia*. He has contributed hundreds of biographical and critical entries to reference books, including both editions of *The Encyclopedia of Science Fiction* and several editions of the library guide, *Anatomy of Wonder*. He has also translated numerous novels from the French language, including several by the feuilletonist Paul Féval and various classics of French scientific romance.

www.ingramcontent.com/pod-product-compliance
Lightning Source LLC
Chambersburg PA
CBHW020554260626
47157CB00003B/692